AXIOM'S END

AXIOM'S END

END

a novel

LINDSAY ELLIS

TITAN BOOKS

Axiom's End
Print edition ISBN: 9781789095319
E-book edition ISBN: 9781789095418

Published by Titan Books
A division of Titan Publishing Group Ltd
144 Southwark Street, London SE1 0UP
www.titanbooks.com

First Titan edition: July 2020
10 9 8 7 6 5 4 3 2 1

A CIP catalogue record for this title is available from the British Library.

Printed and bound in Great Britain by CPI Group Ltd.

For Elisa

AXIOM'S END

▋▋▋▋

I understand your frustration having so little to work with. If we had any means of getting you more or a better sampling of their language, we would give it to you. But in forty years of watching, waiting, and recording, that ninety-seven seconds is all you have to work with. Sorry.

Between you and me, I am plenty frustrated, too. ▋▋▋▋▋▋▋▋ had given up any hope of communication, or even an *attempt* at communication, from our guests years ago, so that after forty years of *nothing*, we get a minute and a half of blathering, only to be followed by more nothing, it's probably more frustrating than if we'd never gotten a sampling of their language at all.

And no, I cannot answer any questions on their behavior, because for all intents and purposes, there is none. No language-related behavior to study except for that ninety-seven seconds. The only one of them they've gotten moving ("Čefo") responds to human engagement, but doesn't give us language samples. The long and short is this—they cannot *force* the Fremda group to give up language samplings, because they don't know how. If that changes, you'll be the first to know.

I remind you that ███████████ and every single expert and organization who's had anything to do with attempts to establish communication with the Fremda group has had less to work with than you do now. So make do. This may be the most we ever get.

—███████

Ortega, Nils. "Fremda Memo." *The Broken Seal*. August 24, 2007. http://www.thebrokenseal.org.

PART ONE

....

THE OBELUS EVENT

Torrance, California
September 20, 2007
NASDAQ: 2,679.05
Dow Jones Industrial Average: 13,242.85

1

On the morning of the second meteor, Cora's 1989 Toyota Camry gave up the ghost for good. The car was a manual transmission with a stick shift its previous owner had wrapped in duct tape years ago, a time bomb the color of expired baby food that should have gone off sooner than it did. At $800, she had paid more for it than it was worth, but back then, she had been a freshman in college and desperate for a car. In the two years since, she'd grown accustomed to the ever-loudening squealing of the fan belt, but on this morning, after she put her key in the ignition and the engine turned, the squealing turned into a hostile screech. A disheartening *thunk thunk thunk* followed, then a snap, then an angry *whirr*, all before she could react. But by the time she turned off the ignition, it was clear that the car, her first and only car, was dead forever.

And she was already late for work.

As the Camry went into its final death throes, Demi, who was locking the front door on her way to work, froze mid-motion as she beheld the scene, wearing an expression of disappointment, but not surprise. Cora's feeling of horror that this was even happening quickly hopped to embarrassment before settling onto her old standby: numbness. She got out of the car, with no choice but to leave it on the street despite it being street cleaning day, approached her mother, and asked, "Can you give me a ride to work?"

Demi looked at her like she had just lost their house in a drunken bet. "Sure." It was the last word she said to Cora for about half an hour.

In short order, Cora was suffering the indignity of her mother driving her to work through the vehicular sludge of the 110. In any other circumstances, Demi would have told Cora she was shit out of luck, that she should have gotten the car fixed months ago, and that she could find her own damn way up to downtown LA. But it had been through PMT, the temp agency Demi worked for, that Cora had her temp job, and it had been Demi who had vouched for her. And so, here they were, crawling under the 105, Demi sacrificing her own punctuality for her negligent daughter's.

"What happened to that $200 I loaned you?" asked Demi just after they passed Rosecrans, her anger now cooled enough that she was capable of speech. "You were supposed to replace the belt and get your hair done, and you have done neither."

Cora resisted the urge to pull her hair behind her ears, as though that would hide her mess of a dye job. She'd bleached it blond several months ago, before she'd dropped out of college, but about six inches of her natural wet-hay hair color had grown in since.

"I had to use it on gas," lied Cora, keeping her gaze on the passenger-side mirror. "And I had another credit card bill I needed to pay off." The truth was she had used that money on a Neko Case concert, her third this year, but Demi didn't need to know that.

"Sure you did," said Demi. "After today, you take the bus."

Cora did not retort or offer excuses. She knew it was absolutely on her that she had not fixed the car. The fan belt was just the last in a long line of events that only tightened the spiral of powerlessness that was coming to define her existence, and by this point, she was getting used to it. Trying to exert some control over her life was an exercise in futility, so why bother? A good concert was the one place she could genuinely lose herself, have an out-of-body experience and detach from the deteriorating morass that was her life. And if it meant getting bitched at by her mother and an indefinite period with no car, then oh well. That's life.

That was when she noticed the black Town Car tailing them. It was close, like it was being dragged along on a hitch, so close she could see the faces of the two men in the front seat clearly. On the driver's side was a younger-looking man of East Asian descent, seeming to curse whatever cosmic force had made him be awake this early. His passenger was a slender-faced white guy with black wavy hair, maybe late thirties, though it was hard to tell, as his face was obscured with a cartoonishly large pair of aviators.

"Jesus," said Cora. "What is their problem?"

"What?" Demi looked in her rearview mirror. "Oh, Christ. Those assholes again."

Suddenly, Cora was on alert. "What, you know them?"

"Well, I've seen them," said Demi. "More than once on my way to work. They always tailgate."

"Holy shit," said Cora, a little shocked at Demi's blasé

attitude. Did it not occur to her that these people might be stalking her? Cora had been on guard for that sort of thing well before she dropped out of UCI.

"I've never seen them anywhere else, though," said Demi. "I figure they leave for work around when I do."

Cora turned around to study them, but they didn't seem to notice her at all. Probably just a couple of guys who were late for work, thoughtlessly tailgating Demi's car like it would get them there any sooner. That wasn't so abnormal, but the fact that the car didn't have a front plate caught her attention. Only out-of-state cars lacked a front plate, and a commuter wouldn't be from out-of-state.

She hadn't really been paying attention to NPR's *Morning Edition,* which had been reporting something about the previous day's wild fluctuation of the Dow Jones, but their next segment made her shoot to attention. "In the three years since it was founded," said the newscaster, "*The Broken Seal* has gone from fledgling website to the forefront of the transparency movement."

The words "*The Broken Seal*" sent a sharp icicle through her chest, and she momentarily forgot about the tail.

"But one month after the website's most infamous and controversial leak gave *The Broken Seal* and its founder, Nils Ortega—"

Demi reflexively slapped a button to change the station, and a Fergie song piped innocuously from KIIS-FM. Cora shot her a look. "I'm sorry," said Demi, smiling coldly. "It's too early."

Cora didn't know how to respond. On the one hand, she felt like it might be a good idea to know why "*The Broken Seal* and its founder, Nils Ortega," were in the news, but on the other hand, there was no subject she wanted to hear about less.

"It's okay," said Cora, glancing again at the Town Car behind them. "I don't want to think about it, either."

She turned to face forward, watching the tall buildings of downtown LA sprouting up like distant spires in the haze, and tried to put thoughts of *The Broken Seal* and stalkers from her mind. But the tailgaters, bored though they looked, were not letting up.

"Mom," she said, "ever feel like we're being spied on?"

"By who?"

"I don't know," said Cora. "Like . . . paparazzi or the government or something."

Demi blinked hard but didn't look at her daughter. "What, because of Nils?"

"Yeah?"

Demi snorted. "Maybe, but anyone who follows us would be on the wrong trail."

"Well, *I* know that," said Cora, unconsciously bopping along to "Fergalicious," her movements restrained by her too-small business casual button-up shirt. She had bought it for an interview a year ago, but she had gained a size since then. "But maybe they don't. Maybe they think we know something. And that's why they're, you know, spying on us."

"I try every day not to think about it." Demi tried to laugh, but it came out more a sigh. "If they are, I'd rather not know."

Cora bit her lip and looked behind them again. "Really?"

"I have enough to deal with," she said. "I feel like if I knew I was being spied on or phone tapped or followed, I wouldn't even know how to function."

"I guess," said Cora, eyes still on the car behind them. She switched the station back to NPR, but the report on *The Broken Seal* had already come and gone. "Lu says we're always being monitored."

"I know she does," said Demi coldly. "I know."

Cora decided to drop it and tried to keep her focus on the Dodge Stratus in front of them. Living under *The Broken Seal*'s shadow was a source of chronic fear that had only worsened since the Ampersand Event and subsequent leak of the Fremda Memo. Like the fan belt on the verge of snapping, *The Broken Seal* was a time bomb that would inevitably blow up in their faces. Again, she looked into the passenger-side mirror for the Town Car but saw that it had vanished. She couldn't shake the dread that this was the day the bomb would go off.

Once Demi had dropped her off at the Kaiser building downtown, Cora tried not to think about the Town Car, trudging through four hours of mind-numbing data entry during which, owing to company policy, she was not allowed any internet access. On her way to lunch, however, the dread only now starting to subside, she spared a glance out the window, at the roof deck of the parking garage several stories below.

There was the Town Car.

Seeing the car briefly stunned her into a stupor; she had not actually expected to see anything there. Why hadn't she turned the station back to NPR? Why, God, why had she listened to "Fergalicious" instead of the news?

She whirled around, scanning the mostly empty cubicles, half expecting the Town Car guys around any corner to throw a bag over her head and stuff her in their trunk. She considered leaving work altogether before deciding it would reflect poorly on Demi, and she was already on Demi's shit list. Besides, the Town Car was there, the men were not. They were likely somewhere in the building. Perhaps they were waiting for her to leave. Probably, this was nothing.

Possibly, it wasn't.

Cora stiffly brushed past the few other people in their cubicles who had decided to work through lunch. By the time she made it to the elevator, half convinced a couple of FBI agents were waiting in ambush at the exit, she decided to go to the cafeteria on the third floor rather than find lunch anywhere half-decent. But when the elevator doors opened, a large brick of a person stood on the other side. His face lit up upon seeing her, and Cora struggled not to wince in return.

"Sabino!" It was Eli Gerrard, one of the only people at Kaiser she knew by name. Eli was not a temp but a college graduate who worked in IT. "You okay?"

"Um," she managed. The door began to close, but Eli smashed the Door Open button, smiling like he'd done her a big favor as the door bounced back open. He fancied himself part of the hacktivist crowd, and, like most of his peers, he adored Nils Ortega.

"What's going on?" he asked.

She wasn't sure whether Eli was the best person she could have bumped into or the worst. She grimaced, conscious of how suspicious she looked, and moved inside the elevator. "Well . . ."

His eyes lit up as the doors closed behind her. "Is it something to do with *The Broken Seal*?"

"Maybe?" she said, now kicking herself for being in a situation where she was trapped in an elevator with this man. Even at a distance of a couple of feet, his eagerness, his overfamiliarity, felt like a violation of her personal space.

Eli was a scene kid, the type that was just a little too into Panic! at the Disco to be trusted. Ever since she'd started temping here a couple of weeks ago, Eli had been one of the first people who had taken a special interest in her, and for the worst possible reasons. At first, he saw her as an in where *The Broken*

Seal was concerned and then, when he realized she wasn't, he turned cold. She saw him sometimes talking to other people while staring at her. She was always waiting for him to accuse her of being a traitor to the cause, an enemy of free speech.

Hell, people like Eli were more than their share of the reason she was so paranoid. Back in July, she'd made the mistake of doing an interview for the *Los Angeles Times*. She'd answered their questions as diplomatically as possible—had Nils Ortega been a good father to her, her brother, and her sister? No. No, he had not. There was a reason he hadn't been in their lives for half a decade. Oh, the outrage in the hacktivist community that she had dared insinuate that their god-king was fallible. She'd had to delete all her online profiles, both the ones with her current legal name as well as the old ones that still bore the name "Cora Ortega."

But Eli had never been *beastly* to her as so many others had, at least not to her face. She figured she may as well see what he knew. After all, he actually followed this junk. "I think I'm being followed."

His eyes twinkled. "Really? By who?"

"I don't know," she said, "but I'm a little freaked out."

"Where?"

"They're outside. Or at least their car is."

"Is it the feds?"

"Maybe? Probably? I don't know."

"Oh, man, this could be huge," he said as the door to the third floor at long, long last opened. Cora all but fell out of the elevator, and he followed. "All that shady stuff the feds have done that's come out—up in Altadena and Pomona. You know?"

Cora stopped in front of the women's room and restrained the urge to roll her eyes. "I've heard rumors."

"People saw some stuff. *Real* witnesses after the Ampersand

Event. But then the government fried their brains and erased their memories so they couldn't say what they saw."

"Yeah, I heard that one."

"Why would that have happened if they didn't see something they weren't supposed to see?"

Despite deliberately trying to avoid all things Nils-related for her own sanity, she was well aware of that conspiracy theory. People like Eli thought the Ampersand Event was a spaceship or something, a UFO or a scout, or at the very least a probe. Cora, like most people, believed it was a rock that fell out of the sky and landed in the hills north of Pasadena. "I don't think that has anything to do with who's in the parking lot."

"It might," he said. "What makes you think they're following you?"

Cora almost started moving toward the cafeteria, but stayed put next to the women's room in case she needed a place to escape where he wouldn't follow. "They were behind our car on the way here. Then, just now, I saw the car parked on the roof of the parking garage."

"And you assume they're here because of you?"

Another batch of people unloaded from the elevator, and Cora kept her voice down. "I don't know, maybe? I mean, there was something on the news this morning."

"Oh, right. That." He watched her while she waited for him to continue, a tiny smile starting to form.

The spike of fear, the same one that always came with the mention of Nils, prodded her in the gut again. "What?"

"You don't know?"

"Eli, *The Broken Seal* is at the top of my list of things that I try not to think about if I can help it," she said. "Did he say something about me?"

He ignored her question. "I just can't believe you don't know. If I were you—"

"You're not me."

Eli took a deep breath, like he was about to bungee jump for the first time. "Dude. If *my* dad released the most important leak in human history, no, the most important *discovery* in human history—"

She snorted and started to respond, but he cut her off.

"I'd be all over it," he said. "You're an inch away from some of the most important stuff that's ever happened on this planet. I would be *on it*. Every hour, on the hour. I'd know what's up."

"You *are* on it, Eli. And that's why the sky gods gave you to me. So just tell me what you know or leave me alone."

"Did you ever read it?" he asked. "The Fremda Memo?"

That caught her off guard. "What the hell does *that* have to do with anything?"

"It has *everything* to do with why the feds might be following you!" he said. "It has *everything* to do with these cover-ups!"

She was by now alone with him in a long, empty hallway, and her fear had chipped her patience down to the marrow. "I'd better go."

"I don't get you, Sabino," he said, not even giving her the chance to turn to leave. "This is a big deal. Let's ignore the biggest discovery in human history that is being hidden from us as we speak. What about the civil liberties aspect? Don't we have a right to know? And those disappearances—five people *that we know of* disappear for a few days, when they come back, none of them have any memory of where they were. And all of them have brain damage. *All* of them. One guy has complete and total amnesia of his entire life. He can't even *talk*. So if some government guys *are* tailing you, the world needs to know. This is infring—"

"*No!*" It came out as a shout. "Dude, the *last* thing I want is anything to do with him! Can you appreciate that?"

He smiled and shook his head. "You're amazing. You don't care. You don't care what Ortega is trying to do or what he's uncovered. You're too caught up in your anti-daddy agenda."

Cora just stood there, mouth agape. Eli shifted uncomfortably, seeming to glean he'd crossed a line, but then doubled down. "Why do you hate him so much anyway?"

"I'm going to step away," she managed, turning before he could respond and darting inside the women's room, shoving the doorstop behind the closed door just in case. She half expected him to try to force his way in, but by some unseen mercy, he did not.

She ambled into the stall farthest from the door, leaving the doorstop in place, giving not one fuck if there was anyone out there who might actually need to use the restroom. She fell onto the toilet, pants still on, rested her elbows on her knees, and stared at the dirty tile of the bathroom floor. There were so many black hairline cracks in the tile she could read shapes into them like a Rorschach test. A whimsical cartoon *T. rex*. A volcano erupting into pyroclastic flow. A broken fan belt.

She'd been staring at the floor for a few minutes before she realized how hard her heart was beating, and then the *thump* of her pulse in her head was all she could hear. It was stupid of her to even ask Eli what he knew. Stupid to think that people like Eli even saw her as anything but a brick in the castle Nils built. Nils was only getting more famous, and this was getting worse. So, so much worse.

It took her nearly twenty minutes before she got off the toilet, the cacophonous thumping in her head only just starting to quiet. By that point, at least five frustrated parties had tried and failed to get into the bathroom, and she knew she had to leave or risk being discovered. She didn't bother going to lunch. Eli might still be in the cafeteria, and besides, she wasn't hungry.

She made a beeline for the elevator and took it back up to the fourteenth floor, where she found an internet-accessible computer that was not occupied. She pulled up Nils's website through a proxy, steeling herself for whatever he had written. She found it immediately, and the title alone made her put off reading it for another minute—"These Disparate Lives." *Ugh. Ugh. Ugh.* Once again shooting for a Pulitzer for achievement in pretentiousness.

Leaks on *The Broken Seal* always came with a bright red header labeled LEAK, but "These Disparate Lives" did not, meaning it was probably one of Nils's op-eds. Sometimes they ran in mainstream publications like *The New York Times,* but just as often, he preferred to keep it in-house so as not to be edited by The Man. He released his articles two or three times a week, mostly polemics on the state of free speech, transparency, his hatred of Bush, or how evil the mainstream media and government were for trying to silence him. She was hoping for something along this line. The worst thing it could be was personal.

Which, of course, it was.

Hello, Friends and Strangers,

Drink with me, or celebrate as your personal tradition dictates. Today marks the one-month anniversary of the leak that has come to be known as the "Fremda Memo," and we have not yet been brought down. In fact, next month will be our four-year anniversary, and, defying all odds, our little dog and pony show still stands. But with any increase of attention, regardless of the moral rightness of an endeavor, comes controversy.

The word of the day coming from the White House this morning: "thief." Others have built on this narrative—is *The Broken Seal* an organization of thieves?

Why steal secrets that are not yours to share?

To which I would counter, can one actually steal a secret?

Anyone who's worked with free speech advocacy, regardless of their hopes for society, has a personal reason for doing so. Do I have a personal motivation? In brief, I do. Three of them, in fact. My children.

Cora stopped breathing. Nils mentioning them in a public forum was the thing she'd been living in fear of for at least two years, but she hadn't expected it to take this form. The form that implied that they were still on good terms, that he was doing *them* a favor.

She noticed one of the white-collars watching her, a fortysomething woman with more pictures of cats than her children in her cubicle. The woman's look could be one of generic mom-judginess, or it could be one of recognition. Did she know who Cora was? Was it just fringe conspiracy crazies who had read "These Disparate Lives," or had this been the national news that Demi had flipped away from in favor of Fergie?

It should go without saying that I don't do this for myself but for the pursuit of a world that will allow them to live their lives without fear from one's government, media, or society for speaking the truth. My children are all in school in California, right near where the Ampersand Event occurred. And I'm not allowed to see them, nor even allowed to set foot in my own country.

This was, perhaps, an inevitability, but if I do have one hope for myself, it will be that I might one day reconcile these two disparate lives. That I may continue to do this work, and be with my children again. I hope I inspire them, as they do me. I hope one day they may be inspired to take up arms and join me.

Her mouth ran dry, her face was growing hot, her fingernails digging into the flesh of her palms. The earth was falling away around her, leaving her in a vacuum, no sound, no air.

Take up arms and join me.

It felt like the atmosphere was changing, and she was so disoriented that, for a split second, she thought she had imagined the blast that came from outside.

The noise startled her out of her stupor, and before she could wonder if they were under attack, a shock wave followed, shattering two of the north-facing windows, glass singing and clinking as it fell down like waterfalls, tiny shards ricocheting off the blinds. The few white-collars sitting near the windows screamed and fell away as the object that had created the blast shot overhead.

Stunned and ears still ringing, Cora slowly approached the window, now with no barrier between her and a hundred feet of open air. The object that had caused the blast had already disappeared, leaving only a bright white vapor trail in the blue-brown sky.

"Is that another meteor?" shrieked one of the women who'd been sitting by the window, now brave enough to approach it.

It sure looked like one. Its trail hung in the sky like a 747's, and where she'd sworn she'd seen it engulfed in flames as it shot overhead, the glow had dulled as it disappeared into the distance. Its trajectory was taking it northward, like it was following the 110 all the way to Pasadena.

In the same direction as the Ampersand Event.

Six minutes ago, a second meteor landed in the Angeles National Forest. It shot *right* over my location, so I want to get this eyewitness account down before they can censor it. We don't have precise geodata, but there are several witness accounts stating, yes, it landed *very* close to Altadena.

That's right. Meteor 2, right next to Altadena, and less than a month after the Altadena Meteorite, code-named the "Ampersand Event" by the CIA.

For the event code-named "Ampersand," we didn't have a sense of direction on the day the "meteorite" landed. *The Broken Seal* didn't leak the Fremda Memo until one day after the Event. We didn't understand its significance on the day that it happened, and by the time we really understood the hugeness of the Event, how deep the conspiracy ran, the dust had already settled. The feds had already cleaned it up.

This time, we know better. This time, we have the upper hand. Are you in the Los Angeles metro area? Don't be a good citizen. Don't be lied to and just take it. Follow the noise.

In the words of Ortega: *Truth is a human right*.

Gerrard, Eli. "Follow the Noise." *DeceptiNation* (blog). September 20, 2007.
http://www.deceptination.com.

2

Cora all but fell upon her front door, fumbling out her keys in a frantic bid to shut herself inside and lock the world out. If traffic was forgiving, it took about half an hour to make it the ten miles home from downtown LA. By bus, it was closer to ninety minutes, but panic on the roads had put today's journey closer to two hours. Cora hadn't been the only person to cut out of work early.

An initial panic had resulted in several fender benders both downtown and on the 110, although by the time Cora made it to her house, it seemed that the traffic was now back to boilerplate rush hour, perhaps slightly exacerbated due to a higher-than-normal number of car crashes. On her way from the Kaiser building to the bus stop, she saw dozens of people tearing by in their vehicles, clogging the streets and one of them nearly hitting her in their fervor, although what they were running to or from, she wasn't sure, and she suspected neither were they. It wasn't like there were any fifteen-mile-wide spaceships hovering over the U.S. Bank Tower that they needed to get out from under.

Despite the time passed, Cora's hands were still shaking as she struggled to get her key into the front door. The Sabinos lived in a three-bedroom house that had been illegally converted to four when they moved in, and that had been the only renovation the house had ever gotten in the forty years since its construction. It still had the same old peeling linoleum, the same old swamp-brown carpet, the same 1960s wallpaper that had been bleached by the sun through the windows. Before they had moved in four years ago, it had been a rental unit owned by Nils's mother that was adjacent to an active oil well. Since the late '90s, most of the oil wells in the South Bay area had dried up and been replaced by million-dollar McMansions, although the McMansion that had gone up on the dried-up oil well next to the Sabino home was probably worth closer to a million five.

Cora made it inside the house, shut the door, and slammed her back into it, exhaling a massive breath. The two family dogs, Thor and Monster Truck, had been whining at the door before she'd even gotten the key in the lock and were happily pawing at her thighs, but her nerves were still too fried to give them any real attention. She was so preoccupied that she didn't even notice that she wasn't the only person in the house.

"What are you doing here?" Cora nearly screamed when she noticed that there was a person on the couch, and that said person was playing her copy of *The Elder Scrolls IV: Oblivion*.

"What are *you* doing here?" Luciana countered, not even pausing the game or turning to look at her. Luciana had a head of rusty-red tight curls that on a good day would be anyone's envy, but lately, she hadn't been taking care of it, and right now, it looked like a crown of drunken tumbleweeds.

Cora's purse slid off her shoulder and fell to the floor. "I live here," she said. It wasn't at all unusual for her aunt to use her spare set of keys to arrive home ahead of Cora or Demi, usually to babysit. It *was* weird that she was here alone. Playing *Oblivion*. She'd thought Luciana hated that game.

"How did you get home?" asked Luciana. "I saw your car still outside. Did you get off early?"

"Our antiquated public transportation system," said Cora, ignoring the second question as she lowered herself into a crouch to give her dogs their desperately sought attention. Monster Truck, a wall-eyed pug who looked older than her eightish years, had already lost interest and returned to the couch next to Luciana. On the other hand, Thor, a mutt who, as best anyone could tell, was a chihuahua-dachshund mix, was insatiable.

"Weren't you supposed to work until six?" asked Luciana.

"Yeah . . . most of the windows shattered on the floor where I was working. So I just left."

"Really?" said Luciana. "I heard that happened in really tall buildings. Downtown is apparently a mess. You took public transportation? All the way from downtown?"

Cora stood up, eyeing her aunt. She had figured that between the confused chaos of a meteor event and Nils making the news with his "I'm fighting for my children" proclamation, Luciana would have reacted with a little more than, you know, nothing. "Yeah, did you not see my car out front?" she asked. "I think it's done for good."

"Oh, yeah, I had wondered about that."

Cora moved herself between the television and Luciana, studying her, starting to humor the idea that her aunt might have been replaced by a body snatcher.

Luciana just leaned over and kept right on playing. "How was traffic?"

"It was really bad," said Cora. "Seemed like more doomsday preppers than usual were heading for the hills."

Luciana stayed silent.

"I can't say I blame them, though," Cora continued. "Two meteorites landing in the same spot in the course of a month makes me think that maybe we should start thinking of shacking up in a cave, too. What do you think?"

Luciana shrugged, paused her game, and at last looked at Cora. "I think the conspiracy crazies are having a good week, and you need to stop listening to talk radio."

"I wasn't listening to talk radio," said Cora, offended at the insinuation. "But I was thinking, it does lend some credibility to Nils."

"What does?"

Cora blinked, her worry deepening. This was international news. Half of Southern California was searching for fallout shelters to die in, and Luciana wouldn't even look up from *Oblivion*. "Lu, a second celestial object just fell from the sky in almost the exact same spot as a nearly identical one did a month ago."

"Yeah, and who knows how long Nils was sitting on the Fremda Memo?" said Luciana. "He only released it after the Altadena Event to make it seem like the two things were connected to give legitimacy to his leak. It doesn't mean that they *are* connected."

Nils had leaked a few days after the Fremda Memo that the Altadena Event had a CIA code name, "Ampersand," which had been colloquially adopted by everyone, even mainstream outlets. Cora found it a little odd that Luciana still called it by its old name.

"So if it's not alien invaders, what is it?"

Luciana shrugged. "Downed satellite? I have no idea, but if I were an alien, I would not conspicuously crash my ship in the mountains next to one of the biggest cities in the world."

"Right," said Cora. It was fantastical, and there was no official explanation from any authorities other than "This is a meteor," which was the current line for both of them. It was frightening, and in times of uncertainty, it was natural to believe something fantastical, but in the end, Luciana was probably right. Occam's meteor—the simplest explanation is probably the correct one. "Well, I tried to call you after it happened. I was kind of freaked out."

"Oh, sorry. I had my phone off." Luciana pulled out her BlackBerry and turned it on. "It's just that with that article Nils released today—"

The phone in the kitchen rang, and Cora moved to answer it.

"Don't," said Luciana. "It's probably the press. You don't want to give a comment."

Cora froze, pulling her hand away from the phone as if it were an electric fence. "The press?"

"Yeah, that's another reason I've had my phone off. Just lie low; with a second Altadena Event, they'll probably move on quickly."

"About that," said Cora, picking up Thor and hugging him tightly. The little dog emitted a beleaguered "urrf." "I think that article Nils published today caught some attention, because I'm pretty sure some guys were spying on me before the meteor hit. There was a black Town Car following us this morning. Demi said it wasn't the first time."

"Oh," said Luciana. For the first time since Cora had gotten home, Luciana finally seemed to be taking something seriously. "That's . . . new."

"Two guys. Followed us all the way to Kaiser, then right before lunch, I saw the car on the roof of the parking garage."

"Are you sure it was the same car?"

"Yeah, it didn't have a front plate, which is, you know, weird. Did you read the article?"

"Yes. That *ass*." Luciana shook her head. "Unbelievable. I'm sorry he's trying to drag you into this."

Cora put her dog down and crossed her arms. "You still haven't told me what you're doing here."

Luciana gestured toward Monster Truck, who, on cue, rolled onto her back in anticipation of incoming belly rubs. "I promised Felix I'd play *Soulcalibur* with him, so I decided to swing by early."

Luciana unpaused the game. A jealous Thor nudged himself between Luciana and Monster Truck, wedging his nervous little head under Luciana's armpit as though he were acting in agreement that, yes, there was nothing more interesting in this world than Thor, dog of questionable ancestry. The *Soulcalibur* excuse, however, was an obvious front; Luciana was doing the Ortega Thing of lying by omission. Luciana's presence in Cora's house might have any number of causes, but she figured since "These Disparate Lives" didn't mention Luciana, it was probably the meteor.

"Are you hiding from the feds again?" asked Cora.

"I am hiding from the *possibility* of the feds."

Cora looked through the window, thinking she heard something approaching, but it looked only to be a delivery boy on a moped. Luciana had her own struggles where Nils's international man of mystery was concerned; the official reason they had given Luciana for firing her was "time card fraud," but everyone knew that the real reason was that being related to Nils

Ortega was not a great thing to be for someone with a job that required government clearance. Cora and her immediate family had it bad, but Luciana had gotten it way worse. At one point over the summer, there had been an entire week when Luciana had disappeared. Luciana said she wasn't allowed to talk about it.

"Won't they be too busy with the meteor to bother with you?" asked Cora.

Luciana chuckled and ran her fingers through her thick mop of copper hair. Cora sometimes found it hard to believe that she was Nils's sister and not some foundling; Nils's features had favored his German side, tall and pale, while Luciana had taken after her father, olive-skinned and petite. "They always find time for me. They were at my door within about three hours of the Altadena Event. Like zombies, hungry for brains and moaning, 'CIA.'"

"Wait, CIA?"

Luciana shrugged. "It's a CIA thing. I dearly hope that's not who was following you."

"I thought CIA wasn't allowed to investigate domestic . . . citizens," said Cora. She couldn't help but get a little nervous at their mention. Before Nils had left for good, he had always had a particular hatred for the CIA and their history of covert abuses of power, and Cora couldn't help but internalize some of that. "Nils said their whole raison d'être was every country besides this one. If we're being spied on, it should be FBI or NSA."

Luciana shrugged. "Well, first, CIA involvement doesn't preclude any other agencies. Second, Nils isn't domestic. He's committing espionage against the U.S. government from a foreign country. Ergo, he is a CIA matter." She looked at Cora, her expression finally changing into something like sympathy. "You okay?"

Cora pursed her lips. "I think he's challenging me."

"Who, Nils?"

"Yeah. With this last article. It felt . . . pointed."

"Well, of course it was pointed. He has never mentioned you before."

"No, I mean, the uh . . ." Cora wrinkled her nose in disgust. "The 'I hope they join me' bit."

"He's challenging all of us."

Cora huffed. "No, I mean *me*. Specifically me."

"Why?"

Cora wanted to give her an honest answer, but there was something in Luciana's tone that put her off. Nils was a difficult subject for all of them, and one they avoided if they could, but Luciana seemed angry that Nils was still the topic of conversation at all, even if it was relevant. "Just a feeling."

"He's a malignant narcissist," said Luciana. "He'll use anyone or anything to bring attention to himself and his agenda, but if we don't respond and nothing comes of it, he'll move on. I suspect he's busy trying to think on how to capitalize on the second meteor. He's probably already forgotten about his 'think of the children' angle."

"I guess."

Cora used to idolize her aunt, the independent older sister she'd never had, the one adult who she felt understood her, especially where matters of Nils were concerned. After Nils left four years ago, they had moved to Torrance to live off the largesse of Nils's mother (who blamed everyone but Nils for her son's decision to skip the country). Luciana, now practically their neighbor, started treating Cora more as her peer, and Cora had learned to think of Luciana as one in turn. For a time, it had been awesome; going to shows with Luciana, even a trip to

Vegas for Cora's twentieth birthday, and Luciana had not been the type to care about legal drinking age. But now that Luciana was unemployed and Cora a college dropout, their adulthood commiseration was just depressing.

Luciana's phone rang, and she snatched it and silenced it in a swift move, barely looking at it. "No Caller ID."

"Probably press, right?" Cora eyed the phone suspiciously, catching the name of who the call was from just as Luciana silenced it; Luciana's old coworker John Lombardi, who went by the name "Bard," almost certainly a D&D reference or something. "No caller ID, huh?"

"He's been calling me all day," said Luciana, her expression falling. Despite Luciana losing her job months ago, she didn't lose Bard, one of the most socially awkward people Cora had ever met. Cora was pretty sure that Bard was actually Luciana's ex, but Luciana would never admit it, and Cora would never ask. "Rough day at work. I'll call him back in a few."

"I see why you wanted to keep it turned off."

"It's not like I have a new job to obsess over," said Luciana. "I'm not quite ready to be out of the loop yet."

Cora sometimes wondered why Luciana still cared about her old job, why she didn't just move on, especially given all the grief it had caused her.

"Sounds like Bard's being illegal, then, since you're not top-secret clearance anymore." Cora stopped, noting the way Luciana slumped her head and rubbed her hands over her face. "Are you okay? Is something wrong?"

"It's not about clearance levels." Luciana sighed. "Bard told me that someone we worked with killed themselves."

"Oh." Cora waited for Luciana to elaborate, but she stayed silent. "Who?"

Luciana shifted a side-eye at Cora. "Someone."

"Right, sorry, forgot." She hadn't, really, but she sometimes hoped Luciana would slip up, although she never did. "Were you close to him? Or her?"

Luciana shook her head. "No. I knew them, but no. But it's surprising. They weren't the type that came off at all as suicidal. I hadn't seen them since I got let go, but it's surprising."

Cora shifted uncomfortably, unsure how to respond with no clue as to who the dead person was, what their relationship was to Luciana, or what drove them to do it in the first place. "Sorry."

Luciana bolted upright on the couch, her attention snapping to the front window. "Someone's here."

Cora moved to look out the window, expecting a cavalcade of black Town Cars barreling in from both directions. There was no Town Car, but there was her mother's Olds Cutlass, and she could feel a thrum of anger waves emanating from it.

"It's Demi."

Luciana caught the undercurrent of dread in Cora's tone. "What's wrong?"

Demi had already caught sight of Cora through the window, slamming the driver's-side door as she helped Felix and Olive out of the car. "She's mad," said Cora.

"Why?"

Cora didn't have a chance to respond. Demi stormed to the door, jerked it open, and glared at her daughter, her other two children trickling in after her. Olive looked like she'd been crying and was on the verge of starting anew, but Felix sauntered in like he'd just scored the winning goal at his soccer match.

"You left work, Cora." Demi's voice was low. "Without a word. I know this because they called me. Because you left."

The first thing Felix said to Cora was a simple, smug, "You're in trouble." He looked toward his aunt fondly. "Hi, Lu!"

"Hi, Felix," said Luciana. "Hi, Olive. Hi, Demi."

"Luciana," said Demi, her voice an ice pick, her eyes still fixed on Cora. Demi *never* addressed Luciana by her full name. This was bad.

"Can we turn on the news?" said Felix, pushing a jumping Thor away from of him. "I hope this is an invasion!"

"Hear me out," said Cora, ignoring Felix. "Did you read the article? About how noble Nils is spearheading this movement for a brighter future for his three beautiful children? Something about that made *someone* decide that I was worth spying on."

"Cora . . ."

"Wait, *what*?" said Felix, losing interest in the television. "Dad mentioned us today?"

"You left without a word," said Demi, ignoring her son. "Without clocking out. Nothing."

"Mom, you didn't tell me Dad mentioned us!" interjected Felix.

Cora's lip curled involuntarily. "Please don't call Nils that."

"I didn't know," said Demi. "And *please*, Felix, not now."

"I assumed everyone would just leave," said Cora.

"They didn't, but you did." Demi's voice was tremulous with anger. "I know because Kaiser called PMT. You have been removed from staffing lists effective immediately because you left without a word during a minor crisis."

"*Minor* crisis?" Cora managed. It had taken her six months to even get the temp job at PMT, making $8.25 an hour, and only with Demi going to bat for her. Six months. "They consider that *minor*?"

"Holy shit," said Felix. "You already got fired?"

"I just . . . Really?" Cora stammered. "Me not clocking out was priority enough for Kaiser to call you on a day like today?"

"Oh, they more than called us," said Demi, the whites of her eyes flashing. "Owing to a less-than-acceptable rate at which temps do not respect standards and practices of our clients, Kaiser Permanente has decided that they will no longer be a client for People for MedTech. Also effective immediately."

Cora's mouth hung open. She thought her jaw might detach and shatter on the floor like glass.

"Wow," commented Felix, pleased at the idea as he flipped to the news. "You are batting a thousand."

"Shut *up*, Felix," Cora snapped, trying to keep her cool for Olive's sake. There were times that it genuinely disturbed her how much Felix reminded her of Nils. While Cora had gotten Nils's gray eyes, neither she nor Olive otherwise resembled him. Cora's hair color, round face, and stature just short of average drew from the Sabino side. Felix, with his lithe frame, black hair, and blue eyes, was looking more and more like a miniature Nils every day. He wasn't worldly enough to be as manipulative as Nils, but she could see him getting there within a decade.

Cora looked at a shaken Olive, then at Demi. "Do we have to have this conversation in front of them?"

"Well, you guys finish your little domestic dispute," said Felix, disappointed to see that the news wasn't on yet, and as they did not have cable, no twenty-four-hour option was available. "I'm going to go online and find out about the aliens that are literally invading our planet."

As Felix departed, Olive turned to her older sister, her blank stare finally betraying fear. "Are the aliens real?" she squeaked.

"No, the aliens aren't real," said Cora with no clue as to the validity of that assertion as she opened her arms to welcome Olive. Olive carefully moved into Cora's embrace, looking at Demi as if to make sure she was allowed to even do so. Cora pulled her sister closer and picked her up. At just shy of six, she was a little small for her age. Cora looked at Luciana and couldn't help but notice that Luciana seemed unusually keen on avoiding this conversation.

"I have a meeting tomorrow with the VP of staffing that may end with my no longer having a job. Because I recommended you to staffing," Demi said, her anger now cold.

"I left during a crisis. The windows in the entire building had shattered."

"Was that the noise?" asked Olive. "The bang?"

"It's okay, butternut. We're safe," said Cora, her tone contradicting her words.

"You still have to play by the rules," said Demi.

"Can we please have this conversation at another time?" begged Cora, not wanting this to end in a scream-out in front of a first grader. Olive hugged her even tighter.

"No!" said Demi. "No, you do not get to duck out of this."

"I'm not trying to duck out of this—this conversation is upsetting your child. Lu?"

Luciana moved like she was about to agree with Cora, but one glance at Demi made her sink back into the couch awkwardly.

"Don't use Olive as a shield," said Demi, the anger turning hot again.

"It never even entered my head that it was in the realm of possibility that one temp leaving during a crisis would cost Kaiser as a client."

"I see that it didn't enter your head," said Demi. "But that's what happened. This isn't high school, where you can just skip half a day and no one will notice. You're an adult, Cora. Actions have consequences."

"Hello?" A man's voice sounded from the still-open front door.

The dogs, caught off guard, now overcompensated by tumbling off the couch in a heap of barks and rampaging toward the door. The three women turned to look at the man standing in the doorframe, looking like he'd caught a fair chunk of that conversation. He was tall and willowy, with full dark hair, a slender face, and a plastic smile.

"Demetra Sabino," he said as he took off his big, shiny aviators. "You prefer Sabino now, right?"

Monster Truck had calmed, but Thor was still challenging the intruder. Cora put Olive down and moved Thor back. She looked at the man again and nearly choked on her own sharp intake of air.

Aviators.

"Yes," said Demi. "I'm not giving any press statements."

"Not with the press." He pulled out a badge. "Special Agent Sol Kaplan, CIA."

It was one of the men from the Town Car.

3

Cora had heard tales of CIA and FBI agents from Luciana (and long, *long* ago from Nils), but she'd never actually met one. He looked to be pushing forty, around Demi's age but more than a head taller than she was, wearing a casual plaid button-down shirt over a Pink Floyd T-shirt, hardly the Man in Black she'd imagined.

"Mind if I come in?" asked Kaplan, ignoring the yappy Thor. Demi shook her head like she'd just snapped out of a spell, and she looked at Cora. Olive stilled, looking like a frightened gerbil. "This won't take a few minutes."

"You," said Cora. "You were . . . at Kaiser today."

"I don't know what you mean," he said, a little too familiar, holding his hand out to her. "You must be Cora."

She looked at Luciana, who was already wearing a tired expression of defeat. Feeling cornered, Cora took his hand briefly, giving it a light squeeze before pulling her hand away.

"Fancy seeing you here," he said, looking at Luciana, his voice walking a line between flirtation and threat.

"Likewise, Special Agent Kaplan," said Luciana.

"Sol," he said, "Special Agent Kaplan is my father." He laughed, indicating to Cora that he meant that to be a joke. But it didn't have the tone of a joke, like he wasn't practiced at joking.

"Olive," said Demi, keeping her eyes on Kaplan. "Could you go wait in your room for a few minutes?"

"Are we in trouble?" Olive blurted.

"We're not in trouble," said Demi, clearly not believing her own words.

Olive looked at Cora, worried, before quietly trudging off to her room.

"Please relax," said Kaplan. "I hate it when I show up and people act like I'm going to throw them into a military prison."

"More a matter of timing," said Luciana coolly.

Demi's eyes darted between them. "Do you two know each other?"

"I've enjoyed the occasional chat with Ortega the Younger," said Kaplan.

Luciana looked at him, and Cora wondered if her aunt wasn't avoiding "the feds," but him specifically.

"So how 'bout that meteor?" he said, looking at Demi. "Last time we had one of those, your ex-husband threw a little party."

"Cora, I think you should go join Felix," said Demi, eyes glued to Kaplan.

"No! I haven't had the pleasure of meeting young Cora. And Ms. Ortega?" he said, nodding toward Luciana. "Glad you're here. Save me a trip." He looked again at Cora and Demi. "Have a seat; this won't take a minute."

Cora obeyed and sat down next to Luciana, trying to look casual. Thor calmed his whining and settled down while Monster Truck curled into a ball next to Luciana. Demi stayed standing.

"As I'm sure you're aware, we are in the process of building a case against your ex-husband," said Kaplan, taking a seat opposite Cora. "But that is far easier said than done, especially as he is very good at protecting his sources." At this, he shot a sharp glance at Luciana, who struggled not to roll her eyes. "Now, I cannot force you to cooperate with this, but I'm hoping I can incentivize you to do so in the event that he tries to contact you."

He looked right at Cora, and that same spike of fear she'd felt that morning at the mention of *The Broken Seal* on the radio began boring through her gut.

"I have no idea what he knows," Demi stated. "I haven't spoken to him in years. The last I heard from him was a letter he sent me in 2003. After that, nothing. Not to me, not to the kids. So I don't have anything for you."

Kaplan shot another glance at Cora before returning his attention to Demi. "I understand that it was messy. Divorce left you with all the debt, he never agreed to pay any child support. But really, nothing in four years? Not even to the kids? And now this 'I'm doing it for the children, I hope they join me' call to action. You've really gotten nothing from him?"

"Nothing," said Demi without pause.

Kaplan looked at Cora. "Same for you?"

The spike of fear sharpened, drilled deeper. She swallowed and replied, "No, nothing."

Kaplan's gaze was implacable, but it lingered on Cora. "That's interesting."

"You know how he is, Sol," said Luciana, the only person in the room who didn't seem remotely threatened by the man. Cora tried to latch onto this; if Luciana knew him and wasn't threatened, there was probably no threat. "It's just PR. He's a showman, not a journalist. But he'll drop that angle immediately if it doesn't go anywhere."

"If they don't respond to it," said Kaplan. He looked again at Cora with that blank canvas of an expression. "Do they plan on responding to it?"

"No," Cora said reflexively. "No, I wouldn't."

Demi shook her head. "*The Broken Seal*'s been enough trouble to me and my family—I include extended family in that as well." She nodded toward Luciana. "We can't help you discredit him. We don't want to turn the world against him. We don't want anything to do with him."

"I know we've had this discussion, but for the record, I feel the same way," Luciana muttered.

"Good. Then if I were to suggest that you don't respond for comment when the press comes knocking, you'd be amenable."

"Of course," said Demi.

He continued eyeing Luciana and Cora as though he had decided Demi was harmless but wasn't so sure about the other two. Finally, he stood up and moved toward the door. Cora let out a breath.

"I do sympathize with all the pain he has caused your family," he said, finally remembering Demi was in the room. "I don't imagine it would surprise you to know that we do want to see *The Broken Seal* disbanded and Ortega extradited to stand trial for espionage."

Demi moved toward the door. "I don't think extraditing Nils will disband *The Broken Seal*."

"Like you said, Nils Ortega is a showman," said Kaplan. "The face of a revolution. There can't be a revolution if it doesn't have a face."

"This isn't the 1960s, Agent Kaplan," said Demi. "Revolutions don't need faces anymore."

"Besides," added Cora, "if the Fremda Memo really isn't legit, that will discredit him anyway."

Kaplan tilted his head toward Cora, amused. "Do *you* think it's legitimate?"

Cora looked at Luciana, who was still planted on the couch, staring into the middle distance. "I don't know," she admitted. "After the Ampersand Event, I thought it was just Nils being an opportunist. Taking a meteorite landing and pretending it was about aliens the whole time, typical conspiracy crap. But now that there's another one—"

"What do you think?" asked Kaplan, cutting her off and looking at Luciana.

"I think I'm under an NDA, and I'm not allowed to comment," said Luciana.

Kaplan smiled, a strange, forced expression, and looked at Demi. "What do you think?"

Demi shrugged. "I don't care."

"You don't care?" He coughed out a humorless laugh. "There's never been a conspiracy theory that's gotten this much media attention in the history of this country."

"Would it change anything?"

He moved toward Demi, resting his arm on the doorframe. Feeling like her mother's personal space was being invaded, Cora stood up, Thor whining as she rose.

"I appreciate your candor," he said. "I dearly hope that you're telling the truth about not having contact with him."

A pulse of worry seemed to weaken Demi's frame. She shook her head and smiled. "I know your agency has kept pretty heavy tabs on me and my family; you know he hasn't tried to contact us."

He leaned in toward her. "I don't know anything about you. I just met you."

Before Demi had a chance to respond, his phone buzzed. His expression changed, his eyes widening for a flash as he read the message on the phone before returning to neutral. He opened the door. "Duty calls," he said. "We'll be in touch."

Neither Luciana, Cora, nor Demi said a word as they watched him walk down the footpath, get into his black Town Car, and drive away. Cora realized how tense she was and released the breath she'd been holding. Luciana seemed slightly reenergized. Demi was still rigid.

"Mom?"

With a grunt, Demi grabbed an empty vase on the table next to the door and dashed it on the driveway. Cora gasped. Demi turned to face her wide-eyed daughter and stupefied ex-sister-in-law, steeled herself.

"I'm fine."

．．．．．

Demi didn't mention the PMT issue or Cora's firing again that night. She managed to put on a happy face for her younger two children after about an hour, and Luciana hung around and helped her drain the boxed wine they had in the fridge. By the time Demi decided to retire, she was so drunk that she stumbled off to bed without even saying good night.

"I'd better go," said Luciana, digging through her purse airily as though she'd misplaced a memory. She hadn't had anywhere near as much to drink as Demi had. "I might be out of town for a few days."

"What's the occasion?" asked Cora.

"I got invited to a friend's cabin, and you know, it's been a while since I went anywhere." She was still digging through her purse, pausing when she found what she was looking for. "I, um . . . I have something for you." She pulled an old flip cell phone out of her purse and handed it to Cora. "I got a couple of these, just in case."

Cora examined it, a cheap flip phone that looked like it came from a vending machine. "I have a phone."

"They've been tapping me for some time now." Luciana gestured to the landline. "I mean, you know, obviously. So I got these burner phones. So if you want to talk or get in contact with me or anyone and you don't want to use a line that might be tapped . . ." She threw a hand up and forced a thin smile. *Ta-da.*

Cora snorted. "Aw, my own Bat-phone. I'm a woman now."

"Bat-phone?"

"You know." She recalled the old '60s *Batman* theme: "*Da-na-na-na-na-na-na-na.*"

Luciana chuckled, but the tension in her voice only made Cora more uneasy. "Ah."

"*Da-na-na-na-na-na-na-na.*" Cora eyed the phone; she'd never even thought to look into burners.

"But only use it to call other burners. Don't call your friends with it."

"It's a good thing I don't have any friends."

"And *especially* don't use it to call landlines. I programmed a couple of my burner numbers in there."

"You think I'll need it?"

Luciana's eyes darted to the window. "You never know."

. . . . .

As Cora was heading for bed, she heard sniffling and loud, heavy breaths coming from her mother's room. *Demi is crying. Demi is drunk and crying. Say words of comfort, you inhuman monster. Say something.*

She didn't know when this wall had erected itself between herself and Demi. Certainly, it had begun construction well before Nils left, as Demi often dealt with conflict by turning cold, and Cora had grown up only knowing how to react in turn. She knew that Demi deserved some compassion and at least an apology for fucking up the Kaiser job.

She stood there a moment, then turned away.

Before she entered Olive's room, she stopped in front of the small hallway mirror, looking at her face and searching for beauty in it as girls so often do. It seemed like the weight she'd gained since last year had made her nose rounder. Looking at the ever-darkening circles under her eyes, she had the thought, *I need new concealer,* followed by, *I wish I could afford new concealer.*

Cora had a routine of singing Olive to sleep, usually when Demi was too drunk to do so herself, which was increasingly often. She did it now more out of enjoyment, nostalgia perhaps, than obligation. Olive was getting too old to expect this anymore.

She grabbed her guitar from her room, parked on the floor next to Olive's bed, and asked, "Requests?"

"'Sk8er Boi,'" said Olive without pause, settling in and pulling the blanket up to her chest.

Cora threw her head back and sighed in resignation. Not

a great choice for acoustic guitar. "Okay, but I'm choosing the next one." Avril Lavigne was not Cora's choice for Artist of the Year, but Olive had weeks ago decided her number-one object of hero worship was now Avril. More than once since school started, they'd had to dissuade her from wearing neckties to school. Usually, singing at night brightened her up, but tonight, even "Sk8er Boi" didn't inspire joy.

"Okay, I did it," said Cora after she finished. "My turn. How about Ani?"

"Ani is boring," declared Olive, looking down at her bedspread.

"That is mean, and one day you will understand that you are wrong," said Cora. "Compromise. 'Hey Jude'?"

"What's wrong with Mom?"

Cora deflated and put the guitar down. "Yeah, she probably just wanted to watch Jay Leno or something."

"She was mad earlier," said Olive.

"I messed up at my job," said Cora, leaning back into the weak wood frame of the bed. "I messed up, and I made her mad."

"Why?"

"I was scared," she said. "I left work without asking permission. I made a mistake."

"Scared of the meteor?"

"Yeah," she lied.

"Was that man looking for Daddy?" asked Olive. Her voice was thin, weak, like she knew Cora didn't want her to ask that question.

"Don't call him that," said Cora, stunned. This was the first time Olive had ever called Nils that. Olive had never known Nils. She was barely a toddler when he left. "Where did you get that?"

Olive shrugged, her eyes still downcast. "That's what Felix calls him."

"That's not what I call him." Cora smiled weakly. "Go to sleep, butternut," she said, kissing her sister on the forehead. Olive hugged her back, but it seemed to Cora a hug of obligation.

Cora went into her own room, which was smaller than those of her siblings, the scraps of square footage relegated to her after a two-year absence. Her room was just big enough for a twin bed, a dresser, a nightstand, and several boxes stacked by the closet. She still hadn't unpacked the boxes she'd brought back from the dorms at Irvine.

She sat on her bed, knees to her chest, quietly resenting the fact that Luciana and Demi had drained what was left of the box wine, and dug out a letter from under her mattress. Almost on instinct, she looked out the window, as if there might be some government spy peeking in. She opened it to read it again. She'd read it dozens of times by now.

The first and only letter she had gotten from Nils in four years.

Dear Cora,

I hope this reaches you well. I've thought at great length how to begin this letter and what to say in it, but after going through several drafts, I've decided the simplest approach is best. I think often about the terms we parted on, how bad it was for both of us, and I regret it.

Abuelita says you've gone to UCI and are studying linguistics. I don't know much about the Language Science department at UCI, but a quick

```
Google search tells me they're one of the best.
What does one do with a degree in linguistics these
days? Now is a good time to be in school—the entire
world economy is about to crash.
```

The letter was postmarked almost two months ago, well after she'd left UCI. He didn't even know she'd been put on academic probation. He didn't even know she'd lost her scholarship and was back at home, living out of unpacked boxes and ruining her mother's career as much as she was her own. Either Abuelita hadn't cared to inform him, or he hadn't cared to ask.

```
By the time you get this, I may have already
released what may be the most important leak we
ever received. We've been working on this one
for months, waiting for the perfect time, or else
people may not give it its due attention, and it
will get buried.
```

She hadn't known it when she'd first gotten this letter back in July, but he must have been referring to the Fremda Memo. Well, he'd gotten his wish. The perfect opportunity had come in the form of the Ampersand Event, and Nils had seized it brilliantly.

```
I write this with the hope that we might
reestablish communication, perhaps even begin to
rebuild a relationship. You were only sixteen the
last time we spoke, and I recognize now that I
should have met you where you were, not where I
wanted you to be.
    I hope you respond to me someday. I don't expect
```

you to agree with what I've done. I know I've hurt
you all. I don't ask for your forgiveness, not yet,
but just understand why I do what I do.

I want a future for us, but I want it on your
terms. Perhaps one day, if I earn your forgiveness,
I may even earn your acceptance. I don't want
you to simply endure what I do. I want you to
understand it, because I think if you understand
me, eventually, you might join me.

                                        Dad

A part of her wanted to burn it. She'd already lied to a CIA
agent about not having heard anything from Nils in four years.
Before, the letter had been a source of cognitive dissonance, but
now it could seriously get her in trouble.

There was a part of her, a part she hated to even acknowledge,
that felt some temptation. The Nils that left them had done so in
a radioactive hailstorm of bad blood. It had seemed at the time
that he was in the wrong, that he was a career failure, and that
Cora was the bright one with a promising future. Now, against
all odds, he had succeeded at everything he had tried to do, and
Cora was the failure with no prospects. There was nothing for
her here anymore, so hitching her cart to that wagon wouldn't
be the most irrational thing.

Nothing for her here, except Olive.

That thought snapped her back to reality—of all of them,
Olive was the one he had abandoned most callously and the one
for whom Cora had picked up the most slack, having to step
in as a surrogate parent when she should have been preparing

to leave the nest. The temptation to respond was fleeting and, ultimately, easy not to give into.

But at the same time, she wanted Nils to know that the message had been received and rejected. His non-apology was bad enough, but coupled with him taking the first opportunity to talk about himself was just arrogant. It was a risk, as there was a chance some government goon might find out she'd lied about the letter, but one she was willing to take. The letter had a return address in Germany, and there it would go.

She decided to slip it in the mail before she went to sleep, despite the fact that it had started raining. As she put up the mail flag and slammed the little aluminum door shut, she caught a flash of something out of the corner of her eye. She looked over into a yard across the street, a house that had been uninhabited for months, adorned with brush and bramble that made the property look feral. She thought she saw something move behind the house, as though the light of the moon had flashed off a bright, reflective surface, and then it ducked behind the unkempt brush in that house's yard.

She gasped, eyes on the dark yard of the empty house, her fingers starting to go numb from the rain and the cool, damp air. It had been such a long, strange day that Cora was prepared to believe anything. She edged toward the brush, beginning to shiver.

"Hello?" she breathed, stopping in the middle of the street.

Nothing.

She gasped as a pair of headlights abruptly rounded the corner, driving far too fast for any residential neighborhood, and she hopped back onto the sidewalk as it zoomed past. Her eyes were now burned from the bright lights, hardly able to see in the darkness. By the time her eyes started to adjust again, she could detect no movement near the house, just light from the streetlamps reflecting off the rain droplets.

She stepped away from the brush, not willing to entertain the ideas that were sprouting in her mind. Whatever she had seen, it was only her subconscious reacting to an unusually stressful day. A big white cat or something. There couldn't be any meteor-related beings in the suburbs, snooping around here looking for Nils, because there was no way her luck was that bad. Right?

There was.

Hello, Friends and Strangers,

With regard to the "meteor" event that occurred on September 20 at 1:13 PDT, I wish I had more for you—the document below reveals little more than what we already knew, plus more code names. "Meteor" event number two they are code-naming Obelus. At least they're keeping it in theme.

Denial is always the first response to upheaval, to any collective trauma, and if these leaks eventually reveal themselves to be legitimate, the revelation of First Contact will be traumatic. Proof positive that we are not alone. Proof positive that authorities do not trust us with this knowledge. Proof positive that authorities cannot be trusted.

I need to impress that this goes beyond injustice, that the biggest cover-up in human history is a crime against all of us. Truth is not freely given in our society; it must be taken. Where walls are built, tear them down. Where borders are drawn, erase the line. Where you see wax, break the seal.

Truth is a human right.

Ortega, Nils. "Obelus." *The Broken Seal*. September 21, 2007.
http://www.thebrokenseal.org.

4

The scuffling in the computer room didn't wake her up; she'd been awake for hours. She'd been trying to clear her mind and get to sleep but always came back to Nils's letter, how it ripped open wounds she'd deluded herself into thinking had healed years ago. She didn't know why she had kept it for the last two months; it was too uncomfortable to merit introspection. She wondered what he wanted, what he really, honestly expected her to do. Those thoughts led her to replaying the act of putting the letter in the mailbox. The thought that the letter was still there, just sitting there. That the U.S. Postal Service, a branch of the U.S. government, was going to ferry that letter, and that they might not deliver it to Germany, but to Sol Kaplan. Going back and forth over what she'd seen in the yard across the street.

This cycle continued until she looked over to her digital alarm and saw that it was nearly 4:00 A.M. She rolled onto her back and threw off her sheet, now coated in a thin layer of sweat. The dorms at Irvine had air-conditioning; this house did not.

She still wasn't tired. Not that it mattered—she didn't exactly have to be ready for work soon.

Then she heard something, a clink of a dropped object, as if there were some nocturnal animal going through the kitchen trash can. After a few seconds of stillness, she heard the scuffle again, and an intense dread bloomed, the dread that accompanies the suspicion that your house is in the process of being robbed.

Or that the flash of white in the neighbor's yard she'd seen earlier had followed her inside.

She shook her head, tried to shake it off, reminded herself that that was absurd. She opened her eyes and saw Monster Truck attentive, facing toward the bedroom door. Cora heard it again, and Monster Truck heard it, too, signaling alertness with a tiny *bork*. Cora sat up, and shook her head, trying to push away the thought that opening her bedroom door would reveal a gunman or a government agent (or perhaps some combination of the two).

Or an alien.

The sound was definitely too large to be a mouse. A rat, perhaps? A rat named Felix? Felix knew he wasn't supposed to be playing games this late—and he'd used the barely operational desktop for his illicit gaming needs before.

Cora fell out of bed, opened her door, and peeked down the hall toward the living room and kitchen area. There did indeed seem to be a light emanating from the computer room that had not been emanating when she went to bed. She stilled for a few breaths, waiting to see if she could hear anything else. The family desktop was nestled in a small pseudo-room next to the living room that was too small to be considered a bedroom. When she didn't hear anything, she shuffled the few feet from her bedroom door to the computer room.

"Felix," she whispered, hoping to God he was the culprit. "Felix? You know you're not supposed to be in there, you little pervert."

No answer.

"Felix?" she whispered again, placing a hand on the doorframe to the computer room, then looking inside. The monitor to the computer was on, a dull blank light emanating from it, but the computer itself seemed to have been dismantled. It was up and running, but its shell had been removed, and was now on the floor.

Not Felix.

She tried to contain the well of fear that was springing up. She again recalled the thing she'd imagined in the neighbor's yard, beginning to entertain the idea that she might not have imagined it. She backed away from the computer room, into the living room, and against the sliding door that led to the backyard—not only was it unlocked, it was slightly ajar.

"Cora?" It was Felix. Now he was out of his room, looking alternately at her and at the computer. "Did you do that?"

Not wanting to cause a panic, Cora answered, "Felix? How about you go into Mom's room?"

"Why?" he asked, rubbing his eyes.

"Because . . . I asked you to." She looked at Felix. He caught her intensity and started backing toward Demi's room.

The exchange brought Olive out of her room. She didn't speak, instead looking at Cora expectantly. Cora shut the door to the backyard and approached the computer room, standing in the doorframe as if there were a land mine somewhere under the floor right in front of her.

"Go with Felix," whispered Cora.

"What's going on?" demanded Felix.

"You're bowing to my will is what's going on," whispered Cora, unable to come up with a reason less panic-inducing than *I think someone, or something, broke into the house.* "Please go into Mom's room for a second while I check on this."

Felix and Olive backed down the hall; Olive did as she was told, but Felix did not go all the way into Demi's room, instead keeping his eyes on Cora. Slowly, like a technician preparing to defuse a bomb, she approached the computer. *This is insane,* she thought. All evidence pointed to someone having broken and entered the house, and she couldn't stop fretting over whether or not she'd seen a space monster. *Someone broke in. They're looking for dirt on Nils or something. Call the police.*

"I think we should call the police," she finally managed.

"What?" she heard her mother's groggy voice from her bedroom.

"I think we should call the police," said Cora again, louder this time. She stood up and backed away from the computer as though the undetonated bomb were still a threat. "I think someone—"

For the space of a heartbeat, she thought she saw a dark silhouette on the other side of the living room, distinctly inhuman, a massive reptoid thing in a crouch. She definitely saw eyes, black orbs imbued with the faintest of golden glows.

In the space of another heartbeat, she was screaming and running in the opposite direction, summoning a strength she was heretofore unaware of to lift her thirteen-year-old brother off the ground and force him into their mother's bedroom, where their confused mother and sister awaited. Felix was too shocked to protest. Monster Truck had followed them on instinct. Cora had already slammed the bedroom door shut before she saw that Thor had not.

"What is going on?" shrieked Demi, shooting out of bed.

"*Something's in the house!*" Cora yelled. Demi had a dresser next to the bedroom door, nearly as tall as an adult and twice as wide, which Cora toppled on its side to block the door, spilling jewelry boxes, pill bottles, and all manner of mom detritus onto the floor.

"What are you doing?" yelled Demi. Olive was screaming. Monster Truck was barking madly, and Cora could hear Thor doing the same on the other side of the door.

"There's something in the house!" repeated Cora.

Demi's face contorted as though she were about to excoriate Cora or at least demand a better explanation, when the door started shaking. Cora backed away from it, wondering if that thing could be held back by a door and a dresser if it really wanted to get in. She turned and looked at the one small window in the room, wondering if there was a glimmer of hope of getting all four of them and the dog out through the window before that thing broke down the door, when she felt a high-frequency noise ringing inside her head. She tried to say something but fell to her knees. She sensed the dog stop barking, her sister stop crying. The noise was telling her to close her eyes, go to sleep.

5

Monster Truck was awake and alert by the time Cora regained consciousness, snorting bravely in pug. Olive was also awake, sitting on the floor next to her, breath heavy but even, eyes glued to the window. The sky was starting to turn a dark cerulean blue with the approaching sunrise.

"Olive," she gasped, shaking off her grogginess. "You see anything?"

Olive shook her head.

"Felix?" Cora blurted, realizing Felix had not yet moved or spoken. Cora shook him, and Felix's eyes creaked open.

"Wha—" Felix shot up.

Demi, who had collapsed next to the bed, began to stir, looking up at the door—dresser barricade still in place, still closed.

"Did you see anything outside the window?" Cora asked.

"No," said Olive.

"What was that?" asked Demi absently.

"I . . . don't know," said Cora. She shook her head and looked up at the window, carefully standing on the bed to peek outside. "How long do you think we've been out?"

"Not long," replied Demi.

"You said the aliens aren't real," said Olive, looking at Cora, betrayed.

"I . . ." Cora shook her head. "I didn't think that they were."

"That was one of them, wasn't it?" said Felix. "Did you see it?"

Cora's breaths were still trembling, her gaze running over all the spilled items on the floor, wondering if it all had really happened. "I don't know."

"I saw it," he said. "It looked like it was crouched, but I saw it. It was huge."

Cora shook her head. She thought she had seen something, or at least imagined it, but she wouldn't characterize it as "huge." "Are you sure?"

Felix nodded fervently. "That email Dad leaked was true. The meteors aren't really meteors. They're spaceships. It's all true."

"You said there wasn't an invasion," said Olive, leveling an accusatory glare at Cora. "You said the aliens aren't real."

"This doesn't prove anything," said Cora.

"I think it does," said Felix, his voice urgent. "Where's Thor?"

Olive's expression of betrayal turned to one of alarm. "Where's Thor?" she asked, matching Felix's intensity.

"He's just on the other side of the door, sweetie," said Demi, now alert, her voice shaking.

Cora sprang to her feet and tried to lift the dresser, but quickly gave up, as it was much easier to topple than it was to stand back up. Even so, they didn't know what was on the other side of that door. "Shit."

"He isn't barking anymore," said Felix, looking at Cora like she personally had killed the family dog.

"Where is Thor?" cried Olive, now unable to hold back tears.

"I'll find him," said Cora, slipping on a pair of Demi's tennis shoes.

"Cora," said Demi, grabbing Cora by the arm. "What are you doing?"

"I'm going outside to look for Thor," she said as she finished lacing up her shoe. "I need to see if whatever did this is gone."

"Fuck," said Felix, the implication of the whole situation hitting him.

"*Cool it!*" snapped Demi. "We're calling the police." Demi jabbed the phone cradle repeatedly, then slowly hung it up. "Line's down."

"Cell phone's dead, too," said Felix, holding up Demi's cell phone and impotently mashing the power button.

Cora finished lacing her shoes. "I'll be back."

"Cora, I am dead serious," said Demi, taking her phone from Felix. "Don't even think—"

"Keep trying with the cell. Olive, it's okay. I'm going to look for Thor, okay?"

Olive shook her head, tears streaming. She had such a strange way of crying for a child her age. It was almost always silent.

"Not okay!" said Demi. "What if that thing's still out there?"

"What do you think it's going to do, interrogate me? 'Hey, sorry you went to all that trouble and exposed yourself, but I really don't know where my father is.'"

"Cora, we don't know that's what it wanted."

"What else could it want? Why *us*?"

"What if it's after Luciana?" volunteered Felix. "What if it has something to do with that time they took her into custody—"

"Or that thing's gone because it dug through our computer and sees we don't know where Nils is." Cora opened the window and started to climb out. At that moment, she was more concerned with her dog's well-being than the broad, sweeping philosophical implications of the existence of extraterrestrial life, or the even more profound implication of Nils's lifework and reason for abandoning his family in the first place being completely validated.

"Cora!" Demi stood up and grabbed her daughter by the pajamas as she tried to slip out the window.

"No!" said Olive, snapping out of her stupor. "It'll get you, too!"

Cora continued her squeeze outside. "It won't get me," she grunted, pulling her legs up over the windowsill and turning her head to peek back in.

Olive clearly didn't believe her, and her face turned livid. "*You* said the aliens aren't real!"

"We don't know that's what it was, Olive!" said Cora, not believing her own words as she rounded the corner into the backyard.

She trotted to the other side of the house and peeked into the window of the den; the computer had indeed been carelessly left in pieces. No sign of a space alien, though. She opened the unlocked back door. "Thor?"

From what she could tell, the creature must have gotten in and out the old-fashioned way: through the front door. It being the dead of night, it may have done so without being seen. She slipped back into the house and ducked into her room, throwing on her old, peach-colored Disneyland hoodie and grabbing her cell phone. She noticed that the front door had also been left open. She started toward it, then doubled back, dug the Bat-phone and her wallet out of her nightstand, and stuffed them in her pocket.

Cora peeked into every room in the house that she considered big enough to hide a creature before Demi and Felix succeeded in removing the dresser from the bedroom door and opened it.

"It's gone," Cora said to Demi. "Whatever it was." She could see a furious Olive down on the floor of Demi's room, back turned to her. "But Thor's gone, too. I'm going to go look for him."

"You just said you were going to check the house," said Demi.

"And I did. I have my cell phone. If I don't find Thor in a few minutes, start knocking on neighbors' doors." She turned and all but sprinted out the front door, the adrenaline coursing through her veins begging to be burned off.

She called for Thor, turning right and jogging to the corner. "Thor!" she bellowed, past the point of worrying about bothering the neighbors. At this point, she was starting to panic. "*Thor, come!*" she called again. What hideous lies movies peddle, she thought, the idea that dogs survive home invasions. If there was a yappy dog making all that noise, drawing unwanted attention, why *wouldn't* an alien kill it?

The thought filled the pit of her stomach with ice. She didn't accept that yet—if the creature had killed her dog, there would be a body or at least a dog-sized pile of ash. No, that was a thought she could not entertain. Olive would never forgive her for that. After a few more minutes and another block scoured, she turned another corner.

There was Thor, sniffing something in one of the rich neighbors' corner yards.

"Thor!" she cried, and the dog lost interest in whatever he was sniffing, ears perked up and happy to see her for one hot second, before doubling back to whatever he was sniffing.

Cora sprinted to her painfully stupid yet mercifully still-living dog. She was now on a block that graduated from upper-middle class to nouveau riche. Some of the homes here forsook lawns in favor of trendy, drought-proof yards dotted with smooth stones, succulents, and sand. "Since the alien didn't kill you, I might have to," she said to Thor before she saw what the dog was sniffing.

It looked like part of a footprint.

She shook her head, thinking her mind was seeing what she *thought* an alien footprint might look like. It looked like a bird's footprint, if the bird weighed three hundred pounds and only walked on its toes. It had a texture to it, upon examination, like creases, joints leaving their imprint in the sand.

And it was fresh, clearly from after the rain had stopped.

"Go home," she told Thor.

Thor's ears perked up in the direction of her house at the sound of Felix and Olive calling for him, sounding much more desperate and frightened than Cora had.

"Go on," she said, kneeling down to get a better look at the footprint. "Go home."

Thor whined at her.

"Go," she repeated, more assertively.

Thor yipped, confused, before heading toward the call of Cora's two younger siblings. Cora looked up to see that Thor had paused at the corner. "Go on!" she commanded. Thor scampered toward home.

She examined the "footprint" for several minutes, alternately trying to convince herself that seeing a footprint here was projection, a mind trick akin to seeing the face of Jesus on a piece of toast. But she had seen *something* in the dark of her living room, something that looked big and alien enough to match this footprint.

In a daze, she started walking in the direction the footprint pointed, wondering if it had been planted deliberately, an invitation to follow. Surely, if there was some sort of alien intelligence capable of interstellar travel, it would be capable of covering tracks in the dirt.

As she neared Sepulveda, however, she caught the distant blues and reds of police lights about to round the corner toward her. On instinct, she ducked into a yard, slipping through an unlocked gate and hiding behind the brick wall that bordered the house. Through the wrought iron gate, she saw the vehicles glide by—not police cars but big, black SUVs. They were heading toward her house.

The letter.

A string of cold wire wrapped around her stomach and squeezed; what if they found that returned letter to Nils in the mailbox? Forget alien home invasions; what would they do if they had found out she'd lied about Nils never contacting her? She flipped out her cell phone and called her mother's phone— straight to voice mail. "Shit," she hissed, dialing the landline. Also out of service. "Shit, shit, *shit!*"

It took another three tries on her mother's cell before it stopped going to voice mail and actually rang. Her mother picked up almost immediately. "Where are you?" she demanded without salutation.

"I'm up—" She stopped herself, remembering what Luciana said about their lines probably being tapped. "I'm right outside."

"Cora, come home, now. Thor came back."

"Is anything going on?" she asked, carefully sliding through the wrought iron gate and out of this person's yard before anyone noticed her. She headed back toward Sepulveda. "Do you see anyone in the driveway? I worry we're about to get another visit from that Kaplan guy."

"Oh, God, Cora, come back here right now!" Demi's voice was strained in a way Cora had never heard it before, not even in the worst fights she'd had with Nils before he left.

By now, she had almost reached Sepulveda and didn't see any more Men in Black headed her way. "I'm serious, I just saw—"

"Oh, God, Cora, I don't—" Demi cut herself off.

Cora froze where she stood. The light changed, and a pre-rush hour flood of cars flew past. "Mom?"

"Someone's here."

"Some*one*? Some-human-one?"

"Yes."

Cora held her breath, waiting for Demi to respond. "Black SUVs?"

"Stay put," said Demi after a pause.

"Stay *put*?"

Demi had cut the line. Cora stood there, staring at her phone dumbly. The wave of commuters passed, and once again, Sepulveda was a wide, empty lake of asphalt. She stayed rooted in place, torn between running away from whatever was happening at her house and running toward it. But whatever was going down, what could she possibly do to stop it?

There was a nature preserve on the opposite corner to where she stood, a small wetland that had managed to fend off developers. Jaywalking laws be damned, she ran across Sepulveda and toward the marsh. On the opposite side of the marsh was the Circuit City and then the mall. Both wildernesses seemed like good places to lose anyone tracking her.

She had only made it a few hundred feet into the marsh before she discerned the sound of a distant helicopter through the noises of her own huffing and panting. Distant, but growing closer by the second. She stopped running and plastered herself against a tree, her default assumption that they were looking for her. But surely they weren't—they must be looking for the thing that broke into their house. Why on earth would they be looking for *her*?

Because I am a witness.

And then she thought about what Eli Gerrard had said the government had been doing to witnesses, the giddy way he'd said it. Witnesses disappeared. When they came back, if they came back at all, their memory was gone. Sometimes permanently.

Cora felt in her pocket for the Bat-phone and started to call Demi, but stopped, remembering what Luciana had said about calling landlines. She instead used her regular cell phone. The phone rang once, twice, three times. Then someone picked up.

"Cora." The voice belonged to Demi, but Cora could tell from her tone that there was someone else there.

"Mom?" She didn't know what to say; they hadn't established any kind of code for this sort of situation. "I'm safe."

"Good," Demi replied. Then she was silent, as though on the other end of the line there were some maniac with a gun to her head. Then Demi whispered, "Run."

Cora froze, unsure whether she had heard her mother correctly, then threw her phone into the marsh, stumbling back into the brush, powering through the long, tall grass. A part of her wondered if she might inadvertently smack into the very thing she had been following, but her senses were tuned to things that might sound human: voices, vehicles, helicopters. Hell, especially the helicopter. She had no idea how to hide herself from a helicopter. What if it had an infrared camera?

She had to get out of the marsh.

She started back toward the direction of the Circuit City, or at least what she *thought* was the direction of the Circuit City, before she stumbled into the marsh part of the marsh. Her feet plunged into cold, wet clay, trapping her where she was. She tried to back out of it, only to discover that in her haste, she had surrounded herself with it. In the distance, a few egrets looked at her bemusedly before flying away. She struggled to free herself from the mud and had only just made it back onto solid ground before an unseen force pushed her back into the muck, flat on her face.

She tried to scream, but it was as though the air in her lungs had frozen solid, the muscles around her throat refusing to come together in the manner required of screaming. The more she tried to thrash, the greater the force that held her in place, as if her body were turned to plaster. She tried to cry out, but nothing came. She convulsed as though electricity were flowing through her, turning her nerves into jelly. She felt a deep pressure on her neck as though something were trying to burrow in between her vertebrae. Her brain demanded that her voice produce some noise, any noise, but her body wouldn't obey.

6

Cora's eyes shot open, and she released the scream she'd been trying to produce. She clapped her hand over her mouth and shot to her knees, breathing hungrily. She'd blacked out, but only for a few seconds, perhaps. She slapped her hand on the back of her neck where she'd felt the pressure, feeling a sticky, warm substance. She looked at her fingers. Blood. Not a lot, but her skin was broken.

She coughed in horror, scanning the marsh to look for where the thing had gone, seeing nothing. That thing had caught her and let her go, tagged her like an animal. Then she saw footprints in the mud—the very same she'd seen in her neighbor's yard.

She stood up, choking on her own ragged breathing as she rose, her legs wobbling. Was it just a tag? Something benign? The seed of a pandemic, or a larva that might lead to the eruption of a face hugger? She smacked the back of her neck, now unable to shake the idea that the thing had laid eggs in it.

She stopped, remembering that she was also on the run from human parties. It was just before sunrise, and she could hear the distant traffic on either side of her, but nothing that sounded like some militarized police apparatus in hot pursuit. She tried to fling off the mud that clung to her right side and torso. Landing in grass had saved her legs, although her shoes were caked into wet bricks, and her right jaw was covered in mud. Between the flowing lavender pajamas, the Disneyland hoodie, and the filth, she couldn't have been more conspicuous if she had been wearing clown makeup.

She whirled around, searching frantically for the creature, neither seeing nor hearing anything. Where before she had second-guessed herself, this time there had been real contact. Real, *physical* contact.

She wanted to run back into the arms of the Men in Black, screaming that an alien had just injected her with *something* and she'd give up just about any measure of civil liberties if they would please get it out. She probably would have if she didn't have what Eli Gerrard said about the disappearances and government-induced brain damage banging about in her mind like a pinball. If all those stories were true, and if just being in the wrong place at the wrong time could get your brain fried by the government, what would actual *contact* net her?

If any time was the time for a Bat-phone, it was now. She flipped it out, began marching in the direction she thought the mall was, and dialed the preprogrammed number for Luciana's burner.

Luciana didn't answer on the first try. Or the second. There were two preprogrammed numbers for burner phones, so Cora tried the second number, and Luciana picked up on the fourth ring this time. "Hello?" grumbled her aunt. She sounded exhausted, but not groggy. It didn't sound like she'd just woken up. "Cora?"

"Lu!" gasped Cora, struggling through the tall grass. "The thing was in our house."

Luciana took a moment before responding. "The what now?"

"The thing, the . . . alien thing. It was after Nils. It was in our house!"

"Where are you?"

"I'm in the marsh," she said, at last stumbling onto a footpath. "The thing was in our house, and then it wasn't, and then Thor was gone, and then I went to look for Thor, and then the Men in Black showed up, and then the thing, the alien thing—" Even saying those words out loud felt ridiculous. "I assume it was an alien thing, I didn't get a good look at it, it . . . I don't know, it followed me to the marsh, and it grabbed me? It—"

"Slow down!" said Luciana, audibly roused by Cora's panic.

"And when I was out looking for Thor, I saw the Men in Black going toward the house, and I called Mom and she told me to run away, so I did, and then I was in the marsh, and it caught me, and it tagged me. And Mom told me to run. I think they've been taken into custody by the feds. Are you there? Are you home? I'm freaking out!"

Silence on the other end of the line. Cora stopped walking, worrying that the line had been cut. "Custody?" asked Luciana, confused. "They arrested Demi and the kids?"

"I don't know!" said Cora, trying and failing not to yell. "Demi told me to run! Can you please come get me?"

"No, I can't," said Luciana. "I'm out of town."

"Where are you?"

"I'm . . ." She heard Luciana put her hand over the receiver, talking to someone else. "Hold on. I'm going to call you back."

"What? No!" pleaded Cora. "Please don't hang up on me, I'm

in the middle of the marsh, and there's an alien out here, and I'm alone, and I'm covered in mud, and I have nowhere to go. Please don't leave me alone!"

"Okay!" said Luciana. "I won't hang up. Just give me a few minutes."

"Where are you?"

"Give me a few minutes."

Cora trudged on, phone glued to her ear, until she reached the Circuit City parking lot. By this point, she had been on hold for about five minutes. When she stopped and calmed her breathing long enough to listen, she could hear Luciana engaged in an animated discussion, but the voices were too faint to make anything out.

Everywhere felt conspicuous, and not knowing where else to go, she headed toward the new open-air renovation of the mall, despite knowing it was infested with security cameras. Of *course* it was—it was a mall. A locked mall, at that. But she'd be easily spotted on the street if so much as one black SUV made the rounds. She had wandered into the mall parking garage before at long, long last, Luciana came back.

"Are you still there?" Luciana asked.

"Yes!" said Cora, trying to rein in her desperation. "Where are you?"

"I'm not going to tell you over the phone, but I'm sending someone to come get you."

"Why can't you?"

"Because I'm out of town, and I don't want to tell you where, *just in case.* Do you get me?"

Cora reminded her body that not every muscle needed to be clenched all at once. "I get you."

"Just stay safe. I'm sending someone to get you."

"I am . . . very conspicuous," she said. "I am covered in mud, and nothing is open."

"Denny's is open."

"Denny's?" repeated Cora, incredulous.

"Denny's is always open!" She spoke as if she were being held at knifepoint and failing to mask her concern. "Just go to the one up on Hawthorne."

"It's 5:00 A.M., and I am covered in mud."

"*Then wash it off!*" The exhaustion in Luciana's voice was palpable. "Trust me when I say this is the very best I can do for you right now. If what you're telling me is true about some feds showing up at your house, you're right, Demi and the kids probably *are* in custody, and you and I are probably in the same boat. Do you get me?"

Cora began the trudge through the empty acres of parking lots in the direction of the Denny's. "I get you."

"I'm sending Bard. He hasn't left LA yet."

"Bard?" whined Cora. She hadn't meant for it to be a whine.

"He'll be in a white cargo van."

"So when I see Bard's murdervan coming around the bend, my prince has come for me."

"I repeat," said Luciana, her patience past the breaking point. "If you want my help, this is the best I can do for you right now."

"Okay," said Cora. "Denny's on Hawthorne. Keep an eye out for Bard's murdervan."

"He'll be about half an hour."

"Got it," Cora said and hung up.

It took another ten minutes or so to make it all the way up to the Denny's. Indeed, when she gave the host a sob story about waiting for the bus to take her to her father's apartment in El Segundo but she tripped and fell in the mud and she couldn't possibly get on the bus looking like that so could she *please* use the bathroom, the host had absolutely no problem letting her. About twenty minutes later, she got a text from Luciana's burner—*He's outside.*

Cora, her mud-shell situation only slightly improved, exited the bathroom and made a beeline for the door, not returning the odd glances of anyone in the establishment as she did. There was the white van, plain in its dirtiness except for one patch of rust that looked like a fish, and there was Bard. She'd only met the guy a couple of times before Luciana got fired, and both times, it was a test of her basic human decency. This guy drove her *nuts.*

She opened the door, and he stared down at her. "What happened to you?"

He had the voice of the captain of a high school debate team. Her initial impulse was to tell the truth about some otherworldly cosmic force pulling her into the muck before violating her person via injection, but she opted instead for, "I fell in the mud," and got in the van.

Bard shrugged and put the van into gear. He seemed even less thrilled to have her as a passenger than she was to be there. Before long, they were on the freeway. He merged into the rush-hour traffic, staying put in the right lane.

Of course Bard would not bother to utilize the HOV lane. Of course.

"So," he said after a solid ten minutes on the 405. "Luciana says you saw something."

"There was something in our living room," she said, looking at the window, praying that he would just get in the damn HOV lane so they'd get out of this nightmare marginally sooner.

Bard glanced at her sidelong. "Well?"

"Well, what?"

"Well, what did it look like? How big was it? What color?"

"I don't know; it was dark. But it was big, and it wasn't shaped like a human."

They rode along in silence for a couple of minutes. Then Bard contributed, "You still haven't told me what you saw."

Cora tried to grasp for what she hadn't really seen. "I think it was white? Although that might have been the moonlight. I saw this sliver of white from over the hedge across the street, and I assumed my mind was playing tricks on me. But then I saw it again in the living room, and I didn't stick around to get a look at it."

Bard sucked on the inside of his lips, considering. "How do you know it wasn't a white person? Like a white human person?"

"I don't mean white as in race; I mean white as in the color *white*."

"White's not a color."

Why did it have to be Bard? Cora lamented. *Why does Luciana need to surround herself with such pedants?* "It looked white. Like a sheet of paper."

"And how do you know it wasn't human if you didn't get a look at it?"

"Because it . . ." She shook her head and again fell back into the pit of second-guessing herself. *Could* it have been some crazy stalker, and her imagination, wanting it to be an alien, filled in the blanks? Still, seared into her mind was what she thought had to be an alien face, an alien head. "It wasn't *shaped* like a person! It had these big eyes," she said. "They glowed."

Bard seemed half-interested. "Glowed."

"I think. I only saw it for a split second before I got the hell out of there. And then when I was out in the marsh, something pushed me down. Some . . . force."

"Like someone pushed you to the ground."

"No, like a magnet *pulled* me to the ground."

"I see."

"If nothing happened, then why did the feds show up?" she demanded. "And why have you all left town? Why won't Luciana tell me where she is?"

"San José," he said. "She's in San José. She couldn't tell you over the phone."

Six-hour drive, Cora thought miserably. *Eight with rush-hour traffic.* "Why are you all going to San José?"

"To lie low."

"Why?" she asked. "Why now?"

"Because everyone at ROSA was laid off yesterday, and some of our colleagues never came home last night," he said. "That's why."

By this point, she hadn't yet been able to process the now-obvious fact that Luciana and her former coworkers had everything to do with the Fremda Memo. That the "refugee" element of the Refugee Organizational and Settlement Agency was very likely not, as she had always been told, high-profile or sensitive political refugees seeking asylum from countries like Iran and Ethiopia. Nor had she even begun to process the betrayal that implied, all the things Luciana had lied to her about.

If Luciana hadn't been directly responsible for the leak to Nils, she'd at least had something to do with it.

She looked at Bard, who did not strike her as believing a single word she said. Surely, someone who was in on whatever secret government alien thing was going on would show at least a little interest in her claims, right?

It had happened, right?

She spent most of the rest of the miserable drive in silence, staring out the window at the vast acres of bovine that stretched out from the 5 up into Central California, wondering why, if the leaks were true, nobody believed her.

Through Nils Ortega's blog entries, his writing, and his weekly webcast, the world has gotten to know him very intimately, very quickly. He seems considerably less interested, however, in the world knowing his family. Yesterday's mention of children is the first he's ever made since the launch of *The Broken Seal*. But in regard to his family, my interest is not in his ex-wife or his children but rather his sister.

Where Nils Ortega has taken great pains to build a cult of personality over his image and crusade, Luciana Ortega has done the opposite. Here we have a woman with virtually no online presence—no social media, no phone book records, nothing. The closest we can come to even confirming that she exists are public records, a few online role-playing accounts, and that she was, until March 15 of 2007, on the payroll of the Department of Health and Human Services.

But most fascinating about this woman, sister to the world's most infamous whistleblowing advocate, is that she began collecting unemployment insurance barely six months before Nils Ortega's now-infamous "Fremda Memo." It's difficult to believe that these facts about the two siblings are coincidental.

Perhaps the question should be expanded. We already know who Nils Ortega is (if anything, he won't allow us to forget it). My question now: Who is Luciana Ortega?

Siegel, Douglas. "Expanding the Scope of Ortega." *New York Post*. September 21, 2007.

7

The house was not *in* San José. In fact, it wasn't fair to even call it *near* San José—it was closer to Santa Cruz, up in the mountains between the two metro areas on one of those back roads where the second homes of wealthy Silicon Valley folks were comfortably separated by large, vacation-sized distances. It was late afternoon when they arrived at the cottage, which looked like it had been neglected for a few seasons. The woods surrounded it, creeping in from all sides, tree branches carelessly draped over the roof. The lawn, such as it was, was a brown, dead bramble covered in twigs. This was a fire marshal's nightmare.

Luciana was out on the porch before Bard's van had come to a full stop, her eyes wide and her hair even messier than before, a rusty dandelion that had had a rough night. She glided down the stairs from the porch to greet them as Cora got out of the van; Luciana gawked at her niece like her skin had been removed in its entirety. By now, the mud had dried and she was able to brush most of it off, but she still looked like she'd been living on the streets for a few weeks.

Luciana stopped in front of Cora, offering nothing more intimate than an awkward wave. Bard approached them and crossed his arms as if he were entitled to a place in this conversation.

"Everyone's waiting upstairs," said Luciana, looking at Bard.

"Okay," he said. "Shall we?"

"We should talk first," said Luciana.

"I agree," he said.

Luciana waited for him to catch on, and when he didn't, she stated, "I need to talk to Cora alone."

Bard looked at both of them suspiciously. "What are you going to tell her?"

"Nothing," said Luciana. "But I am hoping she will tell *me* things—namely, what's happened to my niece, nephew, and sister-in-law."

"Technically, she's not your sister-in-law anymore," said Bard. Despite her already-low expectations, Cora was stunned that he would exhibit a display of such useless, unnecessary pedantry at a time like this. He shot her an "I'm watching you" look before heading up the stairs.

Luciana took her by the arm and led her away from the house. "Let's go for a walk."

"It injected me with something," Cora blurted before they had made it two steps.

Luciana froze. "It what?"

"Were you not listening to me on the phone?" she said, her voice shaking. Cora lifted her hair and showed her the injection site. "I said, it *injected* me with something."

Luciana examined the back of Cora's neck. "Are you sure this isn't a mosquito bite?"

Cora rounded on her aunt. "Are you kidding me?"

Luciana threw her hands up, contrite. "No, no."

"It threw me down. It held me to the ground."

"I'm sorry, Cora, that's not what I meant . . ."

"And *injected* me with something."

Luciana watched her, lips pursed, eyes like dinner plates.

"You have to tell me what's going on," said Cora.

"I can't," said Luciana without pause.

"You *can't*?"

"I could be thrown in jail for the rest of my life for even being here, let alone for telling you anything."

"But you were fired—"

"The NDA I signed wasn't."

Cora threw up her hands, exasperated. "Then why are you here? Does this have anything to do with Ampersand II?"

"Obelus."

"*What?*"

Luciana pinched the bridge of her nose and sighed. "This one's called Obelus."

"This *one*?" said Cora. "This one *alien*?"

"This one celestial object. And . . . we don't know. Everyone I worked with at ROSA was let go without notice yesterday afternoon."

"Bard told me."

"Odds are good that, yes, that had something to do with the Obelus Event. So given the recent tensions—as well as the fact that some of our coworkers have mysteriously disappeared into black vans—some of us thought it might be wise to go off the radar for a few days to figure out a next step. A post-employment retreat, as it were. That's why I gave you the burner. Although I didn't think you would need it so . . . immediately."

Cora hugged herself, took a breath. "Okay, so we've all gone varying degrees of rogue on the U.S. government. So I'll say it one more time. An alien pushed me down onto the ground. And injected something into my neck."

"I understand that, but I cannot share anything with you—"

The shock from the whole ordeal finally began to melt into hurt. Luciana wasn't budging, wasn't showing even a hint of sympathy. "You don't believe me."

Luciana sighed. "I don't *dis*believe you."

"Then why—"

"Because we've never encountered anything like what you're describing!" said Luciana. "It doesn't align with what we know."

"Which part doesn't align with what you know?"

Luciana's hands started making wild gestures as though they were trying to explain something their owner could not. "Any of it!"

"So you're saying the aliens you've encountered are not the sort that telekinetically force people to the ground before injecting their necks with mysterious substances?"

Luciana looked at Cora pleadingly, then shrugged.

"Then tell me what you *have* encountered."

"I can't do that," said Luciana. "This is top level. We should probably be on a plane to Hong Kong already—"

"If we're all on the run from the government already, *what difference does it make*?" Cora thundered, her words reverberating through the trees, through the atmosphere, through the entire galaxy, through space, through time and into eternity.

Luciana's shoulders drew into her body, and she glared at Cora through hooded eyes. "We won't be on the run for much longer if you keep pulling shit like that."

Cora buried her filthy face in her filthy hands, her shoulders collapsing. She knew she was capable of better self-control than this, but she'd been on the edge for a long time, she hadn't even realized she'd flown off it and was now plummeting into the void, and there was no one to catch her.

"Come on upstairs. Take a shower. Get this mud off." Luciana placed an awkward hand on Cora's shoulder, guiding her upstairs. "I'll talk to everyone here; maybe . . ."

Cora turned to her as they approached the door. "Maybe what?"

Luciana deflated, and she shook her head. "We'll see."

Luciana led Cora into the living room, which was crowded with several thirty- and fortysomethings and one older man who had the sort of agelessness that could have put him at forty or seventy, and but for his eyebrows he had no hair on his head. Cora noticed him not only for his age but because he was the only person in the room who didn't look like his house had just been repossessed. "Hi, there," he said. Everyone else looked at her like she'd just crashed a wedding she was not invited to.

"Everyone," said Luciana, "this is Cora, my niece. She's had a . . . rough morning." She gestured to her ex-coworkers in turn. "Cora, these are some of my former coworkers: Harris, Shaun, Natalie, Stevie, Dan-O, David, Joel, Sarah, Maria, and Dr. Sev."

"Sevak Ghasabian," said Dr. Sev, standing to greet her. "Dr. Sev by company tradition, but you can call me whatever you feel comfortable with."

"Dr. Sev," Cora repeated. He nodded at her warmly and shook her hand, and she couldn't help but get tripped on whatever Dr. Phil-by-way-of-California persona he was going for.

"I hear a nonhuman entity may have paid you a visit this morning," said Dr. Sev, sitting back down on the couch.

"Process of elimination. I'm not *sure* that's what happened," she said.

"It helps to be sure," said Dr. Sev.

The woman Luciana had introduced as Stevie also stood up and approached Cora. "Come on," she said, gesturing for Cora to follow her. She was short and lithe, with long, wavy black hair, dark skin, and a short, sharp nose. "Let's get you cleaned up."

Luciana followed Stevie and Cora into the master suite. The house belonged to Stevie's parents, they told her, one of several of their investment properties. Stevie gave her a towel, showed her to the bathroom, and told her to use whatever clothes she found in the closet.

Cora showered off, then went hunting for clothes, a much more time-consuming endeavor than she had anticipated. None of the clothes fit—she was too big for all of them. It took several minutes of digging through a closet, an exercise that itself felt like going back in time, before she stumbled upon a tiered chiffon maxi dress from the 1970s. It was cream colored, draped over her like a bellflower and layered in a way that made her feel like a wedding cake.

"Are you okay?" said Luciana, knocking on the door.

Cora opened it and let her in, just as she finished buttoning up the maxi dress. Luciana couldn't help but smile. "Nice," she said. "After we're done here, we need to find you a field full of flowers to dance in."

"What are these people, fairies?" whispered Cora, the layers of chiffon rippling with her exasperation. "Everything here is like a size 0 petite!"

"Stevie's mom was a model in the '70s and '80s. The wardrobe reflects that, I'm afraid. Come on."

Luciana had Cora calmly, carefully rehash the whole thing

again for everyone in the room. Now having had the time to calm down and run through it in her mind, she was better able to explain what happened.

Did the entity make eye contact? She couldn't be sure; she'd run away. Did it actually touch her? She couldn't be sure; it felt more like a magnetic force than being touched. Did it show interest in the computer? Yes, it had dismantled the computer. She saw it hiding in the neighbor's yard when she was at the mailbox? She couldn't be sure—at the time, she thought she'd imagined it. Did it make any noise? She didn't think so, but she couldn't be sure. Did it make any bid to communicate? She didn't think so, but she couldn't be sure.

With all this ambiguity, she was starting to see why Luciana and Bard were skeptical.

She didn't get a sense of antipathy from the group. It seemed as though what she was saying just didn't compute. Like they had been expecting an invading Hun army, but she was describing a horde of invading spiders. But what was more noteworthy wasn't the way they treated her but the way they treated Luciana—the way they interrupted her and disputed or stepped over her questions and comments made it seem like Luciana was on thin ice.

Luciana sent Cora back outside onto the porch while the grown-ups talked over what she'd just told them. During that five or so minutes, Cora rolled over the looks the company had given Luciana in her mind and figured they must have come to the same conclusion she had. Just like the infinitesimal odds of two "celestial objects" landing in almost the exact same spot one month apart, the likelihood that Nils had acquired the Fremda Memo on his own while his own sister just *happened* to work for the alien-hiding government was improbable to the point of impossibility.

Luciana opened the door and slipped outside, startling Cora from her thoughts. "Hey," she said. "So . . ."

"Was it you?" asked Cora, sounding more accusatory than she'd intended.

"Was what me?"

"Did you leak the Fremda Memo?"

Luciana jolted like Cora had hit her. "No! The people on those email chains, I don't know them. I've never interacted with them . . ."

"How would that preclude you from leaking it?"

"Look at the send dates!" she sputtered, incredulous. "They were from *after* I got fired!"

"I don't know what's real," said Cora. "Everything you've ever told me, now I have to second-guess it. Was there really a dead suicide 'coworker,' or was that also just some made-up bullshit?"

Luciana's expression grew cold. "Yes, someone did die yesterday."

"Some*one*?" asked Cora. "Or some*thing*?"

Luciana looked at her blankly. "I don't know why you think I might lie to you about this, but I promise I know *nothing* that would shine any light on what you're describing. Plus you couldn't really describe what it looked like."

Cora felt heat leaving her body. "You still don't believe me."

"There is no precedent for anything like this. We're just figuring out how to reconcile what you've told us with—"

"No *precedent*?"

"No!" Luciana clapped back, surprising Cora. "Did you read the Fremda Memo? They don't engage with us! They don't touch us, they don't look at us, they don't talk to us! We're not even sure if they *can* communicate with us. And they sure as hell don't understand English!"

Cora backed down. This was the first time Luciana, or indeed anyone with any position of authority, had finally admitted that the Fremda Memo was real.

That *any* of this was real.

"You've tried?" she asked.

Luciana's eyes popped. "My job for *seven years* was to *try*." She tightened her fists into balls and closed her eyes, and her shoulders fell. "Fuck."

The silence that engulfed them was instantly oppressive. There it was. Luciana had worked with whatever Nils had discovered. And despite all that, she still didn't believe Cora. "Guess you're going to jail for the rest of your life, now."

Luciana took a deep breath and shook her head. "Listen, just give me a few minutes to go over everything with them, okay?"

"You want me to just wait out here?"

"Or you can go downstairs."

Cora hesitated, already hearing how stupid the question she wanted to ask sounded in her mind. "What about the mind stuff?"

"The what?"

"Those people who disappeared up around Pasadena and came back with like . . . amnesia and brain damage."

Luciana looked at her, an expression of worry forming. "I've heard of it. Nils's fans think the government did it?"

"I thought it was nonsense, too, but it did get some mainstream media coverage. It *happened*. And now Demi and Olive and Felix are in custody, and you said yourself that some of your former coworkers disappeared into black vans . . ."

"That's not a thing," said Luciana.

This was not the response Cora expected. "You don't even

think it might be in the realm of possibility?"

"I'm pretty sure if that technology existed, I'd at least have heard of it."

"You think you know the dirty doings of every single branch of the government?"

"Oh, God," laughed Luciana. "You sound like Nils."

The words bit Cora like a wasp sting. Luciana's eyes flashed for a moment as though she realized it, then moved on as if it were nothing. "I just know if that technology had been developed, we'd know. Give me a few minutes, okay?"

"Sure," said Cora, still reeling as Luciana closed the door behind her. Maybe Luciana didn't grasp what a huge insult comparing her to Nils like that was.

No. She did.

Carefully, she leaned her ear on the door on the off chance she might be able to hear a part of the conversation. It was an old, thin wooden door, and she could make out some of it.

"I don't know," said one of them. "It throws a wrench in the works."

"Well, discovery is scary like that." That was Dr. Sev. "It doesn't always follow expectations."

"You think what happened at the Sabino house has to do with Čefo?" A voice she couldn't place.

"I'm sure everything that's happened in the last forty-eight hours relates back to Čefo. I'm just not sure what she saw had to do with it or if she even saw what she thinks she saw."

"There are a lot of holes in her story." Bard's smug voice. "It is entirely possible it was a break-in and her imagination ran away with it."

"It just doesn't track."

"There were elements of her description that did."

"And if something was able to knock an entire family of four unconscious from the other side of a door . . ."

"If an entity really did break into the house of Nils Ortega's ex-wife, the only logical conclusion is that it was interested in those individuals, meaning that it is capable of understanding human language and, therefore, communicating."

"Which we know they can't."

"We know they *won't*." Finally, Luciana had spoken up. "It doesn't mean that they can't."

Cora pulled her ear away from the door, frustrated. Maybe what had happened to her didn't line up with what they knew or expected, but it didn't contradict anything. Like Luciana said, these alien beings *won't* communicate; it doesn't mean they *can't.*

Cora walked down the wood stairs of the deck and onto the driveway, taking a short walk to clear her head. This time, she was so distracted that she missed the flash of iridescent skin slinking back into the trees.

8

The gravel of the driveway crunched under Cora's feet as she ambled toward the road. She had by now reached the point where the driveway met the road, but as it was probably not a good idea to present the opportunity to be seen by passersby, she turned back toward the cottage. She thought of her family in custody, their brains getting scrambled by the Men in Black, the indifference and incredulity Luciana had shown to the mere idea. Was there indeed some sort of memory-altering protocol for something like this? Would Demi, Olive, and Felix be spared this procedure because they hadn't *seen* anything like Cora had?

She had to do something. Unfortunately, the most obvious course of action was also the most unsavory: Nils.

Nils was at a point of media notoriety right now where him getting a colonoscopy would make news. If she could find a way to get to him and tell him what had happened, he'd move heaven and earth to do something about it. Of course, he would only do it to benefit himself and elevate his own public profile, but something would be *done*. The enemy of my enemy, and all that.

Ignoring the logistical question of how she could even get to him in Germany without a passport, the question really was whether he could *do* anything other than cause a big stink without any documents to leak, his stock and trade. Cora had only had her own testimony, which, as Luciana had callously demonstrated, was not *proof* of anything.

Cora looked out into the forest, and the solemn realization of being surrounded by just nature calmed her. It had been so long since she'd been in the woods, the smell was downright nostalgic. The sun had only just set, and there was a haze in the trees. These weren't redwoods, more like the opening act for real redwoods, tall pines that jutted out of the earth like arrows. She was too deep in the woods to see any mountains, but the line of the trees alone against the azure and pink of the setting sky was breathtaking.

A memory pushed itself to the front of her mind. Another forest, a different time. A deciduous forest of the East Coast, not the pine pillars of Northern California. A camping trip, one with just her and Felix before Olive was even born. The shorter trees of the Adirondacks had felt as mighty and imposing as the pines did to her here and now. She'd been thirteen, Felix only six. If there had been a favorite child, it had been Felix, the only one of the Ortega children who was not jokingly referred to as an "accident." Back then, she'd not begrudged him that. He was really into *Beast Machines* at the time, and she remembered him spending much of that trip transforming his toys. Did that count as a happy memory? She couldn't be sure. Nils had been there, but his mind wasn't. It never was.

Nils would use her, weaponize her family's plight, use them

to elevate his cultural cachet, but if serving his evil would prevent the greater evil of the government doing actual harm to her family, it had to be done. The question then—how to get away from these people and get in touch with him without getting caught? She lowered her gaze from the halo of dark pines beneath the sky, and that was when she saw it, between the trees, stony and still, staring at her from about fifty feet away.

It was the creature. The alien. In full view and, this time, unmistakable.

She stilled like a rabbit that had spotted a predator, doubting for several long seconds that she wasn't imagining this. The creature was tall, even in a crouch, firmly inhuman, with a shell that shone silvery white in the twilight. Its body leaned forward like a raptor, despite the lack of anything behind it like a tail to balance its center of gravity, with long arms curled in front of it like a praying mantis. It had an oblong head like a dragon, if the dragon had no jaw and no nose, and even had a sort of crest that jutted out from the back of its head like a feather headdress. But it was the eyes that were most striking, the only part of it that wasn't some shade of that iridescent white silver, big almond-shaped things situated on the sides of its head like a wasp, amber colored and seeming to glow as if there were a dim, internal light illuminating a gemstone, and those eyes were focused on her.

Her conscious brain took control before her lizard brain could do something stupid. She'd felt what it had done in the marsh and knew if she tried to scream or run, it wouldn't let her. But she didn't feel anything like a giant magnet. Not yet. It was just watching her, fixated and intent, perhaps even a little curious. In some ways, it was exactly what she'd expect an alien to look like, animalistic and sophisticated, yet nothing like what she'd expect. It didn't resemble the prototypical Roswell alien at all, save perhaps in its color and even then only distantly. It was in the strange construction of its joints, the construction of its hands, which sported six digits that resembled spider legs rather than fingers, the shell-like nature of its skin. It didn't seem to have a mouth at all.

Her mind leaped to all measure of things she should or should not be doing—*Avert eye contact; it could be seen as a sign of aggression. Don't avert eye contact; that is equally as likely to be seen as an act of aggression. Moving is an act of aggression. Not moving is an act of aggression.*

It was a few moments before the creature even moved, showed signs that, yes, it was indeed alive and active, cocking its head slightly, the glow in its eyes narrowing. Following her. *Tracking* her, and she'd led it exactly where it wanted her to go—not to Nils Ortega but to Luciana and her colleagues.

She had led the alien right to them.

I'm not dead, she reminded herself. If her only purpose was to lead this thing to its quarry and then be disposed, it would have killed her without her even knowing it was there. But instead, it just stood there, staring at her. Slowly, carefully, she put her hands up and searched for something to say.

What, she wondered, would she want to hear if she were some sort of unfathomable intelligence on some backwater alien planet? It took a step toward her, using the avian foot that had unmistakably made the prints she'd followed that morning. Her breath increased and deepened, her skin prickled, and the creature's eyes sharpened like a laser about to fire, and it began moving toward her.

"We don't want to hurt you," she stammered, barely a whisper, so it couldn't be mistaken as a cry for help.

The creature stilled. She lowered her hands a bit, shocked that saying something had gotten a reaction at all. Hopeful, even, that there might be a possibility of reasoning with the creature, that Luciana was wrong about "they sure as hell don't understand English." It stayed still for seconds at most before it started toward her again.

Cora whimpered unconsciously. "We don't want to hurt you," she managed again, louder this time. By this point, it was all but standing over her. Only now was she getting a real grasp on how big it was and wondered how it had even managed to get inside her house. Even in a crouch, it towered over her by more than three feet, so standing up to its full height, even with that birdlike, forward-leaning center of gravity, would have put it at a comfortable eight or nine feet.

It blinked, slowly, languidly, like melted wax sliding over the amber gems of its eyes, then receding. It looked at her but didn't move. She couldn't help but read this as hesitation. She slowly let her hands fall to her sides. "Are you alone?" she whispered.

Nothing.

"Can you understand me?"

She was so transfixed on its eyes, she felt the injection just beneath her left jawbone before she even saw the syringe. She moved to grab her neck where the thing had injected her, but her hands were held in place by the same force she'd felt back in the marsh. But the panicked need to swat away the injection faded within seconds, even as the creature used its other hand to grab her firmly around the torso, now moving sharply, swiftly, a spider wrapping its prey in its webbing. It felt like she'd been doused with a bucket of warm water, a calming sensation flowing to every extremity. It was as though she had never even known what it was to be frightened, or upset, or happy.

It held her in place as her muscles relaxed, fiber by fiber, until she was lolling in its grasp like a rag doll. The creature laid her down onto her back, and she saw a small, complex tool in its fingers; it gently tilted Cora's head to one side and implanted something in her ear. For a few seconds, she could only hear the goings-on in her ear canal; it sounded like a machine was crawling inside her head, involving thousands, even millions of tiny parts. Then the mechanism in her ear spoke to her:

"*Still.*"

Her body became still.

The word was phonetic and mechanical. Though the voice wasn't human, the software certainly was—the alien must have co-opted text-to-talk technology. It sounded like the voice from a standard Macintosh. As the creature stepped away from her, her gaze drifted back up to the sky, but her body obeyed the voice and did not move.

"So you *can* understand English," she whispered.

"*Silent.*"

She couldn't speak, not that she had any particular inclination to. She reached into her memory, trying to recall what only a couple of minutes ago had her so concerned. Something to do with a family, perhaps, a family whose names she couldn't recall.

PART TWO

. . . .

BILLIONS OF
FLESH-EATING ALIENS

Mountain View, California
September 24, 2007
NASDAQ: 2,241.05
Dow Jones Industrial Average: 11,572.16

Little attention has been paid to one of the more significant implications presented in the Fremda Memo, which is the suggestion that, despite the fact that these ETIs are ostensibly alive, there has been no successful attempt at communication. This raises a multitude of questions wholly separate from issues of government transparency, some technological, some ethical, some philosophical. They do not respond to our attempts to communicate, despite the fact that the greatest minds that have succeeded in slipping through the filter of government clearance have been trying to get them to respond for decades. Why?

I find the explanation that we are unable to fathom any intelligence advanced enough to develop interstellar travel reductive and inadequate. If I can teach my dog to high-five, an alien smart enough to travel hundreds if not thousands of light-years can at least bang out five notes on a Casio. This barest minimum should be possible if there were curiosity or intent on the part of the ETIs, if there were a desire to communicate, but there appears to be none. And if that is the case, why? It's an exercise in futility to speculate, of course, but it does open the door for some civilization-wide self-reflection on our part.

If these ETIs really do exist, most of us would have to admit that they have terrible timing. Humanity is fractured, bellicose, paranoid. It's the cosmological equivalent of having a guest come to the door when you're in the middle of a knock-down, drag-out fight with your spouse, there are lines of coke on the coffee table, and your pants are down around your ankles. It isn't the failure to communicate that fascinates me; it's the implication that these ETIs appear to have no interest in communication at all. And we humans, vain, egotistical creatures that we are, can't help but take that a little personally.

It may well be that, regardless of why these ETIs are allowing themselves to be held in federal custody, they are well aware that at this stage in our development, we are not yet ready for First Contact. If that is the case, we can probably assume that our guests will not start talking to us anytime soon.

And if that is the case, there is probably a good reason.

Mazandarani, Kaveh. "Is Humanity Ready for First Contact?" *The New Yorker*. October 15, 2007.

9

Cora was following a man wearing dark navy slacks and a light blue T-shirt. To her left, an army of young people at their desks, to her right, a glass barrier on the other side of an enormous open foyer several stories tall. On the dark laminate floor a few stories below, she saw rainbow-colored obelisks snaking up like monsters rising out of the ocean. The obelisks were letters. A *G*, an *O* . . .

Where the hell am I?

Her emotions were still off-line, but she thought that given the situation, logically, she *should* be frightened. But although the idea of fear came to her like an image from a long-forgotten picture book, she couldn't remember what the sensation of being afraid felt like.

Then a voice in her ear spoke: "*Enter the door; follow the man in the blue apparel.*" Computerized, mechanical. It sounded like Stephen Hawking's synth speech.

Am I in the future? she wondered, utterly disconnected. *Am I still on Earth?*

She continued to follow the man in the blue slacks, her dilated eyes burning from the bright sunlight pouring in through the huge plate glass windows. The desks were metallic, new, strangely clean, the dozens of workers all hunched at laptops with cultlike devotion. No offices, but instead one giant open-air mega-office. She looked through one of the grand, multistory windows, saw a groomed green lawn, perfect topiaries, an impossibly blue sky.

Another giant yellow letter crept out of the floor: *O.*

"*Speak: I am searching for the main servers for Southern California.*"

"I am searching for the main servers for Southern California." A sensation of surprise came and went. The machine in her ear had told her to speak, and she had complied. But with that faint dash of shock, she felt her emotions returning.

Cora Sabino is my name.

The man looked at her, confused. "We don't have . . . 'servers' here. Do you work here?"

"*Speak: No, I am a visitor.*"

My name is Cora, and I'm under alien mind control; please help me.

"No, I am a visitor."

Again, she looked toward the big letters reaching out from the floor on the foyer below like plastic flames against a bright blue sky. *G-O-O-G*, the rainbow letter-statues spelled, and she realized she was on the Google campus. She wasn't on another planet or in the future. She hadn't even left the Bay Area. She was on the new campus for the biggest search engine in the world. The "Googleplex."

"You're not even on the right floor, I think," said the man. He had soft brown eyes and dark skin. She tried to wiggle her pinkie and succeeded.

"*Speak: Which floor?*"

Please, man who is probably not an alien, help me.

Cora spied a bag of peanuts on a desk nearby where one of the only women in the room was working. "Which floor?" were the words that came out of her mouth, flat and disconcerting.

"They're in the basement," he said.

"*Speak: How does one travel to the basement?*"

Peanut. She tried to say only one word that was hers. *Peanut, peanut, peanut!*

"How does one travel to the peanut?"

Now Cora felt adrenaline begin to bubble in her blood. Success. She was breaking out of the spell.

"I'm sorry?" he said.

"How does one travel to the basement?"

He looked concerned, perhaps more than anything concerned that someone was playing a prank on him. Cora looked down, and she could feel her neck turning red with embarrassment. She was still in that too-short chiffon tiered maxi dress. She wasn't even wearing a bra. She could smell herself, a funk resultant of god-knows-how-many days without bathing. Without washing her hair for who knows how long, it must have looked like two flavors of ice cream melted together.

Cracks in this alien's plan, whatever it was, were beginning to show.

"Down the hall, go to the end of it, then on the right," said the man, unsure. He must have thought she was high as hell.

Or under alien mind control.

"*Travel to the location described.*"

She turned from the man without another word. She was almost feeling secondhand embarrassment for the alien; this was going *terribly*. What was this thing trying to do with her? Frightened though she was that the device it had put in her ear contained some kind of self-destruct mechanism, it clearly didn't know enough about human culture to pull off whatever kind of infiltration it was attempting.

But at the same time, she was clearly dealing with something powerful. Maybe it didn't get tiny day-to-day human ceremonials like courtesy or wearing a bra, but she was still dealing with technology she couldn't begin to comprehend. Her excitement would raise her heart rate, change her breathing, and in all likelihood it was monitoring everything she was doing. Hell, maybe it could even read her mind.

No, she decided. If it could read her mind, it would know that she should have at least said, "Thank you," before leaving that guy. It would know that she should be wearing a bra, that she shouldn't have gone days without a shower or brushing her teeth, and that tiered chiffon maxi dresses were not a thing someone who was not acting in a '70s period piece would ever wear for any reason. So it could control her body, but it could not read her mind.

But that didn't mean it couldn't tell its control was slipping.

"*Stop,*" said the voice. She obeyed, but a hair slower than she had done earlier.

"Excuse me?" said a voice from behind her, a human voice. She turned and saw an older Asian American man in a security uniform was approaching her. His name tag read "Finch." That young fellow with the brown eyes must have reported her. She didn't blame him; she would have reported her, too.

Finch stopped in front of her. "Can I help you with something?"

"*Speak: How does one travel to the basement?*" instructed the apparatus in her ear.

"How does one travel to the basement?" she repeated in as impartial a tone as she could muster. The creature's eyes were on her now. They had to be. This one little incident could ruin its entire operation.

"Which . . . basement?" asked the guard.

Cora knew that she had to make a decision right now. If the creature hadn't realized that she was back in control of her body before, it had now. Between her breathing, her heart rate, and any manner of things Cora couldn't control, her body was rebelling. This was it. Either way, she had to make her escape right now.

"*Speak: I am looking for my cousin,*" said the voice in her ear. She repeated it, but the words came out forced, nervous.

"What department does your cousin work in?"

The most obvious thing to do would be to turn herself in right here and now, but then she traced that possibility to its logical conclusion; she'd beg sanctuary from the security guard, then from the police, then she would fall right into the hands of the feds, another pawn in their epic war against Nils. At best, she'd have no memory of any of this; at worst, her whole family would have their brains scrambled. And if they took her mother and siblings away for practically nothing, what would they do to *her*? That thought alone made her tempted to just ride this out.

But on the other hand, was it any wiser to throw herself on the possible mercy of the alien, a creature that, for all she knew, was the first of a swarm of superbeings bent on world domination? In any circumstance, it was a creature that did not look at humans as *persons*. The careless way it had already treated her told her that much. And if Cora was an individual on whom its marionette trick didn't work, then she was a liability. Possibly a dead one.

It might well be that this creature would be too preoccupied with whatever greater endeavor it was trying to accomplish than to bother tracking down and neutralizing the liability of Cora Sabino, but did the government of her own country pose a greater threat to her, really? Indefinite detention, yes. Craven dishonesty, yes. Illegal memory modifications, maybe. But were they more likely to kill her than an alien was?

Probably not. This assumption might well prove to be embarrassingly, stupidly wrong, but at that moment, being in federal custody seemed like a lesser evil to being in alien custody. But she couldn't just declare to this guy she was an alien's captive. She'd have to try something else.

Cora steeled herself, took a deep breath, and said, "There's a bomb in the building."

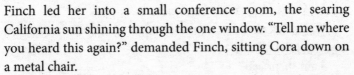

10

Finch led her into a small conference room, the searing California sun shining through the one window. "Tell me where you heard this again?" demanded Finch, sitting Cora down on a metal chair.

"I heard it in the hallway just before you showed up," Cora improvised.

"From whom?"

"These, uh . . . guys with accents." She could not stop herself from wincing at her own bad lie.

"What kind of accents?" asked Finch.

"Indian?"

"This is Silicon Valley," he said. "You just described half the workforce."

"I know that," she said, fidgeting. "Sorry if I'm not being descriptive enough. It was from a few feet away."

Finch folded his arms. "There is no bomb, is there?" he

asked matter-of-factly. "No bomb, no bomb threat. You didn't hear anything."

Cora darted her eyes around the room. "No."

"Then why did you say that there was?"

She pursed her lips, unable to talk her way out of the hole she'd dug for herself. She looked at her hands.

"Are you in some kind of trouble?" asked Finch.

Some kind of trouble! She kept her eyes fixed on her hands.

Finch pulled a chair out, swung it around in front of Cora, and straddled the back of it as he sat down. "So at present, you are the third person to walk in today, looking all dazed and confused and disoriented, with the apparent intention of breaking into our private servers to steal encrypted information about where the government is hiding aliens."

Cora looked up at him, stunned. "I . . . see."

Finch looked at her, eyebrows high on his forehead. "You seem surprised."

"I am surprised."

"Well?"

"Well, what?"

"Well, you look like you just stepped out of the 1973 J. C. Penney's catalog and appear to be about sixteen."

"I'm twenty-one."

Finch nodded curtly. "I feel either way that I'd rather get your story before we call the police, because a drugged-out looking college student is a little more worrisome."

Cora just stared at him. In a way, she was flattered he'd incorrectly clocked her as college *student*.

"You didn't know that other people had come here today, wearing the same dazed expression and asking the same weird questions about servers?"

"No," she all but whispered. "I really, honestly did not."

"I see," he said, studying her.

She cleared her throat. "What day is it?"

"Monday."

"Monday . . . the what?"

Finch paused, and his look of concern deepened. "Monday, September 24."

Cora gawked at him, unsure whether she should be relieved or horrified that she could not account for two whole days. When she didn't respond promptly, Finch added, "September 24, 2007."

"That's good," Cora decided.

"Who instructed you to do this?" he asked. She stayed quiet. "Did they offer to pay you?"

"I don't know how to answer that."

Finch stood up. "Either this is a part of some strange false-flag campaign meant to divert security's attention, or this is the worst organized break-in attempt in the history of Google."

Cora shut her mouth, only now realizing it was hanging open. "I think that may be exactly what it is."

Finch narrowed his eyes.

"So the other people who . . . did what I did, they got arrested," said Cora carefully, realizing that the creature must have done to Luciana and her colleagues what it had done to her. "They aren't . . . dead."

Finch's eyes narrowed further. "Not as far as I know."

Cora breathed a deep, long sigh of relief. If the creature hadn't killed them, it probably wouldn't kill her.

"I'll ask you again," said Finch. "Are you in trouble?"

She looked up at him, lost. "Yes. But is there any way I can reason with you not to call the police?"

"Why?"

Cora opened her mouth but was still feeling foggy. Normally, she was a quick liar, but she couldn't think of anything besides the truth, and the truth sounded absurd.

Finch started to leave the room. "Stay here."

"Wait!" cried Cora, standing up. "You can't leave me alone."

"Why not?"

"What if I try to escape?" asked Cora, panic creeping into her voice.

Finch regarded her like he'd suddenly decided she was not only the source of the bomb threat but possibly a bomb herself. "You stay here," he said again, and was gone.

Cora ran up to the closed door, twisting the knob and finding it locked. She kicked the door and turned to the bright, tiny room, which now felt like it was running out of air. She ran to the window, trying to open it but finding it also locked. It wouldn't have mattered at any rate; she was several stories up with nothing but hot asphalt to break a potential fall.

The fluorescent light bulbs overhead made the room buzz. She backed herself into a corner, sliding down the wall until she was balled up on the floor, knees to her chest. "Hello?" she managed. "Are you still listening?" But the apparatus in her ear stayed silent. She put her head down on her knees.

After about five minutes, she still hadn't moved from her spot. Her muscles, steel-reinforced by fear, started to relax. Maybe the creature was cutting its losses. She only now remembered to check her pockets; her wallet was still there, transferred from her Disneyland hoodie, and she had never felt such relief as the feeling of her Bat-phone. She flipped it open, jammed the power button, but got no response. Though the creature hadn't taken it, the phone's battery was very, very dead.

She looked up at the tile ceiling, wondering if when Finch returned, it would be with a police escort. This wasn't a brig. It wasn't meant to hold prisoners. It was just unused office space, locked from the outside. Those ceiling tiles were held in place only by gravity, and she could fit through one of the holes easily. She hopped up and then hoisted herself onto the table, poised to lift up one of those ceiling tiles.

Then, from nowhere and everywhere, a flash of light.

It felt like it originated from inside her own eyeballs, like her retinas had caught fire. She didn't quite lose consciousness, but she stumbled and fell to the table she was standing on. She forced herself to stand, shaking off the fog. The lights were out. All the power was out. Her first thought was that a nuclear blast had gone off somewhere nearby.

She had to get out.

Without another thought, she hopped up on the table and forced a ceiling tile out of its holding, then jumped up and grabbed the edges, mustering all her strength into one mighty pull-up, hoping against hope the frame of the ceiling tile would hold her not inconsiderable weight. Snaking her way as quickly and quietly as she could through the ceiling tiles, she followed one of the air ducts to another room. She picked an escape tile at random, kicking it out and sliding down into another empty meeting area and then bursting back outside into the wide-open art deco megachurch. The power was completely out, even the exit signs. A few people looked at her, confused, but most people seemed disoriented, rubbing their heads and asking each other if their computers had just shut down, too.

She soon found the stairs, skipping down them as fast as she could, her dress billowing out in all directions as she powered past the myriad Google employees and out into the bright

California morning. She followed the signs for the parking garage, assuming that would also be the direction of the exit to the campus. The outage seemed to have affected everything in sight; nothing seemed to be operating, even cars. She saw a few other people on the sidewalk pulling themselves up, asking each other what had happened.

She all but sprinted to the nearest parking garage, feeling naked in the open, stopping by a stone column to catch her breath. One car had slammed into another one on the bottom level. It looked like the driver had coasted right into some other poor schmuck's SUV. The guy in the smashed car was trying to start it. Cora turned from the wreck, trying to scratch together a plan; cars weren't working, the only way out was on foot. But where in the hell would she go?

Then, she spotted it on the other end of the garage. That awful, ugly white van that had driven them to San José, the only van she'd ever seen with a patch of rust on the side that looked like a fish.

The murdervan.

She dashed toward it. Perhaps Bard and Luciana were still in control of their faculties and had come looking for her, or maybe they were being held there, tied up in the back of the van, next in line after Cora failed to break in to Google.

When she reached it, prepared to break into the van in unorthodox ways, she was surprised to find the back door already unlocked. She tore it open, finding not a helpless Luciana or even Bard.

The creature was crumpled on the floor of the van.

11

She'd catapulted herself against another parked car before she even knew she was screaming. It took her just as long to realize that the thing she was screaming at wasn't moving. She stood up, still stumbling backward between two parked cars. Its eyes were glassy, open, focused on nothing, no longer oppressive and scrutinizing. They no longer had that amber glow to them, now dim and lifeless. It looked dead.

She clasped a hand to her mouth. Whatever had just struck the whole of the Googleplex, whatever had taken out the power and blacked everyone out, had either killed or incapacitated the creature as well. Her first instinct was the Nils instinct—that the government had done this. But the staggering amount of power it must have taken to pull this off, let alone do something like this to the creature, surely was beyond human potential. Right? Brain scrambling and excessive use of force and indefinite detention—that was one thing. But they weren't God.

Right?

"You okay?" a voice called from elsewhere in the garage. She turned to see a garage attendant helping the guy who had crashed into the SUV.

"Yeah," she said, crawling out from between the two cars. "Spider. Big spider."

The guy arched an eyebrow and returned his attention to the fender bender. She heard the noise of a dead battery clicking as the driver of the SUV continued to try to start the engine. She could hear the repeated, futile click, a dead battery sound that she was very familiar with thanks to her now-deceased Toyota Camry. The engine wasn't turning.

Now that she could see the creature up close and immobile, it seemed to her even more unnatural. The color of its skin seemed even more a thing not found in nature, at least not on Earth, but now she could really get a look at its texture. More than anything, it reminded her of canvas or perhaps some kind of polymer. From what she could tell, this was not a being of flesh and blood but something else, perhaps some kind of machine.

She felt a strong animal impulse to run, but now that she was getting a good look at it, the calculating part of her brain started to kick into motion. What to do with an unconscious, and possibly dead, alien? She looked past the creature, into the front seat, and saw a key hanging in the ignition.

Her stomach felt like she'd swallowed a tornado, and she wondered how long it had been since she'd eaten. She got up, approached the creature, reached a shaking hand out to touch one of its toes. Like the skin, there was something manufactured about the structure of its feet, like an engineer had reinterpreted something nature had done wrong the first time. If there were an Earth comparison to its feet, it would probably be eagle talons, but the talons had been reimagined by Steve Jobs and filed to sleek, willowy nubs. She jerked her hand away before she could work up the nerve to touch it.

She waited; it didn't move.

The key dangled in the ignition, and again, she wondered where Luciana was and if she was okay. She pulled out the Bat-phone, quadruple-checking that it was, in fact, still dead, before putting it back in her pocket. Her next thought was to just take the van, cargo and all. If she wanted the van, she *had* to take the creature with her. She was loath to touch the thing, but just eyeballing it, it was probably too big to shove out of the van either way. And she couldn't see that ending well in the best of circumstances.

She closed her eyes and shut the back doors to the van, crawled into the front seat, and turned the key in the ignition; given what had happened with the other cars, she didn't expect the engine to turn, and she was prepared for the battery to likewise be shorted out, for her to figure out another way out on foot.

But the engine turned on the first try.

· · · · ·

She drove east.

The first couple of hours of driving, she turned her head to check on the body so many times she nearly ran off the road twice. She had no idea what to do with the alien in the back when or if it did wake up. At one point, she pulled over, intending to dump it and run, but there were people around, and she was afraid to go far enough into the woods that there would be no human witnesses. She had a good friend from the internet who lived in Salt Lake City. Failing to account for the fact that with half a tank and about eighty dollars in her wallet, she did not have enough gas money to make it that far, she headed in that direction.

She had made it past Sacramento on the 80 and its rush-hour traffic before she came to terms with the fact that her helpful-Mormon-welcome-in-Utah plan was no good unless she came into some cash. Probably for the best, really—how do you explain to someone you felt quite close to but had *technically* never met that there was a possibly unconscious but probably dead alien in the back of your murdervan? She spent about twenty dollars on gas and another five dollars on a cheeseburger and milkshake from an In-N-Out on the outskirts of Sacramento, chawing on the burger slowly while she stayed perched in the driver's seat, watching the lifeless extraterrestrial body on the floor of the van for any sign of movement. The milkshake made her queasy.

The body had jostled from the drive, of course. As she gnawed on the burger, she noticed the creature's left limb had twisted under its body, with the right limb stretching out toward the front as if it were trying to hit the Snooze button on an alarm clock. Its two birdlike legs spread out behind it, and its big eyes had sealed shut under what looked like wax. The eyes closing was a development, and a disturbing one, but otherwise it hadn't moved. If this had ever been a living thing, it was no longer.

She continued driving east. By the time the sun began to set, she was sure the creature was dead. She didn't know what that meant for her. There was the possibility she could use the alien corpse as blackmail to force whoever had taken her family to release them from whatever form of indefinite detention they were in, but somehow, she felt that was more likely to backfire. It wasn't exactly leverage—what would stop the feds from just taking the corpse and locking her away forever?

The mountains rose before her as she drove, jagged and dotted with tall, dark pines. It was cooler up here, but the climb was killing her gas mileage. Wildernesses like this almost evoked a sense of nostalgia; camping—great for a family on a budget—had been a favorite Ortega bonding practice before the divorce. Those whispers of memory led again to thoughts of Nils, how effectively he had sealed himself off from the threat of "censorship" by the U.S. government. Like Demi, Cora had always thought him a deluded paranoiac on that front. Now it was looking like getting inside of the walls of the virtual fortress he had built would be the only thing that would keep her from certain indefinite detention, if not worse.

The corpse was a liability, and she had to get rid of it, even if it meant braving being alone in the woods with it where no one would see her dump it. As she closed in on the Nevada border, she pulled off toward the Donner Lake exit.

She'd never been here before, but she had a pretty good guess as to why the place was called "Donner Lake." She'd had no idea it was now a popular resort destination with ski slopes and golf courses, and she wondered what the lake's namesakes would think of that. She pulled away from the interstate and drove about a mile into the state park before stopping on the side of the road.

Even this short distance into the woods the darkness was unnerving, isolating, as if she were in the deepest uncharted wilderness and not less than a mile from a major highway. She sat there, listening to the van creak as it settled and the engine cooled and the crickets sang outside, before she worked up the courage to get out of the driver's seat and into the back of the van.

The creature had jostled a little more since Sacramento from the back and forth of driving up mountain roads, but was otherwise unmoved. Its limbs were still awkwardly sprawled, its eyes sealed shut.

"You *must* be dead," she muttered, kneeling next to the creature. She sat down, shaking her head. "What do I do now, buddy? You were the one who got me into this."

The corpse stayed corpselike.

She hesitated to touch it; she wasn't sure why. Perhaps it was the fear that it might carry unknown diseases or that it might be radioactive. Perhaps it was even out of respect. Still, she didn't know how else to verify whether or not it actually *was* dead. She leaned in closely to see if she could hear anything (although she was at a loss for what she could be listening for), but got nothing. She reached out awkwardly, not sure what she should be checking for. You'd check for a pulse in a human, what does one check for in a . . . "Fremda"?

She reached out for the side of its neck, a rough approximation of where one would check for a pulse in a human. Before she could touch it, the waxy gray seal over the eyes tore open. She jerked her hand away as the creature bleated something, some screeching, clicking alien language like dozens of forks scraping and stabbing old frying pans.

Cora threw herself screaming against the back door of the van, fumbling for the handle to let her out. She shoved it open, all but fell onto the road, and tore off away from the van and into the night. She was so terrified, she'd already made it several steps before she noticed the police lights she was running toward.

She skidded to a stop, heaving deep, ugly breaths, not quite halfway between the murdervan and a state trooper. Two state troopers, in fact, both of whom were getting out of the vehicle.

She just stood there, trying to get a grip on her breathing.

"Evening," brayed one of them, the older of the two. He was a mustachioed, walrusine guy in his forties with a tag that read "Tallman." She turned to look back inside the van, back doors half-open and the inside of the van shrouded in shadow.

She turned back toward them. "Officer," she stammered.

The trooper had a partner, a younger man with a name tag that read "Sandoval." He looked much more concerned than Tallman.

"You all right?" asked Tallman.

Still breathing heavily, Cora shook her head curtly.

"Is this vehicle yours?"

"No."

"Did you know it was reported stolen?"

She stopped breathing. "No."

Sandoval looked worried, even annoyed, but Tallman, now standing over her, looked at Cora as if he were reeling in a mighty big catch. "Do you have any identification?"

"No," she lied on reflex.

He nodded, the hint of a smile appearing beneath his bush of a mustache. "All right," he said. "Call it in."

"This doesn't feel right," she heard Sandoval mutter.

Tallman took her by the arm and guided her toward the blinding lights of his state trooper SUV. His radio scratched static as he called for backup.

"No," said Cora, coming to her senses.

Tallman rounded on her, and she heard a clinking sound and felt a metal bracelet close around one wrist behind her, then the other. "You have the right to remain silent—"

"No!" She looked at Sandoval. "You've got to stay away from that van."

"Anything you say can and will be used against you," he continued. "Anything you say can be used against you in a court of law."

She turned around to see Officer Sandoval had arrived at the back of the van and was peeking inside. Tallman noticed the wide-eyed look of horror on Cora's face. "You have a right to an attorney—"

"*Holy shit!*" Officer Sandoval stumbled away from the back of the van, his gun trained on the dark interior. Tallman whipped his gun toward the van while Cora moved away from them, backing into the grille of the police car. Then Tallman made a choking sound and dropped the gun.

For an instant, the two police officers were frozen, then they were spasmodic, like thousands of volts of electricity were coursing through their bodies, and their guns flew into the darkness of the woods as though to escape the scene. The creature stepped out of the back of the van, steadied itself, and turned its attention on the state troopers.

"No!" She felt the word escape and go ignored.

The men fell to the ground, their eyes turned upward and their bodies jerking like they were having seizures, not a peep emitting from their vocal cords. Their bodies were stiff, soundlessly jolting, and it seemed as if their tongues were blocking their airways.

"Please, don't kill them!" she begged.

The alien ignored her. The two state troopers were still in that rigid, unnatural position, their faces twisted into awful horror masks.

"I'm begging you, please don't kill them!"

It leaned over each of them, turning their bodies over. From the tips of its fingers, a syringe-like tool formed itself, as though it slipped from the tips like liquid metal, a latticed, weblike thing, and then injected something into their necks just below their jaws. The syringe stopped the convulsing and their horrified expressions calmed, and their bodies became still, their jaws slack.

"Please don't kill them," she whispered. "They called for backup. The backup will be here any second."

It turned its attention to Cora.

She stood erect, hands still bound behind her back, rooted like a tree between the headlights of the cop car. The creature approached her, its amber eyes blazing like magma from the reflection of the bright headlights.

She looked up at it, trying to soften her heavy breathing. Its left hand slid its long, arachnoid fingers around her torso, the two thumb-like appendages securing her front while the other four fingers locked around her back, holding her in place like a clamp. It still had that syringe-like device it had used to subdue, possibly kill, the two police officers. She tried to close her eyes, but she couldn't. She was transfixed, terrified, unable to think straight.

With its right hand, it placed the little syringe against her neck and held it there. The red-and-blue lights flashed against the iridescent gray shell of the creature. It didn't move, the only sounds the distant hum of the freeway, the whip of wind in the trees and occasional static of the police scanner asking for an update on the situation. Cora forced her eyes shut, no longer able to bear looking at the thing.

Then she felt the pressure leave her neck. She opened her eyes just in time to see the syringe turn back into liquid spiderweb and slide back into the tips of its fingers. Then it forced her around, and she all but fell face-first on the hood of the police car. Every bit of her tensed, her shaking breath turning into vapor illuminated by the headlights, and she struggled not to cry like a child from the terror and helplessness of it. Then she heard a *click* and then the delicate clink of the cuffs falling to the ground.

She stood up slowly, her breath quick and heavy, her shoulders glued to her earlobes, careful not to make any sudden movements. She didn't turn to face it, but looked to the ground, as if to make sure that's where the cuffs had ended up. Then she felt the tips of its sharp fingers shove her in her lower back, not hard enough to knock her down but unmistakably an intimidation gesture.

She'd barely turned around before it shoved her again, this time in her stomach, pushing her away from the police car. "*Van*," said the computerized voice in her ear. It shoved her again before she could move to avoid it. She started backing away in a trot to avoid more shoves, nearly tripping over Officer Sandoval. It followed her, hunched forward, tracking her like a tiger.

"*Van*," it said again.

She turned and stumbled toward the driver's side of the van, opening the door and hoisting herself inside. She turned to see that the creature had helped itself into the back and shut the door behind it.

"*Drive.*"

She swallowed. "Where?"

"*Drive.*"

She turned the ignition and made a U-turn, heading back toward the interstate, continuing eastbound on the 80, toward the Nevada border.

She hadn't been on the interstate for a mile before red-and-blue lights came flying down the highway in the westbound direction, no doubt responding to the call the state troopers had made. Had they reported the plate number for the stolen van? She couldn't remember if they had, but if so, there would be an army of police lights bearing down on them before long.

But the red-and-blue lights in her rearview mirror never materialized. She crossed the border. Then another twenty minutes passed. She'd made it all the way through Reno before she accepted that the state troopers had failed to report what they'd come across, and no one was looking for her.

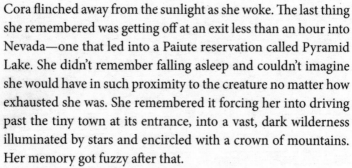

12

Cora flinched away from the sunlight as she woke. The last thing she remembered was getting off at an exit less than an hour into Nevada—one that led into a Paiute reservation called Pyramid Lake. She didn't remember falling asleep and couldn't imagine she would have in such proximity to the creature no matter how exhausted she was. She remembered it forcing her into driving past the tiny town at its entrance, into a vast, dark wilderness illuminated by stars and encircled with a crown of mountains. Her memory got fuzzy after that.

Alert, she stood up and dusted herself off. She saw neither the van, nor any tire tracks leading to where a van might have gone, nor any alien footprints. She didn't know whether to feel horror or relief at the thought that the alien had abandoned her in the middle of the desert. She looked out at the vast expanse of wilderness, an ocean of sand and shrubs rimmed with jagged hills, dread beginning to pool in her at the thought of how far she must be from the nearest gas station, the nearest human.

The nearest *water.*

"*Consume.*"

She shot to attention at the sound of the computerized voice in her ear and turned around to see the source of the voice perched on a large rock about twenty feet away, the reflection off its "skin" so bright it almost glowed in the early-morning sun, save those amber eyes that seemed to suck up the sunlight. In the daylight, its carapace was more off-white than gray, but the iridescence brought out the shadows in sharp contrast. Every fiber of her being screamed to run, but she commanded herself to stay still.

"*Consume.*"

"What?" Her breath grew quick and shallow. She could feel the adrenaline building in her muscles, despite the logical part of her brain knowing that tearing off into the desert would net her nothing but dying of exposure. Whether it intended on abandoning her, killing her, or any other myriad cruelties, she was completely at its mercy.

"*Consume.*"

She allowed herself to take stock of her surroundings, and she noticed the grocery bag plopped not five feet away from her, the thin, rumpled plastic rustling in the desert breeze.

"*Consume.*"

Cora slowly lowered herself into a crouch next to the bag and reached out to examine its contents. In it she saw a sixteen-ounce bottle of canola oil, a box of brownie mix, a jar of black olives, a jar of Cheez Whiz, a jar of pimentos, and a can of corn.

"*Consume.*"

It was a bag of groceries.

"*Consume.*"

An as-yet-unpacked bag of groceries, snatched from . . . somewhere.

"*Consume.*"

She looked back at the creature, incredulous. It must have grabbed the bag from someone's car or house after she'd blacked out. Reached in through someone's kitchen window and snatched it as though any bag of groceries was interchangeable with any other bag of groceries. Grabbed a bag of groceries, determined that the number of calories inside the bag of groceries was commensurate with what a grown human would consume within its predetermined time period, and decided, "Good enough." Then tossed it at her as if it were dumping seeds in a hamster cage.

"*Consume.*"

She stayed in a squat, her mouth hanging open, her eyes darting around, searching for the correct way to respond to this situation. "I . . ."

"*Consume.*"

"I can't," she said, holding out the can of corn as if she were showing off her third grade science project. "I don't have any way to open it."

The creature regarded her, and she shrank away as it stood up on its perch and slid off, gliding like some non-Newtonian fluid, its body a straight line in the air with every step, its huge hands still folded in front of it in that mantid way. She fell onto her knees, keeping her hands low, her body language as unaggressive as possible. It stopped in front of her, squatting down as her shaking hand continued to hold up that can of corn.

She tried not to flinch away from its gaze. Now that she could see its eyes up close, she could see that the bits that seemed to glow were actually reflected light like a cat's eye, but instead of one retina, there were thousands, perhaps millions, clustered in a nuclear mass in the middle and thinning out on the edges.

They moved like solar panels, catching light as the creature changed its focus.

It stared at her as she held out the can of corn, and she figured it didn't want to take the can from her hand directly. She put it on the ground and backed away from it, her eyes instinctively darting down to the bag of groceries. The flimsy, white plastic film of the grocery bag strained at the seams with its contents. The box of brownie mix peeked out, the Pillsbury Doughboy smiling gleefully at her predicament. Then spindly fingers placed the can of corn, now sans top, next to the bag.

She slowly reached for the can of corn, glancing up at the alien's overwhelming, unblinking eyes as she ran through the logistics of getting anything out of the can. Given her lack of utensils with which to get any corn into her person, she imagined trying to slurp it directly from the razor-sharp edges of the aluminum can and blanched at the thought.

She managed to look back up at the creature, glad at least it wasn't yammering at her every five seconds to *consume* anymore. "Thank you," she managed, words of gratitude that no human could mistake as sincere. She looked mournfully into the can of corn, bitter yellow pebbles lying in wait beneath an insidious, smoky fluid.

She forced a weak smile and decided there was no way she was going to be able to get the contents of the can inside her body without getting most of it all over herself. She tilted the can awkwardly, braced herself, and downed what little of the hideous corn water she could get into her mouth. When she'd managed as much of that as she could, she started the process of shoveling corn out of the aluminum can and into her face.

She'd gone through the rigamarole of public school lunches her entire life, so she couldn't say it was the *worst* corn she'd ever experienced. It lacked the stale, oily taste corn could only acquire after a few hours in a steam tray. She'd made it only a few hideous shovelfuls when she noticed that the creature had picked up the jar of black olives and was trying to figure out how to open it. Before she could protest, she heard the *pop* of the metal lid, and it placed the little jar of black olives next to the bag.

Black olives. The answer to the eternal quandary of what if one were to combine snails and old tires into a foodstuff. The only way the creature could have punished her more brutally was if it had forced celery on her.

Her hand shook as she took the jar of black olives, less now from fear than disgust. She looked up at the creature, a plea, but found only implacable alien eyes looking at her as if she were a squirrel that should be grateful for the stale bread it had been tossed. She managed one evil black sliver of an olive, then another, then another, before she decided that no alien-contrived torture was worth this and put the jar down.

"Where are we?" she asked.

The creature backed away, slowly lowering its body into a sort of roost. Once it settled, its posture reminded her more of a deer than a dragon, its arms folded neatly under its midsection, its head raised high and its long, slender neck curved into a slight S. "*Nevada.*"

Cora looked into the vast expanse of desert, the lack of human movement. She looked down at the half-eaten can of corn and the barely touched jar of black olives. She was creeping up to the million-dollar question, but she wasn't sure if she was ready for the answer. Given the creature's sad attempt at feeding her, she figured it didn't want her dead, that it had some plan for her. But there was plenty an alien could do with a person without killing them.

She crushed her eyes closed as if preparing for a blow and asked, "What are you going to do with me?"

She opened her eyes and looked at the creature. Still, nothing. Then, "*Why?*"

"Why, what?"

"*Why did you remove my person from the Google campus?*"

She felt the blood drain from her face, and her mind went completely blank. "I . . . I don't know."

"*Why did you remove my person from the Google campus?*" the voice in her ear repeated. "*Where were you taking me?*"

"I needed the van."

"*Where were you taking me?*"

"I don't know! I didn't have a plan. I was just trying to get as far away from there as possible. You were in the van. I needed the van to get away."

The creature remained still, impartial, impossible to read. "*You could have removed my person from the van.*"

She was shaking her head, dazed. "I don't know."

The creature was still. Its ability to freeze like a statue was unnerving. "*Why?*"

"I don't know!" she said. "I didn't have a choice; I couldn't just dump a dead alien in a parking garage without people noticing!"

"*I wasn't dead.*"

"You *looked* dead," she said, forcing herself to breathe slower, figuring that if it understood something as complex as spoken language, it knew a bit about human body language as well. She crossed her legs, slid her hands over her forearms, and grabbed her elbows, all but curling herself into a nonthreatening ball. She kept her eyes to the ground, looking at the long shadow she cast in the morning sun. "But either way . . . When you found me in the woods—before you *kidnapped* me," she added with some bitterness, "I saw you and I told you that we didn't want to hurt you, and it seemed like you were listening to me. So . . . I figured that at least you understood me."

She looked at the creature again. It stayed still, but its focus seemed to be narrowing like its eyes were lasers about to fire. With all she had seen in the last twenty-four hours, that ability wouldn't have in the least surprised her.

"I don't know why you're here," she continued, eyes darting again to the ground. "Or what you want, but I don't think you want to hurt us. If you did, you'd be going about this"— she looked at the sad, unplanned, stolen bag of groceries— "differently. And I don't know what happened at the Google campus, but I figured that if you were unconscious in the back of a van and all the power was out . . . then you weren't the cause of the outage. So I took the van with you in it."

She closed her eyes, waited for the voice in her ear to respond, but it stayed silent.

"What was it?" she asked. "The blast that knocked out the power at Google. Was it human?"

She looked again into the creature's eyes, and perhaps it was her imagination, but it seemed like the thousands of reflective surfaces were relaxing their focus. Softening, perhaps. "*No.*"

"Was it you?"

"*No.*"

"Who was it?"

A pause. "*Similars.*"

"Similars?"

"*High-ranking military caste. Similars. One higher-ranking Similar, and their subordinates, code-named by your Central Intelligence Agency as entity or entities known as Obelus. Military caste.* Homoioi." The software it was using to communicate made its speech awkwardly slow. "*Similars.*"

She thought this might be some sort of mistranslation but went along with it. "So if Obelus was the cause of the power going out, does that make you . . . the Ampersand Event?"

"*Yes.*"

"Should I call you 'Ampersand'?"

Its eyes shifted, and she considered that maybe she should stop thinking of it as an "it." She wondered if she should bring up the gender question, but given the way the reflection in the creature's eyes was shifting, it seemed to be having a difficult enough time with nomenclature. *He,* she decided, since the voice in her ear sounded male. If she survived this encounter and he decided to enlighten her on how aliens conceived gender, she could straighten that out later.

"Do you have a name?" she asked.

"*Yes.*"

"Yes?"

"*You should call me 'Ampersand.'*"

"Ampersand," she breathed. "What happened at Google? That bright light—"

"*An energy pulse,*" he said. "*What occurred was a specialized frequency, targeted for amygdaline bodies, cast for a large area, where the precise location of the target is not known. A side effect is disabling some human-made devices with active electric currents.*"

"It . . . whatever took out the power, it was there for you, wasn't it?" she asked. "The Similars. They didn't care about us; they were after you."

"*Yes.*"

Cora gritted her teeth behind her pursed lips and took a

deep breath. "Who are you?" she asked. "Why are you here?"

The creature's stillness broke, and he cocked his head ever so slightly to the side like a dog. "*An individual amygdaline, a former technocrat Oligarch of the Superorganism your Central Intelligence Agency has code-named 'Pequod.' I was summoned by one person of the Fremda group in custody at ROSA, code-named 'Čefo.'*"

"Was," Cora repeated, and something in her clicked. Čefo had been mentioned in the Fremda Memo. She'd overheard this name Čefo from the ROSA team in San José. The way they talked about Čefo in the past tense, with such urgency.

Luciana's mysterious coworker who had "committed suicide" the day of the Obelus Event.

"He's dead," she whispered. "He died, didn't he?"

"*Yes,*" said the voice in her ear. "*I seek to learn how he died. I seek to know why. I seek to locate the Fremda group, as I do not know their current location. I seek to take custody of what remains of the Fremda group and remove them to safety before any more of them die or before the Obelus Similars find them and extradite them.*"

"Extradite?"

He paused as though rethinking his translation. "*Extradite.*"

While she knew it probably wasn't a one-to-one translation, "extradite" was such a specific term in English and generally only referred to criminality. "What have you done?" she whispered, fear creeping back into her voice.

Ampersand seemed to be thinking it over, as though trying to carefully craft an adequate explanation. "*Subrace Fremda,*" he said. "*Of species code-named 'Pequod.' English designations, crude ones.*"

"Pequod?"

"*Pequod—the code name for our species utilized by the Central*

Intelligence Agency." She shook her head—the only memo she'd gotten was the Fremda one, and she had assumed "Fremda," not "Pequod," was the term for Ampersand's species.

He paused again like a slow-loading web page, not quite looking at her. "*Crude designations are all I have in the English language. Inaccurate.*"

"It's okay," said Cora, trying to sound reassuring, despite her confusion. "You . . . call yourself an 'amygdaline'?"

"*This is the term utilized by ROSA for individuals of species 'Pequod.'*" His speech software awkwardly spelled it R-O-S-A rather than pronouncing it like a word as Luciana always had.

"Okay," she breathed. "What is 'Fremda,' then?"

"*Čefo's group sought asylum on this planet and was bred into a subrace of our species. The term Luciana Ortega uses for our refugee group is Fremda. This 'Fremdan' subrace of civilization 'Pequod' was the target of extermination due to the possession of undesirable traits.*"

"So . . . you're all survivors of a genocide."

Ampersand deliberated. "*Genetic purge.*"

"Genetic purge," she repeated, skeptical. Her first thought was that humans actually *did* have a term for that in English— "ethnic cleansing"—but assumed that part of his frustration was that there was something about that term that was "crude" or "inaccurate."

"Why here?" she asked. "Why Earth?"

"*I do not know,*" said Ampersand. "*I surmise that Earth was chosen because it was known to the Superorganism, and therefore to Čefo's group, as having an oxygen-rich, stable climate—*"

She blinked. "Superorganism?"

"*—and had likely not been colonized or consumed by transients.*"

If there was any blood left in her face, it was now gone. "'Transients'?"

Ampersand looked away again, into the not-quite-middle distance, and then rephrased: "*My educated guess would be that Čefo's group of Fremdan refugees chose Earth because the planet was known to the Pequod Superorganism as having an oxygen-rich, stable climate and had likely not been colonized or consumed by other exoterrans.*"

"How many exoterran species are there?"

"*Trillions.*"

Cora nearly swooned. There was no other word for it. She was dangerously close to swooning. If she'd had a chaise longue handy, she would have.

"*There are millions on Earth alone.*"

She tried to steady herself, trying to grab for the correct word. "I mean *spacefaring* extraterrestrial species."

"*Three distinct known spacefaring civilizations,*" said Ampersand. "*Two post-natural, one post-biological.*"

"Oh, so *only* three, then," she said, rubbing her face, feeling that there was a nonzero chance she was about to projectile vomit corn, black olives, and bile all over an alien. "And only one post-biological civilization floating around out there. That's reassuring. Is that you?"

"*I am not post-biological,*" he said as though it should be the most obvious thing in the world.

"And the fact that this planet was already occupied didn't factor into them choosing *our* planet to flee to?"

"*There are hundreds of known planets that support life,*" said Ampersand. "*Human industrialization and globalization are recent, and the locus of the Superorganism is nearly one hundred light-years from Earth. The Superorganism's most recent intelligence regarding planet Earth is from what you would call the preindustrial era—655 years, subjective. Even that recently, the human population was roughly 4 percent of what it is today. The Fremda group would have known of a preindustrial linguistic primate species on this planet. They would not have known about humanity's rapid technological development, nor would they have known that the population had increased twentyfold in such a short amount of time.*"

Cora paused, reminded herself that the situation was still extremely precarious, and she needed to choose her words carefully. "You mean . . . your . . . 'Superorganism' doesn't even know how humanity has advanced in the last few hundred years?"

"*No.*"

She sighed, trying not to let these existential alterations to the very fabric of humanity's place in the universe overwhelm her.

"*I would have considered such a population increase impossible for a natural species,*" Ampersand continued. "*Were it my choice, for that reason alone, I would have sought another planet. I do not know why they chose to seek asylum on a war-torn planet populated by seven billion flesh-eaters.*"

She looked around, feeling like she was missing something. "You mean . . . us?"

"*You do eat flesh,*" he said. "*You did it in front of me. Yesterday.*"

It took her a moment to realize he was referring to the burger she'd gotten at In-N-Out just outside of Sacramento. "That's . . . beef," she said gently.

Ampersand continued to glare at her, and that dragon crest on the back of his head stood up a little, fanning out like palm fronds. It was hard for her not to read accusation in that glare, and slowly, she came upon a realization. "You're afraid of us."

Ampersand just kept staring.

She couldn't help but laugh, and she shook her head. "*You're* afraid of *us.*"

"*Would you consider a fear of billions of flesh-eating aliens illogical?*"

"No," she said, growing contrite. "No, it's . . . I guess it's logical, but you see . . . You are . . . very intimidating by human standards. I'm surprised that you're afraid of anything."

Ampersand was silent for several long seconds. Then: "*I am alone on an alien planet. I have neither resources nor means to communicate with those who summoned me here. I am being hunted by militarists from the Superorganism, and I have no allies. And the dominant species on the planet is billions of aggressive, violent flesh-eaters.*"

Her uncomfortable smile faded. "I'm sorry. I can't imagine what you're going through. But I don't want to hurt you. I had the opportunity when you were unconscious, and I didn't take it. Your concerns are valid, but really, we don't want to hurt you."

"*Why didn't you?*"

"Why didn't I what?"

Ampersand was silent for a long stretch, his eyes growing slightly wider, and she couldn't help but shrink away a little. "*Why didn't you kill me?*"

"Why would I kill you?"

"*You are frightened of me. You perceive me as a threat.*"

"You are frightening, by human standards," said Cora, voice gentle, like she was trying to soothe a baby. "But I meant what I said. I don't want to hurt you. I wouldn't attack you when you're helpless. Would you . . . hurt us?"

He paused. Then, "*Not without due reason.*"

She chewed on this, on the broadness of the implications, what "due reason" might entail, and decided not to push. "So . . . you were using me to try to find where they've stashed the Fremda group."

"*In brief, yes,*" said Ampersand. "*My goal in tracking you was that you might lead me to Luciana Ortega or other employees of ROSA, but they have been released from the project, and the Fremda group has been moved from their previous location; none of the former employees of ROSA know where they have been relocated.*"

"You think the government did it?" she asked. "You think they killed Čefo?"

"*I do not know,*" he said. "*I interrogated all the former ROSA employees when I captured you. They were all under the belief his death was an accident or a suicide. They had no explanation for it. The intelligence I gathered from them suggests that they had Čefo isolated from the other Fremda and then discovered him dead the morning of the Obelus Event.*"

It was around this point she registered that what was happening was an actual conversation. An exchange of information, if not between peers, then at least under that pretense. Fifteen minutes ago, it had been one-worded commands to "*consume.*" Now he was answering her questions, as if he saw a possibility that she might have something valuable to contribute.

As if he saw her as a potential ally instead of a tool.

On the one hand, getting him to believe that she was more valuable both intact and in control of her own faculties was her best chance of getting out of this alive. But on the other hand, there was just as much possibility that his "I'm not here to hurt anyone" act was just a façade, and her offering him aid could hurt people in the long run, human or otherwise.

But from where she sat in the desert sand, the sun high enough now that it no longer cast long, stretched-out shadows, she didn't see a better alternative to get herself out of this situation. "And . . . even though you seem to have a rather low opinion of us . . . you don't want to harm humans. Correct?"

"*You want to know if I would harm living beings for leisure?*"

"Well, you assume I might *eat* you." She regretted it as soon as she said it, remembering that now was not the time to come across as confrontational. She said as calmly as she could manage, "Can we agree, then, that both presumptions are equally ridiculous? I have no interest in eating you, and neither of us want to harm any other living thing without due reason."

Ampersand watched her as though he didn't quite buy that she wasn't ravenous for alien flesh. *Is that why he fed me?* she wondered.

"*I agree,*" he said.

"And . . . the Obelus Similars? Would they seek to harm us?"

"*Obelus's primary purpose here has nothing to do with human civilization. They would not hesitate to harm humans, if humans impeded their objective, but humans are irrelevant to their current objective.*"

"Well, then," she said, her breath shaking, wondering how to properly phrase this. "You aren't completely without allies."

He stared at her, stone still and quiet.

"That is, you don't have to be without allies. I could help you." That niggling sense of dread in her deepened, the fear that aiding him now could lead to bad things happening in the longer term. She quashed it. "Provided you don't try to do the mind control thing on me again," she added in a mutter.

"*How would you aid me?*"

"I could help you navigate this planet, I could talk to humans for you, be your mediator. An interpreter of sorts. I wouldn't be a conspicuous or obvious ally."

"*Explain.*"

"Well," she said, "as a young white female of the species, I'm less likely to be looked at with suspicion by others, especially men. I'm, um, more nonthreatening for what I am, for my place in the social hierarchy. For instance, I'm of the demographic that is most likely to shoplift but least likely to get caught for it. Does that make sense?"

"*Your gender, age, and ethnicity make you seem innocuous.*"

"Something like that." She swallowed. "But on the condition that you don't do mind control or any kind of alteration on me again. And you don't touch me without my consent. And you have to remove whatever tracker you've put on me."

"*I do not accept.*"

"What?"

"*I will need a means to determine your whereabouts if we become separated. I will remove the device when our alliance concludes.*"

The pit of dread in her stomach deepened. "Fine."

"*I concede that provided you are trustworthy, your alliance would benefit me, but I do not understand where the benefit is to you in your offer, save perhaps that you mean to use this as a short-term means of escaping me.*"

She refrained from scowling. "I hope it will benefit me finding my family," she said, deciding there was no good in lying. "CIA or FBI or . . . someone took them into custody. There are these stories of people who've seen things, like my family and I saw you. Around Altadena, Pomona, and one in Orange County. They disappear for a few days, and when they come back, they have no memory. Some of them have brain damage.

One guy had complete and total amnesia of his entire life. This guy I worked with at Kaiser was convinced the government did it, that these people had seen something they weren't supposed to see and the CIA swooped in and wiped their memories."

Ampersand just stared at her.

"I didn't believe it at first," she continued, "but now that they've gone and taken my family because they saw you . . . I don't want them to end up like that. My hope is that I can use my ability to communicate with you . . . as a bargaining chip."

Silence. Confused silence, and she realized that "bargaining chip" was a metaphor, an idiom.

"That is to say, I hope to use my ability to communicate with you as leverage to help my family, who are at present . . . in custody."

More silence. Tense silence. His focus was growing and contracting slowly like a fist slowly contracting and expanding.

"Does that make sense?"

"*Understood,*" he said. "*I accept.*"

13

It took some time for Cora to get used to being stared at as if she were a wild hyena on a leash. She'd assumed that they were far out in the middle of the desert, miles from civilization, so she was surprised to learn that after Ampersand had dumped the van, he'd only taken her about a mile away from the road, on the other side of a mountain ridge just out of sight of automotive passersby, sporadic though they were. He led her to the other side of the hill, and there was the road, less than a mile from where they stood, serving as the bright ring around a brilliant, sapphire-blue lake that extended for miles.

"What's your plan?" asked Cora, transfixed by the sight of the lake. Her mouth was as dry as the ground she was standing on.

"*We require a method of conveyance,*" he responded.

"A car?"

"*I am open to suggestions that would not seem so obvious to our pursuers.*"

Aside from horses or cows, Cora was at a loss. "I don't see what option we'd have out here besides cars."

"*Then we must procure one.*"

Cora couldn't read this as anything other than "steal one," but she did not protest. Someone else's car was not worth more than her life, and she still had no guarantee she would survive this. She had no idea how precarious the situation was in the human world, either, what with two unconscious state troopers—or, worse, two corpses—on a nearby highway. Cora didn't ask about their condition. She didn't want to know the answer.

Whatever means he had been using to get around before he met Cora had been "depleted" because of the energy pulse Obelus deployed at the Googleplex, so for the time being, even he was relegated to walking. And so, Ampersand had her march ahead of him, his eyes fixed on her every move like he expected her to turn on him and attack like a wolf once The Hunger set in.

Cora wearied of this after about a minute and started asking questions not directly related to survival. Ampersand had earlier intimated that Luciana was not one of his two failed break-in attempts that had gotten arrested at Google before Cora, so she was probably still free from parties both human and alien. Cora decided it was permissible to make some small talk.

"So . . . you said you're not 'post-biological'?" she asked.

"'*Post-natural,*'" said Ampersand. "*My body is a combination of a partially organic nervous system and synthetic body.*"

"So, you're mostly . . ." She didn't know what word felt right. She figured "cyborg" was the most accurate term, but that didn't quite sit right with her. Accurate though it might be, it felt too . . . fictive.

"*Engineered biosynthetic.*"

"Wow," she said, wondering why in the hell he was worried

about "billions of flesh-eating aliens" if that were the case. Why worry about flesh-eaters if you yourself do not technically have flesh? She glanced at him, and then turned right back around when he froze like a gazelle about to bolt.

Although he hadn't yet indicated she was asking too many questions, she didn't want to cross the line into annoying. The act of turning to look at him seemed to put him off far more than asking questions did, but it was hard not to look at him since his form was just so, well, alien. In profile, his head reminded her of the heads of the oil well pumps that dotted the near entirety of the greater Los Angeles metro area. The crest on the back of his head was less triceratops and more like half a dozen thick, silvery banana leaves that curled downward like a rosebud when at rest but perked up like the petals of a sunflower when he was alert or excited (which was, at present, always).

But it was his eyes that were the most striking, two glassy smooth almond orbs plopped on the sides of his head like beads of oil on water, a large ridge draping over the top of them. The size and shape of footballs, they weren't exactly bug eyes, but they weren't inlaid like a human's, either. They took up so much facial real estate that there wasn't room for much else, positioned more on the sides of the head like a deer's than front-facing like a human's. The reflected light of the sun made them far more striking than they were at night, and here in the desert under the clearest of skies, they were luminous, a miniature galaxy made of millions of red stars. She could only imagine what those eyes were designed for. If she hadn't been walking through the Valley of the Shadow of Death, she might have considered them the most beautiful thing she'd ever seen.

Which was to say nothing of his other apparent abilities. She hadn't seen him use any sort of telekinesis since yesterday, but she was always on edge, watching for him to use it. Was his species just so hyperintelligent their brains developed psychic powers naturally, or was there some kind of technology that his species had devised that ended up with the ability to manipulate matter remotely? She suspected it was the latter, that an "amygdaline" was the logical conclusion to truly fusing a living body with a machine.

"And these Obelus 'Similars,'" she continued, trudging onward, trying to keep her eyes on the lake, "did they follow you here or the Fremda group?"

"*They followed the same distress call that I did.*"

"If they're after the Fremda group, why did they send an energy pulse targeting you?"

"*They endeavor to apprehend me, not kill me.*"

"What makes you special to them?"

"*My intelligence.*"

"That's how you learned English so quickly?"

"*I have studied human language before. All human languages are similarly structured. I created an algorithm that, with enough context, can decode any human language.*"

Cora stopped walking. "Studied our language before? When?"

"*Centuries ago.*"

She bit her inner cheek and turned to look at Ampersand. He had stopped as well, what he must have considered a safe distance away, about ten feet. "How old are you?"

"*I have a relativistic age and a subjective age.*"

She turned back toward the road and kept walking. "Relativistic age . . ."

"*From my time in near–light speed transit. Time is relative. The English term is 'relativity.'*"

She didn't want to admit that she didn't know what the theory of special relativity actually explained, except for something broadly related to space-time and whatever E=MC^2 meant. She tried to recall anything from her high school physics class. *C is the speed of light. M is mass. E is energy.* Ugh, but she hadn't really been paying attention. She had been going through a breakup with her girlfriend, that starburst of a teenage affair that had lasted all of six weeks, and that was before Nils's international celebrity, those halcyon days when high school breakups were the ultimate source of angst. Now it felt less than quaint. "What are your ages?"

"*It has been approximately 962 Terran years since my creation, Superorganism-relative. In subjective time, I am 612 Terran years.*"

"I see," she lied and decided not to push lest she reveal her ignorance any further—after all, to a human, the difference between a six-hundred-year-old alien and a nine-hundred-year-old alien was nominal.

It took them about fifteen minutes to reach the road, and in that fifteen minutes, Cora had seen not one car. Figuring her best bet to staying on his good side was to be subservient, she kept at a respectable distance with her eyes to the ground, and asked, "What would you like me to do?"

"*Would a motorist stop at your request?*"

Cora paled, having figured that was where this was going. "Probably. I'd say if I ran out in the middle of the road dressed like this that there's maybe a 70 percent chance of whoever sees me stopping."

"*There is a motorist approaching from less than two miles. Solo in his vehicle. Stop the vehicle and lure the motorist out of the cab.*"

"*Lure* the motorist out of the cab?" she repeated. "What are you going to do—" She turned around to see only a long, empty two-lane highway and a vast blue lake. Ampersand was gone.

She stood dumb in the middle of the road, the buzz of the approaching car engine turning into a hum. No, not a car. A truck.

"Ampersand?" she said, knowing that he wouldn't respond unless she did what he said. *Your gender, age, and ethnicity make you seem innocuous.* Indeed they did, but she didn't think that the first lesson Ampersand would take was how to weaponize it.

A pickup truck rounded a curve, perhaps thirty seconds from where she stood. Why, *why* had she not asked him what had become of those cops? She knew full well that he had the capacity to render a human unconscious, even control them for a short while, but she'd only seen him do that when he'd had a use for them. What would stop him from killing a human he had no use for?

Why in God's name had she agreed to this?

The car was ten seconds away. She stepped into the road, limply waving her arms over her head. Of course, the driver had already slowed upon seeing her. A white girl out here in the desert in a tiered chiffon maxi dress was sure to draw attention. *It's a setup, you idiot,* she thought. *Keep going.*

He didn't, stopping just in front of her. She restrained the urge to apologize as soon as the man hopped out of the cab. She didn't even have to try to lure him out.

"You all right?" he asked in a concerned drawl. He was in his forties, dark, tawny hair not unlike Cora's natural color peeking out from under a small-brimmed straw cowboy hat. He seemed to be on his way either to or from some delivery, his old red-and-gray Ford F-150 sporting stability poles in the back, as well as a tarpaulin draping over the side.

"No," she said.

"What are you doing out here in the middle of nowhere?"

"I . . . I don't know how I got here." Not completely untrue. As she said it, she noticed a shadow behind the man's truck. In short order, the owner of the shadow rounded the edge of the truck and stood behind the man.

"No cell service out here," the man said. "But if you hop in the cab, I can give you a ride to town if you need to call the police."

It was only as he reached the word "police" that he noticed Cora's growing look of horror, not at him but at something behind him. He didn't get the chance to turn and look before the thing snatched him around the neck, holding him and using the other hand to inject him with something. Ampersand's movements were terrifyingly swift, and the whole thing happened in less than half a second.

Cora stumbled back reflexively and barely stopped herself from screaming. The alien held the man tightly as he struggled, jerking like a rat in the death throes of a snake's coils. Ampersand didn't allow the man to get a look at what had grabbed him as the injection took its effect. Instead, the man's blue eyes, with whites rapidly turning red, stayed on Cora. Then they closed, and Ampersand let him fall to the ground.

For an instant, Cora stared at the man, slack-jawed. Then she looked at Ampersand, and his gaze alone made her feel like every cell in her body was contracting in on itself. There was an unmistakable challenge in his eyes, and she struggled once again not to think of the creature as an "it."

"Is he dead?" she blurted, voice cracking.

Ampersand grabbed the man's boot by the tips of his long, sharp fingers, dragging him around the truck and tossing him in the ditch next to the road. "*No.*"

"Fuck," Cora muttered, choking down bile, her lizard brain screaming at her to run away from this monster. She restrained the urge to ask or say anything else as he rounded the back of the truck and looked at her, keeping that safe distance of about ten feet.

Once again, she was being appraised. She kept her mouth shut and forced herself to stand up straight. What was done was done. This was what she'd signed up for. If she protested, he'd do the same to her. "What do you need me to do now?" she asked, her voice weak.

"*Drive*," he said, and then he turned around, helped himself into the truck bed, and covered himself with the tarpaulin.

Cora only allowed herself to stand there for a few seconds before she hopped in the cab and did as she was told. As she drove away, she caught a glimpse of the man in the ditch, his boots pointed upward, his hat covering his face.

LONG: You've been the target of several investigations, and you are now facing accusations of treason. Why do you continue to do what you do with *The Broken Seal*?

ORTEGA: I've been working in media my entire life, and the media I see is not by the people, for the people. Media companies, like any industry that is complicit with a great lie at the expense of its own consumers, are complicit in murder.

LONG: If we should expect complete transparency from our government, isn't it logical to expect the same from citizens or from corporations? Where is the line drawn?

ORTEGA: I think we may need to get used to the idea that we are entering a post-private world.

LONG: Would you say that you believe that most or all problems can be solved by free information and transparency?

ORTEGA: I'm not that naive. I'm aware that dropping our guns in some countries, removing our spies in others—that would cause chaos. But there is a sickness in my country and my culture—a sickness of manipulating the masses, of hiding the truth from them. Immediate transparency wouldn't cure us of them, but the doing of deeds that even need to be hidden in the first place—that is our sickness.

LONG: Five days ago, you released an article on your website stating that the reason you persist, despite all the resistance against *The Broken Seal,* is because of your children.

ORTEGA: That's correct.

LONG: Your family hasn't responded for comment. Multiple news organizations haven't been able to make contact with them. They seem to have gone off the grid altogether.

ORTEGA: I see.

LONG: Were you aware?

ORTEGA: No, I wasn't.

LONG: Have you had regular contact with your children, or any contact?

ORTEGA: I've tried to.

LONG: How so?

ORTEGA: I've reached out, but I haven't gotten any response.

LONG: Might it be possible that they do not want any contact with you?

ORTEGA: It's more than possible. It's disappointing, but it's understandable. No matter how motivated one's ambitions are, it's difficult to empathize with them when those ambitions end up causing pain to your loved ones.

LONG: So you admit that the work you do comes at a cost.

ORTEGA: It comes at a great cost. It may have burned bridges beyond repair.

LONG: If you could say anything to your children right now, what would you say?

ORTEGA: That I hope we can have a relationship one day. That I hope you can forgive me for the pain and difficulty I've caused. That whatever you want to do with your life, you'll accept my help and support, and you'll let me be a part of it.

LONG: So if you had it to do over, would you do it differently?

ORTEGA: No. I wouldn't.

Ortega, Nils. "Entering the Era of Post-Privacy: An Interview with Nils Ortega." Interview by Stephen Long. *MSNBC Live*. MSNBC, September 24, 2007.

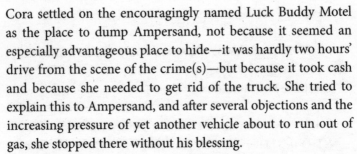

14

Cora settled on the encouragingly named Luck Buddy Motel as the place to dump Ampersand, not because it seemed an especially advantageous place to hide—it was hardly two hours' drive from the scene of the crime(s)—but because it took cash and because she needed to get rid of the truck. She tried to explain this to Ampersand, and after several objections and the increasing pressure of yet another vehicle about to run out of gas, she stopped there without his blessing.

She parked the truck on the opposite side of the reception near the motel dumpster. "Stay here," she said to the tarpaulin in the back of the truck as she hopped out of the cab. "I'm going to get us a room to hide in."

"There is no information to be mined here."

"We need a place to hide while we figure out what our plan is," she said, all but running across the parking lot toward what passed for the reception in this place. It reminded her more of a tollbooth than a motel reception. Mercifully, the man in the booth kept his eyes on his little old VCR/TV hybrid rather than her as she paid for the room. This alone gave her one hot moment of relief before she saw what the man was watching.

"The arrival of a second celestial object," said a familiar voice, "has brought about a deluge of documents."

Cora's eyes shot to the television while the receptionist's back was turned as he plucked her room key off his wall of keys. There was her dad giving a remote interview on MSNBC, with his ice-blue eyes, geometric black hair, and of course, a black turtleneck.

Always the black turtleneck.

"It's also brought a deluge of donations, which is fantastic," Nils continued. "It means that we can pay for the best vetters and fact-checkers. We'll be able to hold ourselves to the highest standards of journalistic integrity, and we'll be able to do so in an expedient fashion."

"Members of Congress are asking for a hearing to find out what the president knows," said the interviewer. "What do you think is your part in all of this?"

"The revelation of truths shouldn't be cause for sworn depositions. If our leaks lead us to a big enough outrage that Congress demands answers, it could mean that we change the course of history."

I could just leave.

It was a dangerous thought, but a tempting one. Ampersand's interest in cooperating with her was tenuous at best. If she ran now, resumed her plan to find a way to get to Nils in Germany, Ampersand might just decide she wasn't worth the trouble and let her go.

But no, there was still the matter of the tracker he'd planted on her and refused to remove. Sticking with Ampersand was probably going to do the opposite of help where her imprisoned family was concerned, but her survival was the most pressing issue, and that was far from assured.

"That guy's changing the world, you know," said the receptionist, noting how transfixed she was on the TV. He looked like the type who probably had a doomsday bunker buried in the hill behind the motel.

She shook her head, returning to the here and now. "Yeah."

"You know Area 51 is down the road, few hours south from here. That's where they're keeping 'em." He pointed out the window behind her.

"I know," she said. He raised his eyebrows. What she meant was, "I know where Area 51 is," but he seemed to take it to mean that she agreed with him.

She ran back to the truck just as the parking lot lights flickered on for the evening, hesitating at the tarpaulin as though looking beneath it might have the same face-melting effect as opening the Ark of the Covenant. She lifted the tarp, carefully, as if it were wet paper that might rip, half expecting him not to be there. But there he was, coiled like a giant rattlesnake, the crest on the back of his head lying flat like an angry cat.

"We need to get rid of this truck," she said.

"*I have not had adequate time to recharge,*" he said. "*We need a method of conveyance.*"

"Then maybe we can find another, less-stolen one. But we need to get rid of *this* truck. *This* is evidence. And if the police find us, we are *both* fucked. They are probably already looking for the truck."

"*An acceptable risk to having no method of conveyance.*"

"Listen," said Cora sternly. "Right now, we are in possession of a stolen vehicle, which makes two stolen vehicles in the last twenty-four hours. When someone finds that guy on the side of the road at Pyramid Lake and he tells them what happened, they're going to immediately call the police, and they will find this truck very, very quickly, and we are guilty of grand theft auto *and* assault. The other, much worse possibility is if they find that man *dead* on the side of the road, his truck apparently stolen, they're going to be looking for the truck with even more zeal, because we are now guilty of *murder*." She choked on the last word. "So we need to get rid of this truck as quickly as possible and get it far away from us."

"*How far?*"

"I'm not sure. Maybe a few miles? I'll leave it in a parking lot or something."

"*Parking lots will have surveillance.*"

"Then I'll leave it in the desert somewhere."

"*Conspicuous.*"

"I'll figure out something!" she cried, at the end of her rope. "*Please* get out of the truck. I got a room to hide you in. I'll be back soon."

"*How will you return after you dispose of the truck?*"

"I don't know. I'll hitchhike."

"*Witnesses.*"

"Then I'll walk."

"*That will waste time.*"

"I'll figure it out!" she nearly yelled. "We are wasting time. *Please* get out of the truck."

At this point, she didn't expect him to cooperate and was surprised to see him move to get up. The only way she could think to get him in the motel room was to keep him under the tarpaulin and herd him inside on a Hail Mary that no one would be looking. Yes, it would look like she was smuggling an ostrich with a tarp on it into a motel room, but this also looked like the type of establishment to not particularly judge for that sort of thing.

But then, something spread over Ampersand like liquid, and in the span of about three seconds, he disappeared. The tarpaulin deflated, and the truck heaved as the invisible monster stepped off it. He was still there; Cora could feel his *mass* right next to her, but she could not see him.

Well, that explains a lot.

"Okay," she said, rolling with it. She trotted around the corner of the motel to their room, giving Ampersand a wide berth, hoping that he'd actually followed her. The door slammed shut with what she assumed was a telekinetic shove, and the invisibility cloak slid off the creature. Those glowing eyes stared at her like they belonged to a lion tamer in a cage with the world's most dangerous big cat.

The motel room was in rough shape. The particleboard on the table was chipped, and the ancient polyester bedspread had more than a few stains. Cora half stumbled into the bathroom, which was accented with torn wallpaper and a cracked, prehistoric sink that also looked to be made of particleboard. She splashed her face, washed her hands, and came back out into the main room, seeing Ampersand sandwiched between the two beds.

"Will you wait here while I get rid of the truck?"

Ampersand kept staring at her in that tense, guarded way of his, waiting for her to strike. Then he said, "*I will wait two hours.*"

Cora sighed, figuring that him conceding to the loss of the truck was as far as he was willing to be pushed. "Fine."

Leaving a truck in the middle of the desert would have been the height of conspicuousness, so she stopped the next town over and left the truck next to an ancient U-Stor-It. She was about ten miles from the motel by this point, and though walking in the dark was probably the safer option, it would have taken a fair bit more than two hours.

It was thus that Cora had her first experience hitchhiking. She had expected it to take longer than it did, but the second trucker she tried pulled over. To her even greater surprise, the trucker didn't pry any further than where she was headed, and she asked him to drop her off at a diner about a quarter mile from the Luck Buddy Motel. On the way, she stopped at a gas station and bought a charger for the burner phone.

She made it back just inside the two-hour window, now well past dark. She opened the door to the room and slid inside. Ampersand had taken up residence on the bed adjacent to the opposite wall, curled up like a tailless dragon on a hoard of stained bedspread. Even roosting like that, his legs tucked next to him, his arms tucked under him, and his head upright, his body took up almost the entire length of the bed. Technological sophistication notwithstanding, his nonhumanness made him seem animalistic at times. Right here, nested in the rumpled-up bedspread, he reminded her of her dogs. Her dear, stupid, helpless dogs. Her heart sank. Had they been taken, too? Had they been abandoned in the house or put in a shelter?

Cora sat down on the other bed and plugged the phone in to charge. Hunger clawed around inside her; she hadn't eaten since that half can of corn and three olive slivers that morning. "How are you holding up?"

"*I don't understand the question.*"

She shook her head. "Never mind. What do you suggest we do now?"

"*I need to locate the whereabouts of the Fremda group and extract them from federal custody.*"

"You want to break in and take them by force?"

"*If necessary.*"

She tried to find a diplomatic way to explain that this was a terrible idea. "Extrapolating from what I've seen you do, I have no doubt that you are capable of incapacitating an entire government compound. That said, I've also witnessed a certain . . ." She bit her lip, trying to think of how to phrase this as inoffensively as possible. "Inattention to detail."

Ampersand stared at her. He was either rapt or furious. Possibly both.

"I . . . deduce that perhaps you haven't had enough time to gather the adequate intelligence on the minutiae of human culture, let alone government securities, to safely pull off such an operation."

"*I agree,*" said the voice in her ear almost immediately.

She blinked. "Really?"

"*I have not had adequate time to gather sufficient intelligence on either American culture, human behavior, or government securities to safely accomplish such an operation.*"

"Okay," said Cora. "Then we need to contact my aunt."

Ampersand's expression did not change, but the air in the room *felt* colder.

"She's the only lead I have on finding where they took the Fremda group. This burner phone isn't tapped. I think."

"*We should not reveal our position.*"

"I'll tell her to meet me at the diner up the road."

"*I do not intend on collaborating with prison wardens.*"

"I don't know how else I can help you. Do the Obelus Similars have your algorithm? The one that you used to learn English?"

"*The primary Obelus, the leader of the Similars, does have such an algorithm.*"

"So there is a chance they can figure out how to understand English and find the Fremda group before you do?"

He paused before responding. "*Yes.*"

"Ampersand," she said, keeping her voice gentle and supportive. "Do you see any realistic scenario where we succeed in liberating the Fremda group *without* negotiating with the government?"

"*Contact Luciana Ortega. Reveal only your location. Do not mention me.*"

Cora nodded and stepped outside to call Luciana.

Luciana was shocked to learn where Cora was but accepted the excuse that Cora could not tell her *why* she was there. That, of course, would come later. Luciana said she'd be there before dawn. That taken care of, Cora drained her last couple of dollars on candy bars from a nearby vending machine, slipped back into the motel room, and then went wordlessly into the bathroom. She felt disgusting, aching for a shower but ill at ease with the idea of getting naked with an alien in the next room. She compromised by showering with her underwear still on. She sat in the old, grimy bathtub with her knees huddled to herself, one eye always to the door while hot water washed over her. The water had a slight septic bouquet. Reasonable or no, she just couldn't bring herself to strip down all the way.

It took her nearly an hour to tear herself out of the shower. With nothing else to wear, she slipped back into the now-filthy maxi dress and crawled into the bed to get a little sleep before Luciana arrived. She thought there was no way she would get any rest—she could still feel the alien *staring* at her—but she was asleep within minutes.

· · · · ·

She gasped herself awake sometime later, coated with a sheet of slimy sweat. She had a vision of fingers like spider legs over her, reaching for her, holding her down, binding her. She jerked her face to Ampersand, who didn't seem to have moved, as if he had been sitting there staring at her the entire few hours she'd been asleep.

She heard voices outside and grew tense with fear that the feds had found them. The voices out there passed quickly, and they seemed to be a man and a woman speaking jovial Spanish. Probably not the feds.

Cora released a breath and fell back into the pillows, tearing off the bedsheets, which now felt stifling. She looked at the clock—it was a few minutes to 4:00. She looked over at Ampersand, who was still staring at her as though she could possibly pose *any* threat of harm to this being. Where did this come from? She was, in every respect imaginable, completely at his mercy.

"Why are you afraid of us?" she asked, more thinking out loud than because she'd meant to ask it.

Ampersand stayed silent.

"I understand that we're dangerous to each other, but to you?"

Nothing.

"I just don't see how a human could hurt you without considerable weaponry."

"*When I was recovering from the pulse, I was vulnerable. You could have killed me easily.*"

Are you often left incapacitated by an energy pulse? she wondered before her brain-mouth filter caught the question. Cora rolled onto her side with her back to Ampersand, burying her head into the flat brick of a pillow. "Have you ever seen a human before?" she mumbled. "Before you came to Earth?"

She heard only the gentle fan of the air conditioner, the distant sound of a truck passing by on the highway. Then, "*Yes.*"

Cora's eyes shot open. "When?"

"*Long ago.*"

"Oh." She rolled onto her back. "So you've been to Earth before."

"*Not I,*" said Ampersand. "*Others.*"

"When?"

"*Centuries ago.*"

"Oh," she said, the implications of that sinking in slowly. "Others?"

"*Similars. Explorers.*"

"Had you ever left your . . . Superorganism before the genetic purge?"

"*No.*"

She took a breath, and it trembled. "So Similars . . . brought humans back to your Superorganism. Centuries ago."

He was taking longer and longer to respond. "*Yes.*"

"Why did Similars bring human specimens back to your Superorganism?" she asked, metering each word, not taking her eyes off the ceiling.

"*Study.*"

"Study," she breathed, feeling like her eyes were being held open with forceps. "Were these . . . objects of study . . . volunteers?"

"*No.*"

She wondered if it was wise to continue in this line of questioning. She could feel his gaze on her, all but challenging her, daring her to judge him for being a part of a civilization that had done this thing. A part of her wanted to ask for reassurance that he wouldn't do the same to her or anyone else, but she knew that wouldn't do any good. The knowledge that he had been a part of a species that had knowingly and deliberately made humans, even ancient humans, into guinea pigs was bad enough.

How hypocritical, she could imagine him saying. *Even if we did something bad to a group of human specimens, it's a drop in the ocean compared to the horrors humans have wrought on each other.*

And he wouldn't be wrong.

"Study what?" she asked.

"*Language.*"

She turned to meet his gaze, glowing softly in the darkness like a cat's eye. "What happened to them?" she whispered.

Ampersand was stone still, and Cora realized she was very afraid. His silence told her everything she needed to know.

Then her phone buzzed. She grabbed it, sat up, and read the message. "Luciana's here."

15

Luciana was seated a few booths down from the door when Cora arrived at Verity's Diner, the sort of mom-and-pop joint that only flourished in towns too small for an IHOP. She looked as if she were casing the establishment for a sniper, her eyes bloodshot, her hair a heavy bramble. Cora sat down across from her aunt, who looked at her as though she might be a changeling. She was still wearing the same navy-blue cardigan over a yellow camisole she'd worn the last time Cora had seen her.

"Are you okay?" asked Luciana.

Cora settled into the booth, picking up the menu in a failed bid to look inconspicuous. "Yes. Are you?"

"Yes," said Luciana, fear creeping into her voice as if she just realized she'd been lured into an ambush. "Why are we in Nevada?"

Cora opened her mouth to speak, then snapped it shut. "Actually, I think it's maybe time you answered some questions."

Luciana stared at her, her mouth pursed in a concerned *O*. "I'm not the one who needs a ride from a diner in the middle of nowhere."

"Yes, well," Cora said, leveling herself, "I was pretty freaked out over an incident in my house when last we spoke. I asked you to give me some context, and you didn't. So I ask you again to please give me context."

"What does context have to do with how you ended up in Nevada?"

"I drove," said Cora tersely. "And consider it a trust exercise. You have to tell me everything before I tell you anything."

"*Trust* exercise?" said Luciana, now growing angry. "Is this about Nils?"

"No, this is not about Nils or the leak. I don't care about the leak. You have to tell me what you've been doing with your life for the last seven years. You have to tell me all about ROSA. You have to tell me how Čefo died."

The air stilled, and it seemed like the diner had gone silent.

"You have to tell me everything before I tell you anything," said Cora. "I'm not some random citizen. I've been exposed to your Pequod, and now I'm a fugitive because of it." At mention of the word "Pequod," Luciana's lips grew thin. "You can't keep secrets from me anymore."

"How did you know that—"

"I'll tell you," said Cora. "But first, you have to tell me. Quid pro quo."

Luciana was hard ice, staring at Cora until a waitress broke the tension by asking if she could get them anything. "Coffee, please," she said, not taking her eyes off Cora.

"I want every pancake in the great state of Nevada," said Cora to the waitress. "And coffee. Please."

The waitress beat a hasty retreat, and Luciana relaxed. "It was 1971," she mumbled.

"What?"

"It was 1971," she repeated. "That's when they were discovered. In Guam, of all places."

"Discovered?"

"They had a landing site in Guam. They may have been there, inside their vessel, for a while, but it wasn't more than a few days before someone from the nearby naval base found them. Our scientists believe they surrendered intentionally. So the government had to very hastily form a secret organization to take care of what appeared to be a nearly inert group of extraterrestrial refugees. While a division of the CIA was tasked with gathering intelligence on the state of extraterrestrial activity, a division of the Department of Health and Human Services with some assistance from a division of NASA was created to look after and study this refugee group—the Refugee Organizational and Settlement Agency. ROSA." She held up spirit fingers. *Ta-da!*

"And from that day, until three days ago, ROSA has been headquartered in a compound near Riverside. And in all this time, our primary goal was to open the gates of communication, but they either cannot or will not communicate with humans. So for more than forty years, they just . . . existed. Silent."

"How do you know they surrendered if they don't communicate with you?" asked Cora. "How do you know they weren't taken prisoner?"

Luciana shrugged. "Well, we can't know what's in their minds, but when they were discovered, Čefo—we think that he was the leader of the group, or one of them—went down into a posture we interpret as submissive. Then they all did.

Head bowed, body crouched to the ground, hands behind his back. That's the closest we've ever gotten to communication from them."

"But you guys have no idea *why* they won't communicate with you," said Cora.

"Right. Either they don't want to communicate or they can't. And the more accepted belief is that they can't, because if they could communicate with us, but didn't want to, why? Why put yourself in such proximity to a species you don't want to communicate with?"

Cora wondered if she looked as sheet white as she felt. She wondered what Luciana would do with the information that species Pequod had visited Earth before and had taken human specimens back to their world. And you would never guess what the subject of the study was.

Language.

Cora decided to keep that tidbit to herself. For now. "What's the difference between 'Pequod' and 'Fremda'?"

"Just different terms referring to different things," said Luciana. "DHHS called the group 'Fremda' because ROSA uses Esperanto code words. 'Pequod' is a CIA code word. So are 'Ampersand,' 'Obelus,' and so on. ROSA called the Guam group the 'Fremda group,' because that's the code name we use for that landing in 1971—'Fremda.' But they also needed a code name for this hypothetical civilization that they come from, so that's Pequod."

"Hypothetical," Cora repeated.

"Again, we don't know if they're the first of trillions or the last survivors of a dying race. We don't know anything about their civilization, if it even exists."

It struck Cora how strange it was that she knew more

about this hypothetical civilization than Luciana did. "And what about 'amygdaline'?"

Luciana blanched. "How did you . . ." She shook her head. "Okay, fine. That's just the name we have for this species at ROSA. You and I are humans, the Fremda group are amygdalines."

"Where did you get that word?"

Luciana heaved an exhausted shrug. "It's just a word that means 'almond.' They have almond-shaped eyes. Dr. Sev named them that back in the '70s."

"How many in the Fremda group?"

"Originally, forty-four."

"Forty-four? That's it?"

"Thirteen have died since arrival."

"Of what?"

"We don't know." Luciana pressed her fingernails to her teeth and looked outside into the gloaming. "We don't know. They're kept inside a clean room, but it could be anything. Pathogens, Earth's gravity, lack of adequate nutrition."

"You feed them?"

"They feed themselves," said Luciana. "They seem to have a . . . store."

"Looking at the dead bodies didn't tell you anything?"

"Čefo is the first dead body they have at ROSA. Esperas—he's the other one besides Čefo we assume to be higher in the hierarchy than the others—incinerated all the other dead bodies."

"I suppose not letting you look at the bodies is a form of communication."

Luciana cracked a tiny smile. "That it is. And that's why it's so frustrating. They know we're here, but they ignore us unless there's something they *don't* want us to do. They take advantage of our hospitality but won't even tell us why they're here."

"Čefo tried," said Cora. "Didn't he?"

Luciana looked out the window again at the blue haze just starting to appear over the mountains and nodded. The waitress came, slid their coffees and Cora's tall stack in front of them, and exited without a word.

"What happened to Čefo?" asked Cora, dumping some off-brand Aunt Jemima onto her pancakes. She'd barely put the syrup down before she started tearing into the pancakes, hardly bothering to chew.

Luciana's gaze sharpened as she saw how ravenous Cora was. "What are you doing in Nevada?"

"I'll tell you after you tell me what happened to Čefo," said Cora, mouth full.

Luciana faced the window again but kept her gaze on Cora. "Why?"

"Because." She swallowed her unnecessarily large bite of pancake. "Because I think he's a pretty big piece of the puzzle."

"Piece of the puzzle!" Luciana laughed, emptying three packs of sugar into her cup of coffee. It was an ugly, tired laugh. It wasn't unnatural on her, but it was unnatural for it to be directed at Cora. "I didn't join the team until 2000, long after the attempts at communication became regular housekeeping. The Fremda group have surveillance on them 24-7, but at night, they also keep a bare-bones security staff watching them through a feed. So one night, March 2 of this year, Čefo and Esperas started . . . a heated conversation."

Cora downed another, less huge bite of pancake. "In . . . alien language?"

"Noises, out loud. Language, we presume. We'd never heard their language before. They don't have mouths, per se, but we knew they had some means of vocalization apparatus." She gestured to the sides of her neck. "But the consensus was that those were vestigial and any communication they did with each other was some form of internal network, or maybe even telepathy, or something else entirely that we just haven't conceived.

"But there they were, talking, and this was heated. To do something I'm not supposed to do, and anthropomorphize, it looked like an argument. I'd never seen anything like this. No one had. It lasted for about ninety seconds, then stopped. Then it was like nothing had happened.

"Part of my job was that every day I had to do the regular check-in, which I did with Stevie. That morning we went into their clean room, and nothing seemed off, but something was different. Tense. Then all of a sudden, Čefo got up and started talking again to Esperas, right in front of us. And then it started again, the back-and-forth. I was a little scared, but Dr. Sev, he's the director at ROSA—*was* the director—just told me and Stevie to stay put." She laughed to herself and took a sip of the sweet, black liquid. "So we did. But then Čefo looked right at *me* and continued making that noise. He was speaking to *me*.

"Bear in mind, none of them had ever even acknowledged a human presence before, let alone . . . this! And all I could think was . . . if this being was a real intelligence, not a drone, and he'd been cooped up in this facility for forty years, he'd finally lost his mind! Because he knew I didn't understand him."

Having also been on the wrong end of a screaming amygdaline, Cora empathized. "What do you think he wanted?"

"His demands were pretty obvious," she said, chuckling to herself. "He wanted to leave the clean room. And for the longest time, I thought that there wasn't a clear way to read emotions on these guys, if they even had emotions." Her eyes grew big. "They have emotion. I learned that day they have at least one emotion, because Esperas was *pissed*. Meanwhile, the teams of scientists down in Texas and Florida were trying to see if they could make anything out of the language that they'd recorded—that didn't go anywhere. You might as well try to translate dolphin song without a dolphin-to-English dictionary."

"What happened then?" asked Cora.

Luciana's face fell. "We got our linguistics experts on the phone . . . we removed Čefo from the clean room, separated him altogether, gave him everything we thought might be useful. Books, movies, immersive language courses. He was clearly trying to learn English." She grew distant. "But they let me go not long after that, so . . . that's where my part in this little story ends."

"Why *did* your part in 'this little story' end?"

"I don't know. Why don't you ask Nils?" asked Luciana, her voice a mélange of exhaustion and bitterness.

"You really don't know why they let you go." A statement rather than a question.

Luciana put her coffee down, the cup clinking onto the plate from jittery hands. She crossed her arms and again stared out the window.

"And Čefo?" asked Cora, deciding to drop it. "Did they get anywhere with him?"

"Math," said Luciana. "Very basic math. Some nouns, but I don't think he understood how we use symbols. Bard told me they got to a point where he was very eager to try to re-create written language using pencils, but they never got any sense that he understood it. There was never an epiphany point—"

She cut herself off upon the realization that Nils's face was now plastered across the TV screens behind the counter. "Oh, Jesus," said Luciana.

Cora looked up at the TV over the bar; the chyron read

ORTEGA DEMANDS CONGRESSIONAL HEARING.

"He could order a goddamn latte and it would make news," said Luciana.

"I haven't been able to keep up," said Cora, keeping her eyes on CNN. It looked like the same interview footage from last night. "What's he doing?"

"He's pushing real hard for a hearing. And his approval ratings are higher than anyone in Congress, so congressional liberals are pushing for it, too, especially for Bush to testify about whether he knows anything."

"Why?" asked Cora, turning away from the television.

"I assume because he knows they'll deny everything," said Luciana. "And knowing Nils . . . he's probably sitting on something—"

"Just like the Fremda Memo," said Cora, finishing Luciana's sentence. "It's not just about what you leak, it's when you leak it."

Luciana planted her elbows on the table, running her hands over her face and through her hair.

"What do you think he has?" asked Cora.

"Is that another accusation?"

Cora frowned, now beginning to regret that she'd been so overtly suspicious about Luciana's role in all this. "No, just asking for your expert opinion."

Luciana shook her head slowly, then chuckled. "Nils's first and only priority is making Nils the center of all conversations, so if he can use it to raise his profile, he will. But what does it matter?"

Cora was a little surprised, maybe even a little ashamed, that her first thought wasn't *How will this affect Demi, Olive, and Felix?* but *Ampersand will not like that.* Every interaction she'd had with him told her in no uncertain terms that he wanted as little contact with humanity as possible—Nils blowing the lid open, which he was clearly positioning himself to do, would only make things more difficult.

And that was ignoring the existence of the Obelus entities running around out there, assuming Ampersand was telling the truth about their nefarious intent. If Nils really was sitting on something potentially revelatory, his leaks and the inevitable international attention they'd get could mean very bad things for the Fremda group.

Cora gulped down the last bit of pancake, already starting to ache from having very rapidly eaten the whole plate. The *whole* plate. "Okay."

"Okay?"

"I do have something I need to show you, but I have to make sure I have my ducks in a row first."

"Cora . . ."

"I need to make sure my hard evidence will cooperate," she said. "Recent history has shown that without hard evidence, I may not be believed."

Luciana's expression cooled.

"I need to check on something first," said Cora, getting up. "Come with me. Let me make sure everything's okay. Then quid pro quo."

16

Cora only entertained a moment of panic when she opened the door to the motel room and found it empty. First, the terror of once again not being believed by Luciana, then the much bigger, broader terror of *What now?* Grand theft auto twice over, plus accessory to an assault that was quite possibly a murder, and after all this, no evidence to show for it.

She closed the door behind her and continued into the room. No, she decided. She would not panic. It didn't make sense for him to just up and run unless she'd told Luciana something he didn't want her to know. Either way, she still had the tracker in her neck, as well as the earbud.

"Ampersand?"

She scratched the back of her neck and noticed that a fold in the bedspread on the bed opposite to the window was crumpled up in an unnatural way, like part of it was resting on an invisible shelf.

She backed herself up against the dresser. "I know you're still here."

The room remained still, silent. Then the invisibility cloak melted away, and there was Ampersand on the floor, wedged between the two beds like an angry cat that had backed itself into a corner. Cora stared, considering the wisdom of asking why he was doing this thing before deciding that he had his alien reasons and letting it lie. She calmly lowered herself into a crouch. "I talked to my aunt. I assume you heard the discussion?"

"*Yes.*"

"So right now, I know you're worried about time being of the essence."

Ampersand hesitated. "*Explain.*"

"I mean, we don't have much time. We think that Nils has something potentially incriminating and that he's waiting for the right time to release it. When he does, whatever he releases might end up being useful in tracking down the Fremda group, and you tell me you need to find them before Obelus does."

"*When will Nils Ortega release these leaks?*" His speech software pronounced Nils's name as "kneels."

"We don't know. Probably after they do a congressional hearing. It might be in a couple days, it might be in a couple weeks. I think you should talk to my aunt, and then we can work out whether there's a way you can work with the government to release them."

"*You suggest I collude with their captors.*"

"Luciana is under the impression that the Fremda group are not captives."

"*Čefo died a captive.*"

She sighed. "Okay, let's assume that's true. Let's assume the worst all around. We have to work with what we've got. If they are captives, maybe you can negotiate their release. But we have to do it carefully; you have to approach them like you aren't a threat. And Luciana knows these people; she'll be able to advise on how best to go about doing that."

Ampersand finally got off the floor. "*Bring her in.*"

"Okay," said Cora, shooting up off the ground, a new enthusiasm fueled by pancakes. "Here's my suggestion: you speak through me, and I'll act as your interpreter."

"*Agreed.*"

He said it without hesitation, and she felt a weight begin to lift. Uncertainty of the situation notwithstanding, this was exciting. "But I have conditions. No mind control on Luciana. No incapacitating. No neck injections. Okay?"

"*I do not agree,*" said Ampersand. "*I will defend myself at need.*"

She almost groaned. "Okay, can you agree at least that you will *only* do these things in self-defense?"

"*Agreed.*"

She huffed a self-reassuring huff, moved to the door, and waved Luciana in. She made sure her body was between her aunt and Ampersand when Luciana's eyes found what Cora had been hiding. Luciana took in a sharp breath that was nearly a scream, clapped her hands over her nose and mouth, and held them there, her eyes wide, her eyebrows disappearing beneath her bangs.

"It's okay," said Cora, reaching around Luciana to shut the door. She kept her hands on Luciana's shoulders, careful to keep herself between Luciana and Ampersand, and hastily guided her aunt to the chair next to the window.

Luciana stayed in her position of shock even after Cora seated her, as if turned to stone by a gorgon. Ampersand had backed himself up on the opposite bed next to the wall, standing on it in a crouch with his back almost parallel to the floor, his hands up and open like bear traps, hovering on his haunches like he was about to pounce. Not a good look for deescalating tension.

Cora approached him. "Hey, buddy, let's put our hands down. Can you maybe sit down on the bed? Then we can all sit down."

She was surprised when he did what she said without protest or hesitation, curling his hands inward and relaxing into his roost along the length of the bed, head turned at such a sharp angle to look at her it was almost backward. "*She is frightened.*"

"She's surprised," said Cora. "Just give her a second."

"He understands you," whispered Luciana through her fingers.

Cora turned and took a seat on her own bed, right in the middle of the room. "Ampersand, this is my aunt Luciana."

"*I know her name.*"

"I know, but this is called an introduction. It's a thing we do. The mediating party provides an introduction. Luciana, this is . . . the Ampersand Event." She gestured at him weakly. "But I've just been calling him 'Ampersand.'"

Slowly, Luciana let her hands slip off her face and into her lap. She stared at Ampersand for some time, slack jawed. This was something Luciana had been waiting years for and probably hadn't seen going down in a moldy motel room out in brothel country.

"He speaks to me through a device he put in my ear," Cora explained.

"Device?" Luciana looked like she was going to be sick.

"It's like a very, very tiny earbud. That I can't see or feel."

"They can learn our language," said Luciana, her eyes still fixed on Ampersand. "They could the whole time."

"No, they couldn't," said Cora. "He says that he was the only one that had some kind of algorithm that could decode human languages."

"He came after you to get to Nils?"

"No, he was after *you*. He doesn't care about Nils. He never cared about Nils. You and your coworkers, who he presumed would know where the Fremda group is. But you didn't know."

Luciana shook her head slowly, still in a daze.

"Okay," said Cora, singsong. "Let's talk."

She waited in awkward silence for nearly thirty seconds before Ampersand spoke. "*Why has the governing body kept the Fremda group alive?*"

Cora furrowed her brow. He was still having difficulty wrapping his unfathomable mind around why the Fremda group wasn't devoured by ravenous, bellicose primates at the moment of their discovery.

"So," she said, clapping her hands in front of her, "our friend here has been on Earth for a month, and while he has not yet been able to make contact with the Fremda group at ROSA, for reasons he has not disclosed to me, he is under the impression that they are being held against their will. He also seems kind of surprised that upon discovering this amazing alien species, ROSA didn't just . . . kill them. He wants to know why you didn't."

Luciana's mouth was still hanging open, but her expression of shock had now been replaced with hurt. "Why would he think that?"

"Well," said Cora, "he seems to have a bit of a low opinion of humanity. For what it's worth, that might also be why all the others except Čefo refused ROSA's bids for communication."

"*Why do you not ask my question directly?*"

"It's called diplomacy," she whispered. "Things need context."

"I . . . I don't know how to answer that question," she stammered at length.

Cora switched tactics. "So to answer your earlier question about how he knows alien language, his culture—former culture—has actually done some studies on the languages of alien species, humans among them, a long time ago. And I think his conception of what human civilization is like is somewhat . . . outdated?"

"How outdated?"

"Ballpark . . . a thousand years or so."

The tension in Luciana's posture began to loosen. "So in that case, it's fair to wonder why a bunch of religious zealots didn't immediately declare a group of extraterrestrials demons and stone them to death."

"I think so, yes," said Cora.

"Well," said Luciana, her voice still a bit shaky. "Human civilization has changed. Our government is, in theory anyway, secular. We also strive to be both compassionate and curious. So when the Fremda group surrendered themselves, we kept them secret, but we kept them comfortable to the best of our abilities."

"*You kept them as captives.*"

"He still thinks they're being held against their will."

"Well, they might be," said Luciana. "They might be staying compliant out of fear. We don't know what their will is. They won't respond to our bids for communication. Which is especially troublesome now that we know it's possible for them to learn our language, if not for us to learn theirs."

"Possible, but extremely difficult," said Cora. "I think Čefo was making a good-faith effort to figure out English, but he didn't have the human language algorithm that Ampersand has."

"*Describe the captives to me.*"

"Can you tell him what the Fremda group looks like, physically?" asked Cora.

"Most of them are a lot smaller than Ampersand," said Luciana. "In a neutral stance, five and a half feet to six, about the height of your average human. Čefo and Esperas were on the taller end, around six and a half feet. And the two big ones, Kruro and Brako, they're bigger than Ampersand. Their neutral stance is . . . well, they'd struggle to fit in this room. Let's put it that way."

"*Similars,*" said Ampersand.

"What does that mean?" whispered Cora.

"*It means that it is unlikely that they are being held against their will. Similars could easily overpower human weapons. I was not aware Čefo had smuggled out militarists.*"

"Are they dangerous?" asked Cora.

"*They are militarists. Militarists are designed to be dangerous.*"

"What's he saying?" asked Luciana, noting the increasing alarm on Cora's face.

"Oh, he says the two big ones are like . . . the heavies. Security guards."

"We figured that," said Luciana. "What does he want?"

"He wants to . . . go to the Fremda group," said Cora, choosing her words carefully.

"For what?"

"He says they're his responsibility and, uh . . . the Similars—that's his term for the big ones, the ones like Brako and . . . ?"

"Kruro."

"Kruro," she repeated, wondering where in the hell they'd

come up with these names. She figured it wasn't alien language, but it sure sounded like one. "He says the Obelus Event is also full of Similars, and they want to . . . the word he used was 'extradite' the Fremda group."

Luciana's eyebrows popped at that word. "What makes them special to these Similars?"

"He's adopted 'Fremda' as the term to describe a sort of genetic subsect of his species that he and all of them belong to. Apparently, they are enemies of the state owing to . . . genetic differences."

"*This Fremda group is also in possession of a Genome that carries Fremdan genetic information. The Obelus Similars will not leave this planet without retrieving it.*" Cora repeated him.

"What's a Genome?" asked Luciana.

"*Genetic information.*"

Cora repeated him and shrugged. "It's a Genome."

"Jesus Christ." Luciana faced the floor, running her fingers through her hair, and considered for a few moments. "My suggestion, based on my limited intelligence," she said at length, "is that we turn ourselves in and ask that they take us to the Fremda group."

"Turn ourselves in . . . to whom?" asked Cora.

"Well . . . probably the CIA."

"*CIA. Militarists.*"

"Not . . . quite," said Cora. "They're intelligence. Technically. Though they work with the military . . . often."

"*I would be in custody of militarists.*"

Cora was starting to worry about his aversion to the military. "Kind of difficult to avoid—your friends happened to get caught by the country with the biggest one." She looked at Luciana. "But how can we make sure we aren't just going to be thrown in jail? Held indefinitely, without trial, CIA mind-altering experiments?"

Luciana shook her head, shooting Cora a worried look like she'd just sprouted horns. "I don't see what else we can do. As far as the United States government is concerned, Ampersand is the single most valuable asset on the planet."

"You're sure they won't try to . . . capture him?" she asked. "Indefinitely detain him, too?"

"Not for lack of wanting to, but they wouldn't know how," said Luciana. "In the grand scheme, we have almost no intelligence at a time when intelligence is vital. I think they'd do just about anything to keep the Fremda group a secret, but the big unknown is what else might be coming or what else might be here already. In exchange for knowing that, I think they'd give him, and us, just about anything."

"*I wish to do an autopsy on Čefo,*" stated Ampersand. "*But first, all Fremdan amygdalines must be moved to a new, secure location.*"

"You think they'd let him do an autopsy?"

"Oh boy," said Luciana. "I don't want to be misleading. It's totally a CIA operation now since they kicked all of HHS and NASA out. I don't know that they haven't already done something with the body. They might? It depends on how the initial negotiations go. We may want to bury that lede."

"But it's possible?" asked Cora.

Luciana shrugged. "Of course it's possible." She looked at Cora, then back to Ampersand, directing her question specifically at him. "Who was he? Who was Čefo?"

Ampersand hesitated. "*A technocrat Oligarch.*"

Cora paused before repeating this, unsure if "Oligarch" was really the term he wanted to stick with.

"Are you all Oligarchs? The Fremda group?" asked Luciana.

"*No. There are three living former Oligarchs on this planet now, to my knowledge. I am one of them.*" Cora repeated him.

He was silent, unmoving except for his gaze. Cora flinched when it fell on her. "*We will turn ourselves in to the CIA, but to make myself more accessible to other humans, I have made an agreement with you to be my interpreter. But be clear, any assistance you give me, you do of your own volition, and you will make this clear to the intelligence agency. And the militarists.*"

Cora gave a curt nod and looked at Luciana. "He'll do it."

"Okay, then," said Luciana. "We'll have to do it through me, since I know the protocol. If he just shows up with no warning, it may not go well."

"What's the protocol?" asked Cora.

"We have codes for every eventuality we've dreamed up. It's been a while, but I think I remember the pertinent ones: 2290 is contact, general; 5208 is contact, hostile; 2512 is contact, nonhostile; 2548 is contact, shows sign of understanding human language. Boy, is that one I thought I'd never use."

"Who do we reach out to?"

Luciana sighed and looked apologetically at Cora. "Better call Sol."

"*Him?* Really?"

"Really."

"That motherfucker arrested my fucking family for—" She whipped an incredulous hand toward Ampersand, who was still parked placidly on the bed. The crest on his head was now relaxed like a flower that hadn't yet bloomed. He looked like he was no longer even paying attention.

"Good lord, you don't know it was him." Luciana had already pulled out one of her several cell phones. "Besides, who else do you think we'd be turning ourselves in to? Give me your burner."

Cora reached into her pocket and handed over her burner phone, which Luciana used to dial a number stored in one of hers. "Hi, Sol," said Luciana after he apparently picked up before the first ring. "Surprised you're awake. Yeah, I know. No, don't bother. We're going to come to you. Yes, 'we,' me and Cora and . . . a 2512. No, I'm not. No, it's not." She rolled her eyes. "Just tell me where to go. Okay, thank you. See you soon." She clapped the phone closed and turned it off.

"So where are we going?" asked Cora.

"Not where I was expecting." Luciana stood up, her expression bewildered, but not surprised. "Santa Barbara."

It's easy to assign blame to the American government for the global financial catastrophe we are witnessing unfold, and that is not wrong. Lies on this scale being uncovered were bound to cause mass existential crises, and what better way to exemplify mass existential crises in our neoliberal capitalist dystopia than a series of bank runs? But although these leaks may have shaken things up, the world banking system was already weakened beyond repair. Believe me, dear reader, this was always going to happen, First Contact or no. A string of shortsighted, greedy decisions that date all the way back to the 1970s are to blame for this financial crisis, not "the aliens." Of course, we will never know how, or when, such a crisis would have unfolded without these precipitating factors causing massive societal upheaval, but rest assured, this was inevitable. JPMorgan Chase may have been the first big bank to fall, but it won't be the last. Who do you think will be next? Leave us a comment below (my money's on Lehman Brothers).

Outrage at being lied to is, of course, perfectly valid; I share your anger. But it is important that your anger stay focused on where it belongs: on the powerful who have wronged you. It's good that the president is being held to the barest minimum of account and that we will be seeing a congressional hearing of the very same kind we saw when our previous president got called out for a very different, much more embarrassing, and much less ruinous abuse of his own power. The deposition is scheduled to go ahead on Monday. What a profound system of accountability we have. Nevertheless, it's better than nothing. I can't wait to see what El Presidente says.

I've seen many point to me as the individual responsible for their retirement savings disappearing overnight, for their stocks dropping double-digit percentages, for the fact that if they don't already owe more on their houses than they're worth, then they will, and soon. I may have dropped the rocks that triggered the avalanche, but the avalanche was always coming, dear reader. The question is not who is to blame but rather, what would it take for the old order to fall? For the powerful people who caused all this pain and anguish to really, truly be held to account?

Where's the revolution?

Ortega, Nils. "Where's the Revolution?" *The Broken Seal*. September 26, 2007. http://www.thebrokenseal.org.

17

The journey south to Vandenberg Air Force Base in Santa Barbara County wound through hundreds of miles of Sierra Nevada. It took some time until they came upon a town with a Wal-Mart, and at long last the opportunity came for Cora to replace the tiered chiffon maxi dress with jeans and a My Chemical Romance T-shirt on clearance. Which, okay. Fine. At least it wasn't Nickelback.

Ampersand had effectively told them they were on their own as far as getting to Vandenberg. Whatever had been hindering his "method of conveyance" earlier, the "power cores" that were slow to recharge, had been remedied. He told her that he would reveal himself at Vandenberg only after they had prepared whoever was there for him, but *only* when he felt it was safe to do so.

Eventually, the pine-covered mountains opened up into the vast desert of Southern California. The trip was quiet, Luciana was pensive and exhausted, and Cora, having not slept well, wasn't faring much better. It was on one of these silent, tense stretches of desert, the car walled on both sides by steep, red mountains, that Cora came to the realization that she was humanity's foremost expert on extraterrestrial life.

She didn't share this epiphany with Luciana, figuring that she had probably come to this realization hours ago. She wondered if her aunt was bitter about it, if she was upset or even relieved that Cora had been deemed the gatekeeper to the secrets of the universe, not Luciana, who'd dedicated half of her adult life to the Fremda group. No adult relationships, no real friends outside of ROSA, and in the end, once *real* First Contact finally happened, none of that mattered. Nearly every meaningful language unit that had been exchanged between human and nonhuman had happened between Cora and Ampersand.

Now that it was no longer a life-or-death situation and she was getting some distance from it, it was hard not to be excited about it. She didn't know what to expect upon reaching the base at Vandenberg, but she couldn't help but spend the drive mulling on arguments that would allow her to stay on as Ampersand's interpreter. She tried to rationalize this as a selfless act, that as long as she was not in danger of government memory modification, Demi, Olive, and Felix would not be, either. But deep down, she knew it wasn't that. She'd been privy to information given to no other human in history, and she hadn't even scratched the surface of all there was to know. She could rationalize it as a selfless, necessary act all she wanted, but it wasn't the truth.

She wanted to know more.

Nils's rejoinder popped into her head: *Truth is a human right.* Pretentious though it was, it was certainly compelling. And if Nils's lifework had taught her anything, it was that knowledge could be stupefyingly, spectacularly dangerous. And if she were to view knowledge as a commodity like Nils did, like the government did, hell, even like Ampersand did, then what to do with something so valuable?

She'd chewed the dry flesh around her fingernails to the point of bleeding and made herself stop. What *would* Nils do in her position? Would there ever come a point where she might have no choice but to involve him in whatever she might learn from Ampersand?

And if that were the case, then regardless of her contentious relationship with Nils, maybe leaking to *The Broken Seal* might be the *right* thing to do? Ampersand had revealed so little, but what little he had let slip through might be very relevant to humanity's interests. There were, after all, not one, not two, but *three* spacefaring civilizations out there, at least one of which had visited Earth before.

Truth is a human right.

By the time they reached Vandenberg, it was midafternoon, the sun high in the sky. Having expected them, security told Luciana to leave her car at the gate, patted the two of them down, and scanned them with metal detectors. Then they were loaded into the back of a jeep, transported to another sand block of a building, and an even more serious set of people patted them down yet again. Ampersand had yet to make his presence known.

Security ushered Cora and Luciana into a big conference room in one of the administrative buildings. "Wait here," said one of the ushers, a disquietingly young marine with strawberry-blond hair and splotchy red skin. He and his partner stood on either side of the exit, decked out in full military regalia, complete with full semiautomatic weapons.

Oh, he will not like that.

"Have you heard anything?" asked Luciana under her breath, turning from the two marines.

Cora approached the window and whispered, "Ampersand, can you hear me?"

No answer.

Then the optimism and excitement she'd been allowing herself to feel cracked. *Oh, God, what have we done?*

She looked at Luciana, her tension blooming into fear. "I think we may have made a huge mistake."

Luciana, for her part, seemed far from panicking. She took a deep, centering breath and said, "Let's wait and see."

"Well, well!"

Cora and Luciana turned to see that a new player had entered the game. Special Agent Sol Kaplan stood between the two marines, looking so innocuous with his lean face, relaxed-fit jeans, and button-up plaid shirt resting over an Our Lady Peace T-shirt. He looked more like a try-hard, just-one-of-the-guys Silicon Valley CEO than a CIA agent.

"Hi," said Luciana, surprising Cora with how relieved she sounded.

"Hi, indeed," said Kaplan, taking off his aviators and resting them on his wavy black hair. "So 2512."

"Actually, 2548," said Luciana casually, taking a seat at the conference table.

"Uh-huh," he said, skeptical but not ready to completely write her off. He sauntered to the other side of the table and sat down. "Is it related to Ampersand, or Obelus, or something else?"

"Ampersand," said Luciana.

"And what about the also-ran?" he asked, gesturing to Cora but not looking at her. Cora stayed put next to the window.

"He's designated her as his interpreter," said Luciana. "His 'voice.'"

Cora waved at him stiffly but didn't smile. Her anxiety over not having heard from Ampersand had not abated, and she was doing a poor job of hiding it.

"*He?*" His expression finally drifted to Cora, then back to Luciana. "Familia Ortega. You're like the Kennedys with aliens."

"Don't be patronizing," said Luciana. "We have nothing to gain by lying about this."

"I didn't say you were lying," he said, one of his eyebrows reaching for the heavens. "'Lying' is not the word that comes to mind."

"*Tell the militarists to remove their arms.*"

Cora nearly collapsed with relief at the sound of the computerized voice in her ear, and she put her hand to her chest, grabbing the windowsill for support. "Oh, thank God."

"What is it?" asked Kaplan. "What's wrong with her?"

"Nothing," said Cora, collecting herself and standing upright. "It's 2548, right?"

Kaplan's expression relaxed as though he might finally be humoring them. "I know what 2548 means. Do you?"

"He's speaking to me," she said. "Ampersand. The Ampersand Event is, um, one. One . . . individual. I've just been calling him 'Ampersand.' He says he wants the soldiers to get rid of their guns."

"He speaks through you?" asked Kaplan. "Right now?"

Cora nodded nervously.

"How?"

Cora tapped her ear. "He uses computer software through a little speaker he implanted in my ear."

"*Implanted?*" Kaplan's expression grew more incredulous. "Computer software? Like man-made?"

"That's what it sounds like."

"Why you?"

Saying "It's a long story" felt like a bad idea, because then she would eventually be expected to tell the long story. Ampersand's forced tracker implantation, breaking into her house, knocking out a dozen ROSA employees and "interrogating" them, kidnapping Cora (*twice!*), to say nothing of two state troopers and one grand theft auto victim she did not know the status of.

"I offered to," she said, "and since he was having trouble locating the Fremda group, he decided having a human intermediary would be a good idea."

"That's not an answer," said Kaplan. "If he's talking to you right now, why does he need an interpreter?"

"It's not just about repeating his words; someone needs to be the middleman for context, idioms, metaphors. There are all sorts of confusing quirks peculiar to human language."

Kaplan's eyes darted to the window. "Where is . . . 'he'?"

Cora looked up at the ceiling. "Ampersand, can you at least tell me where you are?"

"*Near.*"

"Can you be more specific?"

Silence.

"He's not going to come into a closed space with, um . . ." Cora looked at the marine with the strawberry-blond hair and what looked to her like an AK-47. Jesus Christ, he looked younger than she was. "Guns."

"Sol," said Luciana. It struck Cora yet again how familiar Luciana acted around him, like these two had a history. "Do you think maybe we could talk outside?"

He nodded and got up out of his chair. "You guys can take a

break," he said to the two marines. They exited ahead of Kaplan, who gestured for Cora and Luciana to follow. Exiting the cold air-conditioning of the building into the warm, late-summer air felt like moving from a gas state into plasma. Kaplan led them around the side of the building.

"Okay, now that we are alone," he said. "What is this?"

"Please be patient," said Luciana. "This is real, I swear. I've seen him."

"I'm really still stuck on 'him,'" said Kaplan.

"What, gendered pronouns?"

"Yes, gendered pronouns."

"We've used gendered pronouns ever since I worked there," said Luciana. Cora couldn't help but feel like they were getting off topic and scanned the tops of buildings, half expecting to see Ampersand perched atop one of them like a falcon.

"Yes, and that's *always* been weird to me," said Kaplan.

"I can use 'zhe' if you want."

"How about 'xe' if you're going to be a smart-ass about it."

Cora turned from the pronoun conversation, putting her hand to her ear as though that might help anything. "Ampersand, please," she said, trying and failing to speak quietly enough that Kaplan wouldn't hear her. "We're outside and there's no 'militarists.' Would you please, please show yourself?"

When she didn't hear anything, she turned around, that helpless terror she'd felt when she hadn't heard from him for hours returning. She started to offer an explanation but stopped when Kaplan's cool expression morphed into utter shock. She felt a shadow fall over her.

She turned around, and there he was not three feet away from her. She felt like she might cry with relief. "Oh, there you are."

Kaplan slowly, carefully detached a walkie-talkie from his belt buckle, raised it to his mouth as if he were defusing a bomb, and said, "We've got a 2548."

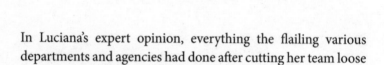

18

In Luciana's expert opinion, everything the flailing various departments and agencies had done after cutting her team loose was, to use the technical term, a total shit show.

ROSA had had contingencies for every contact-related eventuality the human imagination could concoct, since they were in charge of the day-to-day study of the Fremda group. They didn't have a specific protocol for one of them showing up making demands, but at least that sort of thing could be accommodated.

But the current setup was a haphazard hodgepodge of CIA, NSA, and military, all of whom had zero interest in the study of what they had in their custody. They had managed to coax the Fremda group onto transports to Vandenberg with the intent of airlifting them, but it was here where the aliens ceased cooperating. They'd had them locked away in a basement for two days and had found out the hard way that, like Ampersand, the members of the Fremda group had ways of defending themselves. Kaplan said the only way to describe it was like a force field, an ability that they had never exhibited until after the Obelus Event. No one could get in.

Worse still, to Luciana's outrage, four of them had died. That precious group of thirty-one was now down to twenty-seven. Because of these extenuating circumstances and the complete collapse of protocol where contact was concerned, Kaplan had this entire section of the base cleared of anyone without top-secret clearance and directed Cora, Luciana, and Ampersand straight to where the Fremda group was being held.

Ampersand had intimated that nothing *bad* would happen, that these were not two antagonistic parties about to enter into One Final Battle. Despite his tepid reassurances, the prospect of the initial meeting between Ampersand and the rest of the Fremda group made Cora extremely nervous. If Dr. Sev were still in charge, according to Luciana, there would be a whole slew of protocol to go through before they could acquiesce to Ampersand's requests, but this was, after all, a total shit show.

A group of airmen led them into the underground facility where the Fremda group was being held, and there it was, this pitiful refugee group, confused and holed up in a basement, so strange, so foreign in contrast with the drab 1960s military chic of the base. Twenty-seven, plus Ampersand. No corpses, however. Kaplan said the corpses had simply disappeared.

Luciana had described them as closer in size to a human, but it was still jarring to see the (comparatively) little guys after spending so much time with Ampersand. Most were perhaps a little taller than she was, despite that forward-leaning posture that was more velociraptor than human. All of them had smaller eyes and hands than Ampersand in proportion to the rest of their bodies, but having grown accustomed to Ampersand's defensive, almost antagonistic body language, she was surprised to see how meek they all looked. All of them had eyes half closed, turned away from the door, positioned in a half squat, hands folded underneath them like shy praying mantises. All but one of them.

This one stood upright and stepped forward, his eyes bright and focused. "That one's Esperas," whispered Luciana.

There were two more flanking Esperas, and these two struggled to fit under this ceiling. The sight of them triggered a deep, fleeting prey-animal instinct in Cora's brain, the instinct to *run*. She immediately recognized them as the Similars. The "militarists." They were roughly the size of sedans. In addition to flanking Esperas, they also appeared to be guarding something on the floor behind them, a big lumpy thing the same color as their skin, roughly the size and shape of a beanbag chair.

Esperas and Ampersand approached each other cautiously. Esperas was smaller than Ampersand by about two feet, and his grapefruit-sized eyes looked almost beady by comparison. The intensity of his gaze might have been even more overwhelming than Ampersand's had he actually looked at anyone.

Then the two started speaking in their own language.

Cora hadn't heard the language before. Amygdalines had two openings on either side of their necks about the size of a deflated balloon that allowed air in and out, and it was from there the noises came, layering on top of each other like drums. There were a few recognizable noises in there, the occasional *tsh, k,* and *g.* If there were a human analogue, some South African languages like Xhosa might be very, very distant cousins, but there were no vowel sounds at all. Their language was beyond the ability of even the most versatile of polyglots to replicate. It sounded more like low-frequency dolphin language than human language.

As Ampersand and Esperas were left to converse, Kaplan

urged Cora and Luciana outside into the hallway. Cora took the opportunity to give Kaplan an abridged rundown; what she had gathered about their hierarchy, that this entire group was some sort of refugee group owing to "genetic differences," that Ampersand described them as "amygdalines of the Superorganism you have code-named 'Pequod.'" Kaplan jolted a little at the word "Superorganism." "His word, not mine," Cora explained, by now gaining some confidence in her role.

But in her mind, the most important thing she had learned from Ampersand was that the Obelus Event was responsible for the power outage at the Google campus in a failed attempt to capture Ampersand alive and that the Obelus Event brought with it a few Similars who were keen on killing the rest of the Fremda group and absconding with their "Genome." Going by Kaplan's expression, she may as well have told him they had already infected the water supply with space anthrax.

After about twenty minutes, a flood of bureaucrats arrived, most of them military higher-ups. One of them introduced himself as Colonel Keith, an older gentleman who seemed to Cora what Keanu Reeves might look like if he had aged twenty years, gained fifty pounds, and lost all his charisma. When Kaplan debriefed him on the last couple of hours, the man simply could not mask his horror that it was Cora, Nils Ortega's own flesh and blood, who had been appointed as the first and sole mediator between humanity and extraterrestrial intelligence. She tried to be polite regardless.

"Cora, can you come with me?" said one of Keith's subordinates, a friendly blond woman with a tight bun. She reminded Cora of Meg Ryan. "While we wait to see how this plays out, we need to give you a quick evaluation."

"What kind of evaluation?" asked Luciana.

"A physical as well as a mental evaluation. Nothing major," she said. "Also a CT scan."

Cora moved to follow the woman but stopped dead in her tracks when the voice in her ear said, "*No.*"

"What do you mean?" she asked.

"*Tell them no CT scan.*"

"Why?"

"*It is possible that is not all they intend to do.*"

She took in a quick breath. She'd gotten so caught up in being a good mediator, she'd all but forgotten why she'd agreed to do this in the first place. She hadn't even given a thought to what the process of government memory modification might entail. She peeked back in the room and saw that Ampersand and Esperas were still conversing. He wasn't even looking in her direction.

"He says I'm to remain near him at all times," said Cora. "If you want to evaluate me, you can do it here."

"There's nothing to be afraid of," said shady Meg Ryan. "It's just a quick procedure, in and out."

"*No CT scan.*"

She could feel Kaplan studying her, scrutiny radiating off him like heat off a hot stove. "He says no. I have to stay here. I'm sorry."

The woman looked like she didn't know what to do with this and moved to discuss the matter with Keith.

"*They will try to instate one of their own as your replacement.*"

"He's also adamant that it's me who speaks for him, not anyone else."

"Why?" asked Kaplan.

"Because he doesn't want to waste time training anyone new," she improvised. "He's already trained me, and he doesn't want to do it again."

It seemed that with every word she spoke, the pupils of Kaplan's eyes became smaller.

"*Come.*"

"He's asking for me." Cora ducked back into the room, relieved to be in here with dozens of extraterrestrials, some of whom were pushing twelve feet in height, than out there with the G-men.

Ampersand finally turned from Esperas and looked at her. "*Your assessment.*"

Fuck if I know! she thought. "I think they, um . . . I think if we ask nicely, they'll give you whatever you want, provided it doesn't reveal your existence to the public or hurt anyone."

"'*Nicely.*'" Ampersand said something to Esperas in their language, presumably translating her message.

"Where are the four that died yesterday?"

"*Incinerated.*"

"Aha." She looked at the timid group behind him. "Can you tell me what happened to them? The ones that died?"

"*Čefo's subordinates. A phyle. A collective suicide.*"

She blinked. "Why?"

"*Because their superior is gone. Without their superior, they mutually concluded they had come to the end of their purpose.*"

"Oh." Cora pointed to the beanbag chair–looking thing the two Similars were guarding. Now that she was closer to it, she could see that it seemed to have the same "skin" that the rest of them had, an iridescent off-white silvery color. "What is that?"

"*That is our Genome.*"

She had assumed the Genome would be much smaller, like a computer program or a test tube. It looked like a sackful of ostrich eggs. Pequod amygdalines seemed to have very little in the way of material possessions, and if they needed something, they seemed to will it into existence either from their bodies or from pure energy, as Ampersand had with his "syringe." Given the size of the Genome relative to the size of their other belongings, she figured that it must contain *literal* genetic information like stem cells or embryos.

Or eggs. Lots of them.

"Sabino," said Kaplan. Cora turned her attention to the group of humans who were filtering in. She noticed that Esperas, though not looking at any of the humans, was backing away as though he felt cornered. "What do they want from us?"

"*We will require shelter in the short term.*"

"Well, in the short term, they're happy to take advantage of shelter, if you'll let them," said Cora.

"*I will also do an autopsy on the one you have named Čefo.*"

She paused, ruminating on the most diplomatic way to word this. "He wants to know how Čefo died. Čefo is the one who summoned him here. To find out, he'll need to do an autopsy."

Every human within earshot stopped moving.

"He says, an amygdaline autopsy is a procedure that he is the only individual on this planet qualified to perform," she said, paraphrasing. The part that gave her pause was when he said, "*As his next of kin, the body belongs to me.*"

This "next of kin" thing was . . . new.

It took her a moment to decide how she wanted to go about this. "After the procedure, were this corpse human, it would then be relinquished to the next of kin, or lacking that, the state, correct?"

"If it were human," said Keith.

"Then, as his next of kin, the body should then be handed over to Ampersand."

An awkward silence flooded the room like poison gas and lingered there.

"You're his next of kin?" asked Kaplan at length.

"*Our social structure is based on the practice of dynamic fusion bonding. Čefo was my symphyle.*"

"He says he had a 'dynamic fusion bond' with Čefo," said Cora, her voice softened by confusion. "Čefo is his 'symphyle.' As an aside, this is news to me, too."

"'Dynamic fusion bond,'" Kaplan repeated, looking pitifully at Cora as if she were bombing on stage during improv night.

"There's no term for it in English, so he made one up."

"Your biological family?" asked Luciana.

"Amygdalines don't have biological families," said Cora, continuing to paraphrase. "He says, 'We do not have parents, or spouses, or siblings—we have symphyles, but if you find 'family' or 'sibling' more appropriate, you may use those terms instead. Your language has no terms for these concepts.'"

The long pause resumed, broken only by tense whispering between Keith, his subordinates, and Kaplan. "I'll have to confer with others in my department," said Keith at length. "How long will you need shelter?"

"*Either until I am able to prepare an adequate evacuation, or until I believe we can no longer be concealed from Obelus. A few days, weeks at most.*" Cora repeated him.

"What happens after that?" asked Kaplan.

"*You will release us from custody, and we will depart this planet.*"

Cora repeated him again, but this time with a sort of surprised dismay. She didn't know what she had expected, but she hadn't expected them to just up and leave so quickly.

"Why?" asked Keith.

"*Obelus possesses the same human language algorithm I do,*" he said, and Cora continued paraphrasing. "*And with that in mind, my estimate is that it will take him between two and three weeks to have a firm enough understanding of both English language and binary code language to break into any man-made computer system. You must immediately arrange for a transport, according to your original plan. But we cannot risk staying in your custody long enough for Obelus to learn your language. Once Obelus learns your language, he will break into your computer systems with ease.*

"Esperas and I are in agreement that, regardless of what we do after, it is detrimental both for our small group and for human civilization that any amygdaline remain on this planet. We understand that you wish to keep our existence undisclosed to the public. We can best accommodate that by removing ourselves from the planet altogether. If we depart, Obelus will depart as well. There will no longer be any amygdaline presence on Earth. You may propagandize with regard to our existence as you see fit." Cora omitted that last sentence.

Keith looked desperately relieved. She couldn't read Kaplan's expression at all. He seemed to have gone completely blank. "I think we can come to an agreement," said Keith. "Wait here. I need to make some calls." Keith, his subordinates, Kaplan, and most of the others then departed, leaving Cora and Luciana alone in the room with the rest of the Fremda group. Ampersand and Esperas began to confer again, ignoring the two women.

"You think they'll give Ampersand what he wants?" asked Cora.

"I don't know," said Luciana. "I just know this is huge."

"What do you mean?"

"If Ampersand really just leaves with the Fremda group when he says he will, and Obelus follows them and never makes contact with us," Luciana looked at Cora with a strange intensity, "there's still a chance they can keep this all under wraps."

That possibility had not even entered Cora's mind. Regardless of what became of her, her family, or even human civilization as a whole, from the instant she laid eyes on Ampersand, she had assumed that the worldwide Truthening was inevitable. And here was the chance to send it all back into the fringe world of conspiracy. To let the Fremda Memo fade, to discredit Nils Ortega. To deprive humanity knowledge of the single greatest discovery in history.

Truth is a human right.

"This is a huge existential truth that totally alters humanity's position in the universe," said Cora. "We are not alone. Don't people have a right to know that?"

"We aren't really here for ethical questions about what the populace has a right to know," said Luciana, annoyed that Cora would even ask something so asinine.

We. Cora kept forgetting that Luciana had been one of *them* up until very recently. "But after all this"—Cora gestured to the group of aliens not fifty feet away from them—"why do they even *want* to keep this a secret?"

"Because they're covering their asses," said Luciana. "They don't want a huge lie and a metric fuckton of stupid mistakes to be made public. We're heading into an election year. They'd rather just put off the consequences if it means not having to deal with them now."

Cora looked again at the twenty-eight odd existential alterations to the very fabric of the reality standing right in front of her. An election year? A goddamn *election* year?

Who gives a shit!?

"Sabino!" Kaplan had reappeared in the doorframe,

gesturing for her to come with him. Gathering the dregs of her willpower, she followed.

"So," he said once he had her in the hallway, crossing his arms and leaning against the wall, those goofy aviators still parked on top of his wavy black hair. "I get to be the bearer of good news. Here's the deal: they're going to allow this. I think it's a terrible idea, but they are very, very eager not to piss off any aliens or risk them being seen by the public, so they're going to allow you to stay on as his interpreter and see how it shakes out. If he cooperates and things go smoothly, fantastic. They'll let you stay on until they leave."

Cora had unconsciously backed herself against the opposite wall. "What happens after they leave?"

"You sign a strict NDA."

"And my family?"

"They'll sign a similarly strict NDA."

"And that's it?"

"That's it."

She felt a weight lifting from her, ascending into the heavens, allowing her to breathe for the first time in days.

"But if things don't go smoothly," he said, approaching her, "if we find out that you're misrepresenting him, or worse, that this whole interpreter thing is a ruse, then oh boy. Oh *boy*. I know you are your father's daughter, but even you would be shocked at the civil liberties we can violate."

The weight, from which she was only just liberated, bore back down. "I don't think I'd be that shocked."

"But the big thing is," he said, leaning in uncomfortably close, "if I ever, ever catch wind that you are either in contact, have been in contact, or intend to be in contact with your father, things will get very, very bad for you. And it will get even worse for the other members of your family we have in custody."

"They didn't do anything," she said, cringing at the naivete of her words even as they came out.

Kaplan's mouth hung open, his brows knitting as though he was confused. Then he stated, "I don't care."

His shamelessness, how unapologetic he was about the total lack of due process, chilled her. Nils had always distrusted government agencies for myriad reasons, but she was beginning to understand the unique hatred he reserved for the CIA.

"Am I in custody?" she asked.

"No, you are not," he said, straining a smile. "You are now a consultant. Again, I think this is a terrible idea, but I have to work with it, so I'm choosing to look at this as an opportunity. These guys?" He gestured to Keith and his colleagues, who were now approaching them. "They're going to ship us off to a secure location and wait for the controversial thing to go away. That's all they care about."

"Wouldn't want First Contact going public during an election year," she said bitterly.

"Yep!" said Kaplan without pause. "That's the bullshit. But what *I* want is intelligence, and you are our conduit for that. So whatever you find out about them—their culture, their intentions, their civilization, anything—I want you to tell me. You work for *me* now. We clear?"

"This feels like a threat."

"I mean, it kind of is?"

Her shoulders collapsed, and she nodded. "Does that mean I'm getting paid, at least?"

He looked at her again with that patronizing, confused expression. Then he cracked a smile, let out a breath that almost sounded like a laugh. Cora thought it must be the first and only wisp of sincerity she'd seen from the man.

Keith walked past them to enter the room containing the Fremda group, and Cora and Kaplan followed. "We will grant your requests," he said. "Čefo's body is in storage, on ice, and has not been tampered with besides superficial scans. You may handle the autopsy, provided Special Agent Kaplan and any agents he requests also be present."

"He accepts that," said Cora.

"Also, at Special Agent Kaplan's request, all former ROSA employees will be reinstated for the duration of your stay." Keith looked at Luciana, and his tone made it clear that this was a begrudging concession. "All of them."

Luciana went blank with puzzlement. She looked at Kaplan, who was wearing a calm, satisfied smirk. Cora didn't know what her aunt had expected to happen, but this was clearly not it. "Thank you, Colonel."

Cora moved toward Ampersand, stopping at that respectable distance of about ten feet he seemed to prefer. "Is there anything you'd like to tell them?" she asked him.

"*I am relieved that your government has refrained from slaughtering this group.*"

Cora managed to maintain the plastic, neutral expression she had been cultivating since this morning. "He thanks you for your hospitality."

"*Esperas and I are now co-hegemons.*"

"He wants you to recognize that he and Esperas are in charge of the group."

"*We control access to our inferiors, and we grant you none.*"

"All communication will flow through him—that is to say, through me—and they want you to leave the other ones alone."

"*In exchange for shelter and protection, we will concede*

to granting you limited information about us, where I deem it relevant."

"As long as they're here, he'll grant you limited intelligence about their species, but only where he decides it's relevant."

"Agreed," said Keith. "We'll arrange to have you transported within the hour."

"Where are you taking them?" asked Cora.

"The securest bunker in the world," said Keith.

"*A military installation.*"

"If you want shelter from them and you want someplace secure, military installations are your only option," she whispered. Ampersand didn't respond, which she took as begrudging acceptance.

"One more thing," said Kaplan, stepping forward. "The most important piece of intelligence you can give us is what to expect after you leave. Clearly, your 'Superorganism' knows about Earth. What can we expect from them, and when can we expect it?"

"*The Superorganism will never make contact with your civilization.*" Cora repeated him, taken aback at such a simple answer.

Kaplan clearly was, too, and his gaze sharpened, the muscles in his neck stiffening. "Ignoring contact, is there even a remote chance of invasion?"

"He says the Superorganism would never invade Earth," said Cora, repeating him verbatim. "It poses no strategic advantage."

"Would there ever be a point where your species might come for our resources?" asked Kaplan.

"He says no," said Cora. "Earth's resources are unremarkable and abundant throughout this spiral of the galaxy, and Earth is too far from the Superorganism to mine regardless."

By now, Ampersand and Kaplan were engaged in a staring contest. The ridge over Ampersand's eyes made him look surprised, alert, or angry, depending on the angle you looked at him. Right now, he was tilting his head down, hooding his eyes in a way that made it look as if he were about to charge, his focus collecting in a concentrated mass like tiny suns, the crest on the back of his head fanning out like flames. Kaplan was completely unfazed.

"So to be clear, before we go any further with this," said Kaplan, his dark brown eyes unblinking, "can you guarantee us that there is no possibility of invasion, or even of contact, from the Superorganism?"

Cora looked at Ampersand and noticed that his hands had begun to curl up in that pose she now recognized as defensive, a tarantula preparing to strike out against a threat. But the voice in her ear responded without even a second of hesitation:

"*There is no possibility of invasion, or even of contact, from the Superorganism.*"

PART THREE

. . . . .

THE GREAT FILTER

El Paso County, Colorado
September 26, 2007
NASDAQ: 2,057.68
Dow Jones Industrial Average: 10,664.46

And I saw when the Lamb opened one of the seals,
and I heard, as it were the noise of thunder, one of
the four beasts saying, Come and see. And I saw,
and behold a white horse: and he that sat on him
had a bow; and a crown was given unto him: and
he went forth conquering, and to conquer.

(Revelation 6:1–2)

Ortega, an avowed atheist, won't come out and say it, but he has delivered the message to us loud and clear. It's obvious that he doesn't view these happenings as a literal biblical interpretation of events—there are no *literal* horsemen—but it's hard not to catch his meaning. The events of Revelation need not be literal, or even religious, to carry some meaning as to what we are seeing before us.

And what we are seeing is unmistakable.

The fall of the Ampersand Event came with "the noise of thunder." The Ampersand Event was the breaking of the first seal.

The "broken seal" is the first seal. Conquest on a white horse.

The real terror isn't that our government lied. The real terror isn't that our government hosted living extraterrestrial beings.

The real terror is that others are joining them.

The first seal is broken. And it is only the beginning.

What we are seeing here on Earth is the beginning of the end.

The only thing we can do now is rise up against the reptiles who lied to us. Ortega asks, "Where's the revolution?" I have to ask the same thing.

The Judgment is coming, that cannot be negotiated. What can be negotiated is how we rise to meet it.

Callum, Lewis. "The Revelation of Nils Ortega." *DeceptiNation* (blog). September 26, 2007. http://www.deceptination.com.

19

They moved the Fremda group to the bunker at the Cheyenne Mountain Complex.

Cora didn't know much about NORAD except that it was the most well-known, well-fortified military bunker in the world and a setting for an old Matthew Broderick movie she had not seen. After she got patted down, groped, and all but cavity searched in the parking lot outside of the complex, she was loaded into a van that took them more than a mile into a tunnel carved out of the mountain, with Ampersand and the Fremda group coming in on some other transport behind them. She was seated in between Luciana and Vincent Park, a junior CIA agent whom she recognized as the other man who had been spying on her with Kaplan the morning of the Obelus Event, roughly three eternities ago (less than a week for those out there keeping track).

"So obviously, this was built during the height of the Cold War," said Vincent, small-talking as if he were chaperoning a school field trip. He was younger than Kaplan by at least a decade, fresh and accessible, and, well, *cute,* much as she hated to admit it. Unlike Kaplan, Vincent had the good sense not to wear T-shirts of bands he obviously did not listen to.

"Kind of poetic that we're holing up in a doomsday bunker," Vincent continued. It was already obvious to Cora that Vincent Park and Special Agent Kaplan had a calculated dynamic setup, with Park as the good cop to Kaplan's bad cop, and she hated how effective it was. She couldn't help but be charmed by Vincent Park.

"At least Cold War doomsday never came," said Cora.

"Yeah, *that* particular doomsday, but *this* bunker is prepared for a lot of different doomsday scenarios. All sorts of new horrors have revealed themselves since the Cold War."

"I see," said Cora, her gaze floating in the direction of the transport carrying the Fremda group behind them.

"Exactly," said Vincent. "Who knows how many new doomsday scenarios we're going to have to prepare for?"

"Is that what you're expecting?" asked Cora, feeling a little defensive. "Ampersand is lying and they really do have some nefarious ulterior motives?"

"Well, you know what they say," said Vincent, unwavering in his calm, optimistic tone. "Hope for the best; prepare for the worst."

It was late at night when they arrived, and the complex had been cleared of nearly everyone but the people they came in with. The intent was for most of the people who worked in the complex to not even know the Fremda group was there.

Giant blast doors that looked like bank vaults formed the entry to the complex itself. Inside the blast doors, the complex opened into a giant hollowed-out cavern clogged with machinery, with lights hanging from cords that stretched back and forth beneath the ceiling. One hall led to the reservoirs for water and fuel, but the complex proper looked like a giant trailer, a three-story block of a building with no windows, only one small set of metal steps leading to a lonely door.

Cora waited there with Luciana and the G-men for the Fremda group to arrive in case Ampersand needed her to communicate anything. Once their transport arrived, the Fremda group obediently followed the airmen leading them to where they would be held. They really did look like machines. The Similars in particular were terrifying to behold now that she could see them in motion. They must have weighed a thousand pounds each, though they certainly didn't move like creatures that heavy, moving instead like they were gliding through shallow water and the laws of gravity did not apply. They were taller than Ampersand but also wider, making the rest of the group look skinny and svelte.

The others marched along in a comical, profane alien death march, lockstep in pairs behind Esperas and the two Similars with Ampersand bringing up the rear, eyes to the ground like they were afraid of being whipped for disobedience, except two of them.

These two were toward the back of the train and were among the smallest of the bunch, shorter than Cora, even. Unlike the others, with their dim eyes focused on the floor in front of them, these two were bright-eyed, curious, surveying the cavernous surroundings like tourists excited to arrive at their destination. Their eyes found hers in unison, and they stared at her for a moment before resuming their survey of the bunker. She wondered at the pair, the only ones who showed anything resembling curiosity, or at least the only ones who indulged in it. *Woodward and Bernstein,* she thought. Perhaps a bit too charitable to interpret their curiosity as "investigative," but something about them smacked to her of subverting what was clearly a very strict hierarchy.

Before she followed the group through the lonely door into the labyrinth of the complex, she looked again at the exit. What bothered her wasn't the blast doors—it was the idea that once they were closed, if they ever closed, they were sealed in with no way out. The blast doors to the facility always stayed open when they weren't in lockdown or doing a drill, they assured her, but it still felt like a cage. Hundreds of rats backed into a circuitous, state-of-the-art rat hole.

The group was led to the very back of the complex, a place that was seldom used and wasn't likely to be accidentally stumbled upon by any nonessential personnel.

"Will we be guaranteed privacy in this section of the complex?" asked Ampersand. It was the first time he'd spoken to her since they arrived.

"He wants to know if you can guarantee them privacy." She noticed a security camera peeking out of the corner of the ceiling as she said this.

"We can respect that," said Vincent Park.

"Leave us. Take the militarists with you."

As it was by now almost midnight, everyone who was not stationed at the complex, including Luciana, Kaplan, and Vincent Park, was taken off-site to a local hotel. Cora, however, had to stay on-site, as she needed to be easily accessible to Ampersand at all times.

A couple of tight-lipped airmen showed Cora where she would be sleeping, explaining that she could not sleep in any of the bunks that housed staff that overnighted in the bunker, of which there weren't many—most people who worked here lived in nearby Colorado Springs, and few actually *slept* here. They led her a couple of hallways away from where they stashed the Fremda group, into one of the empty bunks.

The room was perhaps thirty feet wide by sixty feet long and was designed to sleep forty people. It contained ten sets of doubled-up twin metal bunk beds, painted a delicate baby-poo brown that time had chipped away. Perhaps 60 percent of the fluorescent lights in the room were still operational, and one of them flickered aggressively. All forty mattresses sat naked and unmade, save for one bunk upon which sat two blankets, two sheets, and one pillow that was the size, shape, and firmness of a textbook. The blankets and sheets more closely resembled plastic than cotton.

This portion of the bunker was designed to house several hundred people for years, but said doomsday scenario had yet to materialize, and here these rooms of unused bunk beds sat. This room had been more or less empty since the bunker's construction, they told her, and was generally only accessed for very, very occasional maintenance.

Then they left, the door shutting with a heavy metallic *thud*. She stood alone, no pajamas, no toothbrush, no possessions at all except for the clothes on her back, utterly stupefied. The moment did not last long, as pure exhaustion collapsed her onto one of the crunchy plastic mattresses with the crunchy plastic sheets. She barely mustered the energy to spread them out underneath her before falling asleep, the flickering lights still on.

．　．　．　．　．

The theater for Čefo's autopsy was improvised without Ampersand's input. It was one of the rooms that were interconnected with the space they had allocated for the Fremda group on the second floor of a three-story building, but Ampersand and Esperas had sealed themselves off. Ampersand gave her no instruction as to when, where, or what he needed for his autopsy. Fortunately, the powers that be had taken care of it, and the next morning, a room had been cleared out, and there was an alien corpse in the middle of it. Čefo.

It was surreal seeing it (him?) lying there on its stomach, legs pulled in, head forward, arms tucked under the head, eyes glazed. They had a camera set up over it and a television broadcasting a live feed to the room. Čefo was bigger than Esperas, but still considerably smaller than Ampersand, who was much closer to the Similars in size and stature than to any of the others. It didn't feel like she was looking at an actual corpse; it felt more like looking at a wax sculpture of a movie monster.

Kaplan and three of his agents had arrived ahead of her, including, to her relief, Vincent Park. Luciana arrived soon after, and she nearly cried with gratitude when she saw the Wal-Mart bags her aunt had in tow; they contained some changes of clothes, a pair of pajamas, toothbrush and toothpaste, and other basic amenities. Cora was so relieved, she nearly hugged Luciana.

Eventually, Dr. Sev arrived with several of the ROSA people she'd met in Santa Cruz, now looking considerably less hostile and, thankfully, now Bard-less (apparently, he had been one of the three failed Googleplex infiltration attempts before hers). She didn't remember most of their names, except for Stevie, the tiny person with tiny clothes. When Dr. Sev entered the room, he set down a large leather satchel and a plastic tube full of large printouts and approached Cora without a moment of pause.

"You," said Dr. Sev, grabbing Cora's shoulder. "You did it."

Cora forced a smile. "I was just in the right place at the right time."

"Incredible. How does it feel when he speaks to you?"

"Intrusive," she said honestly. "It feels like he implanted Stephen Hawking's voice in my head."

"*Prepare to dictate,*" said the intrusive computerized voice in her earpiece, startling her. "*I require a receptacle for waste.*"

Cora gasped and turned to see that he was already in the room. A knot formed in her throat, and she wished he'd given her time to go over what he needed before a bunch of people showed up. "Can anyone get me a bucket?"

One of Kaplan's underlings obliged, departing and returning shortly with a large white plastic paint bucket. She picked it up and faced everyone. "Best practice, for their comfort, is be sure to keep your distance," she said. He hadn't stated this outright, but she could read between the lines and figured it best to play it safe. "Stay back a solid fifteen feet."

"What about you?" asked Kaplan.

"I'm his interpreter." She approached Ampersand and handed him the bucket.

He took it and placed it on the floor below Čefo. Then, he started speaking. "*Understand that the terms I choose will not be a one-to-one translation, as the English language has neither the vocabulary nor the precision of Pequod-phonemic. We are a post-natural species. You, to us, are considered natural. This autopsy will focus mostly on the nervous system, as it is the only portion of the body that is alive.*" Cora repeated him verbatim.

"*The carapace protects a semi-organic synthetic endoskeleton, which houses the nervous system. These bodies are designed to exist on alien worlds and are energized by power cores, not natural metabolism. Fremda have a higher quantity of organic nervous system relative to inorganic than other, non-Fremdan amygdalines, as well as some organic body parts outside of the nervous system and a unique microbiome. This makes us unique among the Superorganism."*

"Superorganism," said Dr. Sev. "You've used this term several times. Can you elaborate on it? Your species?"

"This information is irrelevant to human interests."

Cora bit her lip. "He says he wants to focus on the autopsy."

He didn't have a scalpel, but the already sharp tips of his fingers seemed to have sharpened into blades, slicing into the back of the carapace and pulling it apart lengthwise. Between this and the "syringe" he had materialized and used on her before, Cora decided that Ampersand had at least some limited shape-shifting ability. Not extensive, but he was certainly able to modify the shape of his fingers based on his task. He sliced the carapace open like butter, revealing an internal network no human had yet seen.

Čefo's body, the "inorganic" portions that housed the nervous system, was a machine so complex it almost resembled a living thing. It looked nothing like human machinery, nothing metallic or mechanical as she might recognize it. She could see the structure inside, not like big, clunky human vertebrae but dozens of structural supports that pulled back like hammers inside a piano. Then the dozens of supports opened, and there really was organic matter. *His brain.*

She didn't know how to feel. It was honestly too strange, too foreign, too unfamiliar to be disgusting. "He says he lacks English terminology for amygdaline body parts," said Cora.

"It must be difficult having a conversation in an alien language and performing a delicate operation at the same time," commented Dr. Sev.

"He says he's not 'speaking,'" said Cora. "His language runs through an algorithm that translates our language into Pequod-phonemic and back, which he delivers to his interpreter."

"How do you know human language?"

"*Experimentation on human subjects.*"

Cora nearly choked on her spit, which Kaplan clearly noticed. "Research," she said. Ampersand didn't even look up.

"Why did Esperas and Čefo incinerate the bodies of all the other Fremda who died before Čefo?" asked Dr. Sev.

"He says that was their prerogative," said Cora. "'Esperas believed, and continues to believe, that the situation called for a policy of nonengagement with Terran natives.'"

"Why?"

"*Esperas believes that our history as an advanced civilization has proven that interspecies communication is futile.*" Cora changed that last word to "risky."

"What is your policy?" asked Kaplan.

"*Full engagement with natural aliens is not possible.*"

Cora strained not to grimace, and said, "Cautious engagement."

"*Decomposition has already set in,*" he said. "*I will not be able to retrieve any recent memories.*" She repeated him. The room went silent for a few minutes, watching Ampersand's long, delicate fingers move, opening those myriad support structures farther. There was the equivalent of a spinal cord, along with dozens of dark tubes of sizes ranging from cable to a hair's width plugged into and around it.

"He says the cause of Čefo's death is starvation," said Cora.

"Starvation?" said Dr. Sev.

"Should we be concerned?" asked Stevie.

"It's not pandemic," Cora relayed. "Amygdalines don't have

fat stores off which to live. Čefo cut off his own supply of glucose, and he was dead within approximately six minutes."

"Can you tell us if someone killed him?" asked Dr. Sev.

"*I see no evidence that this was anything but a suicide. This concludes the biological autopsy. I will attempt now to dissect portions of his non-organic memory and see if there is any viable information.*" She repeated him.

He raised his forefingers in front of him, steepling them into a triangle, and the entire organic portion of the body, brain, nerves, and all, lifted itself out of the body bit by bit, until it was hanging in the air like a gelatinous cloud nebula. A couple of the ROSA people braced themselves as though it might explode.

As a whole, it didn't look so dissimilar from a human nervous system. The brain looked wildly different from a human brain, yellow-gray, smooth, and more hammer-shaped than the purple-gray, wrinkled, and spherical human brain, but the makeup of the nervous system was the same, with the "spinal cord" splitting like tree limbs into branches and twigs of nerves.

Then there was a light like a camera flash, and in an instant, the decomposing, gelatinous mass suspended in the air had been incinerated, gray slime turned to gray ash. Ampersand directed the ash ingloriously into the bucket with a barely audible *plop*. He used a light telekinetic nudge to scoot the bucket toward Cora's feet and then turned his attention to the now-empty shell. "*Tell them to dispose of this as they see fit.*"

Dumbfounded, Cora picked up the bucket, glancing at the crumbled bits of carbon. "He says you can do whatever you want with it," she said, holding out the bucket to Dr. Sev, who ingested this before calmly taking the bucket with a smile and handing it off to a stunned Stevie.

"Thank you," he said politely. He picked up the leather satchel and removed a heavy manila folder from it. "I have something that may be of interest to you as well. As you may know, Čefo spent the last few months of his life in isolation from the rest of the Fremda group, trying to learn to communicate with us. We spent some time on aural and spoken languages, but most of the attempts revolved around written language. Would you like to see what he did?"

Ampersand didn't respond immediately, and when Cora turned to look at him, he wasn't even looking at them but down at the empty shell that once housed Čefo. At length, he said, "*Show me.*"

"You should give that to me," said Cora. Dr. Sev obliged, smiling like an overworked mall Santa. As she approached Ampersand, she opened it and leafed through the pages.

They were photocopies, not priceless originals of an alien trying to replicate human writing, but they made her stop in her tracks all the same. Čefo's "handwriting" was as close as one could get to replicating Times New Roman using only a pencil. Some of it was copied verbatim from other texts. Two pages she recognized as direct copies of pages from *Moby Dick*. Most of it was nonsense. There were dozens of pages of letters in isolation, letters combining into complete gibberish words, pages upon pages of "lorem ipsum."

"This is incredible," Cora breathed, handing the pages to Ampersand. He took them, his fingers now back to their normal state, seeming almost hesitant. She watched the strange way his fingers moved as he leafed through the photocopies, like a spider using its forelimbs to place silk in its web.

"It seems to us that he never got any kind of hold on human

language structure, although it gives us some idea as to the mechanics of your language," said Dr. Sev.

"*It seems that he conceived of English as purely polysynthetic, as our languages are,*" said Ampersand. "*This likely confused him—there are some polysynthetic elements to some human languages, including English, but no natural human language is purely polysynthetic as is Pequod-phonemic. It seems that he mistook individual letters as representative of individual phonemes, which they are not. Phonemes in human languages do not necessarily convey meaning, as all phonemes do in our written and spoken languages.*" Cora repeated him.

She had only really started on her linguistics major the year she dropped out but knew enough to understand that the school of linguistics wasn't equipped at all to tackle nonhuman languages. The study of phonemics alone was so specifically attuned to the sounds the human mouth made—glottal stops, lingual fricatives, velar fricatives, sonorants, sibilants—all noises of tongue and teeth, neither of which amygdalines possessed. The Pequod-phonemic language didn't involve amygdaline "mouths" at all but the small openings on their necks used for breathing. Overlap sound-wise was near nonexistent; she could only imagine how different amygdaline syntax was.

"I find it particularly interesting that you describe your language as polysynthetic," said Dr. Sev. "We note that Čefo made thousands of attempts to combine letters together, but he never seemed to understand how letters combined to form words. Is there anything you can tell us about what he might have been trying to tell us, based on what you see?"

Ampersand continued to leaf through the pages, faster now, more the movements of a machine than a living thing. Then he stopped and all but slapped the leather binder shut. He handed it back to Cora.

"*Čefo was clearly trying to impart something he believed would be comprehensible to humans, but I cannot know his intent.*" Cora repeated him. "*This concludes our agreement with regard to the autopsy. Tell them to leave.*"

"He says he's done here, and he wants some privacy now," said Cora. "Please."

Dr. Sev held his ground. "There is one more thing that might interest you," he said, unslinging the plastic tube full of paper scrolls around his shoulder, shaking them out. More photocopies, a few dozen of them about two feet by eighteen inches.

"After a few months, not long before your . . . arrival, Čefo appeared to have given up on trying to crack the code of our written language and opted instead to try for visual representations instead. Drawings." He gave the rolled-up photocopies to Cora. She unrolled them to see an almost photorealistic drawing of a red planet, but one that looked like it had been drawn with colored pencils. It looked like Mars. The page beneath it was the likeness of a blue planet, Earthlike, but the shapes of the landmasses meant it couldn't be Earth. The entire stack of papers seemed to be depictions of the same two planets over and over again, from different angles, distances, even exposures, but with far more versions of the red planet. She held the papers up for Ampersand, who took them gingerly.

"He drew variations on these two images more often than he did anything, but he seemed especially interested in this Mars-like planet. We've been calling it Erythrá." Dr. Sev paused at this, watched Ampersand, as though he suspected something revelatory were about to emerge. "We thought that perhaps one of these planets was your planet of origin."

"*The Superorganism is not based on a planet. It is a construct. A Superstructure.*" Cora repeated him.

"I see," said Dr. Sev. "But of course, without context, even a highly detailed drawing of a red planet is meaningless. Čefo was obviously trying to tell us something." His soft, patient expression finally hardened, waiting for some reaction, some indication that Ampersand recognized this. "Can you surmise what he was trying to tell us?"

Unlike the previous mass of papers, Ampersand paused on each one of these photocopies, taking in the details of each page. Seconds extended into tense, silent minutes as every human in the room watched him leafing through the curled papers, waiting for some response. After he had gone through each of the photocopies, he curled them back into scrolls and foisted them back onto Cora. "*I cannot know Čefo's intent with regard to these drawings. Tell the militarists to leave now.*"

Cora sighed. "He says he doesn't know."

Luciana almost looked relieved, Kaplan stone-faced. Dr. Sev's patient demeanor had returned, and he nodded curtly as though this were more or less exactly what he'd expected. "Thank you for your time," he said and turned to leave. "Please let us know if there's anything you need."

Not wanting to overstay her welcome, Cora moved to follow the rest of the group.

"*You stay.*"

She turned to Ampersand, waiting for further instruction as everyone else filtered out, but he kept his attention on the corpse, his meticulous fingers digging around inside the neck. Cora stood there awkwardly for about two minutes, before she finally took a seat in one of the chairs. After about another minute of waiting, he spoke to her: "*I inquire an explanation as to your changes in my word choice."*

"Things are tense," she said, nervousness clapping her like a bear trap. "It's hard enough for them to trust you with you only giving partial information, but then you say things that I *know* they won't like. And my job as your interpreter wasn't just to make you more comprehensible but more, well, relatable. Less threatening, correct?"

"*Correct,*" he replied, not looking up from the body.

"But you can't say things like 'I experimented on live humans to learn your language' and not expect them to get a little perturbed. So I decided to paraphrase." He didn't respond. "Like you said, it wasn't a lie; it just needed to be rephrased in a way that sounds less threatening."

Still nothing.

She looked down at her feet, clasping her clammy hands behind her. "Was that wrong?"

"*No, you have done a commendable job interpreting.*"

She looked up. "Really?"

"*I believe your word choice in paraphrasing and reasoning for doing so was well founded. I simply inquired an explanation.*"

She waited a moment to see if he would expound on that with a 'but,' but he didn't. She watched Ampersand as he dug around in Čefo's now-empty head and wondered at what Ampersand had said about "phyles," the "family" alternative. He rooted around in Čefo as if he were a car he'd found in a scrap yard, not a beloved family member. She imagined herself doing an autopsy on Olive, cutting her open, pulling her little brain out, hanging it in the air and incinerating it. The mere mental image made her muscles jerk in revulsion. "Can I ask you something?" she asked.

"*Yes.*"

"I want to know about dynamic fusion bonding," she said. "How is it different from our biological families?"

"*The two are hardly analogous,*" said Ampersand, his focus still on Čefo. "*Dynamic fusion bonding has roots in biological phyles of our ancient ancestors. On Earth, the closest analogue to a phyle might be a pride of lions or a troop of chimpanzees. Protoamygdaline nymphs were raised and then purged from their birth phyle, forming new phyles as adults containing five to ten symphyles. Protoamygdaline symphyles were not biologically related to each other but instead fusion-bonded upon reaching sexual maturity, creating a new phyle.*"

"Why do you call it 'dynamic fusion bonding'?"

"*In contrast to fission-fusion social groups. It is nonmonogamous pair bonding. Modern amygdalines retain the dynamic fusion bonding practice despite no longer practicing sexual reproduction. Fusion bonds are lifelong. Once the physiological bond is formed, it lasts until death.*"

"Lasts until death," she repeated. Interesting implications for a species that lived so long. "Did you have a phyle?"

"*Oligarchs do not form phyles,*" he explained. "*Lower castes form phyles.*"

Cora looked at the corpse on the table, confused. "Well, you had symphyles, right?"

Ampersand paused. "*I had seven.*"

"Had?" It took her a moment to catch the implication of "had." "Are any of your symphyles still alive?"

Ampersand went silent, removing his hands from the corpse and curling them in front of him, but not looking at Cora. "*Two.*"

"Where are they?" she asked.

"*I do not know.*"

"Then how do you know they're alive?"

He cut her off. *"That is enough questions."*

She shrank away. "I'm sorry."

"Leave now," he said. *"I have no more use for you."*

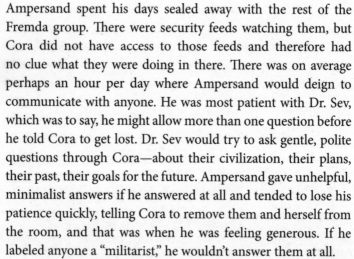

20

Ampersand spent his days sealed away with the rest of the Fremda group. There were security feeds watching them, but Cora did not have access to those feeds and therefore had no clue what they were doing in there. There was on average perhaps an hour per day where Ampersand would deign to communicate with anyone. He was most patient with Dr. Sev, which was to say, he might allow more than one question before he told Cora to get lost. Dr. Sev would try to ask gentle, polite questions through Cora—about their civilization, their plans, their past, their goals for the future. Ampersand gave unhelpful, minimalist answers if he answered at all and tended to lose his patience quickly, telling Cora to remove them and herself from the room, and that was when he was feeling generous. If he labeled anyone a "militarist," he wouldn't answer them at all.

From what Cora could tell, the loyalty of the Fremda group seemed nearly split down the middle between Ampersand and Esperas, with Ampersand holding an ever-so-slight majority; Cora learned through dictating that most of these were technocratic underlings: chemical engineers, electrical engineers, physicists, or the amygdaline rough equivalents thereof. More specifically, Čefo's subordinates (the ones who did not elect to end their lives, at least). The others, about ten of them called "diplocrats," spent their days cowering behind Esperas. Unlike the technocrats, the diplocrats refused to so much as look at Cora, and she almost never saw them, and the same held true of the two Similars. Like golems, they seemed to exist only as statues waiting to be brought to life, and from what she could tell, only Esperas held the power to do that.

Ampersand allowed that one unique trait of the Fremda group was that they seemed to specialize in the arts or sciences, at least as a human might conceive it. No grunts, no peons, no worker bees—all seemed born (well, "born") and bred thinkers. Even the Similars were primarily designed for exploration and intelligence gathering, not "militarism." The origin of the word "Similar" she couldn't figure out, but some of the other terms Ampersand used were beginning to make sense. Cora had been assigning the word "phyle" as "file," and had assumed it a translation error until Dr. Sev suggested that it was actually derived from a Greek word meaning "clan" or "tribe." So, too, with the prefix "sym"—"symphyle" literally, "within the tribe," a fellow tribesman.

Pequod-phonemic, what Ampersand called the "common language," was the closest analogue to human language, as it was spoken aurally and had a written corollary. This was all Ampersand was able to use among the Fremda group at present, a major point of contention with Esperas, who seemed to hate using the "common language."

Esperas's preferred method of communication Ampersand

called "network language," which, though related to Pequod-phonemic, was not spoken out loud and was more akin to telepathy. Ampersand, however, was unable to communicate through network language at present, relegating everyone to spoken Pequod-phonemic. At some point since the Fremdan genetic purge, someone (or something) had removed Ampersand's telepathic capability.

Who removed his telepathy? "*Slavers. Similars. Militarists.*" What did they do to him? "*Exploitation. Slavery. Torture.*" How did he escape? "*By chance.*" He refused to elaborate on any of these points, as knowing the details would not aid any human in their current objectives.

"*Irrelevant.*"

"Network language" wasn't *really* telepathy, not in the sense humans conceived it (like amygdaline telekinesis wasn't *really* telekinesis; it had something to do with manipulating electromagnetic fields). Network language was more like a wireless system that was plugged directly into the brain like a thought-powered cellular network. Ampersand even implied that humans might develop such technology within Cora's lifetime.

There was a third language in their repertoire—Ampersand called it "high language," but owing to its intimate nature, this one was not being employed by any of the Fremda group at this time. When Cora asked him what made "high language" different from the other two, he responded that it was "*irrelevant to humans.*" A human could neither comprehend it, nor engage in it, and therefore, it was a waste of time to try to explain it.

Then he told her to leave.

As she exited the room, she all but smacked into Kaplan, who had been waiting for her. "Time for debrief!" he declared. She followed him into another office near the center of the complex.

It wasn't near the command center—neither Cora nor anyone at ROSA, nor apparently even Kaplan, were allowed near that. This was yet another area of in-flux office space. The bunker was, for the most part, more reminiscent of a junior college two years before shutting down than *Dr. Strangelove's* War Room. Vincent Park was already waiting for them, and he smiled at her when he saw her, a balm to the dread Kaplan induced. She frowned at him as she took a seat, but he only smiled at her more warmly.

"You need to get 'him' to agree to talk to people," said Kaplan, flicking a ballpoint pen back and forth between his fingers. "Not just Ghasabian and his cronies."

"Like who?" asked Cora.

"Several departments want to send their higher-ups," said Vincent. "We're not obligated to grant access to *all* of them, but . . ."

"What departments?"

"Well, Defense is the loudest at the moment."

She groaned and let her head fall forward. "That's what I was afraid of."

Kaplan flicked the ballpoint pen across the room. "Can you negotiate?"

She shook her head. "That's the one department he won't even humor talking to."

"But he's happy taking shelter inside a military bunker," said Kaplan. He paused, then shook his head. "What else you got for me?"

Glad to switch topics, she gave the two agents the rundown on what she'd learned about the three different types of language as best she could. Like Cora, Kaplan got hung up on the mystery that was "high language."

"What, is it some kind of thought-speak that transcends space-time?" he asked, more to himself than to either of the other two people in the room.

"Probably," said Cora through a heavy sigh. It wasn't even midafternoon and she was exhausted. It was impossible to sleep in this place. "It might be something he just doesn't know how to explain."

"Bullshit," said Kaplan. "Anything can be explained."

Cora moved to rebut him, to remind him that they were dealing with beings who had evolved wholly different ways of communicating, before thinking better of it. "What is it you want me to find out?"

Kaplan leaned forward. "I want you to find out why they're here."

Cora sat up, confused. "I told you what he told me—"

"No, I want to know why they're *still* here. If the plan is to leave, why wait? Why hang around for a few days? If they're all so put off by the filthy hu-man, and if there really are 'Similars' on this very planet who are here to kill them, why take the risk?"

"I believe him when he says they need our shelter and resources," said Cora. "It's either this or pitch tents in the rain."

"But why wait at all, if Obelus really presents some existential danger?" asked Kaplan.

"Them staying on Earth for a set amount of time wasn't our idea," added Vincent. "If Obelus really does pose a danger to them, they shouldn't be dallying in a bunker."

"The only thing I can gather is that Ampersand and Esperas are in disagreement about . . . something," said Cora. "And they needed a safe place to hash it out before they decide where to go."

"And therefore, it falls to you to find out what that *something* is."

The inside of her nose stung, and her eyes grew hot. "I'm doing the best I can—"

Kaplan cut her off. "Do better."

. . . . .

She had taken for granted that the task of alien interpreter was one she was completely unqualified for, as had every single human she had come in contact with since she'd met Ampersand. But this assumption ignored the fact that there was *no such thing* as a human who was qualified for the task of alien interpreter, because this task was completely unprecedented. And by extension, she was really, *really* fucking sick of people underestimating her. She was determined to give Kaplan what he wanted, not out of fear for herself, or her family, nor even out of love for species or country but out of *spite*.

The best way to get Ampersand talking was to get on his good side. The best way to get on his good side was to help him get what he wanted from humans.

And what he wanted from humans was to be left alone.

Ampersand had told Cora when they first arrived at the bunker that he would summon her "at need." During those first forty-eight hours after the autopsy, he summoned her all of three times, and each time it was for her to tell whatever ROSA scientist, or CIA goon, or military intelligence officer, or whoever to leave him alone. (She, of course, phrased it more nicely than Ampersand's direction to "*Expel these militarists.*")

The morning of the fourth day at the bunker, she decided to preempt Ampersand's summoning by just showing up unbidden. She grabbed a Nutri-Grain bar from the café, a notepad from an office, and a Harry Potter book from the little makeshift library the airmen used, and then she marched on down to the lab space where Ampersand had performed Čefo's autopsy. The "corpse" was still there, as were their Genome on another table, a few of the technocrat underlings, and Ampersand.

All noise ceased when she entered the room, and she noted that Ampersand's underlings seemed to freeze as though they might have to defend themselves against her. As quietly as she could, she pulled a folding chair next to the exit, said, "I'm here if you need me," sat down, and began reading this already-dog-eared copy of *Harry Potter and the Deathly Hallows*. After a few seconds, Ampersand said something to his underlings in Pequod-phonemic, and they went about their business as if she were not even there. For the next few hours, she acted as a bouncer. Someone like Dr. Sev would arrive with the hope of doing some study, or initiating some contact, or asking some question. Cora responded, "If you have a question, I might be able to answer it, but they're in the middle of something. They need to be left alone."

To her astonishment, it worked.

For the most part, if she told people to fuck off on the part of their alien guests, they went with it without much protest, with the exception of Dr. Sev. He seemed to have good instincts as to what he should push for, and he had one thing in particular on his mind. "I do have a question," he told her. This was his second attempt to get a conversation on this topic going. "If you can get an answer out of him, I would appreciate it."

"What is it?" she asked.

"Ask him, can he tell us if there is a Great Filter?"

"A what now?"

"A question, a thought experiment about why intelligent life isn't common in the universe. Statistically, if we exist, and they exist, and in terms of the greater galaxy we are not far apart at all, then intelligent life must not be *that* rare. Therefore, in the thirteen odd billion years of existence before now, the galaxy should have been colonized a hundred times over, or at least recognizably explored, but it hasn't. Let's say the Great Filter is a big philosophical question in astronomy. Either the filter is behind us and intelligence is astronomically rare, or it's in front of us and advanced civilizations just don't last that long. Ask him if they have an answer to this question."

Cora held off on that one.

Ampersand and Esperas seemed to engage in many conversations, but none seemed to involve Great Filters or philosophical black holes, but rather the Genome. It didn't take Cora long to decide that something about their Genome was the main point of disagreement between Ampersand and Esperas. She took a note for Kaplan, despite figuring that he had probably already come to the same conclusion.

Then she started doing something she'd been meaning to do for a little while: math.

It had been Luciana who had explained to her the basics of Einstein's theory of special relativity on the plane to Colorado Springs, using *Ender's Game,* a book Cora had not read, as an example. "See, at the end of *Ender's Game,* Ender is about thirteen," she said. "The sequel, *Speaker for the Dead,* takes place about three thousand years later, but Ender is only in his thirties since he's spent most of the last few thousand years traveling near light speed. Time as perceived for the traveler slows once you start getting close to light speed."

"So a 'relative age' is age as it's relative to, I guess, the basic flow of time," said Cora. "And 'subjective age' is age as it's experienced."

"Correct," said Luciana. "Time is going at a certain speed relative to us here on Earth, but once you start traveling close to the speed of light, time for the traveler starts to slow down. What were his ages again?"

"'Superorganism-relative,' 962 years," said Cora without pause. Those numbers he had given her were too memorable not to be seared into the meat of her brain the moment she'd heard them. "'Subjective,' 612."

"So if he's telling the truth, that's a 350-year age discrepancy," said Luciana. "In lived time, he's 350 years younger than he should be."

Cora looked up from her notepad at Ampersand, who for the first time all day was sparing her a glance now that Esperas was not in the room. She wondered what was going through his head, wondered if he was irritated at her questions about his symphyles or if her faux pas was beneath him to even spare a thought about.

Cora looked down at her notepad and started her equations.

$$2007-962 = 1045$$

Her mouth went dry, and she looked back up at Ampersand, who was now back to acting as though she were not in the room. If those numbers were right, Ampersand was "born" in A.D. 1045.

That thought made her a little light-headed. One thousand years was grand to the point of meaningless until placed in terms of actual dates on the Gregorian calendar. A.D. 1045. Before the Norman invasion of England. Before the printing press. Before the entire birth, life, and death of the transatlantic slave trade. More than seven hundred years before the founding of these United States of America. Hundreds of years before modern English would even evolve into a language. Her plan for today had been to get back into Ampersand's good graces by shooing people away and not to bother him with questions. But since they were alone, she took a chance and asked, "What year, Common Era, was the Fremdan genetic purge?"

She expected the same response of "*Irrelevant.*" Instead, to her surprise, he gave her an answer: "*Approximately 1629 C.E.*"

Esperas soon returned with one of the Similars, who had to practically collapse into himself to fit through the door. The sight of the Similar sent a pulse of adrenaline into Cora's chest. It seemed that Esperas was intimidated by Ampersand, perhaps by his size. Perhaps even by his abilities. She'd assumed that all of them had some telekinesis, but Ampersand was the only one she'd seen use it. Flanked by his heavy, Esperas reminded Cora of a diminutive mob boss calling for his muscle. She looked down at her notepad.

$$2007 - 1629 = 378$$
$$378 - 350 = 28$$

If it happened in 1629, it had been 378 years since the Fremdan genetic purge, but Ampersand had only experienced 28 of those years. That was a lot of time to have stolen by near-light speed travel. The passage of time alone might account for part of the "had" in Ampersand's "*I had seven.*"

This got her thinking of another number—Ampersand had said that the most recent visitation to Earth by the Pequod Superorganism, the one when they'd abducted human subjects for "study," had been "approximately 655 years ago" when the Earth's population was approximately "4 percent of what it is today."

$$2007 - 655 = 1352$$
$$0.04 \times 7{,}000{,}000{,}000 = 280{,}000{,}000$$

Putting a number to the year did further illuminate why Ampersand assumed humans would treat the Fremda group barbarously. She couldn't imagine any alien civilization who had tripped across medieval Europe giving it a charitable interpretation. Still, it had been a while since AP European History, and she couldn't remember what exactly was going on in the world in 1352. She didn't have much, but fortunately the piddlin' little makeshift library in the complex had an old 1980s hardcover edition of *Encyclopædia Britannica*.

The following morning, Cora returned to her post next to the door, now with a Nutri-Grain bar, her notepad, and four volumes of *Encyclopædia Britannica*: the Krasnokamsk-Menadra volume for medieval Europe, the Delusion-Frenssen volume for King Edward III and French history, the Number-Prague volume for Paris and House Plantagenet, and the Bayou-Ceanothus volume for the Black Death.

In her brief research, she remembered what was so noteworthy about the 1350s—it was right after the Black Death had wiped out nearly half the population of Europe and vast swaths of India and China. Had the Pequod Superorganism just abducted their "samples" and run, or did they stay awhile to observe? If they had taken an interest in human language, then surely there must have been some scientific interest in human behavior. She wondered if they understood the context of a post–Black Death world, if they knew that they had arrived just on the tail end of the worst pandemic in human history. If they understood that their projections about human population might be a bit off, as humanity had just lost about a quarter.

But the thing that struck her the most in the *Britannica* entry about the Black Death was how the afflicted reacted to the plague.

> Renewed religious fervor and fanaticism bloomed in the wake of the Black Death. Some Europeans targeted groups such as Jews, foreigners, beggars, lepers, and Romani, thinking that they were to blame. Attacks on Jewish communities became commonplace. In February of 1349, the citizens of Strasbourg murdered half of their population of 2,000 Jews. In August of 1349, the Jewish communities in Mainz and Cologne were exterminated.

As she read this passage, she realized that she was being stared at. She looked up and saw two smaller amygdalines staring at her. They looked like identical twins, perfectly symmetrical, almost Kubrickian. She recognized them as the two who'd dared to look around when they'd first arrived at the bunker. "Woodward and Bernstein." They stood at that "safe" distance of about ten feet, their hands daintily folded in front of them in that mantid way.

She waited for them to do something, move, *anything*, but they just stared at her. "Ampersand?" she whispered, glancing in his direction.

"*They are curious,*" said the voice in her ear. He didn't look up or react, keeping his back to her. "*Stelo and Krias are propagandists. They know your book contains written language. They are curious as to what information it contains.*"

Cora shook her head at his word choice. *Propagandists.* "Would you translate for them?"

He spoke aloud to the two, and the two responded to him

quickly, seemingly in unison. They seemed downright eager.

"*Explain the information in your text.*"

"It's actually really interesting," she said. Ampersand didn't look up from whatever he was doing, quietly translating into Pequod-phonemic. "It's called an encyclopedia. It contains entries about a wide variety of topics. This is an old one. We use mostly digital now."

The two propagandists looked at the book, their bright eyes seeming to widen. These two had a shorter head front to back than Ampersand's and smaller eyes relative to their size, but with broader faces, making these two look a little more wasplike. Their eyes did have that reflective glow to them, but much dimmer than Ampersand's and more of a grayish blue compared to his warm amber. "I know the last time your . . . Superorganism explored Earth would have been somewhere in the 1350s," she said. "If it was in the 1350s, they would have arrived right after the Black Death hit Europe. The plague was—well, *is*—a bacterium, *Yersinia pestis,* and it killed huge swaths of the population in the late 1340s. Almost a quarter of all humans died within about five years. So your people wouldn't have just arrived during a dark period in our development, but the worst disease outbreak in all of human history—"

Ampersand stopped talking, and then Woodward and Bernstein quietly turned their eyes away from her and moved away. She started to ask what the problem was, if perhaps the topic of plague was too gauche or offensive, when Esperas arrived in the room. Esperas and his two Similars.

She closed her book. Esperas started speaking to Ampersand in Pequod-phonemic, Ampersand not even looking up. Trying and failing to look casual, Cora slowly resumed the position of being engrossed in the entry about the plague while they spoke. Ampersand finally turned around to engage Esperas. His "voice" was somehow sharper than Esperas's; their language reminded Cora of rain on a tin roof, but Ampersand's voice was tinnier.

Cora glanced up to see that Woodward and Bernstein had already sneaked out of the room, and none of the others were paying her any attention, which helped blunt the adrenaline spike that accompanied being in the same room as the Similars. She grew even tenser when Esperas all but snapped at Ampersand, and she recalled what Luciana had said about being able to tell when Esperas was pissed.

He was circling the Genome, and Cora wondered if that was the topic of discussion. It was hard to read emotion on something so foreign, but Cora wondered if both she and Luciana misread Esperas. Somehow, this didn't strike Cora as anger but as fear. Perhaps Esperas was afraid. But of what?

Cora looked down as the back-and-forth continued, and she looked up again from the book she was pretending to read just in time to see Ampersand disappear into the next room behind the others. Surprised to be left alone, she didn't move for at least two minutes.

Eventually, she put down the encyclopedia and stood up, approaching the still-open door they'd disappeared into. She didn't see any of them on the other side. She turned and looked at Čefo's corpse, rigid and compacted and looking like it had been wrapped in cling wrap.

And then there was the Genome.

She allowed herself to drift closer to it, if only to see if there were something she might be able to learn about it. It was smooth, uninterrupted, like a real egg sac, and seemed to have the same texture as amygdaline skin, which Cora had never touched. Her hand started drifting toward it almost of its own volition.

There was that part of her brain telling her, *No bueno*. Ampersand would probably not look fondly at a dirty human touching his precious Genome. But on the other hand, how fragile could it be if they just threw it in their allocated laboratory space with nothing protecting it? She never saw the Similars guarding this thing, not the way they shadowed Esperas. And besides, they had knowingly left her alone in the room with it. There was probably no foul if she just touched it.

And that she did.

The texture wasn't completely smooth, but more like a cat's tongue, smooth in one direction but slightly jagged in the other. The Genome-egg was also warm, a little bit warmer than room temperature. It even pulsed a little. She felt stuck somewhere between intrigue and disgust; this thing felt less like a suitcase and more like an external womb, like there was probably something alive in there.

She didn't have much time to mull on this, however, when she was grabbed from behind by a hand with long, hard fingers and yanked away from the egg.

She screamed, more out of shock than fear, trying to get a look at her assailant as it dragged her out of the room. Similar? Definitely not. Ampersand? No, this one wasn't big enough. It was only after he threw her down in the hall and slammed the door that she saw who it was.

Esperas.

He didn't even look at her, not even so much as a glance imparting, "*That'll show you.*" He just flung her against the wall like a bag of dirty laundry, darted back into the lab space, and shut the door behind him.

In no time, a few airmen came running, responding to her scream. She sat crumpled on her back, stunned, embarrassed, and unsure of what to say.

Then the voice in her ear spoke: "*Do not touch the Genome.*"

Hello, Friends and Strangers,

What did the president know, and when did he know it?

Allow me to quote from the president's deposition: "I was asked
questions about the legitimacy of the so-called Fremda Memo, as
well as the purpose of the Refugee Organizational and Settlement
Agency under the Department of Health and Human Services, and
I claimed that it had no connection to the Fremda Memo. While my
answers were accurate based on the information I had at the time,
I now know that that information was not complete. But I only
came to know about a 'Refugee Organizational and Settlement
Agency' this week, and as far as I can tell, it has nothing to do with
the so-called hoax Fremda Memo."

What did the president know, and when did he know it?

The belief that better information-sharing among national
security departments and agencies could have prevented 9/11
motivated the president and Congress to create new institutions
to safeguard the nation against catastrophic terrorist attacks.
Between 2004 and 2007, institutions and safeguards of
interagency intelligence sharing were put in place to prevent a
tragedy on the level of 9/11 ever happening again.

Of course, the agencies that created these new institutions
were unaware of the massive, existential secret other agencies
were sitting on. Agencies that were not designed to contain

such secrets in a post-9/11 world are why we are sitting in this comically leaky boat.

What did the president know? The exact nature and purpose of ROSA.

When did he know it? The following recording shows that he knew as early as 2004.

Your move, Dubya.

Ortega, Nils. "What Did the President Know, and When Did He Know It?" *The Broken Seal*. October 2, 2007. http://www.thebrokenseal.org.

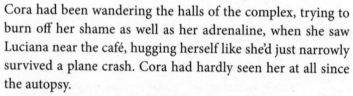

21

Cora had been wandering the halls of the complex, trying to burn off her shame as well as her adrenaline, when she saw Luciana near the café, hugging herself like she'd just narrowly survived a plane crash. Cora had hardly seen her at all since the autopsy.

"Fuck, fuck, fuck," said Cora, approaching her. "I'm so fucked."

"I know, I know," said Luciana, not even looking at Cora, staring at the wall as if she were in the middle of a conversation with it. "This is a disaster. This is just such a mess."

"What?" Cora stopped short. "How do you know?" Esperas had only ingloriously tossed her out of the laboratory space twenty minutes ago. How had Luciana found out?

Luciana looked insulted. "Because I have access to the news?"

Clearly, they were fretting about two very different things. "Oh, Christ. What's he done now?"

Going by Luciana's horrified expression, Nils had apparently started a thermonuclear war. "You don't know?"

"No, I don't," said Cora. "I spend my entire day holed up in a bunker with aliens. I don't have internet access."

Luciana stared at her blankly as though she didn't quite believe her and then she tossed her head, urging Cora to follow her.

Luciana led her to a lounge down several halls and up one flight of stairs. About a dozen airmen were rapt in front of the television, which was tuned to CNN. She could barely hear what Wolf Blitzer was saying, but she didn't need to. The chyron at the bottom of the screen told her everything: LEAK REVEALS PRESIDENT HAD PRIOR KNOWLEDGE OF FIRST CONTACT.

It felt like the blood had been sucked from her face, the air ripped out of her lungs. She all but stumbled back into the hallway, grabbing a handful of hair. Luciana followed suit, shutting the door behind them and grabbing two handfuls.

"What . . . what was it?" asked Cora.

Luciana shook her head. "It was like a phone call or something. From a few years ago. Proves not only that Bush knew but that he lied about knowing, and he lied in a sworn *fucking* deposition. Nils probably had his hands on this before he got the Fremda Memo. He was *waiting* for Bush to disavow knowledge before he dropped this."

"Why?" Cora breathed, despite already knowing the answer.

Luciana laughed dryly. "Because he wanted to be the man who took Bush down."

Cora's hair follicles were starting to tingle, and she let go of the handful of hair, slamming her back against the wall. There it went. There had been a chance they could still keep this under wraps. That had been the hope, the plan, until at the very, very least Cora and her family were free.

Not anymore.

"What does this mean for us?"

"I don't know, I don't know," said Luciana, pacing back and forth in the tiny hallway. "I know the White House is wildly flailing at trying to find a character assassination angle, which is hopeless because Nils is already an international folk hero. Even the major networks are speculating that this could end Bush's presidency. God, he . . ." She buried her face in her hands. "He played this perfectly."

"You really think it will come to that?" Cora asked. "You really think it will work?"

Luciana shook her head, began her circular pacing anew. "A day ago, I would have said never. Never in a million years. Now? I don't know. Half of Congress is calling for his resignation, even some Republicans. Clearly, I don't know anything. I've been wrong about so much. He . . ." She balled her hands in front of her. They were shaking. "It wasn't just a cable or an email. He got a recording. He got the idiot on *tape*."

Luciana finally stopped pacing and leaned her back against the wall. The two stayed in stunned disbelief, the barely audible sounds of Blitzer's breaking news leaking through the door of the lounge.

"I mean, in a way, maybe this is good," said Cora, unable to bear the silence. "Maybe it'll mean the end of the war in Iraq . . ." She stopped, hearing how ridiculous her own words sounded even as she said them.

Luciana shook her head mechanically, still staring at the wall. "It won't. You know it won't."

Cora couldn't help but laugh. Beheld from a distance, the situation was utterly absurd. "This is like Al Capone going down for a parking ticket."

Luciana sighed bitterly. "I do know the White House is in

spin mode. I heard through the grapevine that they're trying to find an angle to go after me, because here I am, already at their mercy, so they may as well."

Cora looked up at her, stunned. "What do they have on you?"

"I don't know. I don't know!" Tears were welling up in her eyes.

"Well, it has to be something."

Luciana finally tore her gaze away from the wall and looked at Cora, hurt. "Why are you bringing this up now?"

"Because you were a willing participant in a massive government cover-up for several years?"

"What benefit is it to me to tell Nils anything? Why would you think I'd have any incentive?"

"I don't know!" said Cora. "You were working for ROSA for a while. I don't know every single thing you did or said while you were there!"

"And why would I jeopardize that by telling *him*?" she demanded. "Nils, before anyone else? Before Demi? Before you? He's never been in my life! Never shown any interest in it. Nicest he ever was to me was for that few months in college when he wanted to fuck my best friend."

Cora's jaw dropped, and she stared at her aunt in disbelief. Luciana backed off right after she said it, realizing how below the belt that was to say.

"I'm sorry about the accident that is my existence," said Cora.

"I didn't mean it like that," said Luciana, contrite. "And I'll always be glad we got you out of the equation." She had never said something so crude or callous, even though the entire family knew it to be true. Even Cora knew that Nils had only started being nice to his younger sister to get close to Demi and that Demi getting knocked up at the age of twenty had resulted in a shotgun wedding to appease two sets of Catholic parents.

They stood in silence as though waiting for someone to break in, informing them that they needed to divert their attention elsewhere, but no one was concerned for them at present. All the airmen were still glued to CNN. Wolf had given way to Anderson Cooper.

"'Truth is a human right,'" said Cora, her voice near a whisper.

"Do you believe that?"

Cora rested her cheek on the cool metal wall. "Right now, I don't care. I just want to survive this."

"Me, too."

Someone in the lounge had turned up Anderson Cooper. Anderson sounded like he was having a great day. "So there's no way they're going to make this scandal go away," said Cora, "even if the Fremda group leaves when they say they will."

"No," agreed Luciana.

"What does that mean for us?"

"Nothing good."

"What do you think it means for Demi and Felix and Olive?" asked Cora, searching desperately for a silver lining. "Maybe they'll just . . . drop this whole thing and let them go, now that there's nothing to hide."

"No," Luciana said airily. "No, I think the opposite is more likely."

Cora felt the tiny sapling of hope that had sprouted inside her shrivel and die. "Why?"

"Because a cover-up is one thing—Demi and the kids are evidence of abuse of power. Worse, civilian evidence. Worse, *children*."

Cora took a deep breath. Now she could feel tears threatening to break down the door. "Are you absolutely sure they don't have the technology to erase memories?"

Luciana closed her eyes and took several more forced, unnatural breaths. "No, I'm not sure."

Cora nodded and looked straight ahead at the wall. "What should I do?"

"Just . . . be compliant," said Luciana. "What were you upset about earlier?"

She had almost forgotten. The incident of fucking up her attempt to get Ampersand talking and getting accosted by Esperas seemed like it had happened years ago. "Nothing."

. . . . .

Cora jolted when a knock on the metal door echoed throughout the giant room of her bunk. "Come in?"

The door opened, and Vincent Park peeked inside. He was wearing a polo and slacks—it always seemed like he tried to keep his aesthetic exactly one notch more professional than Kaplan's. Her eyes lit up when she saw what was in his hand.

An acoustic guitar.

"One of the airmen who's normally stationed here got deployed to Qatar for the next forever or so," he said, holding it out for her. "So they told me this was fine for me to loan you."

Cora reached out for it and took it, trying not to appear too grateful. It was a basic, unremarkable thing. A Yamaha, worn but not loved. Even so, it felt like she'd had a lost limb reattached. "How did you know I played?"

"Oh, you know," he said, casually leaning his shoulder against the doorframe. "You just seem like the type."

Cora waited for him to come clean. "Plus all the spying on me. Right?"

He shrugged. "Technically, that wasn't us. That's the NSA."

"Charming," she said, trying not to let his cavalier attitude toward warrantless government surveillance bother her. "So the NSA never sent you any nudie screenshots from my webcam?"

He kept smiling, but now his smile was forced. She'd finally edged him into discomfort. *Good.*

"To my knowledge, they aren't *that* shameless."

"Sure they aren't," she said coolly. She bit the tip of her tongue, remembering what Luciana said about being compliant. "I didn't mean to imply you did stuff like that."

"Given everything you've learned in the last couple weeks, it's not an unfair assumption. But no webcams have been hacked . . . as far as I know."

"I believe you," she lied.

She sat down, fingering the guitar. Almost on instinct, her fingers found the opening chords to the Beatles' "Blackbird."

"Wow," said Vincent, taking a seat on one of the dozens of empty beds. "You're pretty good."

"Thanks," she said. "This is what happens when you go through a middle school phase where you both have a massive crush on and also want to be Ani DiFranco."

"Who's that?"

She shook her head, not knowing why it surprised her that he didn't know who Ani DiFranco was. "Just a singer." She absently plucked the opening chords to "Not a Pretty Girl." "So . . . since you have some insider info . . ." She looked at him. "Do you know if they have anything on Luciana?"

He crossed his arms and shrugged. "If they did, she would be in the darkest federal prison."

"Not military prison?" she asked, still playing. It was almost shameful how much she missed this.

"You have to be military to end up there. Luciana's a civilian."

"Right."

"For what it's worth, I don't think the flimsy charge they came up with will stick."

Cora stopped playing, snapping her head up. "What do you mean?"

His smile faded. "I thought you knew."

Cora shook her head.

"She's been arrested," he said. "They took her an hour ago."

As lights turned back on across Guam after a massive blackout that hit tens of thousands of people, authorities were still largely in the dark about what caused the collapse of the interconnected grid. Others have pointed to a similar outage that mysteriously affected Mountain View, California, last week, one that similarly had no discernible cause and even went so far as to affect mobile devices and car batteries.

Guam governor Felix J. Pérez Camacho promised a thorough investigation into what he called an "unprecedented" outage—one that raised questions about flaws in Guam's grid. Energy officials said the results of the investigation would be available in ten to fifteen days.

Jackson, Aisha. "Hunt for Cause of Massive Guam Power Outage Begins." *The Washington Post.* October 2, 2007.

2 2

Kaplan had a seriousness about him, an odd mélange of nonchalance and intensity, and the situation in the outside world made it even more unsettling. Luciana hadn't been gone for twenty-four hours, and Cora was convinced that Kaplan was responsible, but he hadn't said a word about it, and either way, that was not the issue at hand right now.

She'd learned about the power outage in Guam from Vincent about forty-five minutes ago, and then two minutes after that, she'd gotten the demand from Kaplan that he needed to talk to Ampersand, *now*. She ran to his quarters and relayed this, reframing it as a request rather than a demand, and to her shock, he granted her request, with one caveat: "*Not here.*" So she asked him to relocate to the room where she'd been doing her debriefs with Kaplan, and he agreed.

That had been fifteen minutes ago. That whole time, she'd been alone in the room with a long conference table, a dozen folding chairs, and Kaplan. Kaplan was seated at the other end of the table holding an accordion folder full of manila files, opening and closing it absently like a bellows and staring at the wall. She had not yet been able to bring herself to sit.

"What are those?" asked Cora, no longer able to bear the brittle silence.

Kaplan opened the accordion folder, closed it again, and then opened it, and finally looked at her. "I'm going to use this as an opportunity." Slowly, mechanically, he began removing his manila files one by one.

"To what?"

"If he's a captive audience, maybe I can get him to look at these." He nodded at his files. "Every account of abductions we consider remotely credible." At the word "credible," his intensity cracked, and he rolled his eyes. "Probably all nonsense. *But.* But."

"Yeah."

She crossed her arms, looking around the room nervously while he continued to play with his accordion folder like it might produce music, and the two just existed in the painful silence. At length, Kaplan had had enough. "*Sit!* Jesus, you're freaking me out."

"Sorry," she said, stumbling into the nearest chair, one catty-corner from where he was sitting. His files now on the table, he'd gone back to bellowing his accordion folder, staring at the wall as though the Four Horsemen were having a board meeting on the other side of it.

"So . . . ," she mumbled. "Sol . . ."

"That's me," he sighed, leaving the accordion folder on the table, stretching out, and crossing one of his long legs over the other.

"Is that short for something?" she asked. "Like Sol the sun-god, or Saul the . . . not-Paul-the-Apostle-yet?"

Kaplan entwined his fingers in front of him and placed them on his lap. "Solomon."

"Oh."

Again, his eyes passed over her, this time his expression much cooler. "I guess you know your New Testament."

"Huh?"

"Saul, who becomes Paul." He looked almost as uncomfortable as she did.

"Oh." She stole a glance at him. "I guess I got the Catholic on me."

Once again, tense silence, the only noise in the room the song of the humming light bulbs.

"So why's he call it *The Broken Seal*?" asked Sol. "Is that, like, a Bible thing, too?"

"Huh?" Where the hell did *that* come from? "I don't know; he's got the Catholic on him, too. Why don't you ask him?"

"Because he won't return my phone calls!"

His tone was bordering on playful. Cora didn't know what to make of it. "You clearly know more about this than I do."

"No, I don't. I got the Jewish on me."

"Well, I'd tell you to ask Luciana, but . . ." She stopped, regretting the words even as she said them, and braced for whatever awful thing he was about to say.

"It wasn't my call," he said. "I had nothing to do with it."

She hesitated, eyeing him. He'd treated her like garbage pretty consistently up to this point, and she couldn't parse whether his turn was sincere or just a mind game. "Do you know where she is?"

"D.C., I think."

Cora sank deeper into her chair. It was late, but not seeing the sun had a way of making one feel displaced in the time stream. "She keeps insisting she had nothing to do with the leak."

He raised an eyebrow. "Let me tell you something about Luciana. There is no question she had nothing to do with the leak. What there *is* a question of is how Nils Ortega knew to go digging for a leak like the Fremda Memo in the first place."

She stared at him blankly. That was an angle she hadn't considered.

The door opened behind her before he could say anything else, and in came Ampersand, already inching toward his antagonistic posture, positively radioactive with the desire not to be in this room. Sol raised an eyebrow to Cora, who stood up and approached Ampersand. "There was a power outage in Guam like the one at the Google campus. Sol wants to know if Obelus did this."

"*Almost certainly.*" She repeated him.

"Can you guess what his goal is?" asked Sol.

"*The same as it was in Mountain View—to disable me for recapture and to disable the two Similars so they cannot mount a defense.*"

Cora repeated him, then added, "Guam was the site where the Fremda group originally surrendered, wasn't it?"

"You think that's why?"

"*It is unlikely Obelus discovered this through human networks or that his algorithm has successfully decoded human languages yet.*" She repeated him.

"How long did it take you to decode our language?"

"*Approximately three weeks. Obelus will likely work more quickly, as he has multiple Similars at his disposal.*"

Sol stood up and studied Ampersand, then Cora. At least he had the good sense not to stare at Ampersand the way he did her when he wanted to intimidate her. "Before you go, I want to go over some reports of other . . . sightings, shall we say," said Sol, gesturing to the files on the table. "These are not amygdaline, and we operate under the assumption that most of them are not legitimate, but I'd like to get your expert opinion."

He opened a couple of the files, which contained what looked like conspiracy theorist rap sheets. Photos, dates, names of witnesses, and artist's depictions for each file, each with a code name—*HISPANIOLA, Sloop John B, Pequod, Flying Dutchman*— ships, she realized. They were all code-named after fictional ships. Some she didn't recognize, such as *Rachel, Covenant, Gloria Scott, Nellie, Surprise, the Ark*. Others, like *Wonkatania, Poseidon, Nautilus,* and *African Queen,* were more familiar.

"*Poseidon*?" she laughed. "As in *The Poseidon Adventure*?"

"As I said, these date back to the seventies."

"And the *Black Pearl*?"

". . . And some are more recent."

A few of the artist's renderings looked familiar to Cora; the file labeled *Flying Dutchman,* a.k.a. "Grays," contained an artist's rendering of the stereotypical humanoid Roswell alien with big black eyes. The file *Nautilus,* a.k.a. "Reptilians," contained a rendering of a half-lizard, half-man. To Cora, they all looked absurd, especially the Reptilians. She couldn't believe they took Reptilians seriously enough to have a file on them.

"Three ETI landings we have confirmed," continued Kaplan. "Fremda, in 1971, and this year, Ampersand in August and Obelus in September. All ETI species code-named 'Pequod.'"

He picked up Ampersand's file. "The ROSA code names, traditionally Esperanto words—Dr. Ghasabian told me yours is"—he cocked his head, stumbling over the word—"'Scio'?"

"We should probably just call him 'Ampersand,'" said Cora.

"He doesn't like it?"

"He doesn't care. He says names are 'arbitrary.' But 'Ampersand' is how everyone knows him now. And that new one's kinda silly."

"Sillier than 'Ampersand'?" Kaplan raised his eyebrows. "He cares about that?"

"No. I do."

Kaplan shrugged. "I figured they'd have dropped the Esperanto names by now anyway. Give you names like 'Dan' or 'Brian.' Guess it doesn't matter. Aside from information we have proof on, we have literally thousands of testimonies from witnesses claiming to have either seen ETI craft or have been abduction victims themselves. Most of these we can prove as hoaxes. For instance, we have no intel to indicate that the Queen of England is a reptile person who needs to consume human blood to maintain her human form."

"He says he doesn't understand the rationale that human blood is a unique or preferable form of sustenance but that we shouldn't preclude the possibility." Cora looked at Ampersand to make sure she got that right, half expecting him to issue a correction.

Kaplan's smirk vanished. "Please tell me he's not talking about Reptilians."

Ampersand's fingers drifted to a file. "Not Reptilians," said Cora. "Sloop John B." Ampersand lifted it, leafing telekinetically through the file.

"That one," said Kaplan, "was of particular interest to us. We have several matching descriptions of a similar-bodied creature over three decades. The description isn't *that* dissimilar to an amygdaline, except for the tail and the"—he gestured to his mouth—"maw."

"This is our sister species."

Cora repeated him, hoping he was mistaken. In all three renderings, the creature had the forward-leaning center of gravity of amygdalines, but these creatures all had dark, segmented tails. Also, unlike amygdalines, these things had mouthparts, big ones, like a grasshopper. Two of the three drawings gave the subject sharp, jagged teeth the same dark color as its skin.

Also, in one of the artist's renderings, the subject appeared to be consuming a human. A cheap sci-fi rendition of Goya's Saturn eating his son. It looked like parody. It had to be. *Ah. Ampersand has discovered humor and is joking. That's nice.*

"Sister species?" asked Kaplan.

"The sister species to modern amygdalines," said Cora. "Transients. They share ancestry with amygdalines. He says, 'I was a political prisoner to a transient pod for several decades, after they took me from a group of Similars.'" Cora's eyebrows rose in surprise even as she said the words, imparting to Kaplan, *Yes, this is news to me, too.* "'This species is nomadic; it is not surprising that they have visited this planet. I find it remarkable that there have been enough incidents that a witness could give such a coherent account.'"

"Might they be here still?" asked Kaplan.

"He says, 'It's possible,'" said Cora. "'Most violent clashes between amygdalines and transients have regarded colonized planets. Planets the Superorganism had mined and then transients . . .'" She looked at Ampersand worriedly. He was looking over the files, utterly detached. "'Consumed.'"

"What would that mean for us?" asked Kaplan, now on alert. He looked at Cora sharply, then back at Ampersand.

Cora said: "'Know that, unlike amygdalines, transients reproduce quickly, have a very high metabolism, and are very difficult to kill. Transients can tear through planetary resources. Transients consume.'"

"What does that mean for us?" asked Kaplan again.

"'I will not advise you on policy,'" said Cora, shrugging. "That's all he said."

The door opened, and Vincent Park stuck his head in the room, breathing heavily like he'd been running. "Sec def is here."

Kaplan's shoulders fell. "Christ. Why didn't they at least warn me?"

Cora's eyes darted between the two of them. "Sec def?"

Vincent smiled at her through his obvious distress as he approached them. "They're not happy." He gestured toward Ampersand. "They want to see him. *Now*."

"What now?" said Cora. "*Right* now? I have to—" She looked at Ampersand, but he was stony and silent.

"*Militarists?*" he asked her at length.

Kaplan noted her reaction. "What did he say?"

A door burst open at the back of the room, causing both Cora and Sol to gasp. Like locusts, men in green uniform began pouring in. Not soldiers but officers. Every single one.

And at the core of the group, right in the middle, was the secretary of defense.

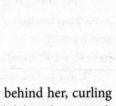

2 3

She could all but feel Ampersand's fingers behind her, curling up like he was trying to strangle the air. He didn't make a sound, but his anger seemed to make the air thick, and Sol noticed it, too, shooting Cora a helpless, even confused expression. She didn't buy it, but whether or not Sol had known these men were in effect planning to ambush them was moot.

"Greetings," said the secretary, casually jogging toward them as if he were a few minutes late to a meeting. The secretary of defense had the kind of calm, confident poker face that took decades to hone. He wasn't a big man, but he did have a commanding presence. At least he wasn't dressed in full, formal uniform.

Cora turned to Ampersand and started when she saw his hands curled up like briars in a wild bush, the crest on his head fanned out like a sunflower. "Hey, put your hands down. That's going to come across as antagonistic."

"*It is intended to be antagonistic,*" he said. "*Tell them not to come any closer.*"

She whirled back around, stammering, "Stop." The men halted intermittently, confused at the breach of protocol, until the secretary himself stopped. "He needs space," she added.

Again, the men seemed not to know how to respond. On the one hand, she was violating protocol (although exactly what protocol, she had no idea). On the other hand, no one was sure how exactly to correct her without it coming across as correcting their extraterrestrial guest.

It was the secretary who broke the silence. "We understand that you are acting as his interpreter," he said. "And we do apologize for this abrupt visit. But our time is limited, and as you know, our bids to actually schedule a time and a place to have this conversation have gone unanswered."

"*I will not negotiate with militarists.*"

Cora suppressed a groan and turned back to him. The silence in the space made her ears ring. It felt like the men in the room had ceased breathing to enhance the quiet. Cora placed her hands together and, as quietly as she could, whispered, "You need to talk to them."

"*This is a breach of our agreement,*" he said. "*I did not agree to talk to the head of the military apparatus.*"

"They're here now, though," she mouthed, her breath shaking. "Let's just hear what they want to say and get this over with."

"*What has you frightened?*" he asked, his focus narrowing into a point.

A whimper crawled up her throat, and she tamped it back down. "These are very powerful men," she mouthed.

"*They represent your own government,*" he said. "*Why are you afraid of your own government?*"

At first, the question struck her as odd, considering why he and the rest of the Fremda group were even on the planet

Earth in the first place. *Sometimes governments do bad things, including yours.* "That's just what it's like on this planet!"

That pinpoint focus drifted from Cora to the secretary, and she thought she saw the man shudder when it found him.

"Is everything all right?" he asked.

Cora's dread faded to anger. "No," she said. "He finds it disrespectful that you showed up here unannounced."

"Understandable," said the secretary, clearly suppressing anger of his own. "But given our multiple bids to schedule a discussion have gone unanswered, we feel we have been left with little choice."

"*Why have your superiors sent the head of the military?*"

"He hasn't responded because he doesn't feel like he has anything to say to the Department of Defense," said Cora.

"Firstly, you are being housed in a military bunker, which is my purview," said the secretary. "Secondly, there's been another power outage on U.S. territory that shares many characteristics with the one that happened in Mountain View. From what intelligence we have, it's likely hostile parties of *your* species, correct?"

"*I have already spoken on this topic and have nothing more to add.*"

"He says that's probably correct, but he can't know for sure."

She thought she saw a muscle in the man's jaw twitch. "At this point, we only want to talk to you about one thing, and that has nothing to do with the military. We want to ask about means of translating your language, not just through communicating through you and your"—he flipped a hand to Cora, like she was the help—"interpreter."

She turned back to Ampersand, her hands unconsciously raised as if she were negotiating a hostage release. "Is that reasonable?" she asked, her voice just above a whisper.

"*What they want is dangerous.*"

Cora's face, which had only draped itself in an expression of modest hope, fell. "How?"

"*Opening communication between our two species will create more danger for both in the long run.*"

She noticed Sol glaring at her. "So is that a no?"

"*I can assign such a task to my technocrat inferiors, but I intend to relay this truth, if they insist on moving forward.*"

"I'm not here to make demands," said the secretary, his voice staid. "I want us to be on the same level. There are clearly others of your kind in this facility who are as anxious to communicate with us as we are them."

"*These individuals are not Oligarchs,*" he said.

"He says they're not as high-ranked as he is; that's why he handles communication."

The secretary was trying to keep his gaze on Ampersand, not Cora. "Here in America, we consider ourselves created equal. We stand on equal ground."

"*Categorically untrue.*"

"He says he feels that's dishonest," said Cora flatly.

Sol stepped forward to intervene. "Mr. Secretary, this is a delicate operation, but try to respect that this is a slow-going process."

"We don't have time for 'slow-going,'" said the secretary, looking past Cora toward Ampersand. "There's a hostile alien presence on the planet attacking American interests, and the human race is on the verge of official confirmation that they're not alone in the universe. We need to understand the language samples we already have and be prepared in the event we need translations after you leave."

"*The secretary doesn't understand what he is asking for,*"

because he has no experience. No human does."

"He says that . . ." Cora paused, gathering her thoughts. "You're asking for something you may not understand because you don't have any firsthand experience with interspecies contact."

The secretary allowed a guarded smile. "We will take every precaution to ensure that things go smoothly and painlessly."

"He says, 'Communication is neither smooth nor painless,'" she stammered. Ampersand's voice was faster, more urgent than it usually was, and she was too nervous and overwhelmed to paraphrase his words to something less threatening. Sol went on red alert. "'It is a dangerous, futile endeavor. I will cooperate, but first I wish to impart the dangers inherent in interspecies communication.'"

The secretary, again, didn't betray any emotion. Sol did, his expression turning cold.

"We'll listen to anything you have to say," said the secretary.

"Well, he doesn't like to be interrupted," said Cora. "So . . . here it is. He says, 'The human fascination with intelligent exoterran species focuses on their *similarity* to humans. Humanity is not prepared for any cultural, biological, or ideological disparities it may encounter. No species is.

"'One species is only comprehensible to another species as it understands itself. But with all species, there are attributes one possesses that the other does not share. Where attributes are not shared, inevitably both parties will try to shape the other into a form they can understand.'"

Cora swallowed, and looked at Ampersand. He was going too fast for her to have time to reword anything. Her palms were sweating, her legs starting to tremble. She continued, "'General, I deduce you are of European descent.'"

"I am."

"'Are you aware, then, how those with a European heritage came to dominate this portion of the continent?'"

"I am," said the secretary without pause.

"'There is a native ethnic group in this country that predates the current dominant European ethnic group that endured many modifications at the hands of the more powerful Europeans. Some modifications to the natives were self-imposed, such as the adoption of horses and ammunition; others forced upon them, such as religion, language, and raiment. But the fact remains that there was a more powerful entity that imposed itself upon the less powerful entity through violent means, cultural imperialism, disease, and otherwise.

"'This phenomenon is not unique to any one species. It is in the nature of all organisms, intelligent and non-intelligent alike, to understand other entities only through their own prism of existence. We understand each other only insofar as we understand ourselves.'"

The secretary's face was stone. "I do follow," he said. "But you may be drawing a false parallel."

Cora continued to spit out Ampersand's words: "'The more powerful superorganism will always try to reshape the less powerful superorganism in its own image. If it does not, the value systems the more powerful superorganism finds repugnant are exterminated or assimilated, or the less powerful superorganism is neutralized altogether.'"

"Neutralized," repeated the secretary. "Is that a threat?"

"No," said Cora, her own word and not Ampersand's. She added his: "'It's a statement of a pattern of history.'"

"Our history," said the secretary.

"Their history, too," said Cora as she gestured toward Ampersand. "He says, 'Our conflict with our transient sister species has been more mutually destructive than I can relate to you with your language. But our long, savage history of communication with our sister species has been a failed attempt by both sides to modify the other. If the values of the transients are repugnant to the Superorganism, the Superorganism will attempt to change them, for the benefit of the transients. Failure of modification leads to—'" She stopped short.

"Leads to what?" asked the secretary, his voice flat. "What did he say?"

The word had turned to dust in her mouth. "Genocide."

She looked straight at the secretary, eyes wide, breath growing heavy. "He wants . . . he wants to know if this sounds familiar to you in the context of human history, General?"

"It does."

"'Human civilization has not yet encountered a superorganism more powerful than its own.'" She paused to get her bearings. She heard a low creak from somewhere deep in the complex, as though the mountain itself was releasing a sigh.

Ampersand stopped, and Cora fell silent. The faces of all in the room were stone walls, especially Kaplan. Defeated, Cora finished, "He says he hopes his wording is comprehensible."

"I think it is," said the secretary.

Cora entwined her fingers together behind her back, slumping her shoulders. She felt helpless, trapped. She felt young. "He also says he's done here, and if you insist on him creating a means with which to translate their spoken language, he will begin that project now."

"I do insist," said the secretary without pause.

"Then he will comply."

She noticed the men were no longer looking behind her, where Ampersand had been, and turned to see that their gaze was following him as he moved out of the room, faster than she'd ever seen him walk and just as silent. In seconds, he was gone. Cora shook her head, numb. "There isn't anything else."

The men murmured among themselves. A few of them whispered to Sol, and then they began to filter out of the room.

"Sabino," said Sol. "With me."

She looked at him, awash in a strange sense of defeat. She felt a test had been sprung on her by every power in the room, and she had failed each one.

"*Go to the laboratory space I have been allocated.*"

She straightened up, now back on alert. "What?"

"*Go to the laboratory space I have been allocated.*"

"Where?"

"*Where Čefo's body is stored.*"

"Sol wants me to go with him." She looked at Sol and explained in a quiet voice, "He's talking to me again."

"Sabino." Sol's voice cut again through the quiet room, a command.

"*Go to the laboratory space I have been allocated.*"

She shook her head back and forth slowly like a pendulum. "I should do what he says."

"Excuse me?"

"He says he needs me to go with him." She didn't give any of them the chance to respond before turning to leave. If Sol moved to stop her, she didn't see it.

She was out of the door and halfway down the hallway before the voice in her ear said, "*I must confer now with Esperas.*"

"And you want me in the laboratory?" she said, dazed. "What do you want me to do there?"

"*Wait.*"

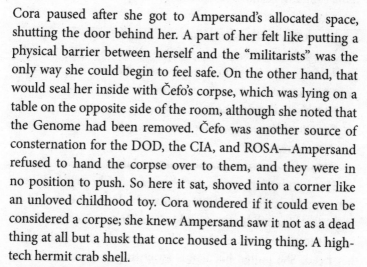

Cora paused after she got to Ampersand's allocated space, shutting the door behind her. A part of her felt like putting a physical barrier between herself and the "militarists" was the only way she could begin to feel safe. On the other hand, that would seal her inside with Čefo's corpse, which was lying on a table on the opposite side of the room, although she noted that the Genome had been removed. Čefo was another source of consternation for the DOD, the CIA, and ROSA—Ampersand refused to hand the corpse over to them, and they were in no position to push. So here it sat, shoved into a corner like an unloved childhood toy. Cora wondered if it could even be considered a corpse; she knew Ampersand saw it not as a dead thing at all but a husk that once housed a living thing. A high-tech hermit crab shell.

She found herself drawn to a cabinet in the corner opposite to where Čefo's corpse lay with a sliding metal door that groaned with the effort of opening. It was empty, like most things in this part of the complex. Without thinking, she slid into the cabinet, drew her knees into her chest, and shut herself into darkness, only thin lines illuminating her. Being inside this cabinet felt natural, more natural than anywhere else in the bunker. At first, all she heard was the eerie breath of the complex itself, what she imagined being entombed deep underwater might sound like.

Then she heard shouting, and she was twelve years old again, not in a cabinet deep inside the Cheyenne Mountain Complex but in her closet in her old house. It was a tiny thing, filled with boxed-up memories from distant childhood, barely leaving room for her small body.

And then there were the voices in the kitchen.

I'm not keeping your name. The kids aren't keeping your name. You can go die in obscurity, because you sure as hell will be dead to us. Is that what you want?

Yes, that's exactly what I want. Are you happy?

Fuck you. I'm dead fucking serious. When you go, you go for good. How many times do I have to make it clear? You can't have your cake and eat it, too. This is insane.

I can't stay in this country.

For what? You really think they're going to come for you over this New Yorker *shit?*

Absolutely. You don't know them like I do.

Her hands were pressed to her ears as she tried to keep her tears back. She was failing Felix. She knew she should go look after him, tell him it would be okay, but she couldn't bring herself to get out of the closet. She retreated even further into her head. She pulled her hands away from her ears just long enough to twist her hair into two identical ropes, which she wrapped around her ears like cinnamon rolls.

This wasn't a closet; it was a holding cell, and she was a

prisoner slated for termination. This wasn't a condominium complex adjacent to Cornell University; it was the Death Star. She was Princess Leia, and she'd just survived torture by Darth Vader. She'd just watched her planet be destroyed. She didn't crack under torture. But she'd be terminated soon. It was okay, though. She did her duty. Leia stayed strong because she was.

Then the door slid open, and a short stormtrooper entered. He told her his name was Luke Skywalker and he was here to rescue her. She wasn't alone anymore. Leia was up and ready at a moment's notice. She even had to help them shoot their way out of this. That's how strong she was. It didn't matter how she'd suffered. She could survive anything.

Soon, they were off the Death Star. Soon, they were charging toward safety, readying a new battle plan. Because they were the Rebellion. Princess Leia was strong. Princess Leia had friends, yes, but she could also fight her way out of anything. Princess Leia was not alone.

Where are you going?

I'm going to stay at Sarah's. I can't stay with you. I can't stand to look at you.

Fine.

You aren't going to abandon our children while I'm away, are you?

Are you irresponsible enough to try me?

Cora Ortega, age twelve, was crying loudly in her closet, but no one else heard her. She was not strong. She was not even strong enough to go find her brother. He was only four. He could hear their parents fighting, too. He fancied himself like Luke, and like Luke, he thought he was here to save the day. All little boys do. But he was the one who needed rescuing, and she couldn't do it. She wasn't brave. Wasn't strong.

On some level, she really believed that if she wished hard enough, this closet would turn into an X-Wing. She'd know how to pilot it innately like Luke did. She'd have an innate knowledge of the Force like Leia did. She wanted to fly away from this place, to a galaxy far, far away. All she needed to do was wish hard enough. She cried harder and wished harder. Then she heard the front door slam.

The door to the cabinet slid open with an angry creak like pewter fingernails on an old chalkboard. Cora gasped, just as surprised by the noise and the bright light as the alien that was staring at her.

She tried to stop the intense heaving of her chest, mop the tears from her face, will the redness from her skin. She hadn't even realized how hard she'd been crying or how desperately she'd needed to cry. She just looked up at him, embarrassed, hands entwined in front of her like she'd been praying.

"*Are you nesting?*" asked the voice in her ear.

"What?" she breathed, sniffing and trying to wipe away the effluvium flooding out of her face.

"*Are you making a den?*"

She had to remind herself that he wasn't trying to insult her and wouldn't be asking her this if he didn't mean it in its most literal sense. In fairness, wasn't that exactly what she was doing? Is that not what children do when they hide in closets and wish to disappear to a galaxy far, far away? Her heart was sore. She gave a barely perceptible shrug and nodded.

The cabinet door shut. Ampersand was so quiet as he walked, the only indication that he had even left were the shadows moving over the thin, white lines of the light peeking in through the cracks in the door.

Pain melted into embarrassment. The adult part of her

brain chided her for even going to this buried memory, a painful, vulnerable place that still burned and ached. But in that moment, when she saw Nils in her mind's eye, she didn't see the enemy she'd spent so much energy in the last four years training herself to hate. She saw her father. The only one she'd ever have, flawed though he was. There was a massive hole in her life, in her entire family's lives, created by his absence. But no amount of hatred could ever fill that hole. It only made the hole deeper.

She took several deep, centering breaths, willing herself to come back to reality. There was a certain pain that came with thinking about Nils; hating him blindly was so much easier than admitting that she was lonely, and lost, and out of her depth, and she needed her father, and she missed him. In any case, he wasn't going to change, and he wasn't coming back.

She shook her head. After all that had happened tonight, why was she thinking about Nils?

Ampersand was back; she could tell not only from the dancing light on the other side of the cracks in the cabinet but now from sound. It was a very light rustling, like he was fiddling with plastic wrap or maybe linens. Then the door to the cabinet shrieked open again, and she saw that was exactly what it had been, more or less: three grab-and-go military-issue sleeping bags, removed from their plastic coverings, and three pillows.

She looked at the pile, confused, and Ampersand crouched to her level. "*Do you consent?*"

Cora looked at him, alarmed. "Consent to what?"

"*Part of our agreement was that I not touch you without your consent. Do you consent?*"

She had completely forgotten about that—at the time, she had been wholly concerned with him not injecting her with any more alien drugs of dubious origin, but him asking permission to open the door of physical contact again was almost a relief. A part of her had wondered why he was so fastidious about *not* touching her and had assumed it was more or less for the same reason you wouldn't touch a wild raccoon. "Sure."

He hesitated, then fluidly he wrapped his fingers around her back and legs and carefully removed her from the cabinet as if he were moving a collectible from its packaging. He placed her on the cold floor and, with rapid efficiency, spread out the three sleeping bags in the cabinet to make a makeshift cushion, followed by the three pillows. Then as fluidly as he'd removed her, he placed her back in her "nest."

She watched him, bemused, as he carefully lowered himself into a roosting position. At length, he asked, "*Are you comfortable?*"

Her breath shuddered. She had allowed herself to get so emotionally raw, she had no more energy left to extrapolate what to do with this. "Yes," she said. "Thank you."

He paused, looking at her like he didn't quite know what to do with this, either. "*You are frightened.*"

She looked down at her hands. She didn't know if she was, really. She felt too drained to *feel* anything. Her brain was a withered balloon. "I . . . I feel alone. I don't know what to do. I'm completely in over my head. I'm worried they're going to fry my family's brains, and mine while we're there. I'm afraid they'll take me away in the night. I don't even know if they're okay, if they haven't already been altered. I don't know what the point is of even continuing to hold them. Is it me? Am I the point?"

"*In part.*"

That had been a rhetorical question; she hadn't expected Ampersand to have the answer. "You know where they are?"

"*Your government will not alter them, mentally or otherwise. They are in no immediate danger. Does this comfort you?*"

She looked up, surprised he'd even ask about something so sentimental as comfort. This was the second time he'd used the word in so many minutes. "Yes," she said, not wanting to sound ungrateful. "I'm still worried about what they'll do with me, but . . . that does help. Thank you."

Business now resolved, she figured he would leave, but he kept staring at her, the glowing focus of his eyes slowly dissipating like fireworks fading in the night sky. "*Do you need to be fed?*"

She blinked. "What?"

"*I can feed you, if you need to be fed.*"

"I'm not hungry," she croaked, utterly bewildered. "But thank you for asking."

Once again, she assumed that would be the end of it and waited for him to say something else, but he just sat there, staring at her. She bit the inside of her cheek and clasped her hands together on her lap.

"*Explain to me the proper method to comfort you.*"

"What?" She nearly did a double take. "Why?"

"*As my interpreter, you are also my charge. I have been an insufficient caretaker, because I see that you are in great distress. I am taking measures to lessen your distress. If you are not hungry and you are not in pain, perhaps you are in need of emotional comfort. But for that, I need instruction.*"

She almost wanted to laugh. "I'm not sure what to tell you. We don't usually have to explain how to comfort each other."

"*Humans naturally intuit means to comfort each other, but I am not human. I do not know if you would accept comfort from me, but if you would, then I need instruction.*"

Cora wondered if he understood what an *un*comfortable position he was putting her in. But she found that the fact that he even asked, even if it was purely a utilitarian move to keep his human tool up and running efficiently, had helped. He didn't know how to properly comfort a human, but he cared enough to ask.

She reached for the long fingers folded in front of him, before she stopped and asked, "Do you consent?"

"*Yes.*"

She hesitated, struck yet again by the strangeness of his digits, striking and majestic and terrifying, like an orb weaver with no abdomen. Her fingers shook a little as she touched his hand where the fingers met, the "palm," and she tried to imagine how to retrofit *those* digits for a task designed for human hands.

She leaned forward and slid the front four digits of his left hand behind her back. She tried to do the same with his right but stopped when they naturally fell on her head. She flinched, an instinctive contraction at the touch of such a foreign thing, then relaxed. "General rule of thumb for comforting but not-too-intimate touching—hand-holding is good, back is okay—above the hips, that is. Try rhythmic motions against the skin. Head is good, though face is a little weird. Not too hard or it hurts; not too soft or it tickles."

"*Rhythmic motions against the skin,*" he repeated. She felt his fingers graze the skin behind her ear, and it was a little breathtaking. The grazing became short and pulsing, like he was scratching an itch, and she couldn't help but smile.

"Longer strokes and longer intervals is good," she said. "Like, maybe ten inches of skin every five seconds."

He moved forward to make the movement more natural for him, but kept his head well outside of the cabinet, seeming to intuit that it wasn't wise to invade a mammal's den. He adhered to her instruction, running two digits from the top of her scalp to just below her ear, uncanny, mechanical—the exact same amount of time over the exact same skin, over and over.

Almost of its own volition, she saw her right hand lifting from her lap toward his "face," toward that space between his eyes where a nose should be. She only just managed to reclaim autonomy over her arm and stop it. She saw the focus in his eyes flashing and changing. Only at this close distance did she see that although there was always one spot in those luminous eyes that was brighter than the rest, he seemed to be able to have multiple focuses. Part of his focus was on her face, but most of it was on her hand.

Then, in a barely perceptible fluid gesture, he leaned into it and closed his eyes.

Cora froze like a bird had landed in her palm. Somehow, she hadn't expected him to do it; comforting a human on his terms was one thing, but given that innate aversion he held for humans, she hadn't expected him to allow her to touch him. But here they were; his long orb weaver fingers still running through her hair at exact five second intervals and her fingers touching his face and him allowing it.

His body didn't pulse in the way human bodies did, pumps opening and closing as hydraulics pushed the fuel that kept the animal going, but instead hummed. She thought she could even feel him breathing, not the in-out of human breath but a constant stream like an air conditioner. His skin had the same cat's tongue texture that the Genome's skin had, albeit much softer and barely perceptible.

He opened his eyes, again with that dual focus, and she was struck suddenly that he wasn't unfathomable at all. They were both made of the same star stuff. The same primordial fires that had coalesced to form their respective planets had been so close, on a grand cosmic scale. A near-infinite universe, and they were practically next-door neighbors. Looking into his eyes was like looking into ten billion years of history, like she could see the particles and rocks and gasses coalesce over eons, until somehow, impossibly, here they both were. Not wanting to overstay her welcome, she removed her hand. "Thank you," she whispered.

The focus of his eyes returned to a single, soft point.

"Am I safe?" she asked. "You think they'll try to take me?"

"Although the militarists are in agreement about their desire to remove you, they also fear that doing so will antagonize me, and that they will not risk. However, I cannot tell you that you are safe."

She looked down at her hands. "You think I'd be safer if I'd just been carted away with the rest of my family."

"I know you would be."

"Because of Obelus."

"Yes."

She looked back up at the creature and reflected with some awe at how long he'd been alive. Hundreds of years old, both subjective and relative, and yet he still seemed primarily motivated by that most primitive of emotions, fear. "Are you frightened of Obelus?"

"Yes."

She smiled sadly. "I'm surprised you haven't . . . engineered out feeling fear. Fear is so primitive."

"No intelligent species has evolved past fear. Least of all my own. Without fear, there would also be no survival. I have much experience with fear and with isolation."

"Isolation?" she said, looking up. "But you at least have . . . your underlings."

"*My experience as a captive sets me apart from them. In some regards, I am as alien to them as I am to you.*"

She hadn't even thought to wonder why he was here with her, when he should be with his own people.

"*Regardless of my success in creating a means of translating language outside of my intelligence-driven algorithm, I would prefer you stay on as my interpreter for the duration of our captivity. But you are not my slave. The decision is yours.*"

She nodded eagerly. "I'll stay with you."

"*You have been a valuable asset,*" he said. "*I shall endeavor to be a better caretaker until we part ways.*"

Until we part ways. With those four words alone, the emptiness came back, and again she ached.

George Walker Bush announced last night that he will resign as the forty-third president of the United States at noon today. Vice President Dick Cheney will take the oath as the new president at noon to complete the remaining one year of Mr. Bush's term.

Bush claimed in his Thursday address to the nation that he had only learned of the true purpose of the Refugee Organizational and Settlement Agency this week. After classified documents leaked by *The Broken Seal* founder Nils Ortega revealed that the president had been aware of the true nature of the agency as early as 2004, President Bush bowed to pressures from the public and leaders of his party to become the second president in American history to resign.

"By taking this action," he said in a television address from the Oval Office, "I hope that I will have hastened the start of the process of healing that is so desperately needed in America."

Vice President Cheney, who spoke a short time later, announced that Secretary of Defense Robert Gates will remain in his cabinet.

The president-to-be praised Mr. Bush's sacrifice for the country and called him "a true patriot who was the nation's rock in some of the darkest hours of its history."

Mr. Bush said he decided he must resign when he concluded that he no longer had "the trust of the American people" to make it possible for him to complete his term of office.

Declaring that he only ever had the nation's best interest in mind, Mr. Bush laments his role in the cover-up and professed a hope that the government can regain the trust of its people.

But "as president, I must put the interests of America first," he said.

O'Carroll, Shannon. "Bush Resigns." *The Washington Post*, October 3, 2007.

25

Cora woke still shut inside the cabinet, and forgetting where she was, she nearly bashed her fist against the door in her initial confusion. She tore open the metal door and spilled onto the cold floor, her neck aching from having slept at an awkward angle. Ampersand was gone, but as soon as she crawled out of the cabinet, the voice in her ear instructed her where to find him.

After a hasty tooth brushing and not bothering with a change of clothes or a shower, Cora stumbled into the back of the complex to find that she was about the tenth human to arrive. Standing awkwardly outside the door as though they were waiting for the bar to open were Stevie, Dr. Sev, several of their coworkers, and, of course, Sol. Good ol' Sol. All the humans greeted her icily, like she'd been keeping them waiting.

"Sabino," said Sol. "Would you ask your . . . boss if he'll let us in?"

Cora's face reddened, and she barged past them. Ampersand

was inside, as were several of his underlings. "I didn't know I was late."

"*You weren't,*" said Ampersand. "*No rendezvous was scheduled. They arrived unbidden. I saw no reason to wake you.*"

"You can come in," she said to the people standing outside, who shuffled in uncomfortably.

"Where were you?" Sol asked. "You weren't in your assigned bunk."

Cora shrank a little. "I was with him," she said, pointing at Ampersand. "But he didn't tell me you were here."

"With *him*, doing what?" asked Sol.

"Talking," said Cora, too quickly, and addressing Ampersand, she asked, "What do you need me to do?"

Ampersand had her transcribe and deliver a list of materials he would need to complete the task of creating a means of translation that would apply not only to the other amygdalines in the complex but to recordings of spoken Pequod-phonemic that human microphones had managed to pick up. Ampersand had decided that the simplest and directest way to go about what they wanted was to create glass tablets that showed written versions of each spoken language on opposite sides of the tablet. "*Crude,*" he said, "*but fulfills the request.*"

To Cora's surprise, Ampersand did have use for most everyone in the lab—effectively reading the dictionary into recorders, which, with enough "intelligence" and "context," would eventually be able to transcribe and translate. They'd been at this for an hour before Sol off-handedly mentioned "the resignation."

Only then did she realize the strange sense that pervaded everyone, like the whole complex was unmoored. "Did . . . Bush resign?" she asked Sol.

He popped an eyebrow. "Didn't you know?"

"I don't find anything out unless someone tells me."

He looked like he hadn't slept. "Looks like Nils got what he wanted."

Somehow, that felt like a threat. "So much for keeping this under wraps, I guess."

"Yep," said Sol. "So much for that."

"Does this mean anything for me?" she asked. "My family?"

Sol pursed his lips, his eyebrows raising contemplatively. "Either way, it will all be over soon."

Around this time, Dr. Sev cornered her. "Did you ever get around to asking my question?" he asked as if it were some minor curiosity.

"Which one?" she asked.

"About the Great Filter."

"Oh, I haven't yet. I've been preoccupied."

He only nodded in response, but she couldn't help but feel like for the rest of the day he was studying her with more scrutiny than he was any of the aliens.

Ampersand was mostly hands-off, instead delegating this particular task to his underlings. She hardly saw him at all that day, save a few times when he needed to give her instructions and once when he was in the adjacent room, having an interaction with Esperas. She saw the Genome, the first time since the Genome Incident. If she had to guess, that was what this discussion (which she couldn't help but read as an argument) was about. In short order, Esperas saw that she was watching them, and the door between them slammed.

· · · · ·

The calluses on Cora's fingers had already started to soften in the short two weeks since she'd last played guitar, so it was a good thing she'd gotten the Yamaha. She'd been in her bunk plucking it for an hour, a length of time that didn't usually make her fingers hurt. Then, without warning, the door to her bunk swung open, revealing on the other side: nothing.

The door swung shut, the air quivered, and then the cloak of invisibility melted off Ampersand, standing at his full height. He was so goddamn big. He only needed to stand up a tiny bit straighter for his head to hit the ceiling.

"Hi," she said, unconsciously drawing the guitar closer to her like it might act as a shield. "Do you need me?"

He eyed the flickering light, his head cocked to the side as if he were trying to decide whether this were a bug or a feature. Then he removed the covering of the light and poked one side of the offending light bulb, and the flickering stopped. Then he replaced the pane of fiberglass.

Moving fluidly, he wove around the other side of the double bunk next to the one Cora was parked on and slid onto the bottom two mattresses, relaxing into a roost and folding his hands politely in front of him, interweaving his fingers like a wicker basket.

"*Describe to me your emotional state.*"

"Better," she said, her voice clipped, relaxing her grip on the guitar. "Much better than last night."

"*You are anxious.*"

Her eyes darted to the door. "Does anyone know you're here?"

"*No.*"

"Do you want them to know you're here?"

"*No.*"

Oh, the implications. If he was just going where he wished

and no one knew, he must have found a way to hack the surveillance. She wondered if he had ways of getting in and out of the bunker. She looked at him again, at those magnificent eyes, cooler under the fluorescent lights. That could either be a good thing or a bad thing, and her imagination was running away with possibilities for both.

"Is there anything you want me to do for you?"

"You have acquired a musical instrument."

She picked up the guitar by the neck. "Vincent lent it to me from one of the air force people who's stationed here sometimes." She placed it in her lap and strummed out a quiet G-chord. "Do you want me to show you how it works?"

"Show me."

She thought of the last time she'd sang for Olive. "Hey Jude." The thought stung, and she pushed "Hey Jude" away. The next thought that popped into her head was "Sloop John B." She'd never played it before, but it was simple enough—basic three chord folk song progression. I-V-I-IV-I.

"Do you know why they code-name transients after this song?" he asked after one verse.

Cora shrugged. "I think it's random. CIA code names seem pretty arbitrary. Like 'Ampersand' and 'Obelus,' I think they just picked those at random. 'Pequod' . . . hmm." There was something somehow un-random about that one, but she couldn't put her finger on what. She set the guitar on the floor. "Is there anything else you'd like to talk about?"

"Yes."

He asked her simple questions on a variety of topics, but his main frustration, one he had apparently been sitting on for a while, was his inability to separate fact from fiction—without a human guide to explain it, trying to divine what was and wasn't real in the human exchange of information known as the internet had been nearly impossible. He told her that it had taken him the better part of the entire month he'd been on Earth to get a firm enough grasp on the English language to use internet search engines, and with the single exception of the Fremda Memo and everything surrounding that, everything relative to his search was either fiction, speculation, or conspiracy theory nonsense.

Cora found answering *why* this was the way of the world difficult, in no small part because she didn't even realize she didn't have the answers until asked. Why did people believe and propagate conspiracy theories? Why was this on the rise? She didn't know, exactly. Yes, the specifics of conspiracy theories were always wrong, but it was in response to a genuine distrust of authority, and a search for alternative explanations wasn't completely baseless. After all, maybe the conspiracy theorists had been wrong about almost every single detail with regard to the alien presence on Earth, but they hadn't been wrong about the presence itself.

"There's something I've been meaning to ask," she said. "Dr. Sev wanted me to ask you something, about a 'Great Filter.'"

He paused as though waiting for her to elaborate. Then, "*I do not understand the meaning of this term.*"

"Just this idea that if life in the universe is common, which you've told me it is, just by virtue of numbers, there should be all sorts of alien civilizations out there, but you tell me there's only three, including yours. Until we met you, we thought we were alone. So his question was, is there a Great Filter preventing civilizations from . . . advancing? Why are there so few?"

Ampersand considered this for an unusually long while. "*Advanced cognition. Intelligence is the filter.*"

"So life is common, intelligent life is not."

"*Yes.*"

She noticed that he'd sidestepped the question of whether he considered humans "intelligent life." "How long have you and your ancestors been . . . intelligent?"

"*Beginning with natural protoamygdaline ancestors, who are analogous to modern humans, approximately 350,000 years.*"

Given that *Homo sapiens* itself was only a couple of hundred thousand years old, she'd expected an answer in the realm of millions of years, not marginally older than humans. "What about you as an individual? How long do you think you'll live?"

He stilled, seemingly surprised by the pivot in topic. "*I do not know. My chosen death date would have placed my death age at 1,126 Terran years, subjective, but the genetic purge would have halved that. As it stands, with my current limited resources, I do not think I could survive more than two hundred more years, subjective.*"

Cora had wondered if these beings were immortal, or at least pursued immortality, and was mildly surprised this wasn't the case. There was certainly something appealing about a death date; one chooses exactly how long one lives, and one knows exactly when one will die. If a civilization could remove uncertainty from their own mortality, why wouldn't they? Perhaps that was an element to why he was always so afraid; he had lived for hundreds of years in a society where his death was under his control; now death could come at any moment. She had thought that Ampersand was just as likely to be considered young as elderly, though he appeared to be middle-aged.

Suddenly, his eyes widened as though something had come to his attention, and he slid out of his bunk bed in one fluid motion, standing over her. She tensed, less from fear than from excitement.

"*Do you consent?*"

"Yes."

He raised his left hand, and two fingers fell on her scalp, tracing her hairline down past her ear twice. Five seconds on, five seconds off. "*We will speak again.*"

. . . . .

The news of Bush's resignation changed the mood of the complex, not so much chaos as bewilderment. It seemed business as usual, but there was an intriguing split between people who were livid at Bush for being dumb enough to lie about something as momentous as First Contact under oath, the people who were trying to suppress their joy at the development, and the people who did not care.

By the second day of the tablet project, Ampersand's underlings had produced something modestly functional, and with that came the beginnings of an understanding as to why it was so impossible to go back and forth between English and Pequod-phonemic directly. The individual phonemes, what he called "morphological units," had pseudo-meaning on their own but only had actual meaning when combined with other phonemes. But the complexity of the combination of phonemes had to be simplified, because at present, the result was total gibberish. The word "table," for instance, apparently translated comprehensibly into the written form of Pequod-phonemic, but when Allogas, one of Ampersand's technocrat underlings, said the translated "word" back, a short blurt of alien phonemes, the resulting translation was *subject-inanimate-subject-noun-function-inanimate-platform-legs-medium-furniture-stand-function-temporal* and went on from there. The first reverse-translation of the phrase "sit on the table" went on for about five hundred words.

That evening, after she returned to her bunk and shut herself inside, she was all nerves, hoping he would come back again. *Afraid* that he would come back again. She had swiped an old playing card deck and was trying to distract herself with solitaire, feeling each second as a century, trying to resist the urge to go back to the lab and ask the alien superintelligence for whom she had been tasked as interpreter if he wanted to come play cards with her.

She had a hard time rationalizing why she wanted to be alone with him, considering how stilted and awkward their interactions tended to be—there was the thrill of having a secret, of course. That she was able to have entirely frivolous conversations with an extraterrestrial intelligence was its own charming kind of exciting. A part of her acknowledged that she was lonely, and it was nice that someone was showing concern for her well-being and interest in whatever she had to say. But most of all, these conversations felt like they could lead to Cora finally learning something of real consequence about the Fremda group and why they were still even here at all.

Ampersand finally appeared in her bunk approximately fifty years later, positioning himself on the bunk opposite hers, and opened with, "*Describe to me your emotional state.*"

Cora perked up, surprised. "Better. Thank you. I wish I could go outside, though. Claustrophobic in here. We humans go a little nuts if we don't see the sun for too long." She cracked a smile. "Would you like to play a game?"

Ampersand went along with it, although not eagerly. Cora shuffled and dealt, having placed a stool in between the bunks for them to play on, and explained the rules of Crazy Eights. He seemed annoyed, maybe even a little frustrated, that she would suggest this activity, a game much more suited to human hands than long, pointed, machinelike fingers. He hesitated every time he drew a card, as though the mere act of playing this game was a form of debasement. She figured it couldn't be too bad, though; if he wasn't willing to try, he would say something or just leave.

Multitasking did not seem to come naturally, and she had to explain that card games were primarily designed to have an activity to do with one's hands while verbally socializing. Soon, they found themselves on the topic of human sexuality, which, given humanity's obsession with it, Cora was surprised it hadn't come up sooner. Ampersand showed all the delicacy of a person who had never lived in a confused, puritanical culture infusing that confusion into all conversation. Which was to say, none.

Of course, trying to learn English using the internet meant having to wade through mountains and mountains of pornography, and this appeared to comprise the majority of what he understood about human reproduction. "*It seems violent and painful,*" he observed. "*Especially for the females.*"

"I can see where you'd come to that conclusion. But, um . . . It isn't. Well, it isn't *supposed* to be. Most of the time."

Cora thought she read skepticism in his glance. "*It is not painful.*"

"It never has been for me."

"*Then why do the actors perform the affect of pain?*"

Cora folded her cards and looked at the ceiling, smiling as she felt her face turn red. She had thought that she wouldn't get embarrassed about this topic, since Ampersand's only sexual point of reference was purely scientific, but the Catholic Shame was strong. "It's a fine distinction, I figure, for an outsider. But those aren't pain noises. They're, um, happy noises." She laughed despite herself, wishing she weren't explaining this as if she were having the Talk with a six-year-old.

"*This is a taboo,*" he observed. He still had his cards up awkwardly, aping the way she'd been holding them earlier. "*You feel you should not discuss this.*"

"No, no!" she said. "It's just a deep cultural shame thing. It's not rational. You can talk to me about me anything you want. I may feel a little bit embarrassed, but I'll get over it. I know it's just . . . exobiology to you." She bit her lip and tried to shake off that shame. "Those are actors, you are right about that. But they are performing the affect of pleasure noises, not pain noises. They're heightened for the performance aspect. In real life, it's not *usually* that loud."

Seeing that she had ceased the game, Ampersand put his cards down and folded his hands in front of him. Relaxed in his roosting posture on those two bunk beds, he reminded her of a cat. "*Our protoamygdaline ancestors never experienced sexual attraction as humans do. Reproduction was instinctual, not pleasurable.*"

"Wow," said Cora, stopping herself from adding, "that sucks."

"*I understand that relationships and sexuality are a source of great emotional angst, but I still do not understand the dichotomy of the obsession and the taboo with regard to reproduction.*"

"Maybe it's rooted in the bigness of the ability to create life," Cora postulated, "and the taboo is something of a holdover."

"*Protoamygdalines evolved no such taboos surrounding repro- duction.*"

"And your Genome?" Cora asked carefully. It was the first time she'd brought it up since the Incident.

Ampersand hesitated before responding, "*No taboos surrounding Genomes. To your perspective, more surrounding emotions. We would never express love verbally, for instance.*"

"That's what 'high language' is reserved for," Cora deduced.

"*In part.*"

"Is love with dynamic fusion bonding different from human love?"

"*I do not know the lived experience of human love.*" He paused, then a block of words: "*Can you subjectively explain to me what sexual pleasure feels like? Or what it is to have a sense of smell? I can understand these things in concept, but I cannot understand them subjectively. Fusion bonding incorporates the other's energy, their brain waves, and it becomes a vital part of one's nervous system.*"

"So fusion bonding means you can read each other's minds?"

"*No,*" he all but snapped. "*'Mind reading,' as you conceive it is not possible.*"

She stiffened, stifling the instinct to apologize for even asking.

"*It is more a sensory experience, one to which humans have no point of reference. Bonding allows one to sense the energies of another, not read thoughts. To lose a symphyle isn't merely to lose a loved one; it is to lose a piece of your mind and all the psychological and physiological instability that accompanies. There is no biological human point of reference for fusion bonding. But this is a shallow, inaccurate explanation. I haven't the adequate language.*"

This was as much as he'd ever allowed as far as "high language" was concerned, but it always seemed to frustrate him, so she decided to drop it. "Are genetic purges common?"

"*Yes, but not like this,*" he said. "*Typically, they are decided hundreds of years in advance. Ours was sudden. Politically motivated.*"

"Genocide," said Cora airily. She waited for him to correct her word use as he was wont to do, but he just looked at her. "What was your life like before the genetic purge?"

"*My life from before the purge may be disconcerting or frightening to you. My life after was difficult and painful.*"

"It's not about hearing happy stories," she said. "It's just about knowing."

"*There are many things about our culture you would find abhorrent.*"

"There are a *ton* of things about our culture you find abhorrent. At least you know what they are."

She let it sit for a while, pulling her knees up to her chest, waiting. At length, he asked, "*Tell me what you want to know.*"

"Okay," she said, crossing her legs and leaning forward. "You said that you, Čefo, and Esperas were Oligarchs. Do you mean like Russian oligarchs?"

"*An amygdaline Oligarch is more analogous to a senator, although amygdaline Oligarchs are not elected and do not have the power to perform checks over an Autocrat.*"

"I suppose that's why he's called an 'Autocrat,'" she said. "Were you . . . 'bred' to be an Oligarch?"

"*Yes. The Superorganism operates on a strict caste system. Not all who are bred to be Oligarchs ascend. Approximately one in sixty do. But only those bred to that caste ascend. Tell me why this topic interests you.*"

She gave a shaky smile, unsure of the answer herself. She didn't want him to think that she was mining intel for Sol, because right now, it honestly was not the case. "I suppose because there was a point in time where you had great power. I'm curious what you did with power when you had it."

"*I've never considered my time in power in terms of personal philosophy that dictated decisions.*"

"Don't have a lot of political philosophers?" she asked with a slight chuckle.

"*No. I could detail a list of decisions I've made, large and small, and they would number in the millions. But I could not say any overarching philosophy governed them, save of course what I considered the greatest good for the Superorganism."*

"Only for the Superorganism? Not for yourself, or for . . ." She hesitated. "Other alien species?"

At this, he focused on her, and Cora thought she read something like suspicion in that glance. *"For us, all knowledge is in service of the protection of the Superorganism. However, maintaining stability and attaining knowledge creates ethical problems, as you will inevitably have to weigh the value of the life of your own species against the value of another. The value of in-group life versus the value of out-group life. Humans do this constantly—this is how you justify war.*

"My time in power came to be dictated by our Superorganism's conflict with our sister species. Not only had transients discovered how to knock out Similar power cores using remote energy pulses specific to amygdaline energy signatures—a technology that Obelus has co-opted in his attempts to recapture me—they were using it to become aggressive. Then a group of Similars reported a relatively remote planet, sixty-two light-years from the Superorganism, which the transients had consumed."

Cora frowned, again tripped by his word choice. "When you say 'consumed' . . ."

"They had consumed that planet, in the way humans have consumed Earth."

She couldn't help but take a little offense at that. "I see."

"That consumption led to a stable population explosion. Hundreds of millions of transients. Most Oligarchs believed the only way to protect the Superorganism in the long term was to wipe out this population."

The muscles in her face grew slack, and the muscles in her shoulders grew tense. "Did you?"

"*I did not,*" he said. "*I and other Oligarchs petitioned that merely existing in a stable population was not a crime enough to warrant genocide. But other Oligarchs, the Autocrat, and stratocrats like Obelus, believed that a large, stable population of transients was in and of itself a threat.*"

"What did they do?"

"*They sterilized it,*" he said. "*The entire planet. Not just transients—all life. Even single-celled organisms. The oceans boiled. Nothing survived.*"

The complex groaned distantly like creaking in a massive ship. The air felt thick, stale, oppressive. Cora stared at Ampersand, mouth hanging open like a dead fish.

"*I recognize human expression well enough now to know that you are upset.*"

"Of course I'm upset. Your . . . The Superorganism . . . wiped out an entire planet."

"*You inquired about my time in power. The transient sterilization was the most consequential event of said time.*"

Cora closed her mouth. "What happened after?"

"*After the sterilization, the Autocrat solicited 'studies' to determine what it was about the dissenting Oligarchs, and indeed, the segment of the population at large, that so opposed the idea of genocide. The studies concluded that this segment of the population that we label 'Fremdan' has an inherent biological defect owing to their breeding.*"

"Opposing genocide is a defect?"

"*Any viewpoint that might place the lives of aliens at equal value to that of our own was considered a defect. Therefore, in the interest of finishing the transient genocide, the Fremdan population must be purged.*"

She braced herself. "How many?"

"*Approximately 6,860,000.*"

Cora felt hollow, and her gaze drifted to the foot of her bed. Such a terrible, dramatic number, but no more terrible than the "hundreds of millions" of transients. It was an abstraction, a statistic.

"*Does this comfort you?*" he asked.

She looked up at him, realizing he was upset that she had even asked, and the picture of why he was wasting his time with his pet human came into place. It wasn't strategy that brought him here at night—he did it because he liked it. Because it comforted *him,* because compared to his own people, she was simple. She didn't challenge him like Esperas did but instead hungrily scrambled for any scraps of information or affection he deigned to toss her way.

And then his pet turned on his own desires and challenged him, even in the simple way that she had—asking him to tell her about his past.

"Yes," she said. "It does comfort me. Sharing painful memories is difficult. But it's necessary for creating empathy. Do you agree?"

At length, he replied, "*That depends on the circumstance.*"

Cora picked her cards back up, deciding now was a good time to change the subject. "Do you like this game?"

"*No,*" he said.

She chuckled, still tense from the conversation. "Why?"

"*Because it offers little opportunity to strategize. It is mostly a game of chance.*"

"The same could be said about life," offered Cora.

"*Yes,*" he said. "*That is why I don't like it.*"

26

The following morning, as she was grabbing breakfast, she didn't see Sol when she entered the cafeteria, and she had only just let her guard down when he found her about to dig into a bowl of oatmeal with a generous crust of brown sugar. He sat down across from her, straddling his seat with the seat back in front of him, rubbing his eyes. "It never ends," he mumbled, sliding his hands over his face. There were dark shale deposits just under the skin beneath his eyes.

"What's going on?"

"There was another mysterious power outage today. About an hour ago. This one was at Vandenberg Air Force Base."

She froze, her oatmeal-laden spoon midair, her mouth hanging open. A plume of fear blossomed in her chest. "Where we were last week," she said, putting the spoonful of oatmeal down.

"Yep," said Sol. "Where we were last week."

The two sat in tense silence for a few minutes while others in the cafeteria went about their business, ignoring them. Cora couldn't help but look at the exit of this room, trace the path in her mind to the only exit, the blast doors that were so far from where they were sitting. The only escape. "Does this mean they need to leave?"

"I'm not supposed to encourage that," said Sol. "But . . . this whole thing being made public means every agency under the sun is trying to find out what's going on and, more specifically, *where* they are. Every day, more people know we're here, and these people seem to think labeling their emails 'classified' and sending them from .gov addresses will shield them from hostile ETIs finding and reading them." He sighed again and dragged his fingers through his messy hair. He needed a haircut. "And he hasn't told you what Obelus is capable of."

"He won't even tell me what *he's* capable of."

"Is there anything you have learned that might ameliorate this situation?"

Even single-celled organisms. The oceans boiled. Nothing survived. Cora ran through a mental simulation of her telling Sol the tale of an alien Superorganism's preemptive sterilization of an entire planet and no good coming from it.

"Going by the look on your face, I'm guessing the opposite is true."

Cora relaxed into her chair. "If an alien species has the power and technology to even get here, then it stands to reason that they have the power and technology to do terrible things. That doesn't mean terrible things are inevitable or that we'd see them in our lifetime. But what do we do with the knowledge that terrible things are possible, if not inevitable?"

"This goes beyond national security," he said with a dry chuckle. "This is existential." He started rubbing his face with his hands, up and down, until the skin around his nose started turning red. "Has he said anything to you about this? About the . . . 'energy pulse' in Vandenberg?"

"No, he hasn't spoken to me at all today."

He leaned back, and Cora could all but see the train tracks in his mind switching. "Did Dr. Sev tell you that the tablets are functional? That they have some translations?"

"No," said Cora. "Have you gotten anything?"

Sol nodded at her slowly. "Why don't you go pay him a visit?"

· · · · ·

Dr. Sev was alone in an unused room in the back of the complex when Cora found him. He turned to look at her, his bright brown eyes shining like he'd been expecting her. "Miss Sabino!"

"Dr. Sev," she said, bemused. "I asked him about the Great Filter."

"Indeed!" his eyes lit up. "Thank you. Did you get an answer?"

"Yeah, he said it's 'intelligence.'"

"Meaning 'intelligence' is the barrier that is rarely, if ever, crossed by living things?"

"That's what he indicated to me."

His left eyebrow was raised ever so slightly as though he suspected her of a little white lie, a playful one. "And their Superorganism so close to Earth, relative to the hugeness of the Milky Way galaxy, and yet with the exception of their hated transients and an unnamed third party, no other civilizations exist. How very improbable."

She didn't quite know what he was getting at or how to respond. She took a seat, waiting for him to get on with it. He had one of the translation tablets in his hand and was waggling it between his fingers absently as he studied her.

"Is something troubling you?" he asked.

"Nothing." She gestured to the tablet. "Sol told me that you'd translated some recordings."

Dr. Sev arched an eyebrow. "We're calling Special Agent Kaplan 'Sol' now?"

Cora shrugged. She couldn't begin to define the nature of their relationship, but whatever it was, it had become too personal to warrant a surname anymore.

"Well, we might have some new insights into our old friend Čefo . . ." He eyed her, then rolled his chair over to another table and picked up a file folder. "I think this might interest you."

"What's that?" she asked.

"Transcripts," said Dr. Sev. "We did manage to transcribe some of our security feeds of the Fremda group."

"Really?" said Cora, brightening. "Does it tell you anything about how their language works?"

Dr. Sev belly laughed. "The only thing we've learned about their language is the beginnings of what we don't understand. These tablets are a software, one that translates a very base simple version of their language, and one I suspect is hardly accurate at all. I think what he's given us is an extremely poor man's Yahoo! Babel Fish."

Cora held up the tablet. It looked like a pane of glass with a metal rim, about the size of a picture frame. "Maybe we can build a better software."

"Oh, I don't think we'll be at that point for a long, long time," said Dr. Sev. "Man-made computers can't even accurately translate one human language to another. I'm not saying it's impossible to develop an algorithm as sophisticated as the one Ampersand uses to understand human language, but I am saying I likely won't live to see it."

He reached out for the tablet, and Cora handed it back to him. "In all likelihood, he's designed these to translate very, very selectively, so what we have managed to translate is extremely bare bones, but maybe you'll have some insight."

"I'll try," she said.

"So," continued Dr. Sev, "as a result of the inadequacy of modern human microphones, there were large portions of the recordings that were untranslatable. But we do have precious few that give us partial translations. I'll start with a sample from September 27, a conversation between 'Esperas' and 'Ampersand.'" He added finger quotations to their names. "Paraphrased, of course."

He cleared his throat. "Says Esperas: 'In forcing us to stay in their custody'—we assume he's addressing Ampersand—'you are consigning us to death.'" He looked at Cora.

Cora unconsciously grabbed the back of her neck. "I . . . would assume that has to do with their worry over their culture clashing with human culture."

"You warned the secretary of defense about that the other day when you were interpreting." He nodded slowly to himself, then continued, "Here's another snippet, September 29. Esperas: 'There is no legacy outside the context of a superorganism. The issue cannot be mere survival. Survival to what end? No function within a greater superorganism? If our endeavor is survival with no legacy, what reason is there to live?'" He looked again at Cora. "What do you suppose he means by 'legacy'?"

Cora pondered. "Ampersand once told me their Genome contains genetic information. Like, he sounded almost defensive about it. That makes me think it's *capable* of reproducing. It sounds to me like . . . there is some controversy over whether or not they should use it. I assume that's why they smuggled it out in the first place and why Obelus wants it."

Dr. Sev continued, "Esperas: 'The Genome is our only hope for a legacy of Fremda. If we surrender it to Obelus, we are accepting death and the void. No legacy.'" He smiled and looked at her. "I think I might draw the same conclusion, Miss Sabino. On that note, here is a sample from March 2. A conversation between 'Esperas' and the late 'Čefo.'"

"Luciana told me about that," said Cora. "That was the first time anyone heard them speaking in Pequod-phonemic. It happened during the night shift and then again when Luciana and Stevie were in the clean room with them. That was the ninety-second recording Mr. Redacted was talking about in the Fremda Memo."

"Correct." He licked his lips, straightened out the paper, and read, "Says Čefo: 'The Superorganism has attained our location.'" Cora felt her skin tighten, which Dr. Sev clearly noticed. "There's much here that didn't really translate. From what we can tell, Esperas and Čefo were debating as to whether they should try to communicate with us."

"That seems to be a running theme," said Cora.

"Ah, but we did get a clear translation of this gem, courtesy of Čefo: 'If we don't communicate with human civilization, we are consigning them and ourselves to death.'

"Them *and* ourselves," he repeated. Cora drew in a long breath through her nose. He smiled knowingly and continued reading. "Says Čefo: 'We have little time before Similars arrive; I must learn to communicate with human civilization.'

"Says Esperas: 'The Superorganism will sterilize Earth if it discovers that there has been any communication with us. To avoid sterilization, do not attempt to communicate.'

"Sayeth Čefo: 'Earth will be sterilized regardless.'"

Cora felt like the air had slunk out of the room to avoid the conversation. Dr. Sev watched her. He seemed amused. "Your expression might read as guilty to some."

She allowed herself some time to respond. The "hundreds of millions of transients" had been an abstract horror, but one she hadn't thought to apply as a possibility to Earth. "Yeah, Ampersand implied something along those lines."

"And what did our friend imply?"

"That that there is a precedent for the Superorganism sterilizing entire planets," she said, her horror growing with each word. "And the knowledge that humanity had had contact with a fugitive purge group might make it . . . more . . ."

"More?"

"More likely than it might have been otherwise."

"Make what more likely?" He was still smiling, but his eyes were growing serious.

"Planetary sterilization," she stammered. "But this is all really speculative. The sterilization he told me about was against a planet of transients, and they have a long, painful history with them. They have *no* history with us. Their Superorganism doesn't know we're here. Or rather, they don't know we've advanced. As far as the Superorganism knows, it's A.D. 1180 and we're still keeping our population in check with siege warfare."

Dr. Sev shook his head and chuckled. "The impression I get is that Čefo believed that their Superorganism will see us as a threat no matter what happens once they find out we've developed into an advanced civilization. Which, of course, we haven't, but we will. Soon, if we don't kill ourselves first. Esperas, conversely, believed that open communication with the Fremda was what might do humanity in, that the Superorganism would see us as 'tainted' by a genetically defective purge group. Either way, long-term survival for humanity doesn't look good, does it?"

Cora was stunned. "How can you be so calm about this?"

He leaned back on his chair. "Well, the Pequod Superorganism hasn't figured out faster-than-light travel yet, so sayeth Ampersand. Odds are good I won't live to see contact from the Superorganism if their home base is as far away as Ampersand says it is. About ninety-seven light-years, I think? Don't worry," he said. "You probably won't live to see anything big happen, either."

"But . . . our species?"

Dr. Sev shrugged. "Que será . . ."

Cora's stunned, existential horror melted into indignation and then to anger. *Typical,* she thought. *Of course you don't really get too worked up about issues that won't affect your generation.* Men his age weren't too fussed about the potentiality for man-made climate change to pose an existential threat to human civilization. Why should hostile aliens be any different?

He stood up and gave her a pat on the shoulder, his eyes drifting to the tablet he'd been fiddling with earlier. "Since Ampersand and Esperas control access to their inferiors, we haven't been able to test these out on any live subjects. But since you might be able to get close to them . . ."

Cora took the tablet. "Can you tell me where . . . Stelo and Krias are right now?"

· · · · ·

Cora found the two propagandists in the room interconnected with Ampersand's lab, no Oligarchs or Similars in sight. When she entered with the tablet, they didn't seem surprised to see her; if anything, they seemed to be expecting her.

Adjusting for the fact that they didn't stand fully upright like a human put them around the height of an average woman. The pair approached her in tandem, slowly but confidently, and she went on guard. Being among the smallest of the group, with deep obsidian eyes, these two fell the closest to what one might consider cute, but that accessibility belied something careful, almost conniving. They were, after all, "propagandists." Even if Ampersand's word choice was only half-accurate, part of their raison d'être was finding the best way to push an agenda.

She came within a few feet of them, steadied herself, held up the tablet, and said, "Would the two of you communicate?"

The Pequod-phonemic "written" translation of her words appeared on the opposite side of the tablet; it looked more like freckles than writing. The two responded in Pequod-phonemic immediately, and on Cora's side of the tablet, the translation read:

[SELVES do wish to communicate.]

Cora couldn't help but smile, shocked that this haphazard device actually worked. "What would you like to tell me?"

They were silent and still. She thought they must be communicating through "network language." Then they both spoke. They seemed take turns speaking as though they spoke with one mind:

[Communication access for US/PROPAGANDISTS inhibited because of caste system. System enforced by Esperas and his Similars.]

[Caste system is COUNTERINTUITIVE on Earth.]

[We do wish to communicate.]

The two stepped back, almost in unison, as though they were trying not to invade her personal space. They stood perfectly still when they spoke, but they didn't have those thousands of bright reflective surfaces in their eyes like Ampersand did.

She decided her first angle would be to cross-reference with them things Ampersand had already told her. "Why was there a genetic purge of the Fremda group?" she asked.

[In our lives' duration, SELVES saw the stratocracy, the MILITARISTS, gain much power within the Superorganism, enough to lobby for the purge of us/Fremda.]

[On the basis that we/Fremda value non-amygdaline life over amygdaline life.]

[This supposition is based on our genetics.]

"Is that true?" she asked. "Do you have a different view on . . . natural aliens than the rest of your Superorganism?"

[Biological determinist conclusion on FREMDA is unsubstantiated.]

[We do not know validity of this supposition.]

[We will never know if biological determinist supposition is substantiated.]

[We believe in human personhood.]

[We were told by our superiors our entire lives that naturals are incomprehensible to us. Their ways are alien; they haven't capability for high language.]

[PEQUOD SUPERORGANISM policy against alien life-forms is predicated entirely upon presupposed incomprehensibility.]

[But we/Fremda have been dependent on naturals for nearly forty years.]

[Superior/Esperas maintained that we must not communicate with the naturals; they are incomprehensible to us, and communication is deadly to both parties.]

[Either Esperas was in error or misspoke deliberately.]

[We are communicating with you now.]

[Ampersand communicates through YOU, his human interpreter.]

[You/naturals are not incomprehensible.]

[We/Fremda/humans must communicate, become a part of the human superorganism.]

They took turns but spoke in such a steady stream, not leaving even a breath of a second between each of them speaking. It was only after one of them said they must "become part of the human superorganism" that they stopped, and their heads tilted forward as though they were about to see the finale to a magic trick.

Cora gathered her bearings. What to say to that? It wasn't like they were asking her opinion on the best neighborhoods to rent an apartment in LA. This was *big*. "You . . . you want to stay? You want to live among humans?"

[We/propagandists have no function outside of a superorganism. But we may use our skills to learn from the HUMAN SUPERORGANISM, contribute.]

[We/Fremda have not the resources or genetic diversity to create a new colony, new superorganism.]

[We/Stelo/Krias understand this.]

[Ampersand understands this.]

They paused, and again, the eager lean forward.

"So," she said, wanting to make sure she was understanding them. "Esperas's plan to take the Genome and run . . . He *does* want to breed a new colony. And you think that's a bad idea."

[We/Stelo/Krias believe it is immoral to breed new Fremda; they will have no superorganism and will lead short, miserable lives, if they survive at all.]

[Inevitable. Fremda will go extinct, but we/Fremda may live our lives with purpose within HUMAN SUPERORGANISM.]

[If HUMAN SUPERORGANISM has any hope at all of surviving PEQUOD SUPERORGANISM.]

[Our legacy cannot be through breeding; it must be through other means. Through HUMAN SUPERORGANISM.]

There it was again—the idea that the Pequod Superorganism would pose a threat to humanity. It was clearly at the forefront of their minds, just like it was with Ampersand. "Why would your Superorganism hurt us if we've never hurt them?"

[Preemptive strike.]

"How many times has this happened?" she asked, her skin growing hot. "How many times have they wiped out civilizations as a preemptive strike?"

[Unknown.]

[Consistent, sustained acts of genocide against transients.]

[One known planet sterilized. Possibly more.]

[Transients are monsters, but we share an ancestor with transients.]

[Transients are monsters.]

"So you believe that the genocide against your sister species is justified?" she asked. Cora thought she detected the two of them lean back ever so slightly.

[Humans are not monsters.]
[We do not share an ancestor with humans.]

Clearly, Woodward and Bernstein were not interested in answering that question.

[HUMAN SUPERORGANISM would be the first.]
[HUMAN SUPERORGANISM is not true ADVANCED.]
[But soon, within a few centuries.]
[Perhaps sooner.]
[HUMAN SUPERORGANISM will become true advanced, very soon.]

"Then why would they want to kill us, not even bother setting up diplomatic relations?"

[AUTOCRAT determined never to repeat mistake of allowing transients to flourish.]
[PEQUOD SUPERORGANISM is determined never to make this mistake again.]
[NEVER again.]

Dear Demi,

Your terms are fair, so I agree to them. I'll tell
your lawyer the same thing, but frankly, I don't
want to litigate that right now.

What I want to litigate is why, no matter what
evidence I showed you, no matter how much you used
to support my work, you never stood by me when I
said we needed to leave the country. You performed
support well when it didn't threaten your sense
of domesticity, but hey, it's different now, Demi.
Blinders off, this is the world now, and it's all
gone downhill fast. It's not my fault you can't
accept that.

You didn't believe me when I said they saw me as
an enemy of the state, even if I was "protected by
the First Amendment," formalities that no longer
matter. We call that a "Just World Fallacy." I know
you know this, Demi, because I taught you this term
when I was your TA. You refuse to accept that you
do not live in a just world. Sooner or later, you
will have to.

I feel like I'm taking crazy pills. I've had
colleagues that I've known for years, people I
considered rational thinkers, use the phrase "Saddam
Insane" as they rejoice that we're going to go get

the bad guys. There's no question that Saddam is
a dictator, but I am horrified at how quickly and
easily the whole country has fallen for the line
that Iraq is to blame for terrorist attacks they
had nothing to do with, just so the U.S. will have
someone to invade. That the Patriot Act passes, and
hardly anyone bats an eye. These people who insist
that there is evidence of WMDs in Iraq are just as
bad as the people insisting Bush did 9/11—the only
difference, of course, are that the former are in
power. Bin Laden *hates* Saddam. The administration
knows this, Congress knows this, the CIA knows this,
everyone knows this! It makes me sick.

There is so much more that I don't have hard
evidence on yet, things I've learned from my sister
that make the Iraq invasion look like peanuts by
comparison. But right now, this is what matters,
because people believe it. People want to believe
it, because it gives them an enemy, and that's
all the people want right now. Any enemy will do,
apparently; that's what we've been reduced to.
And I am frightened, Demi. More than that, I am
disappointed that you don't see it the same way.
So, yes, I agree to your terms, and that is the end
of that. I am not sorry. I did the right thing. One
day, you'll see. You all will.

—Nils

Ortega, Nils. Letter to Demetra Ortega, Munich, Germany, May 4,
2003.

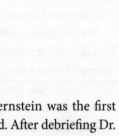

The day she talked to Woodward and Bernstein was the first she neither saw nor heard from Ampersand. After debriefing Dr. Sev about the conversation, she read some books and waited a few hours before awkwardly asking the open air if everything was okay, knowing that he could hear her through her earpiece, but got no response. When she went to the laboratory where they'd been working on the tablets, she found it completely empty, and she began to fear that they had already disappeared without anyone realizing.

She got dinner in the cafeteria and wondered if the tension she felt among the people who worked here was a result of the chaos going on in the outside world or just her projecting. She left without speaking to anyone and returned to her lonely, cavernous bunk room. When she entered, Ampersand was already inside, waiting for her, perched on the bottom bunk next to hers that he had de facto claimed as his own like she had forgotten some appointment they'd made. Cora slammed the door behind her and tensed, worried that she had committed a faux pas by speaking to his inferiors without his permission.

"Hi," she said. "I missed you today."

He watched her, his head tilted to the side ever so slightly. She moved to sit down on her bunk. "*We must depart soon,*" he said after she settled.

Her heart took a dip. "I know. Sol told me there was another power outage at the air force base we were at last week." She paused. "How soon?"

"*Tomorrow evening. Perhaps sooner.*"

He continued watching her, as if he expected her to explain his plan for him. She didn't say what she wanted to say, which was simply, "I'll miss you." She knew he wouldn't reciprocate. Lacking instruction, she reached for her guitar. When he continued to stare at her in silence, she strummed the opening chords to a Neko Case song. The other few times she'd played guitar, he would interrupt her in the middle to either ask a question or make a comment, but this was the first time he sat and watched her make it the whole way through a three-minute song without comment. It might have been the bittersweet tone of the song, but she couldn't help but project melancholy onto him.

"*It is a language,*" he said after she finished.

"What is?"

"*Music.*"

She removed the guitar from her lap and placed it on the floor. "Oh, yes, I suppose it is."

"*Can you translate its meaning?*"

She entwined her fingers in front of her, aping the way he tilted his head. "Well, in the case of this song, she doesn't *literally* wish she was the moon . . ."

"*Do not interpret the lyrics. I do not mean the lyrics; I mean the music. It is a language. It has an aural language, as you demonstrate, and a written corollary, correct?"*

"Yes."

"And the language conveys meaning, correct?"

"Yes."

"Can you translate the meaning of the music, independent of the lyrics?"

Her first impulse was the Sol impulse—*anything can be explained*—but as she reached into the ether to try to find accurate words that translated the meaning of the music, she came up short. With every example that played through her mind, she found she could loosely, very loosely, describe some approximation of the feeling the music was meant to evoke—*melancholy, wistful, longing.* But that barely skimmed the surface in terms of accurately describing the meaning inherent in the music. The descriptions were shallow, inaccurate, just like he described his own frustration at expressing his own concepts in English.

"I don't know how," she admitted at length.

"So you see why I am unable to describe to you high language in a way that would be satisfactory for either of us."

The ghost of a laugh escaped her. There it was. Not everything could be explained, at least not with the limits of spoken language. But there was something comforting to it. Their mutual inability to understand each other leading to a place of understanding.

"Do you still wish to go outside of the bunker?"

Cora snapped to attention. "Are you offering?"

"If you wish it."

Not for the first time, she thought she heard inflection in the voice. Urgency? Nervousness? "Are we escaping?"

"*No, but I can take you somewhere outside of the complex for a short time. I can take you wherever you wish to go, but I advise that you do not share this with the intelligence gatherers.*"

A deep ambivalence bloomed in her; on the one hand, this was the most exciting thing he could offer. On the other hand, it could be a very bad idea. It was at minimum a suspicious and frivolous thing to do with his time. "So we're sneaking out."

"*We are sneaking out.*"

She smiled despite herself, drawing her legs up to her chest, anxious, excited, frightened. "Why?"

His head tilted forward, the crest on his head fanned upward slightly, and it reminded her of the first day he had met Sol, the way he had looked at the man as if he were a bull about to charge. She couldn't read the expression, but this time it didn't feel hostile. It felt filled with intent, but what intent she could not read. "*Because it pleases me.*"

The part of her that was frightened gave way to excitement, and she felt her heart swell. This was an irresponsible thing to do. A dangerous thing to do. "Yes," she breathed.

One of the layers on Ampersand's back cracked open like an insect's wing. A slit opened up, and something resembling a thin metal plate, about the size of a sleeping bag, leaked out. It was solid, but the way it moved suggested plasticity. Ampersand placed it on the floor between the two rows of bunks, and it widened farther like liquid metal. Cora got off the bed and stood at attention, her heart pounding.

"*This is a semiautonomous plate. It is how we travel short distances on high-gravity planets. I program a destination based on the electromagnetic field of the planet, and it takes me there.*" He stepped onto the plate, and instead of sitting, he contracted into himself—head in, feet tight under his body, hands under his head, and neck shortened into practical nonexistence, small enough that he might have been able to fit into the back seat of a car. In a fluid motion, like a wave in the ocean spreading over the sand, the metal spread over his entire body until he was encased in it, and once encased, he disappeared.

"This explains so much," said Cora.

Within seconds, he reappeared, and the metal plate melted off him. As before, the invisibility was an optical illusion, not a means of teleportation, and she could still feel his mass when he wasn't visible. He stood up and revealed a second metal plate from his back compartment, smaller than the first, sliding out in a thin layer like fabric. "Will that work for me?" she asked.

"*Tell me where you wish to go. I can take you anywhere, though I believe it would be wise not to leave the continental United States.*"

"Is there anywhere you need to go?"

"*I go where I need, at need,*" he said, confirming to Cora that this was far from the first time that he'd sneaked out of the complex. "*I will take you where you want to go, within reason.*"

Within reason? She could ask for him to take her wherever they were keeping her family, but that definitely fell out of the purview of "sneaking out" and could land all parties in far more trouble than they were already in. The very thought of Nils brought up so much cognitive dissonance it scrambled her brief good mood entirely, and besides that, he was far outside of the continental United States. Her stomach was tied in knots; this was such a strange and unexpected situation, she was tempted to tell him to take her wherever he wanted. *Wherever it "pleases" you.*

"Can you take me home?" she asked. "I want to see if my dogs are there."

"*Place yourself upon the plate, and make yourself compact, as I demonstrated.*"

A part of her worried that this was made for amygdaline bodies (which weren't so much bodies as Swatches to begin with), but she knew it was absurd to think that Ampersand wouldn't have considered that. She placed one timid foot on the plate, then the other, and looked at him to make sure she was doing this correctly.

"*I won't let any harm come to you.*"

She gave a curt nod and lowered herself onto the plate, drawing herself into a fetal position and drawing her face to her knees. She gasped as she felt the metal moving beneath her, then flowing over her, and she made herself as compact as she could. It was cool on her skin, but not cold like the metal in the complex. But it moved, and breathed, and hummed. One moment, she was in darkness, then the metal fell off her, she opened her eyes and sucked in a gulp of air. Her muscles felt rigid, but her breath was still heavy, her heart still pounding.

She was in her living room.

She stood up on shaky legs, careful not to stand up on the plate, and turned around, disoriented, her mind not caught up yet with her senses. Ampersand stood by the television, perusing the few years' worth of human detritus that had accumulated in the living room—a Gamecube controller, a TV remote, an issue of *People* magazine. Everything was more or less as they'd left it. In the next room, she could see the computer still in pieces, and looking down the hall, she saw the mess from toppling her mother's dresser scattered all over the bedroom and spilling into the hall—jewelry, old cell phone chargers, prescription pill bottles. Somehow, she was surprised she didn't see any signs of a struggle.

She shook herself back to reality. "We should probably

keep the lights off, in case anyone's watching. Thor?" she called weakly, already knowing they weren't here. "Monster Truck?"

Only the distant wail of an ambulance cut through the silence.

They're dead, she thought, and her innards churned. "You, exobiologist, can you tell me if they're in the house, alive or no? I . . . it would be emotionally damaging if I stumble on their dead bodies."

The focus in Ampersand's eyes spread out, and their glow dimmed as he turned his head around like a radar. Then: "*There are mammals, alive in the house. Mice. A skunk. No canids, alive or dead.*"

She'd suggested going home because it felt like the only marginally responsible thing to do; she hadn't been emotionally prepared to do it. She wondered if the people who'd taken her family had tossed the dogs off into a shelter somewhere like they were taking out recycling. A civic duty one does to objects with no real value.

"*You are so concerned with domestic animals,*" he said. "*But these animals you had no intention of consuming.*"

She looked at him and almost said, *Humans don't eat dogs,* before remembering that wasn't always true. There was something deeply unnatural about being here with him. This house was so domestic, so banal, and he was so out of place in it. Even so, the words he had said earlier came to her mind: "*We must depart soon.*" The thought made the excitement that was still boiling in her gut mutate into sadness. She turned from him and wandered into the backyard through the heavy sliding glass doors. There were occasionally nights where the haze and light pollution dissipated enough that stars were visible, but this was not one of them.

She thought of Woodward and Bernstein, who, unlike Ampersand, had not only been on Earth for forty years but had spent those forty years completely sheltered. Ampersand, conversely, had had to fend for himself. Still, he had only been on Earth for six weeks, and not for one second of that time had he let his guard down. Cora wondered when, or even if, he slept. "I had a conversation today. With Stelo and Krias. I don't know how much you heard."

"*I heard it.*"

She turned around and saw that he had followed her outside. "Have they had a conversation like that with you?"

"*No.*"

"Why?"

"*There is no protocol for those of a lower caste to make tactical suggestions to Oligarchs.*"

"In all the time we've been at the complex, two weeks now, you haven't allowed input from anyone but Esperas?"

"*We have imported our caste system, despite no longer being beholden to it. Social dynamics do not simply change when the situation does.*"

They do if you want to survive, she thought. She looked again at the sky, a dark, pink-tinted gray. "Can you take us someplace clear?" she asked. "Someplace where we can see the stars?"

"*Tell me where you would like to go.*"

She looked back up at the sky. "I don't have an exact place in mind," she said. "The desert somewhere, maybe, between here and Colorado. Death Valley, Mojave, Joshua Tree?"

She saw movement at her feet and looked down to see her plate had glided next to her. She touched a toe onto the plate, felt the strange material give under her like syrup, then stop. She stepped onto the plate and got into her fetal position, and the liquid metal enveloped her.

When it melted away, she was in the desert. After the ambient noise of an LA suburb, the sudden stillness and quiet of the desert made her ears ring. But the most disarming thing was the darkness. She had never been this deep in the desert before, and there was no sign of civilization except for a distant ring of light pollution far to the west. Ampersand was standing right beside her, almost over her, tall enough that even standing at her full height she didn't come up to the bottom of his head.

The darkness triggered a residual fear from the last time she'd been alone in the desert with him, when at least then the sun had been up. Now here they were with no light but the infinite stars, and him less than a foot away. As her eyes begin to adjust to the dark, she saw that they were surrounded by brush on all sides. A breeze rustled through the branches, and her lizard brain screamed, *Rattlesnake!*

"I can't see what's in the brush," she said. A part of her wanted to reach out to him for security; another part of her saw him as the thing to be afraid of. "There are some animals out here that are dangerous to humans. Snakes, scorpions . . ."

"*I won't let any harm come to you.*"

The reassurance pulled her back to the present, and she took a few breaths to calm herself. Her vision had adjusted enough now to see a clearing in the brush, and taking him at his word, she sat down in it and looked skyward. She could still feel some warmth from the sun baked into the sand. "I don't think I've ever seen such a clear sky."

He also had his gaze skyward, and she wondered what this sky looked like through his magnificent eyes. She figured that even the clearest night sky to him would be about as exciting as the ficus tree in the backyard was to her. A stippled haze like clouds painted a faint stripe across the eastern sky, and she figured that must be the Milky Way. She'd never seen it with her naked eyes before. Now that her lizard brain had quieted and the fear subsided, a feeling of calm took over. This place was so dark, so vast, and yet so intimate.

Ampersand looked down to examine the brush a few feet away, moved in a circle around her, and then parked himself in a roost right next to her. Again, she thought of the last time they'd been alone in the desert, how on guard he'd been. How fastidious he'd been about keeping her at a safe distance. Now he sat right next to her like it was nothing, like they had been friends for years.

Now that her eyes had adjusted to the dark, she could see the reflected glow of the starlight in his eyes, the only part of him she could see in any detail. He had a distinctly inhuman way of looking at her that couldn't be described as staring, his gaze fading up and down as though he were taking stock of her entire body every few seconds. His eyes soaked up the light of the stars like a sponge, reflecting it back in concentrated brilliance, cooler in the blue starlight than the fiery warmth they gave when in direct sunlight. She desperately wanted to touch him and clasped her hands in front of her, her right hand clamping down on her left as if scolding it for even having the thought.

She looked back up at the sky. "Which one's yours?"

"*It cannot be seen from here.*"

"Why not?"

"*The star the Superstructure orbits is not visible. The Superorganism structure is most analogous to a theoretical human construct called a Dyson sphere. It orbits the star, thereby blocking visible light from reaching Earth.*"

"Where is it?"

"*Do you consent?*"

She nodded. He gently slid his fingers around the back of her head, angling her face upward and a bit to her right. With his other hand, he pointed to a spot in the night sky.

Cora stared at the spot for a while after he had folded his hands on the ground in front of him, at the patch of darkness that was blocking a star, a patch so minuscule and distant her eyes couldn't even begin to make it out. "So when you say you'd never been on an alien planet before the purge, you meant you'd never been on *any* planet before the purge."

He put his hands back down in front of him. "*I hadn't.*"

"How are planets different from being on the Superstructure?"

"*They are wild. Dangerous. Tempestuous. Loud. This one is inhabited by an advancing alien species, which is not something I ever thought I would encounter.*"

She chuckled. "Funny you should think of planets as wild and tempestuous. You adapt well to this one."

"*Only out of necessity. There is no comfort in so alien a place.*"

She looked down at her hands, hands that she could barely make out in the darkness, and clasped them even tighter. "Do you know where you're going to go?"

He didn't respond. Didn't even look at her.

She pursed her lips, trying to screw up her courage, trying to push through this sense of shame she was only starting to acknowledge. "Do you consent?"

"*Yes.*"

Her right hand finally let go of her left, and she reached out to take one of his hands in both of hers. He looked at her, and she thought she saw some of that old fear creep into his posture, the instinct to defend against a wild animal. His hand was awkward to hold in the traditional sense—each of his fingers were at least two feet long, and the palm itself was smaller than a human's. She wrapped her fingers around his palm, looked at him, and whispered, "Please don't leave."

He didn't respond, but the focus in his eyes did begin to concentrate and brighten.

She brought his hand close to her chest. "You are a survivor. I know you don't want to give up on life just yet. And we know the Superorganism is going to be an existential threat to both of us eventually. Maybe the best chance for both of us, the Fremda group and humanity, is if you stay here on Earth."

He continued staring at her, his posture implacable.

"I know that's not what Esperas wants," she continued. "I don't know what else you guys have been discussing, but I can't help but think that just striking out into the wilderness with the intent of breeding new Similars with what I know are very limited resources smacks to me as having a poor chance of success."

"*It has no chance of success. It was a fool's errand conceived when they believed they would be rescued by someone with far more resources than myself.*"

"Then maybe the government keeping your existence a secret because it is politically inexpedient, all while you quietly hop from planet to planet until Obelus inevitably catches you, is exactly what we should *not* be doing."

He removed his hand from her grasp and slowly tucked it back in front of him, but continued to hold her gaze in an unbroken way more characteristic of a human. "*We can neither fight nor outrun Obelus. I believe that a greater danger is posed to humanity if it were obvious to the Superorganism that humanity had had any contact with a fugitive purge group.*"

"But both you and Esperas have already let it slip that the Superorganism will see *any* advancing civilization as a threat. It doesn't matter if they knew you were here or not. I know it might seem counterintuitive to Esperas, but maybe you could, I don't know, reason with Obelus?" The last words tapered off, sounding ridiculous even as she said them. She knew just enough to know that her ignorance on the situation was near total.

"Obelus cannot be reasoned with," he said. *"No one individual with direct instructions from the Autocrat can be negotiated with, and Obelus least of all."*

"Then maybe there is something we can do. There might be *some* fringe benefits to landing in the country with the biggest military."

"There aren't. It is irrelevant. Any destructive capabilities humans possess, Similars can return a thousandfold. They cannot be beaten by any force either your civilization or I myself possess. They can only be outrun."

She shook her head, her desperation beginning to strangle her. "I know you didn't come here to help us. But even if Obelus can't be reasoned with, maybe the best chance for any of us, instead of Esperas's Hail Mary, is for you to stay here. I know we do terrible things, to each other and to animals and probably eventually to aliens, but I think we have the potential to do good things, too. And we could protect you. We just need to know *how*."

He looked at her. She thought she saw something akin to sadness, perhaps imagined it. He slowly rose to his feet. *"I cannot even protect myself from the Superorganism or from our sister species."*

"But you've hardly been here two months. You haven't even begun to explore the possibility—"

"And if I stay here, I fear I will live to see my Superorganism

preemptively exterminate an entire species, and I will again be powerless to stop it."

She stilled, craning her head to look up at him, and again the silence of the vast wilderness rang in her ears. "Are we not worth trying to save?" she asked, her voice cracking.

"Perhaps I understated the significance of discovering your civilization. You are just as great a discovery to us as we are to you."

Cora started, confused, and she stood up to meet him. "Why? You said there were three spacefaring civilizations."

"All descended from the same common ancestor." His eyes burned, the nucleus glowing like dim, distant suns. *"When our ancestors departed a dying home world, it is estimated that hundreds of distinct groups fled to other systems, of which three now have descendants. Of the hundreds of life-supporting exoplanets we have discovered, none had evidence of species we considered even capable of advancing. An axiom developed that planets that support life are so competitive and dangerous that advanced civilizations can never evolve, and advancements such as ours are unlikely to the point of impossibility. This is an idea grounded as much in propaganda as reality, as it places the Superorganism at the top of even hypothetical hierarchies.*

"As I told you, complex life in the galaxy is common, even language is common, but advancement, even the potential for advancement, we have only encountered in species that descend from our own common ancestor. Do you understand?"

Cora's breath shuddered, her mind buzzing, her skin tight. He'd never looked at her with such intensity. "No."

"You are the civilization that disproves this axiom. You would be both the greatest discovery in the history of the Superorganism and the greatest threat to its conception of itself as divinely unique."

"Then help us!" she begged. "You keep alluding to this

apparent inevitability that your Superorganism will wipe out our civilization, then you treat it like I shouldn't care about it because it won't happen in my lifetime."

"*I didn't say you shouldn't care. I said I do not have the power to stop it.*"

"Then maybe it isn't about *you* having the power to stop it. Maybe it should be about empowering *us* to protect ourselves. I just can't help but think that the question of whether or not we survive as a species is being answered right now. But you treat it like a given that there's nothing we can do about it. *Please,*" she begged, entwining her hands and bringing them up to her lips. "I don't want to die knowing humanity's days are numbered."

"*I do not have the power to stop it,*" he said. "*And the Fremda group cannot stay on this planet.*"

2 8

"And we still know next to nothing," said Sol. "Knowing their civilization *might*, hypothetically *maybe* want to destroy us in a few hundred years is probably worse than knowing nothing."

Cora looked up at Sol, seated across the table from her in the conference room they'd been using for debriefing. Sol wasn't in great shape, and he'd quit putting effort into hiding it a while ago. He had been sulking about, to again use the technical term, the total shit show of fallout that had resulted from the presidential resignation. As a result, he'd spent more time putting out fires than getting intel from Cora. He looked positively haggard.

"He was very insistent that there was nothing he could do to affect that outcome, one way or another," said Cora.

"That could be a partial truth."

She shrugged. "It might be."

"Or you could be telling me a partial truth."

Cora grew cold, drew her lips into a thin line. With Ampersand, she had been disappointed, and she did not yet know how to process that disappointment, but she was reaching a breaking point with Sol. "We are on the same side."

"Are we, though?" he asked. "From the second you darkened my doorstep, you have been more invested in protecting him than telling the truth."

Her shell toughened further. "That's not true."

Sol sat up and leaned toward her. "No, I think it very much is. I can see you taking in what he says to you and paraphrasing it, omitting key words."

"If he says something hostile and rude, yeah, I'm going to paraphrase it. Doesn't mean I'm not telling the truth."

Sol huffed as though trying to purge the cynicism from his being, if for only a moment, to force himself to approach the situation from a place of empathy rather than bullying. "Look, I understand that you're . . . that maybe you trust the alien a little more than you trust me."

"You think?"

"You should know better," he said, ignoring her shortness. "They hammer this point home all the time at ROSA—you can't anthropomorphize them."

"And yet I know more about them than the people at ROSA do."

"Which leads you to see him as a being that thinks like a *human*. He isn't."

"We kind of have to anthropomorphize. We have to create a framework. Our human brains have a hard time seeing them as persons if we don't."

"Exactly my point!" he snapped. "To Amps, you aren't a person. Deep down, you know this—you're excess detritus as soon as your usefulness wears out."

She glared at him, daring him to keep going.

Sol placed a thumb and forefinger on the bridge of his nose, and he closed his eyes. "You think I want you out of here just because you're underqualified or because you're not with the agency? This is dangerous."

"But you're okay with 'indefinite detention' for my family, who have done nothing."

Sol scoffed, smiling through his bitterness. "Oh, you sweet summer child, they are far safer than you are. We still have an understanding, don't we?"

"Yes. But you also promised me information on my family."

He arched an eyebrow as though he were about to go on the attack and then relented. "What about them?"

"Are they in any danger?"

"Of course they're not in danger," he groaned. "I keep telling you that. *You* are the one who is in danger."

"That's not what I mean. Are their *minds* in danger?"

A look of utter annoyance washed over him, the childish kind she was accustomed to seeing on Felix when she got on his nerves. "What the *fuck* are you on about?"

"You know what I mean. Those people in Pomona and Altadena who disappeared and eventually reappeared with memory loss and brain damage. Is there any chance of that happening to my mother and brother and sister?"

Sol coughed out a breath and then another. It took Cora a moment to realize that he was laughing. Before she could express her incredulity, his laughter turned into a shameless guffaw.

"What's so fucking funny?" Cora demanded, standing up.

But he was gone, lost in a world of mirth that she was no longer capable of even conceiving. "This explains so much!" he managed between laughs, not cruel but careless. "This explains *so* fucking much. Yes, of course you would believe that. Of course. You almost had me fooled."

"What are you talking about?"

"You act like the apple falls so far from the tree," he said, wiping his eyes. "But you are just like your father. Oh, *don't* give me that look."

Cora couldn't help it. He may as well have slapped her. She was entertaining the idea of slapping him.

Sol took a few deep breaths, calming himself, then asked, "Who do you think started pushing this idea of the government using memory wipes to censor witnesses after the Ampersand Event?"

Cora wanted to hang on to that hot anger, ride it, but it was already growing cold. "I don't know."

"Nils may act like his hands are clean, but he employs and promotes conspiracy theory nutjobs who are the exact kind of people he warns against. But they're his supporters, so he never publicly condemns them. *Fuck* me. You really thought it was us." He started laughing again. "This is a fucking farce."

"So you're saying it didn't happen?" Cora demanded, her voice much angrier than she felt.

"Oh, no, it happened!" said Sol, getting up out of his chair and circling the table, stopping right at her feet. "It absolutely happened. But here, I'm going to let you in on a state secret, and don't you tell anyone." He placed his hands on Cora's shoulders, holding them fast. "We have only *one* suspect for who is responsible for the disappearances in Pomona and Altadena. He's even here! In this very complex!" He leaned into her ear, seeming to savor this, and whispered, "But he sure as hell does not work for the U.S. government."

· · · · ·

Cora shut the door behind her, louder than she'd ever dared before. She'd half expected the Fremda group to be gone, but they were still there—Ampersand and Esperas had been conversing before she walked in but fell silent upon seeing her. "They want me to ask you what your plan is."

"*We plan to depart.*"

Esperas didn't look at her but moved into the adjacent room. She knew he couldn't understand human language, but she couldn't help but read judgment into his movement. Like Ampersand was even less worthy of respect because he was being spoken to like this by his own interpreter.

"When?"

"*Soon.*"

"How soon?"

"*Soon.*"

"Is it true?"

The crown on the back of his head bristled, like massive porcupine spines, eyes widening in an implacable expression.

"What Sol said. The people who disappeared and came back with brain damage. Is it true? Were you responsible for that?"

"*Yes.*"

She tried to tamp down the anger that was bubbling up, but it was strong, demanding. It wasn't even born out of being lied to, that was bad enough. It was born from feeling duped, feeling like an idiot that she hadn't even considered this. It hadn't even occurred to her to question Eli Gerrard's narrative; she had never wondered if he even had any evidence. "Why?"

He slowly approached her, pulling up his hands just slightly, until he was almost directly over her. "*When it became clear to me that I would need to employ human bodies to infiltrate ROSA, I had to hastily learn both how to control human action as well as erase short-term memory."*

"Why didn't I have brain damage?"

"Because after a point, I learned how to modify short-term memory without causing brain damage."

"How many people did you take?"

"Fourteen."

That nearly knocked the wind out of her. *Fourteen!*

"I fail to understand how this is a much greater ethical infraction than what I did to you."

She shook her head, looking up at him incredulously. "You lied to me."

"I did not lie to you."

"You could have told me it was *you* who did those things to those people! There's one man who barely remembers how to speak!"

"You have been consciously avoiding ethical questions. This is why I considered it ill advised to tell you about my life or culture from before the purge."

"I told you that I was afraid that the government was going to fry my family's brains because of the mysterious disappearances near the Ampersand Event. This isn't some irrelevant topic. This is the *entire reason* I even offered to help you in the first place!"

"To maintain any sort of control over you, I had to learn how by experimenting on other human subjects first."

"I didn't know *those* were the human subjects!"

"I fail to see where this is an ethical infraction where using humans as experimental subjects in the more distant past is not."

"You mean the language study," she said, her voice low. "'Centuries ago.'"

He stepped away from her and lowered his head like a bull about to charge, a posture which she now understood communicated a warning to stay back. "*It was imperative for the study of alien language. That study is solely the reason I had an algorithm that enabled me to learn English. Without it, it would have taken months, perhaps years, to learn human language. Similarly, I was in a position where I had no choice but to engage with the natives.*"

"Engage," Cora coughed.

"*Conspiracy theories and fictive narratives made finding information through networks impossible. I had to engage, interrogate, and erase the memory of the interrogation.*"

"Have you killed anyone?"

His hands relaxed a bit, but something about his posture, his entire person, felt even more defensive. "*Don't ask questions to which the answer will only upset you.*"

"Have you killed anyone?"

He stilled, then began to back away from her. "*I have never taken the life of a person where the jurisdiction in which I resided did not allow for it by law.*"

"I didn't ask if you'd ever killed anyone illegally. I asked if you'd ever killed anyone."

He seemed to be measuring her, his focus hardening and softening, almost like a pulse. "*Don't ask questions to which the answer will only upset you.*"

She shook her head. "You know what upsets me? Finding out *you're* responsible for something I'd been blaming on the government. Tell me the truth. Did you kill those state troopers? Have you killed anyone?"

Slowly, he moved toward her until he was towering over her. "*I have killed persons. But I have not killed persons on Earth.*"

"Are humans 'persons'?" Her voice was growing tremulous, an uneasy combination of fear and anger. "Or are we animals?"

He didn't respond, just kept watching her with that angry, defensive posture, and somehow, his silence, his inability to answer that most crucial question, one she'd been sidestepping this entire time—*Are we people to you?*

It was his silence that broke her. She was out of anger, out of strength. She raised a hand to her cheek, stunned, numb, staring into nothing. She looked toward one of the doors and saw Esperas staring back at her. Esperas and the two Similars.

"*You had a prior belief in misinformation created and spread by conspiracy theorists. I did not give you this misinformation; I simply did not correct it. Why would I correct misinformation when it works to my benefit that you believe it?*"

Esperas and Ampersand had a short back-and-forth in Pequod-phonemic, she could only imagine what about. What was more insulting? she wondered. Ampersand, who acted like all ends justified the means and feigned seeing humans as people worthy of respect? Feigned seeing *her* as worthy of respect? Sneaked her out, took her to her house, stargazed with her, but with no more care than one might a dog slated for euthanasia at a shelter?

Or Esperas, who made no pretense of any such thing?

"You aren't staying on Earth, and the thing I was so worried about . . . it isn't even the government's doing. It was yours."

She looked back to the door where Esperas had been, but he and the Similars were gone. "God, maybe you were right. Of course you were right. We can get along where we have similarities, but the stuff we find repugnant about each other's cultures . . . it's a deal breaker, isn't it?"

She looked at him, waiting for a response. Hoping for one. This was inevitable, perhaps. The myriad of traits she didn't yet know about that one culture finds repugnant and the other sees no need to change. He had placed so much stress on the idea of Obelus being the reason they could not stay on Earth; why would the natives be worth going to the trouble of protecting if they weren't even "people"? Billions of flesh-eaters. Ravenous, dangerous things that consumed all they touched. Just like the "transients." Monsters, bogeymen, which, for all she knew, may not even exist.

She turned from him and headed toward the door. "I need to go."

. . . . .

It took a while to get all the way from the back of the complex to the entrance, as one had to wind through a network of hallways that weren't exactly a straight line. She didn't have a destination; she just wanted to get as far from him as possible, and without going through any blast doors, the farthest place was the reservoir.

Her first impulse had been to talk to Sol, to tell him to take her wherever he wanted. But no. They had struck a deal, and the deal was close to over. She didn't know what would happen to her or her family after this, but one way or the other, the only thing that was in her control was being a good little puppet for Sol. She'd done the best she could, and at this point, the only priority was signing that stupid gag order and then being released into the new hellworld that Nils had shaped. Probably not better or worse than the old hellworld, just different.

She didn't think she was supposed to be back here, not that she particularly cared. Even with the light shining from the entrance, the reservoir itself was dark, deep, a long tunnel that led to blackness as though it were the entrance to the underworld. She couldn't see to the bottom of the water, either, millions and millions of gallons of it. She wanted to be petty and throw something in it. Herself, for instance.

This would be over soon, she reminded herself. Hours at the most. She could get through this; all she needed to do was the barest possible minimum. If they needed her to be his interpreter one last time, she could do it. But given how easily he'd sneaked her out of the bunker, it was equally possible that the Fremda group would just disappear, and the people running the joint would have no idea where they had gone or how.

And she would never see him again.

For now, she had no choice to take for granted that they would all be released after this, that the only thing that awaited her was a "strict NDA" just like Luciana's, with the threat of an eternity in solitary confinement in a federal prison if she ever so much as thought about going public. The world would vaguely know that First Contact had happened, but the truth about the Fremda would remain a secret until it was no longer politically inexpedient to do so. Which was to say, never.

No one would ever know the details of the contact. No one would ever know that there was a massive existential threat out there that did not yet even know that human civilization was beginning to advance like they had millennia ago.

She felt a low, deep rumble in the distance, sensed a bright light coming through the tunnel. It made her light-headed, punched her as if a bottle of vodka had flooded her system, and she nearly collapsed. The lights flickered, went out, and then struggled to come back to life.

Then the blast doors began to close.

2 9

The lights coughed, sputtered, went off and on intermittently as the blast doors continued their arduous journey shut. She was close enough to one that she considered jumping through it, because being on *this* side of the blast doors was most definitely the wrong side. Trapped, no way out, no defense from beings that would have no problem getting through them, open or otherwise.

She thought about the two Fremdan Similars, monstrous and terrifying and silent, how their stillness belied power. If Obelus contained a multiplier of Brako and Kruro, then she needed to be as far away from them as possible. Ampersand had implied that the American military would be like swatting away flies—they could turn the whole bunker into a fireball, gas it like they were fumigating for cockroaches.

No, she remembered. They could, but they wanted Ampersand alive and the Genome intact.

The sputtering lights stabilized, and the blast doors sealed shut. She heard voices shouting, and on instinct, she backed away from the voices, back toward the darkness of the reservoir. The door was shut. The only thing to do was wait it out. To hide. To survive.

Then her mind's eye summoned the image of Ampersand in the back of the van after the last energy pulse Obelus had sent. Helpless, unprepared. Her conscience tried to override her will to survive. *You can't leave them alone back there.*

The darkness of the cave held her back, womb-like in its promise of safety. Yes, they had parted on bad terms. She had already begun the process of making peace with the fact that their relationship was over. There was no way in hell he'd do the same for her, but if there was something she could do to protect him, she had to at least try.

Pulled along by the string of her own stupid, maladaptive sense of obligation, she ran back toward the entrance to the complex. By the time she reached the lonely door with the short metal staircase, people were already falling out of it like water through a pinhole. No one she recognized as she steeled herself to push through the crowd of people trying to get out—until Vincent Park's face emerged through the chaos.

"Let me through!" she said, trying to cram herself into an opening. The instant he saw her, his normally gentle demeanor turned to steel, and he grabbed her by the arm as he fell out into the cavern.

"No one gets in," he said.

"We have to get them out of here," she said, counting every second and trying not to fall into panic. "This is the exact same thing that happened on the Google campus. They're probably unconscious. We *have* to get them out of here!"

"We're cut off."

Cora turned to see the source of another familiar voice spilling out of the door. It was Sol, the latest in the train of people. All these people were military or intelligence. Not a single one of Luciana's colleagues. She turned again and saw the person who had grabbed her wrist. It was Vincent Park.

"We can't get any word down there," said Kaplan. "None of our equipment works."

Panic shot through her like a geyser. "We have to get them out of there!"

Cora saw Sol give Vincent a look. "I'm sorry," said Vincent, starting to pull her back toward the blast doors. "This is a button-up. Everyone is at their stations."

"Vincent, *no!*" she cried.

Going by their expressions, both Sol and Vincent believed her, but that didn't mean they weren't slaves to protocol. "We have orders," said Vincent. "It's buttoned up. No one gets back there."

"We don't have more than a few minutes. *We have to get out of here!*" Cora's eyes darted wildly to the blast doors, then to the door to the complex, which had by now stopped spilling out airmen, who had by now all gone to their posts.

Vincent clapped a hand over her mouth. "Calm down!" he snapped in a voice she hadn't thought him capable of.

She tore his hand away. She knew she wasn't helping her case, but she couldn't contain her panic. It was a miracle they'd gotten away from the Google campus—she didn't expect to get away again. "Don't you get it? Those doors aren't going to keep them out!"

"There's nothing we can do," said Vincent, his characteristic calm returning. "Ghasabian is down there; they're not alone."

Then Cora felt a rumble, something deep and quiet like one of the minor earthquakes that one got used to after living in Southern California for a while, barely noticeable. Seconds later, a second tremor, this one strong enough to nearly knock her off her feet. The springs under the main complex creaked and groaned, and the loud chatter of the airmen yelling at each other also ceased. Everyone braced themselves.

Then another rumble shook them, and the three of them fell to their knees. The rock ceiling above split the room with a deafening *crack*. Another rumble, this one louder and closer. Then the sound of a collapse, some machinery falling, metal crunching, airmen barking out orders.

Then the wall of the cavern split, and a deep snapping sound echoed throughout the bunker. Whatever was coming in was already on them, right on the other side of the blast doors. Vincent grabbed Cora, pushed her to her feet and against the wall of the cavern, and then forced her down onto her stomach.

She looked up, down the several-meter causeway to the blast doors, and again the lights flickered. Besides the creaking of the mountain and the echo of water dripping from the rocks, the dark corridor was silent.

She turned to look at the blast door, but it was gone. Not open, just gone. The sputtering lights made it difficult to see, but it was as though the door one moment *was,* then it *wasn't*. It didn't really melt, rather, shrank in on itself, seemed to crumple like ancient, weathered paper. The mass or density of the metal didn't change but rather collapsed, creating a sound like burning wood blown out to its highest decibel. And what stood in its place possessed the body of a Similar.

Obelus.

Cora stopped breathing, and even Sol wore an expression of abject shock. Obelus was huge, bigger than Brako and Kruro, obvious even from her vantage point hundreds of feet away, bigger than a Cadillac, and like the others, he didn't seem to obey the laws of gravity. It was hard to pin down how, but Obelus looked *newer* than the other ones. As he stepped through what remained of the blast doors, he moved as if he were walking through moon gravity, despite his massive size. Then three more Similars appeared behind him, their invisibility cloaks melting away.

The three of them stayed in line behind the leader, the biggest of the bunch. Obelus moved his head like a sonar, scanning, and for one horrible instant, his eyes fell on the cowering mass of humanity that included Cora. These eyes were cool, blue gray, but in terms of brightness and intensity, closer to Ampersand's than she'd seen from any of them, even the two Fremdan Similars.

Obelus approached the side of the main building, stopping in front of the lonely door, and examined it for a few seconds. Then a hole tore itself in the corner of the building as though a laser blast melted a tunnel right through it, but there was no liquefaction, no red glow of hot metal. It just shriveled back like old leaves in the fall and crunched away just as easily, until the side of the building revealed a hole large enough for them to easily slip through.

Then the cloak of invisibility fell over Obelus, and seconds later, the same cloak fell over the other three, all of them unnaturally silent despite their size. No one moved or said a word for about a minute.

"We're going," said Sol, and Vincent Park hoisted Cora up by her waist and onto her feet and shoved her toward where the blast door once was.

The three of them, plus a few others who were not actively stationed, ran through the remains of the blast doors to the parking area on the other side. Vincent shoved her into the back of a jeep, and she shook out of it long enough to realize that Sol had not hopped in the jeep with them. The jeep zoomed out of the complex before she had the chance to brace herself, through the tunnel, out the entrance, and into the crisp evening air. The sun had almost set as the jeep tore down the curves of the mountain. Terror still lit up her veins, and she held her breath as she looked back toward the entrance of the complex, knowing that Obelus could easily destroy the jeep even from deep inside the mountain.

After about five minutes of driving, the jeep stopped at a heliport, and everyone piled out. Several helicopters were headed their way, and one was ready to lift them out, the first group to arrive.

She allowed Vincent to tear her out of the back of the jeep. He led her to the largest of the three helicopters, its blades not even slowing as it waited for them to board. Cora swallowed her bile, her mind reeling at the prospect of putting themselves in this big, tempting target. It was a military helicopter, complete with an array of guns next to the doors. She wondered if they honestly thought those guns would do any damage. Vincent strapped her in, his expression sympathetic as though that was supposed to make up for this.

The chopper engines revved up, preparing to take off. Her muscles were tensed into sinewy, brittle bands, and the image of Čefo's nervous system turning to ash in midair sprang to her mind. She had a vivid mental image of what it would look like for the same to happen to a human body.

"Hold it!" Sol's voice. She turned and saw another jeep pulling up. After he hopped from his jeep, he hauled out a big plastic Sterilite container and jogged over to the helicopter with Cora and Vincent. They jammed the box into the chopper and strapped it in, still fastening it as the helicopter took off. Every second in the helicopter, Cora felt like her terror might break her apart at the seams. Were the CIA field agents used to this sort of thing? If they weren't, they hid it well. They were stressed but clearheaded. By the end of the helicopter ride, she thought she might have even started to get used to constant terror. Vincent unbuckled her when they got to the airport in Colorado Springs. A military jet was waiting for them.

She stayed put while they gathered themselves, her thoughts still with Ampersand, what was happening with him and the rest of the Fremda group. Had he been prepared for this? He had to be. He was far too conniving to be caught unawares. It was only now that the absurdity of her trying to get back into the complex to help him caught up with her. What exactly could she have done, other than stand in the way like an insect to be swatted aside?

Vincent led her away from the helicopter toward the plane. Another airman approached Sol, and the two started yelling to each other to be heard over the din of the chopper, but Cora couldn't hear them over the noise. She then saw Sol and another agent open the big Sterilite container to show the airman what was inside.

It was the Genome.

The plane landed at Dulles somewhere in the space between late and early. Cora hadn't spoken to Vincent, Sol, or anyone the whole flight. After about an hour, she started to entertain the notion that Obelus did not intend to blow them out of the sky, and the less terrified she became, the heavier her heart grew. To Obelus, the humans in the bunker were at most collateral, but best case, something to be ignored altogether. Vermin in the sewer that scurry when a light is shone on them. The humans of Cheyenne Mountain were not what Obelus was after. It was difficult not to think about the small likelihood that any Fremda made it out of that elaborate rabbit hole alive, or any human who got in the way, for that matter. She told herself that Ampersand had been prepared, that he had his ways and had gotten them out.

Either way, she was never going to see him again.

Entering the complex at Langley was like being displaced in the time stream, the corrugated, bright ornamental elegance a world away from the cave ceilings and Spartan, U-boat halls she'd been calling home for the last week. It was sharp, state of the art, open, and bright even in the early-morning hours. There was even a Starbucks. Cora expected to be taken to a cold, uncomfortable interrogation room; instead, Vincent took her into an office with faux-leather seats, a big oak desk, and even a patriotic portrait of Andrew Jackson that took up half the wall. They brought in the Sterilite container with the Genome as well.

She felt like her veins had dried into husks from spending so many hours in terror; it was only now that she had the opportunity to breathe, to an experience an emotion other than the fear that comes with standing on the precipice of death. And all she could think was that she would never see him again. She would spend the rest of her life wondering what had happened to him.

Vincent returned in short order and made a flaccid attempt at small talk before quickly giving up after she refused to reciprocate. She tried to take a nap and nodded off a few times but kept jolting awake, imagining that she heard thumping noises coming from the Sterilite container.

Sol came back just as the sun was starting to peek through the trees outside the window. He was tired, as tired as she was if not more so. He took a seat on the other side of the desk. "Coffee?"

Her position on the opposite side of the desk from Sol, Vincent flanking her left, made her feel like she'd been sent to detention for some girl-drama infraction that may or may not mean the end of the world. Were these people her enemies? Her allies? She couldn't think straight. "Yeah."

Sol nodded to Vincent, who left the room without pause or smile, and forced a smile at her. Not a smug smile, nor a confrontational one. A tired, empty smile.

"Is this your office?" she asked.

"For the moment."

"You know anything?"

Sol shook his head, leaning back in his chair, tapping his fingers against the desk. "Not anything worth knowing."

Her eyes stung; her cheeks grew hot. "What does that mean?"

"Means we've still got intel coming in. Good news and bad news." Cora clenched her jaw. "Bad news is military casualties. Most of them from rubble. No body count yet, but . . . anything greater than nothing is, needless to say, bad. More bad news is the rooms where the Fremda group was housed were completely mowed down. I suppose the good news on that front is that they haven't found any amygdaline bodies, except for Čefo's and one of the Similars. Brako, we think. The bad news is that they haven't found any living ones, either."

Her stomach tightened like a string on a violin about to break. "So they're just . . . gone?"

"It would seem so."

"What about the ROSA people?"

Sol continued to rock in his chair, not meeting her gaze. "A few confirmed deaths."

"Dr. Sev?"

"He's alive."

Cora thought she should feel relief at that, but the first thing that popped into her mind was a sort of indignation. This was a dramatic, terrible thing that had happened, but it wasn't even a taste of what was to come. Dr. Sev had treated the Superorganism as an existential threat, yes, but one that was too far away to get really worked up about, one the current iteration of humanity probably wouldn't even live to see. She wondered if he was still taking such a blasé attitude this morning. "Didn't I warn you?"

"You did warn us," Sol laughed. "I'm CIA; I have no say in what the DOD does. I don't envy the guy who has to write the families."

Cora remembered the blast door. Three feet of solid metal shrinking in on itself like it had been dehydrated, deflated, and then simply *wasn't*. Čefo's nervous system that turned to ash midair.

"Truth is, based on how those airmen died," he said, "Obelus seems to have ways to . . . dissolve the organic matter in the body. They didn't even see them fire anything."

"Please, don't tell me any more."

He shrugged as if this were a weekly thankless debrief that he would forget about in an hour. "My point is, we may never identify any remains down in the compound if they used that method to kill them." He leaned forward to offer her a tissue from the box at the front of the desk. Cora refused it, determined not to let him see her cry.

"On the plus side," he continued, "we're pretty confident if they'd done that to any of the Fremda, it would have left more of a mess. Shells and whatnot, since they're mostly inorganic."

"They'd have a different method to kill other amygdalines," said Cora.

"That may be, but my point is we've only found the remains of one of the Similars, and that one appears to have been taken care of the old-fashioned way."

She looked back up at him, her gaze turned to ice. "Okay, it's over, and we survived. So let me go. Let my family go. We had a deal. I stayed on. I did what I was told. Now give us our NDA, and let us move on with our lives."

Sol tipped his head to the side. "I know you're relatively new to this, but you have to have guessed that it's not going to be as simple as that."

She had. Of course she had, but she felt as if she were being sucked into quicksand all the same, struggling against her own helplessness. Sol pulled out a briefcase, and Cora recognized it as the leather satchel Dr. Sev had with him at Čefo's autopsy. He opened it and pulled out some of Čefo's transcriptions, the pages and pages of "lorem ipsum," alongside some scaled-down photocopies of Čefo's drawing of the two planets. The blue planet. The red planet. "Earth 2" and "Erythrá."

"Why?" she breathed, staring at the photocopies in slight disbelief. "NORAD just got mowed down. Why are we going back over this now?"

"Yeah, well, this is something I had hoped we would be able to go over before the Fremda group left. I've been puzzling over this blue-planet-red-planet thing. I was looking at them, and I noticed something." He slid two photocopies in front of her, side by side. "You notice that the landmasses are kind of shaped the same on both?" He pointed toward the shorelines on Earth 2, and to the outline of mountain shadows on Erythrá. "Just this one has water, and this one doesn't."

She felt a coat of ice spread through her chest as she realized what he was getting at. The landmasses on one, the mountain covering on the other. The haze surrounding one, the lack of atmosphere on the other. These weren't drawings of two planets. This was not an attempt to impart to humanity the beauty and majesty of their home world. These drawings were a before and after.

These were the same planet.

Erythrá was the transient planet that the Superorganism had sterilized. *The oceans boiled. Nothing survived.* These images were a depiction of the Erythrán sterilization, the same planet at different points in time. Čefo had tried at first with a failed attempt to learn written language, and then with an attempt at symbolic language, through drawings. Čefo had been trying to warn them.

And Ampersand had known.

Going by his expression, Sol had come to this conclusion a long time ago. "So now what?"

She shook her head, closed her eyes. She was so, so tired. Something about Ampersand hiding the truth about Čefo's failed attempt to warn humanity about the Erythrán sterilization should have felt like a betrayal, but it didn't. Ampersand had been convinced of his own powerlessness. Perhaps Čefo saw some hope in warning humanity about the possibility, felt that there was some way to avoid Earth coming to the same fate, but Ampersand didn't.

Vincent was back now with a fresh, hot cup of coffee. She took it with shaking hands, feeling like she'd had more coffee these two weeks than she'd had in her entire life. Vincent smiled like an actor who wasn't getting paid and took a seat behind her.

Cora looked at the box with the Genome in it. She had expected something more secure-looking, something along the vein of a safe. The box they'd thrown the Genome in looked like Tupperware blown up to the size of a trunk.

"Shouldn't this be in lockdown in a lab somewhere?" she asked.

"The powers that be are still figuring that out."

"You don't have anywhere better to put it in the meantime, though?" she asked. "Somewhere more secure?"

"The only thing that matters at this particular juncture, as per my recommendation, is keeping the Genome close to you."

Cora straightened. "Why?"

"Because," he said, "owing to the very strange circumstances that have brought us here, you are still the world's foremost expert on extraterrestrial life. And owing to the fact that we have that"—he nodded to the box—"the thing all extraterrestrial parties seemed interested in, my recommendation to the powers that be is that this is not over. Therefore, we keep you and the Genome together at all times."

"Whatever happened to keeping me safe?" asked Cora. "I thought the best thing for me and everyone was that I cease involvement in this whole debacle, go sign a gag order, and go home."

Sol sighed, still maintaining that tired expression, running his hand over his face that by now had gone at least three days without a shave. "I say to you now what I said to you a week ago," he said, a tremor in his voice. "This is existential."

Cora caught his meaning, but a part of her refused to accept that he, or anyone, could see her as being that important, that consequential. "What do you mean?"

The thinnest of smiles carved itself onto his face. "I mean that your personal safety is a somewhat secondary concern next to the survival of human civilization."

She looked at Vincent, for some reason expecting a sympathetic face, but he was stone solemn. "How could I possibly affect that?"

"By knowing," he said. "And sharing that intelligence. You do know where you are, right? This is the agency . . . for central intelligence. You might call it a . . . central intelligence agency."

"Fine." Her voice was shaking. Her fists were shaking. Every part of her being felt as if it were about to shatter. "I'll tell you what he told me a couple of days ago. If all signs point to the Superorganism wanting us wiped out before we can advance enough to pose any kind of threat to them, I begged him to help us. He flat-out told me that even if he wanted to, which I'm not sure he does, he can't. 'I cannot even protect myself from the Superorganism or from our sister species.' That's what he told me, and that's effectively what he left me with. So I don't see what I could possibly offer humanity on an existential level. The only individual in this equation with even the remotest chance of being useful is convinced that he can't influence anything."

"And you're his 'interpreter,'" said Sol. "Believe me, I find it absurd, too. But you're the only bridge we have for communication. And this?" He nodded toward the Genome box. "This isn't over. So I'm keeping you with the Genome. And if that means Obelus finds you with it"—his mouth thinned to a flat line, and he shrugged—"well, who knows? Maybe Obelus will talk to you, too."

Cora shook her head. "Every implication I've gotten is that Obelus has zero interest in talking to us."

"Neither did Ampersand until you convinced him to." He continued to stare at her as he sat back in his chair. "There was a massive protest in D.C. yesterday. Thousands showed up. 'Truth is a human right,' after all. We have your father to thank for that."

She laughed hollowly. "I'm sorry I share genes with that man. But I don't know him. I don't have anything to do with him."

"You really don't." Sol continued to observe her. She looked away, focusing on her coffee. "Remember when I asked you about the name *The Broken Seal*? Why he named it that?"

"I don't want to talk about Nils."

"Well, I do. Yesterday, he was parroting this quote about 'the noise of thunder' from Revelation. Goading these 'The End Is Near' doomsday prepper types. *And I heard, as it were the noise of thunder . . . And I saw, and behold a white horse: and he that sat on him had a bow; and a crown was given unto him: and he went forth conquering, and to conquer.*"

Cora kept staring at her coffee.

"These people think the world is ending. Nils is encouraging them. You think he believes it? You think he knows how close to the truth he is?"

She looked up at him, drained. She felt her face growing hot.

Sol tilted his head at her and chuckled. "He says he doesn't want anything to do with the religious nuts, but he's drumming up their panic and has them marching lockstep behind him. Well, funny thing, based on what we know now, he may not need the crazies to back him up on the whole doomsday thing. He might not be wrong, but he doesn't know that. For him, it's just opportunity. He doesn't care about First Contact. This whole debacle is just scaffolding to his own narcissism. It's just theater to elevate Nils Ortega, and he has no idea that what he's doing right now might be the single most destructive thing any one human has ever done."

"What does that have to do with me?" demanded Cora. "Why are we making this about Nils?"

"Because you and I are not like him," he said, the tiredness in his expression turning to intensity, and he leaned forward. "We know that Nils may not be wrong about secret-keeping, but we also know that the secrets we keep aren't just fodder for the theater of one man's narcissism. This is *fucking* existential. Ampersand's assessment of his own powerlessness isn't the only perspective in the universe. Frankly, I don't accept it. I'm not ready to surrender to genocide. Are you?"

Cora started to speak but thought she heard a noise coming from the Genome box, the same thing she thought she'd heard in her half dreams earlier. Sol seemed to hear it, too. He pulled out a phone, spoke into it, asking for backup. Cora stood up, looking at the box.

"I thought you just took their Genome," said Cora.

"I thought so, too," said Sol.

Again, another noise, this time like scraping. The slightest of bumps, but this time unmistakable. Sol pulled out his handgun, approached the box, and opened it.

The Genome they had brought, the smooth egg sac, was no longer there. In its place was a creature, one that resembled an amygdaline, but this thing was not like the sleek cybernetic creatures they had grown accustomed to. Unlike the others, it had a segmented tail extending from its slender body like a scorpion's, black beady eyes, even a mouth, a mouth covered with some sort of apparatus that stretched to the gills on its neck, covering it completely.

Before she could even begin to conjecture on what it was, it looked at both of them in turn and screamed.

31

The screeching sound drove the three humans against the opposite wall, the living, screaming, and ostensibly thinking contents of the box just as surprised to see a group of humans as they were to see it. The creature stumbled out of the box but collapsed under its own weight as it tried to pull itself toward the window, continuing that awful wail.

It clearly wasn't a true post-natural amygdaline, as it lacked the silvery iridescent skin, the size, the sleek biosynthetic body. This thing had real, living skin that was dark and even splotchy in places, the color of a brick that had been drained of saturation. The skin seemed married at points with the skeleton, which, like the other amygdalines', appeared to be a sort of hybrid of an endoskeleton and an exoskeleton, both beneath the skin and a part of it. Where Ampersand had no lower jaw at all, this thing had something almost mandibular, opening up in a dozen tiny mandibulate mouthparts more like a grasshopper's than a vertebrate's. But it was not the mouth from whence the noises came but the air holes on the side of the neck, same as post-natural amygdalines.

"Humans don't need to know irrelevant stuff, huh?" said Sol.

It managed to get up on its haunches to crawl behind the desk. Cora's attention stayed fixed on the pitiful creature struggling under its own weight. It was hard not to be repulsed by the thing; its natural, biological body made it disgusting in a way that the rest of the Fremda group was not. Based on the repetition of sounds, the way pieces of them sounded like Pequod-phonemic, the Genome seemed to be speaking a language, but it was definitely not Pequod-phonemic. Perhaps this Genome was not capable of network language or even common language.

Cora didn't immediately recognize it because of how different it looked from human clothes, but it was also "clothed" in a way that the post-natural amygdalines, their bodies themselves acting as vehicles, didn't need to be. It looked like a thin sheen that covered her body, clinging to her skin like a sheet of sugary icing.

"'Genetic material.' That lying cyborg sack of shit," said Sol. "Yeah, this is 'genetic material.'"

Cora remembered how Ampersand had responded when she'd confronted him about the disappearances; of *course* he hadn't volunteered that information. Why correct misinformation when it worked to his benefit that she believed misinformation? He had not *lied*. What was this if not more of the same?

"This one of their enemies? The sister species? Sloop John B?" asked Vincent.

"I don't think so," said Cora. "I think it's one of *them,* a natural *them,* or at least as natural as they're going to get."

"What do you mean?" asked Sol.

"She doesn't look completely natural," said Cora. "She's got some of the gray amygdaline cybernetic stuff on her head, see?"

"'*She*'?" He looked at her with such an incredulity one might have thought she'd proposed to marry the creature.

"Why not 'she'?" said Cora. It was hard to make herself heard over the pitiful cries of this thing, like a dolphin and a sheep had a screaming baby.

"Quiet!" whispered Vincent. Cora saw the Genome reach toward the window, peek out, then hide behind the desk again, warbling in that unfamiliar language. "I called for containment."

"No, not more people," said Cora. "She's freaking out."

"We have to do something with it," said Sol.

"Keep your voices down," whispered Cora. "If that egg sac hasn't even been opened since they've been here, she's been in some sort of stasis for at least forty years; she may not even know what planet she's on."

The Genome made a noise like a tiny beached whale. Sol looked at Cora and laughed. "You're right; that thing's some kind of 'natural.' Naturals need food and water. Clearly, something right now is ailing it very much. We have no way of figuring out what that might be and no way to translate its language. The slightest impurity or pathogen could kill it. So it might have behooved us to know a little bit of protocol as to how to deal with this thing, because right now, I don't feel too good about little Genie's survival."

The containment unit, wearing hazmat suits, entered the room with a stretcher. The Genome saw this and protested weakly. She seemed to speak to the agents as they put her on the stretcher, but she didn't fight them. The whole scene made Cora want to cry. The Genome was roughly the size of an eight-year-old girl, and she was being tackled and pinned by half a dozen grown men in hazmats. They tried to put her on her back, but she resisted, forcing herself on her side, mewling intermittently. Before long, she quieted down.

"Let's make sure this *is* an amygdaline and not a prisoner, one of their enemies," said Sol as they pushed her out of the room on the stretcher.

Cora doubted that the Genome was a transient. The witness sketches from the "abduction files" Sol had shown her at NORAD did look more like this little guy than Ampersand, but transients had a different facial structure and skin color, and they seemed *much* larger and more intimidating, Similar-sized rather than child-sized. This was "genetic material." Of course she needed to stay in the body she was born in.

They took the Genome to a clean room elsewhere in the complex. Cora had to shower off first, getting clean before receiving a hazmat suit of her own. The containment team's goal in the short term was to figure out whether little "Genie" was, in fact, a non-biosynthetic, "natural" amygdaline and not some other species. The Genome had a filter over the opening of its air holes like wet cling wrap but also a thin, translucent film over its entire body, presumably to protect from pathogens in the outside world. The film even covered its mouth, but it seemed like it could be permeated through some as-yet-undetermined means; matter, effluvium, excrement could get in and out, but only selectively.

"See if you can get it to react," Sol instructed her.

The clean room reminded her of an ICU, and the Genome looked like a desperately premature infant, complete with a little plastic bed with transparent walls. The Genome wasn't lying on her side anymore but was roosting in that deerlike manner Ampersand did when in repose. Every few seconds, she stole a glance at Cora before staring ahead into nothing. She almost had the obsidian eyes of the propagandists, but there was a bright spot in those eyes, the retinal reflection that unmistakably betrayed what the creature was focusing on. One thing their respective species apparently had in common—staring was an act of aggression, and the Genome was desperately trying not to make eye contact.

Sol told Cora that they had succeeded in giving the creature some distilled water, which she imbibed through the protective film covering her body. Someone had prepared this little guy for travel *before* putting her in that egg. Someone had prepared her for the eventuality that she might be exposed to the pathogens and harsh climate of an alien world.

The Genome seemed to be in shock. While she wasn't making those awful noises anymore, she wasn't making eye contact or moving, either. The feeling of being one of the myriad horrors in a den full of monsters made Cora move even more carefully. By this point, the Genome had decided she had stolen enough glances and now stared straight ahead.

Cora racked her brain for something, anything helpful that would provoke a reaction but not read as aggressive. She hadn't even learned any body language from the Fremda other than the universal baseline that came with being descended from naturally evolving animals: hands up like a spider on the defense was "antagonistic." Head forward was a challenge. She hadn't learned anything that might deescalate.

She pulled up a chair, put it in the Genome's line of sight, and sat down in front of her. Slowly, as if she hoped Cora wouldn't notice, the Genome averted her gaze to the floor but kept her eyes open. The way she moved her head reminded Cora of an abused dog.

She placed her hand into the Genome's line of sight, and this time, the Genome didn't even bother to avert her gaze. Cora tried a few variations on hand movements, holding her right hand up next to her head, then holding it to the plastic walls of the Genome's tiny prison. No reaction.

She hadn't been in the clean room for more than half an hour before she saw Vincent Park on the other side of the window, gesturing for her to come outside. Cora obeyed, leaving the room and taking off her flimsy plastic helmet.

"We've got to get it out of here," said Vincent. "Director just arrived, and after what happened last night, he does not want that creature here. Don't want to risk the Obelus Similars attacking Langley like they did up in the mountains."

"How did Obelus find out where the compound was so quickly?" asked Cora, shimmying out of the rest of the hazmat suit.

Vincent shrugged. "I don't know if we'll ever know. I heard a few guesses floating around this morning. Most popular one is that the DOD left too obvious a paper trail, all those intelligence goons from their department heading up there, sending emails, not encrypting them. Kaplan's sending us away in a small motorcade. Just a couple of vehicles."

"Where are we going?"

He laughed. "I can't tell you because I don't know. He wants to keep you with the Genome, though."

"Yeah," Cora sighed, too exhausted to feel anything. "I know."

Within an hour, the Genome had been strapped on a stretcher, zipped inside of a bag that looked like it was made for dry cleaning, and attached to an oxygen tank. They loaded up into a big blue van shaped like an ambulance, with Cora and Vincent in the back and another two agents in the front, and departed Langley. In all this time, she had only been able to wash off the previous day's terror before she went into the clean room. She still wore the jeans and T-shirt that she'd had for most of her stay at NORAD, still stinking with fear sweat.

Either exhaustion or experience had taken some toll on her, because she wasn't crippled with the debilitating terror she'd experienced in the helicopter. She was even able to steal a bit of sleep during the drive. Not much, but by the time she opened her eyes again, the sun was high in the sky. She had no idea where they were. They seemed to be taking back roads.

They were in farm country, mountains on all sides. They must have gone inland, as they were in the foothills. Cora could see a few houses nearby, but beyond that, they seemed to be firmly in the middle of nowhere.

She looked at the Genome and then at Vincent, who sat across the stretcher from her. He was dead asleep. She looked down at the Genome, now so close to her, eyes closed. Wrapped in plastic, she reminded Cora of Čefo's corpse, a wax sculpture of a movie monster.

He must be alive, she thought. He had to be. Like Sol said, there would have been bodies if they hadn't gotten out. And if he was alive and the tracker he'd implanted was still operational, then he knew where she was. While the tracker in her neck likely didn't have a range limit as long as he was on the planet, the bud he'd put in her ear probably did. But even if it didn't, there was a certain finality to their last interaction. It had been genuine. She had been angry, and he had deliberately kept what he had done to his experimental subjects from her to keep her compliant. Moreover, he did not see anything wrong with what he had done. He never would.

All the same, she worried for him. And she missed him. "Ampersand," she whispered. "Can you hear me?"

Nothing.

Cora thought about whatever non-plan Sol had for them. Find some local black site, stash them there, and wait to see who showed up, she supposed. Obelus or Ampersand, whoever came first.

Cora was considering allowing herself to doze again when a bright light flooded her retinas like milk. Her mind went fuzzy, and she was only jerked violently back into consciousness when the van swerved and crashed into a tree.

The seat belt nearly sliced into her clavicle, and on instinct, she tore it off before the car had even settled. The following instant, the SUV behind them crashed into the back of the van, breaking the glass in both back doors and crushing the SUV's hood.

The SUV engine hissed with steam, and someone in the front seat groaned in pain. As Cora regained her bearings, she snapped quickly back to alertness. She looked across at Vincent, but it looked to her like he'd been injured, his head lolling forward.

The crash had sent the Genome's gurney banging into the wall toward the front of the van. There was movement coming from inside the bag, and in shockingly fast order, the bag ripped open, and the little alien squirmed out of it. The Genome's strange skeletal structure gave her some very sharp fingers, sharp enough to rip right through the plastic film. It was only here that she looked at Cora. As with humans, the pulse clearly did not have an effect on the non-biosynthetic Genome.

Cora recoiled in instinctive revulsion as if a giant spider had crawled out of a burrow in the ground. With swift, surprisingly powerful movements, the Genome had powered her little body through the broken glass and out of the van.

She is going to fucking kill herself.

Cora gaped at the open window, stunned that the Genome was even physically capable of what she'd just done. Vincent stirred, and her mind immediately jumped back to Cheyenne Mountain, her screaming that those blast doors were going to do fuck all, Vincent knowing full well it was true but ignoring her and holding her fast regardless. The way he and the rest of the men had forced her along, not even pausing to listen to her. She, the only person who had lived through one of these pulse attacks before.

Vincent's eyes batted open, and he looked at her in confusion. On impulse, Cora grabbed the side of the gurney the Genome had been on and flipped it over to pin him in place. There was a part of her that realized how hard the shove was, that it had gone farther than she'd meant it to, the sound it had made when it contacted his skull. The sound was like the time she had tried and failed to split open a coconut with a hammer when she was ten. Such a distant memory—long enough ago for it to have been Nils who stepped in and did it correctly.

She was already out of the van when she registered the sound of Vincent retching, but she pushed that away as well. She had to get away. She had seen Obelus before; she never wanted to see it again.

Her eyes scanned the horizon and only just spotted an alien creature making for the tree line, each step more belabored than the last. Cora knew that the safest place for her to be was as far from the Genome as possible, but the creature was clearly acting on instinct, running from the monsters that had captured her with no clear concept of what was at stake, what might be lurking in those woods, or what she was even physically capable of. If someone didn't go after her, either Obelus was going to catch her or she was going to fucking die.

3 2

The Genome had run into a patch of woods about thirty feet from the road, and Cora only just caught a glimpse of her before she disappeared into it. Cora powered after her, shocked at how fast she was able to run considering how labored her movements had been earlier. Even so, the Genome was absolutely no match for a fully grown human.

Cora caught up to the Genome in seconds, grabbing her and nearly wrestling her to the ground, ignoring any caution she felt about the Genome's fragility. Either she had to be tough enough to handle this, or she would die either way. Cora had expected her to crumple like wet origami, but the Genome fought her, flailing to wrench free from her grasp. No noise came forth from her mouth, but the Genome opened it, and Cora spasmed with revulsion. The mouthparts looked like a giant insect, and she had her sharp fingers up in that manner Ampersand did when he was on the defense. It was really hard not to look at this thing and see an animal, a monster, to imagine that there was an intelligence in that head.

Imagine it's Olive, she thought, hoisting up the Genome, shocked to find how light she was, lighter than a human child her size. She was barely heavier than a toddler. The Genome tried to fight her, scratch her neck and pull away, but Cora grabbed her arms. The animal noises coming from the thing triggered the lizard part of Cora's brain—*This is an animal; this is an alien.* Again, she thought of Olive, imagined her sister alone on an alien planet. Imagined some well-meaning idiot alien monster trying to port her off to safety, even if she didn't understand that was what was happening. Reminding herself that this was a *person* she was dealing with, not an animal.

The image of Obelus appearing in the circle of a deconstructed twenty-foot blast door at NORAD flashed in her mind, propelling her forward through the woods. She stole a glance behind her toward the direction she'd just come from and was surprised to see no one was following her. She had two options: hide or keep running. The last time Obelus had used a pulse to attack, it had taken him less than two minutes to show up. Through the trees, less than a couple of city blocks away, she saw the white of a farmhouse. She opted to hide.

When she reached the house, it looked like no one was home. One old car out front, but no sign of life or movement inside. She had made it to the house's back door when the first low-frequency hum, something that could only have come from a blast of some kind, rocked her body.

She didn't bother knocking on the door. Headlocking the Genome in her left arm, she picked up a brick from a pile next to the house and heaved it through the pane of glass in the kitchen door. Keeping her arm locked around the Genome's neck, she reached through the broken shards with her free arm to unlock it from the inside.

The Genome thrashed again, pushing and pulling and trying to get away. Cora held on to her, but the Genome thrashed hard enough to jerk her away from the door, and the shards of newly broken glass ripped a deep tear in the flesh of her forearm.

Cora shrieked, more from shock than pain as her skin opened like a bursting water balloon, blood flooding all over the door. She forced the Genome back toward her as she unlocked it, the windowpane now soaked in her blood. The Genome seemed to know what she had done and fought even harder to get away from Cora. Cora pulled her back and hoisted her up as she finally got the door open.

"Is anyone here?" she called, not waiting for a response as she moved through the kitchen, stopping next to the staircase and huddling there as though preparing for an earthquake, the Genome continuing to fight her.

She kept her uninjured arm locked around the Genome as she moved toward a window in the living room near the house's front door. The pulse had certainly been targeting the caravan, but why use a pulse to target a bunch of humans? Why not just napalm the place, burn them all, destroy any and all possible survivors?

"What makes you special to them?" she had asked Ampersand back in the Nevada desert, the first time they had ever conversed.

"My intelligence."

No, there had to be more to it than that. They wanted Ampersand unharmed, and given that this was always their attack of choice against him, there must have been something dangerous about him—else why try to knock him out before capturing him? The pulse attacks Obelus used must have had the same effect on them as it had on Ampersand if directly exposed and, therefore, they needed to stay well out of the range of the pulse as well.

That meant Obelus thought Ampersand was *here*.

She dropped the Genome next to the window, and the Genome pulled herself under a table, moaning softly, and then became still. The living room itself seemed full of hand-me-down furniture. This was not the house of a grandma who had lovingly cared for her belongings for generations but more likely the inheritance thereof. The floor was dusty, the house unkempt, and the grime clung to the viscous filter-membrane that covered the Genome as much as Cora's blood did.

Cora finally allowed herself to collapse for a moment before dragging herself up on her knees and looking out the dusty old single-pane window. She could see the car crash in the distance, the gentle whisper of steam still escaping the front hood of the SUV crashed into the back of the van Cora and the Genome had escaped from. It looked like the driver of the SUV was badly hurt, and the passenger had come to his aid. She had no doubt that the blood she'd left on that kitchen door would give away where she was, whether anyone knew she'd been butchered or not, and she debated whether or not to go clean it up.

Suddenly, both the SUV and the van were dashed into nothingness, as if they been unzipped, their contents gently, *quietly,* turned to ash, falling to the ground like a gentle snowfall. Cora pulled in a breath so loud it was almost a scream, and she clapped her hands over her mouth. The remains of the vehicles looked like burned paper but maintained their mass, their weight, and collapsed into the earth appropriately.

Cora nearly choked on her own scream as she pulled away

from the window. She only now realized how shallow and fast her breathing was.

Vincent.

Then another hum shook the house, accompanied by a bright glow coming from the direction of where the motorcade had stopped, and the same happened to the people standing by the vehicles. A flash like a photo, and then there was nothing but ash floating in the breeze.

Cora managed to stay silent this time, grasping her arm firmly to slow the bleeding as she lowered her face so that only her eyes peered over the windowsill, carefully, slowly moving away from the window, as there was a chance the Similars might hear her. Then one of the Similars took down its cloak.

It was the same one she'd seen the night before. Obelus, the leader of the pack. His feet seemed to be fused to a plate like the ones Ampersand had used to sneak her out of the bunker. He stayed visible for either ten seconds or ten hours, Cora couldn't be sure, then collapsed into himself, was enveloped by his plate, and disappeared.

The Genome was looking out the window now. Cora didn't know if she'd seen the whole thing, but she had at least seen Obelus, glancing furtively between Cora and where the monster outside had been, not half a kilometer away. Cora wondered if the Genome even saw him as the enemy. He was, after all, a representative of the Superorganism. Her home.

The Genome slowly lowered herself away from the window. She looked at Cora, her body growing small, contrite. This could mean any number of things, but Cora chose to interpret this as the Genome understanding that Obelus was a threat and that they shared a common enemy.

Then she heard something, and for a few seconds, she

thought it might be an auditory hallucination before she placed it. *Helicopter.* She definitely heard the distant chopping of a helicopter. A helicopter, she knew, was doomed if it got too close.

But there was nothing she could do for them.

She looked down at her arm, slick and wet with blood, then at the Genome. Captive by an alien species she'd never seen before, likely completely unaware of what planet she was on or who this violent, flesh-eating creature that had taken her captive even was. A true natural alien, something the Genome would have never encountered before in person. What a grotesque monster Cora must have appeared to her.

Cora got up and ran into the bathroom, tearing apart a cabinet looking for first aid, finding some rubbing alcohol and a bit of gauze under the bathroom sink. She stuffed one roll of the gauze in her mouth, and doused the disinfectant on her other arm, squealing her agony into the gauze. Then she ripped open the other roll of gauze, and clumsily dressed her arm as fast as she could. She spied some duct tape on top of a box and used it to seal the gauze.

By now, the helicopter was close. She figured Obelus either had departed or was still looking for Ampersand, and if the latter was true, that helicopter was not long for this world. If she and the Genome had even a mote of a chance to escape, it was now. The helicopter may not have stood a chance against Similars, it might be barreling into a suicide mission, but it might cause enough of a distraction.

She waited for the helicopter to pass overhead before tearing into the woods. After a few more minutes of running, her arms and her lungs were on fire. She couldn't carry the Genome much farther like this. She just didn't have the upper-body strength, and the cuts on her arm burned like hot pokers with every movement. She stood the Genome up, urging her to hop on her back so she could piggyback her. The Genome didn't understand and cried out in pained protest when Cora tried to pull her arms over her shoulders. Trying to do anything with the Genome was difficult, as that translucent filter that covered her entire body was slippery and slid all over her skin. She backed into the Genome, grabbed her legs, tried to hoist her onto her back. Eventually, the Genome gave in.

The sun started to set by the time she allowed herself to approach anything resembling civilization, having only stopped to rest for a few minutes once or twice in the last hour. Her arm, scraping up against the legs of the Genome, was still bleeding, and she was starting to feel faint. Having hardly eaten anything in at least a day, she was fucking ravenous.

Eventually she came to a gas station on a small, out-of-the-way highway. She had no money, no ID, nothing. The only vehicle in the station was a truck. She didn't see the owner; he must have been inside, paying for gas. Not wasting an instant, she pulled herself into the bed of the truck, careful to keep the Genome on her back, and then crawled up toward the cab, sliding the Genome off her and hiding next to a big black toolbox that rested on the walls of the truck bed.

The truck started and left the gas station.

By the time the truck stopped after about twenty minutes of driving, the sun had nearly set, leaving a light blue haze over the still-overcast sky. Cora didn't move for at least ten minutes, waiting until she was absolutely sure that the driver had left the truck for good. Eventually she peeked out of the truck bed and saw that they seemed to have gone even farther into the mountains. She had only the license plate on the truck to indicate what state they were even in: Virginia.

After all this, *how* were they still in Virginia? With all the distance she'd traveled that day, they might as well be in Patagonia. She urged the Genome onto her back, and this time she cooperated more readily. Cora hopped out of the truck, stumbling onto the gravel driveway and moving away as quickly as she could.

But to *where*?

She had to rest, and she figured that right here, right now, this was the safest she'd been in weeks. No paper trail followed her here. No government, no Obelus. Not even Ampersand. The only danger now was that someone might see them and report them. Leave a paper trail that Obelus could follow. The truck had parked next to an orchard, with a big industrial barn adjacent to it. Crippled by exhaustion, she stumbled into the barn, using her last wisps of strength to crawl up into the hayloft. She let the Genome off her back and collapsed in the hay. The two of them lay still for a few minutes. Somewhere through her exhaustion, she laughed. The thought *I want to go home* flitted through her mind, and with it, she was reminded of "Sloop John B."

"*Do you know why they code-name transients after this song?*" Ampersand had asked when she played it for him. *No, sir. No, I do not know. I think it's random like all their code names and operations are. I guess someone thought it was funny.*

The last thoughts that passed through her mind as she lost consciousness were cousins to the thought that had been plaguing her all day: she had no plan. Her plan had been to escape, to survive, but what after that? The slightest wrong move would get her and her new charge caught. No plan. Lost in the wilderness.

"Cora!"

Cora gasped herself awake, flinching in pain as she felt a scab break on her arm. She must have scarcely moved all night, her neck stiffened into a brittle cord. She sat up and stretched it out.

The Genome was roosting a few feet away, avoiding the hay. Cora listened but didn't hear anyone calling for her. Perhaps she had heard a voice in the yard and her dreams had filled in the blanks. She relaxed and looked at the Genome. "You're still here."

The Genome spoke to her in her alien language.

"Yeah," said Cora. "Well, it would have been your funeral anyway."

The Genome spoke back.

"Oh, don't worry about it. It'll heal eventually."

The Genome replied. Cora smiled. Despite zero mutual understanding, they seemed to be on the same page about it being nice to have someone to talk at, if not talk to.

Cora thought she heard people having a conversation

outside. She held her breath and listened. She thought she heard someone say, "I'm looking for my niece. Ran away from home last night." The voice sounded familiar. "About five four, gray-hazel eyes, hair's a . . . well, she needs to touch up her roots."

No way.

Without thinking, she stumbled down the ladder out of the hayloft. Was this some kind of trick? Someone from the CIA had followed her, or Obelus had found a way to synthesize Luciana's voice? Oh, hell, if it was, Obelus deserved to catch her.

"Stay," she told the Genome. Then she ran out of the barn. "*Luciana!*"

The petite redhead standing at the front door of the farmhouse turned to her and all but forgot the property owner she had been speaking to. Luciana ran toward her, stopping short in horror.

"What happened to you?" gasped Luciana. "Your arm?"

"Who cares?" said Cora. "Oh, God, how the hell did you find me?"

"I care!" said Luciana.

The old woman who lived here cleared her throat. Luciana gave Cora a look that stated, *Not now,* as she approached the old woman, explaining that Cora had gotten in a violent fight with one of her siblings (broken home) and had run away, but not to worry, she was going to take her to the hospital now.

The woman didn't seem convinced, but pretended to be, not wanting to be inconvenienced further. Cora didn't recognize Luciana's car—it must have been a rental. Or another stolen one. She didn't ask.

"How in God's name did you find me?" asked Cora, motioning for Luciana to follow her back to the barn.

"I received a text message telling me where you were," said

Luciana, rummaging around in her bag. "I assumed it was you. I'm on the run from the law now, by the way. Well, sort of."

Cora stopped. "Text message? From whom?"

Luciana looked at Cora like she'd been stung with a cattle prod. "It wasn't you?"

Cora shook her head.

"I got this text to my old burner," said Luciana, pulling out her cheap flip phone. "The one you called me on when you were in Nevada. It told me that you were here. At first, I was pretty freaked out because you were the only person who had this number. I wouldn't have followed it, but then I heard about what happened at Cheyenne Mountain. You didn't send this?"

Cora looked back to the house, making sure the woman wasn't spying on them. "It must be Ampersand."

"What makes you say that?"

"Because he is the only person who could have possibly known where I am."

Luciana watched her, bewildered, as Cora turned and walked back into the barn. She climbed the ladder and peeked over the floor of the hayloft. "I'm sorry," she said. "I hope I didn't scare you."

It appeared that the Genome had attempted to bury herself in hay but hadn't gotten far. She looked weak, much weaker than she had even a few hours ago. Perhaps it had been the stress from yesterday or just the cold, but the energy the Genome had shown yesterday had vanished.

"Oh my God," said Luciana's voice from down below. She stood silently while Cora tried to coax the Genome into moving. After a while, after Cora gave up on trying to coax her out and had instead hoisted the moaning, miserable creature over her shoulder, Luciana simply said, "Figures."

. . . . .

Luciana had been just outside of D.C. when her burner had gotten the message. She'd only been held for about thirty-six hours—apparently, they had held her for long enough without evidence. She did not know how or why Demi and the kids were still being held (*still!*), but as best as she could tell, they were not under arrest for anything criminal and were being contained under different circumstances entirely.

After they loaded up the Genome in the back of the car, they quickly agreed that contacting anyone, even the number that had sent the message to Luciana's burner, was a bad idea. The best destination they could agree on was a contact of Luciana's in southwestern Virginia about an hour east in Christiansburg, so they headed in that direction. Not in any way affiliated with ROSA, she said, which Cora took to mean it was another one of her online role-playing buddies. Luciana swore he was trustworthy and wouldn't ask questions, although that didn't mean they would mention that they had an alien breeding unit on them.

Luciana hadn't known about the attack on NORAD until after Ampersand contacted her. Her information was sketchy, but she had heard from Stevie, who was alive. In fact, almost all her ROSA coworkers had gotten out, and all the Fremda group, save one—the Similar, Brako. That was the only body they'd found.

The only human casualties were the ones who'd tried to fight back or who'd gotten in the way. As Ampersand had foretold, Obelus wasn't interested in the natives. Dr. Sev, Stevie, and their colleagues had hidden and were summarily ignored. After the dust had cleared, it appeared as if the Fremda group had completely vanished, and no one could point to how or where until a technician uncovered a small tunnel that had been burrowed into the cave wall behind the complex, a small but smooth tunnel about four feet in diameter that didn't look like it had been dug so much as melted, a tunnel that wound all the way to the other side of the mountain. *Miles* to the other side of the mountain.

All without one single U.S. government official even noticing.

No one knew how the Fremda group avoided being knocked out by the pulse, though Luciana informed her of one aspect about NORAD that Cora, and apparently Obelus as well, had been unaware of—the bunker was built to be EMP-proof. Cora boggled a bit at learning this. Maybe NORAD hadn't been such a stupid place to hide after all.

Cora told Luciana her side of things: the horrible flight, Langley, how the Genome woke up mysteriously, the protective film covering the Genome's body, Obelus attacking with a pulse again. Watching those people die, knowing the Similars' preferred method for easy disposal of "naturals." The hours lost in the woods. She didn't mention Vincent.

The state of the house they pulled up to in Christiansburg, Virginia, confirmed Cora's suspicion—definitely one of Luciana's *World of Warcraft* buddies, another in her online guild string of broken hearts. Cora put on a jacket before introducing herself to Luciana's friend. Having washed the blood off her neck and face, she might have passed for merely a hot mess.

The renter of the house was a bachelor's bachelor, a large, redheaded fellow named Matt. Luciana explained to Matt that Cora was having problems with her famous father and asked if they could use the basement, on the condition that he not tell anyone, *anyone*, that they were there at all. Matt told her that a lot of his friends were having a field day with Nils Ortega and ET-gate. This new nomenclature was news to Cora, and it was all she could do not to gag upon hearing it.

Luciana's explanation seemed good enough for Matt. He acted like hosting Luciana was like having a celebrity in his home—apparently, she was an even bigger name than Cora realized in the *World of Warcraft* scene. Cora got out of the car and wrapped up the Genome, and she and Luciana carried her into the basement when Matt was in the bathroom.

The basement was even more of a bachelor pit than the upstairs. Video games from every era, many, many action figures, a fish tank, and even a pinball machine. At least the basement had a couch, which Cora fell onto gratefully.

Luciana took this opportunity to examine the Genome, who, even in the less than two hours in the car, had visibly deteriorated. The splotchy skin had gotten worse, and her eyes were losing focus.

"I have to admit," said Luciana, pursing her lips. "This was not a challenge I was prepared to encounter today."

Cora's heart dipped. "Did he mention the Genome to you when he contacted you?"

"No."

"Have you contacted him since you found me?"

"No. I turned this burner off. I could turn it on, but then we might be traceable by . . . parties. NSA and otherwise."

"Keep it off, then," said Cora.

"Have *you* tried to contact him?"

"I . . ." Cora's heart dipped farther. She didn't know why she was feeling such a sense of loss. They had parted on such sour terms, but if he had bothered to contact Luciana, one way or the other, he did care if she lived or died. "I think there's a limited range on the communicator he uses with me." She nodded toward the Genome. "He must not know we have her. He must think either Sol has her or Obelus does."

Luciana shook her head. "I've got no idea what is or is not poisonous to a 'natural' amygdaline. So unless their physiology is radically different from ours and they can survive for any length of time without food or water, she's probably starving."

"She took some water at Langley," said Cora. "It was triple, quadruple distilled, though."

The Genome's eyes had clouded over, and she'd stopped being conversational a while ago. Cora hadn't quite grown accustomed to the Genome—her alienness was still off-putting, like a cockroach blown up to the size of a dog—but Cora didn't find her so revolting anymore. She'd fought so hard to keep this creature alive, and not for any real strategic reason, just some latent protective instinct she couldn't really rationalize. She couldn't help but feel some attachment to her, some drive to *keep* her alive.

"I think there's more to her than just reproductive cells," mused Cora. "Otherwise, why not just use stem cells? Frozen embryos?"

"Maybe," said Luciana.

The Genome's breathing hadn't been labored before, but it was now, but not in the familiar way typical of mammals. She jerked in air in spurts, more like a heartbeat. "I don't see any realistic way to get her out of this alive," said Cora, admitting it as much to herself as she was to Luciana.

Luciana brought her hand to her head and sighed. "I did get a set of coordinates with the message telling me where you were," she said. Cora looked at her, a surge of hope pulsing through her. "I think it's latitude and longitude. I assume that's where he is, or at least where he wants you to go."

That emotional dissonance flared in her chest again—she had been done with him, and she'd thought she had made her peace with him. He had laid it out, and she had been his mouthpiece: "*Where attributes are not shared, inevitably both parties will try to shape the other into a form they can understand.*" He had made it clear that he wasn't sorry about all the things he had done and that what she already knew was just the tip of the iceberg.

And she was still sick with worry over what had happened to him. Maybe he was right, that with full knowledge of his past and culture, they couldn't peacefully coexist, but that didn't mean she never wanted to see him again.

"Is it far?" asked Cora, a little too eagerly.

Luciana tilted her head toward Cora, clearly noting the eager tone in her voice. "Pretty far. A couple hours' drive."

Cora peeked at her own wounds, still bound with old gauze and duct tape. She dreaded cutting off the duct tape. She could feel infection already beginning to burn, but she didn't want to see it. "What do you think?"

"What do I think about what?"

"Do we trust him?" asked Cora. "Ampersand?"

"You'd know better than I would." Luciana tilted her head farther, now suspicious. "Did something happen?"

Cora sighed deeply. "I keep finding things out. Things that scare me. Existential things, as Sol would put it." Luciana's face turned stony. "He . . . we're not *people* to him." She nodded to the Genome. "I don't think she is, either."

"And regardless of what is the safe thing to do, there's also the question of what is the right thing to do."

"They don't think like we do. I don't think they'd agree on what the 'right thing' even is." Cora knelt down next to the Genome, her big, wet, cloudy eyes staring into nothing. "He didn't tell us that she was a living, thinking being. But that might be because amygdalines have different definitions of personhood than we do. We aren't persons. The Genome is not a person."

"Do you *know* that?" asked Luciana. "For sure?"

"I don't know," admitted Cora. "I can't tell what he's said and done out of desperation and what he really believes."

"I think it's a mistake to try to separate the two. Good justification or no, he believes what he believes, and he does what he does. And we have to make our best guess for what that is, and either live with it and tell him we have the Genome, or we don't." Luciana looked at the Genome, who was slowly, silently, painfully, pulling up into a roost. Cora wanted to comfort her, give her *some* indication that she did care whether she lived or died, but had no idea how.

"Matt has a fish tank. That means he probably has distilled water," said Luciana.

"I don't think we should risk moving her," said Cora, placing a hand next to the Genome, but not touching her. The Genome didn't even eye it warily. "Look at what that short drive did to her."

"How do you know it was him?" asked Luciana, her neutral, stone expression giving way again to suspicion.

"He still has that tracker on me, and that's the only way anyone could find me right now."

"Tracker?"

"Yeah," said Cora, a bitterness she had buried suddenly rising to the surface. "Remember that thing he injected me with, that I told you about, and you didn't believe me?"

Luciana's expression melted into disbelief. "Jesus Christ, Cora, why didn't you tell anyone?"

"I *did*," said Cora. "*You* didn't believe me."

"You didn't know what it was at the time!" said Luciana. "Now you apparently do know, but you *still* didn't tell anyone."

"Because he and I made an agreement," said Cora, her defenses fully fortified. "I told him he could keep the tracker on me until he left. Apparently, that was a good call. So I'm going to go now."

"*What?*" Luciana shot to her feet. "I hope you don't think I'm going to let you run off alone to find him."

Cora stood up to meet her. "You never had a problem with me being alone with him before."

"We weren't both fugitives from multiple powerful entities, some of them nonhuman, before."

"And that's why I want to go alone. Find out what he wants to do before I let him know where the Genome is."

"You don't *trust* him," said Luciana, raising her voice.

"Yeah, well, what a crop I have to choose from!" The Genome tried to back away but lacked the strength. "All I've gotten from the people in my life for the last few weeks have been lies, half truths, and manipulation. I'm *surrounded* by liars and manipulators. Closest person to honest is Mom, and look where that got her."

"And where does that put me?"

"I didn't say anything about present company being excluded."

Luciana's eyes widened, her lips flattened into a narrow line. "Why don't you go ahead and call me a traitor while you're there?"

Cora forced herself back down, reminding herself that *no* good would come from them fighting right now. "That's not what I meant. You know it."

"Oh, I think I do," said Luciana, standing up. "I've been in interrogation rooms for the better part of three days, which is to say *nothing* of what they put me through before all that. Just come out and say it, Cora. Toe the party line."

"*Fine!*" Cora yelled. "Do you *really* expect me to believe that Nils Ortega's own sister just happened to work in direct contact with aliens and that someone else leaking to him the perfect incriminating document was *just* a coincidence?"

Luciana drew back like she'd been struck, as though she hadn't expected Cora to take the bait. But it was out now, poisoning the air.

"I'm a tool to Sol, I'm a tool to Ampersand, I'm a tool to Nils. I know you never thought I'd ever get involved in this, but I did . . ."

"And I lied to you," said Luciana, her voice near a whisper. "You thought you could trust me, and I lied."

"I knew better than that." Cora winced as she said the words, not meaning them.

"Do you want to know the truth?" Luciana asked, her words frigid.

Cora opened her mouth to rebut but stopped. She didn't honestly want to know right at this point in time, because it did not matter. It was completely irrelevant. The only thing that mattered now was keeping the Genome alive and finding out what happened to Ampersand. Cora had been sitting on her anger and suspicion at Luciana for a while, and her exhaustion had let it leak. But now was not the time.

"No, I was . . . I was angry. I'm sorry I said that," said Cora, pulling back.

Luciana's hands glided to her sides, and she stood up straight, shoulders back. It was as though all the warmth had left her body. "Do you *want* to know the truth? I may never get another chance to tell you."

"Will it in any way aid me?" said Cora, trying to ameliorate the situation, but her voice still tremulous with anger. "Will you divulging the family secrets in *any way* aid me in our endeavors right now?"

She had never seen her aunt so livid, so betrayed. "Cora . . . ," she said, her voice low and shaking. "You're going off to face down an alien being that you do not trust, and you're leaving me with the one thing that all parties involved are willing to kill to get ahold of."

"So?"

Luciana didn't take her eyes off Cora. "So this may be the last time we ever see each other. Do you really want this to be the note we part on?"

Cora said the first thing that popped into her head. When she eventually came to look back on this conversation, she wondered why the most honest thing she could say was also the meanest, the cruelest, the pettiest. "I'm sorry it was me," she said. "I'm sorry he decided to talk through me and not you."

PART FOUR

. . . .

BELOVED

Blountville, Tennessee
October 8, 2007
NASDAQ: 1,884.57
Dow Jones Industrial Average: 7,298.10

3 4

The coordinates led Cora to a long-abandoned warehouse, an old weathered building with a rusted tin roof that might have at some point been a factory farm barn. Upon entering the building, she saw that most of it had been gutted, although there were some rows of gates toward the back of the building, cages that must have once housed pigs. "Hello?" she said, her voice reverberating against the cinder block walls of the building. "Ampersand?"

The late-afternoon sun pouring in through the windows illuminated the dust in sharp parallelograms. The ceiling was high and stippled with rust so severe it had eaten through some parts of it, creating holes for the harsh sunlight to peek through. Metal lamps dangled down every twenty feet or so, themselves so rusted they probably wouldn't even turn on if the building had electricity. It looked like the cages in the barn had been poached for scrap for about three-quarters of the length before the poacher decided it was not worth the trouble to finish.

Cora turned back toward the other half of the building, the half that had been stripped of its equipment. There were a few remnants of cages, bent and broken and not worth the effort to finish stripping. There was also an old, dirty fiberglass washtub. Ampersand was there, too, standing just out of the sunlight near the tub, his eyes soaking up what little light fell on that corner of the building and shining it back in a concentrated, radiant mass. She jumped in surprise upon seeing him and searched herself for what to say, how to feel.

"Where are the others?" she asked, unconsciously crossing her arms to hide her injuries as she approached him.

The voice in her ear spoke: "*Nearby.*"

Hearing the voice made her stop. It was different now, clearer, less mechanical to the point where now it sounded almost human. It even had the touch of an accent to it, placeless yet somehow foreign.

"I'm glad you're safe," she said.

"*I am not safe.*"

"I'm glad you survived, then."

Ampersand approached her in that fluid, snakelike way that he moved, and stopped at a respectable few feet away, observing her. "*I left the Genome in the possession of the militarists. They took it when they took you. Do you know its location?*"

"Luciana has the Genome. She was alive when I left them." Cora emphasized *she*. Ampersand was still, seeming to soak in the implication of Cora describing her as "alive." "But she was very weak. I didn't want to chance moving her again." She slid her hands over the barely scabbed-over wounds on her forearm and squeezed, the pain a catharsis.

"*Do you consent?*"

Without looking up, she nodded. Ampersand delicately took

her right arm with the tips of his fingers, leaning in to examine it as he peeled back the old, dirty jacket sleeve.

Her muscles stiffened at the sting, and she tried to act braver than she felt. "You didn't tell us she was alive."

"*How did this happen?*"

"I . . ." She sighed. "It was an accident."

"*Move next to the washtub.*"

It felt as if he were reprimanding a child who'd soiled her Sunday best. The water that came out initially was brown, like its reservoir had been tainted with old blood, but ran clear after about a minute. He placed one of his digits on the duct tape binding and drew it up the length of her arm, burning the tape away as it went, filling her nostrils with the acrid smell of seared plastic. She gritted her teeth, preparing for him to pull it away and the pain that would come with it, but instead, he placed two of his fingers at the fold of her inner arm, the digits forming a point so sharp it seemed to disappear at the tip, and went into her arm like a syringe. Then her lower arm fell completely numb.

He removed the gauze and tape while Cora closed her eyes and turned away until the deed was done. When she looked at the damage, she realized it wasn't as bad as she'd feared, although the sight of it made her convulse slightly. Angry red flesh surrounded black and brown clots caked like mud all up and down her arm.

He pulled her arm under the cold running water, flushing out her wounds and reopening them even farther, darkening the tub's rusty basin with blood spatter.

"You didn't tell us she was alive," Cora said again. "She was terrified. She had no idea where she was."

He removed her arm from the running water, and she watched, fascinated by the canyon that now decorated most of her right forearm, the burgeoning infection once covered by blood clots now screaming and red. It was as though it were not even hers, a prosthetic, a prop in a cheap horror film.

The focus of his eyes split, equal parts on her eyes and her arms. "*She must have been frightened. She has never seen an alien before, let alone a natural one.*"

Ampersand seemed to be reopening everything that had already clotted, as though nature had done it wrong the first time. The dust swirled around them, catching in the light of the sun, only it wasn't dust, it was steam; some heat she could neither feel nor see was *cooking* something in the wound. She turned away and closed her eyes, no longer able to bear the sight of it.

"Is she natural?" she asked, trying to distract herself by staying on topic.

"*Not a true natural,*" said Ampersand. "*She is engineered. She is post-natural in that regard. But her body is not biosynthetic.*"

She swallowed, demanding her eyes to stay closed. "I think she's dying."

"*Explain.*"

"After I felt the pulse, the van crashed into a tree, and she made a run for it, and I ran after her. She spent a lot of energy trying to get away from me. Then this morning, she was so much weaker."

"*Her body is not engineered to withstand Earth's gravity or rigorous activity.*"

He continued in silence for several minutes, the only sound coming from the birds outside. She finally looked back down at her arm. The walls of her wound-canyons were shiny and pink, stripped of their clotting, but devoid of the blood that normally rushed out when blood clots were torn off.

"What is your plan for her?"

"Esperas's plan with Čefo was to use the Genome to breed more Similars, when resources and aid arrived. Čefo's death complicated Esperas's plans. Aside from myself, Čefo was the only one who could work with genetic material. Without my cooperation, Esperas cannot do anything with the genetic information the Genome carries."

She was so transfixed, sickened by what he was doing to her wound, that it took her a few seconds to realize that he had not answered her question. That he did not intend to.

"What does Obelus want with her?" she asked.

"Obelus has a strategy relating directly to his hierarchy within the Superorganism. He believes recovering the Genome will aid in his ascent. Our species has dangerously low genetic diversity. Even a dangerously flawed Genome is invaluable."

"I thought Similars were just . . . 'militarists.'"

"They are not, but regardless, Obelus was not always a Similar, and Obelus is uniquely ambitious. But his position in the Superorganism is tenuous."

Cora opened her eyes, careful not to look down. "Why?"

"Because he is like me."

Cora furrowed her brow, wondering if she'd misunderstood. She tried to read some recognizable expression into that alien face but found nothing. "You mean Obelus is Fremdan?"

"Yes."

"Then why was he . . . omitted from the purge?"

"His genetic lineage is not known to the majority of the Superorganism. His subordinates most assuredly do not know that he is Fremdan. The Autocrat, however, does know. Retrieving this Genome is a sign of loyalty to the Autocrat."

"How do you know all this and his subordinates don't?"

"I know."

She looked down and saw that he had by now cleared most of the blood out of the cut. It looked like a satellite view of a stinging, fleshy valley. "Why does Obelus want her alive?"

"*She is a living memory.*"

Cora shook her head, confused.

"*Our kind can transfer memories through direct neural contact. This is a part of high language. Some memories are passed down from very distant ancestors. The Genome carries them. I cannot translate an appropriate description for it in English. She carries memories that are not her own. They are also invaluable, potentially dangerous to the wrong parties.*"

"Does she even know what's happening? That there even *was* a genetic purge? That she's on Earth?"

"*I don't know. I've never interacted with her. I don't know what Čefo allowed her to know.*"

His digits were moving the crevasse in her arm back together with a fast, mechanical fluidity that reminded her of a sewing machine. It was as though he were stitching the two flaps of skin together, but there were no stitches. Again, she felt detached, as though this were not happening to her body.

She wanted to push him again, ask him what his plan was. But it was only here that she realized the reason she kept pushing him for a plan was because she had none herself. She was completely lost, looking for someone to tell her where to go, what to do, but no one knew what they were doing, what lay ahead. Everyone now was paying the price for the clumsiness of their own secrets. Luciana. Ampersand. Sol. The goddamn president of the United States of America. No one was flying the plane. Not a game of strategy but a game of chance. She didn't even know what her official status was. Was she on the run from the law? Was she a fugitive? Had she *broken* any laws?

You killed a federal officer. Pretty sure that's illegal.

She shook her head as though Ampersand had accused her of it. From what she could tell, it seemed like no one had gotten out of that wreck before Obelus arrived, everyone staying to help the injured if not injured themselves. But she hadn't seen him die. Maybe Vincent had survived. Maybe he had gotten out of the van, or maybe he had gone undetected.

But she knew that wasn't true.

Then came the rush she'd been holding back; those tears that she'd been fighting for a whole day broke through. Ampersand looked at her, those brilliant amber orbs taking notice of the change in her mood, crushing her between the glass plates of a microscope.

"I think I killed someone." She didn't know why she thought he would care, but right then and there, she felt she would rot away if she didn't tell someone, and he was the only option available. "Vincent—one of the junior CIA agents. I felt the pulse happen, and I wanted to escape, and I wanted to slow him down so he wouldn't follow me, so I shoved a gurney at him, and . . . I don't know. I did it harder than I meant to. It hurt him. It blocked him long enough for me to get away, but I didn't see him follow me. And then Obelus was there, and everyone I saw, everyone down by those cars who didn't run like I did . . ."

His dexterous mending of her wound slowed as he got to the end of the second major gash on her arm, and then stopped. All that remained of the dark, ugly laceration was a fine line. The skin was still swollen, but it looked like the kind of swelling that would go down with a couple of hours with an ice pack. It would scar no more than a cat scratch.

He slid his two forefingers back into the fold of her arm, sliding in the needle again, and feeling flooded back into her forearm. He let her arm go, and a deep, burning heat like boiling water flooded into her veins. She sucked in a few breaths between her teeth as she grew accustomed to the pain. But her breath slowed, and with it, the heat cooled. After about a minute, it still burned, but not unbearably so.

He lifted his hands up, curling them into a neutral, mantid stance. "*Do you consent?*"

Her fists were clenched so tightly her knuckles were almost white. She looked up at him, not sure what else he needed to do. "Yes."

He lifted up his hands, steepling them into a triangle as he did sometimes when he was about to use his telekinesis, and she braced herself for it, but his forefingers gently fell onto her crown, through her messy hair, and then gently glided down toward her ears. His touch was more complete, less mechanical than it had been the last time he had done this. A rhythmic stroking pattern—five seconds on, five seconds off. He grazed his thumbs through the little riverbeds left by the tears on her cheeks. "Do you consent?" she managed.

"*Yes.*"

She hesitated, didn't quite know what she was asking permission for. Then she leaned her face forward, her forehead meeting with his muzzle. Her arms snaked around his frame, and he had to bend over considerably for her to even reach around him, until her hands came to rest on the shell of his back. They just stayed there for a while, the alien continuing to run his fingers through her hair, and the girl weeping softly. She closed her eyes and, for the first time in a long time, just allowed herself to exist.

"*I reacted with anger when you asked me if I had ever killed anyone,*" he said after a few minutes.

She opened her eyes, looked out the window. The sun was no longer sending sharp rays into the building and had fallen beneath the trees. "Who was it?" she asked softly. "Who did you kill?"

"*Transients.*"

"But you said they were monsters."

"*I never said they were monsters. Stelo and Krias described them as such—and Stelo and Krias are propagandists. I said they were our enemies. I was a prisoner of war, but the pod that held me was not inhumane. They were not kind, but they did not torture me. Had they been torturous, I would not have survived.*

"*But when Čefo's message made it to the pod, I made a decision to escape. But I knew this decision would cost the life of at least one of my captors, and it did. It cost the lives of all of them. Transients are very difficult to kill.*"

She knew she needed to let him go, but the knowledge that this would likely be the only time she got to do this held her in place. It was such a strange position to be in; he had never inspired that visceral repulsion in her the Genome had; he was just too machinelike, too far removed from nature to spark disgust. But he was alien all the same; how could one find comfort in so foreign a thing? She couldn't explain it.

"*Empathy and ethics, in a time of great suffering, have a way of being pushed to the side in the interest of survival. I struggle with my memories. I am unique among the Fremda group on Earth in that regard. They neither understand nor empathize with the inherent trauma of torture, of captivity, and of taking lives for survival.*"

She felt him lean into her neck.

"*It was fair for you to want to know if I had killed people, my species or otherwise. I reacted with anger. These are experiences*

I cannot erase from memory, but they cripple my cognition all the same."

"Your cognition?"

"Trauma can cause cognitive impairment in all sapient species."

Cora leaned her face on his shoulder. "Do you regret it?"

"No. But having to make the choice to kill is a traumatic position to be placed in. You have been put in such a position and chose not to kill."

"With Vincent?"

"With me. You chose not to take my life. I envy you that."

"You envy *me*," she coughed, and she pulled him closer to her. "Aren't you glad I didn't?"

"I do not know whether to be grateful. With Čefo died my sole reason for being here. Perhaps it would have been most humane if you had killed me."

The lump in her throat that had only just begun to soften turned again to stone, and her eyes grew hot. "Even if I had known exactly how to kill you, I wouldn't have done it. I don't . . . I wouldn't hurt you." She noticed he had stopped petting her and had his hands draped across her back, stiff, like he wasn't sure how to react. "I wanted to protect you. From the moment I first saw you, I wanted to protect you."

"Maladaptive. I don't understand the reasoning."

She let go of him and backed away to look him in the eye, opened her mouth as though the rational, tactical answer would come spilling out, but it didn't because there was none. Just the honest counterintuitive, maladaptive truth. "Because no one else would."

He stood up a bit, but not to his full height. The focus in his eyes was soft and distant.

"You were right," she said. "About us only being able to understand each other through the prism of our own existence. I want to be able to put you in the right context. The context of your species, of your history. But I can't help but apply human morality to you."

"*Not just human morality. A fast-changing brand of morality, unique to this time, place, and culture. It will be a different morality a day from now. A year from now.*"

She chuckled sadly, looking at the outline of the window from the sunlight on the dirt floor a few feet away. "And I'm still angry. I still . . . What you did to those people was wrong. You not telling me the truth was wrong."

"*It was also necessary. I needed to keep you compliant, and through that compliance, I was able to make contact with the Fremda group without alienating their American hosts. I understand that you see it as a breach of trust.*"

"I tried to come back for you," she said. "Back at Cheyenne Mountain. When I saw what was happening. I tried to come back for you. But Sol's agents took me. They wouldn't let me come back for you."

"*I know.*" His fingers grazed the palm of her hand, stopping on the back of her palm where the hand met the wrist and then lingering there.

"Stay." She heard herself say it before she realized the word was on her tongue. She looked up at him. "Stay on Earth." *Stay with me.*

Ampersand stood up to his full height, his eyes unfocused. "*We cannot. Not with Obelus on Earth.*"

"Kill them," said Cora, her voice regaining its strength. The sudden intensity of Ampersand's gaze shook her, but she didn't look away. "Kill them all. I know you can do it. The Obelus

Similars are afraid of you or they wouldn't be attacking you with energy pulses instead of just taking you head-on."

"*I cannot fight Obelus. No force on this planet can. Even if we could, more Similars would come. Obelus is saving his resources, but he could wipe out your entire species in a matter of days.*"

"So could you."

Ampersand's head tilted like an alert dog's.

"The Superorganism is going to find out there's an advanced civilization on this rock sooner or later," she said, running a finger over her now-mended wounds. "Better for us to be prepared than not. Besides, Obelus followed you here. If you run, he'll just follow you wherever you go."

"*I am aware,*" he said, almost cutting her off.

"And Esperas thinks that humanity knowing about you is only going to reduce our chances of survival. They won't like that we *know*. Is that true?"

"*Do not ask questions to which the answer—*"

"No!" she cut him off. "No. Tell me the truth."

"*I do not know the political situation inside the Superorganism. I have been apart from it too long. But any cultural shift that would make an advancing alien species appear more antagonistic, more belligerent, would give incentive to the Superorganism to sterilize it before it becomes a real threat.*"

Again her eyes fell to her arm. The swelling seemed even tamer than it had five minutes ago.

"*I know what is happening, the shift that is occurring in your culture. They are angry; they are frightened. They are frightened of us.*"

"They're not angry at you. They're angry at the government for keeping you a secret."

"*It's not realistic to assume that anger won't eventually redirect* to us. *Especially if it ever comes to light what the Superorganism has done.*"

She didn't immediately connect what he meant, but then the image of Erythrá flashed in her mind's eye. That sad little colored-pencil drawing. That warning.

"*The Superorganism will see only an advancing civilization that already fears them, one that is already advancing at a far faster pace than our ancestors did.*"

"Of course they'd want to kill it in its crib," she said, defeat sapping the air from her lungs.

"*If I had the choice, I do agree that us choosing to stay on Earth poses the best chance for the survival of both parties in the long term. A slim chance, but a chance. But,*" he said, leaning in closer, "*we do not have that choice. I must retrieve the Genome. And you must depart.*"

"Where?" she breathed.

Cora closed her eyes. She felt a long arachnoid finger touch the bottom of her chin, tilt her head up ever so slightly, and she opened her eyes to meet his. "*It is time for you to go.*"

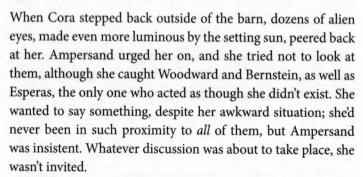

35

When Cora stepped back outside of the barn, dozens of alien eyes, made even more luminous by the setting sun, peered back at her. Ampersand urged her on, and she tried not to look at them, although she caught Woodward and Bernstein, as well as Esperas, the only one who acted as though she didn't exist. She wanted to say something, despite her awkward situation; she'd never been in such proximity to *all* of them, but Ampersand was insistent. Whatever discussion was about to take place, she wasn't invited.

When they were a comfortable distance from the group, Ampersand handed her a translation tablet. She took it, surprised he'd even kept one.

"*It may benefit you at some point in the future,*" he explained. "*It is of no use to me.*"

She nodded, gliding her fingers over the thin, glass-like device in her hand. Physical equipment, she figured, must be something an advanced species evolves past.

"Isn't there anything I can do for you?"

"*Tell me the Genome's location.*"

Cora sighed and gave him Matt's address in Christiansburg. "What are you going to do with her?"

"*Possibly nothing,*" he said. "*But I need the location.*"

"She'll die if you don't—"

"*I am aware,*" he cut her off. She felt an urgency in him, despite his stillness. "*You need to leave.*"

Cora looked to see if she could see Esperas and the others, but they were hidden by the barn. "Ampersand, what's going on?"

"*You need to leave.*"

She deflated a little, looked at the dusty ground. "We're never going to see each other again, are we?"

"*Likely not.*"

His brusqueness stung. "So I guess this is goodbye." She held out her hand to him, fingers spread stiff. "It's been nice being your interpreter."

He looked at her hand as though she were showing him some hitherto undiscovered species of butterfly. "'*Nice.*'"

She smiled softly. "Well, no, it was kind of hell. But it was a riveting sort of hell."

He looked at her outstretched hand, and he shortly acquiesced, enveloping her hand with his long fingers, curling in on themselves like the legs of dying spider.

"*I wish we could have learned more about each other. But you need to leave.*" He let go of her hand.

"Okay, I—"

"*It is for your own safety. Go, or I will force you to go.*" She backed away. "*Do not come back, no matter your inclination.*"

Cora shook her head, her emotions in a blender. "Goodbye,"

she said and turned to run. She didn't look back, and Ampersand didn't say another word.

She didn't stop running; it got some of her tension out. The sun was now sending sharp rays through the trees, peppering her eyes with painful intensity as she ran. She wasn't sure what to feel; she felt like she *should* be angry with him, but she wasn't. All she felt was the sense that she shouldn't have left. She shouldn't have left Ampersand. She shouldn't have left Luciana. She shouldn't have left Demi, Olive, and Felix.

Nils should not have left.

She had left the car at the head of the dirt road, as the road itself looked so neglected it may as well have been a foot trail and did not look safe to drive. It was there still, right where she'd left it. Maybe he wouldn't tell her his plan for the Genome because there wasn't one. Maybe he had abandoned her from their ever-changing schematic entirely. She stood there at the edge of the tree line, shielding her eyes from the sun with her hand and looking at Luciana's rental car. Her chariot to freedom. To aimless freedom in Argentina, with her bitterly resentful aunt and an extended family she hadn't seen since she was ten.

What makes you special to them?

My intelligence.

She wondered why her mind kept jumping to this exchange. There was something about it that felt false. Or perhaps not false but incomplete.

The still of the clearing was cut by distant screaming, and Cora whipped toward the direction of the sound. She'd never heard Pequod-phonemic *screaming* before. It sounded like a dolphin had combined with a Tasmanian devil. It didn't sound agonized or frightened; it sounded livid.

Do not come back, no matter your inclination.

He must have known something like this would happen before she was out of earshot, because her inclination to go back to see what was making that sound was pretty strong. Then the screeching cut through the trees again, but this time, it had more of an edge to it. She was anthropomorphizing, she knew, but it sounded to her like a more frightened edge. Or maybe she was just projecting and looking for an excuse to go back. Then she heard that noise again, ripping through the evening air.

Sol's voice came into her head: "This is *fucking* existential."

If Ampersand had wanted her to listen to him, he should have told her the whole truth. She followed her inclination.

She'd made it about halfway to the barn she before had to slow down. Hands on her knees, her lungs gulping air hungrily, she remembered that she had the translation tablet on her and pulled it out. She could still hear the vocalizations in the distance, and they seemed to become more frantic, but she was too far away for the tablet to pick up any phonemes. She put it back in her jacket and forced herself to keep going. She kept her eyes half-open, bracing for the white flash of the now-familiar pulse that preceded the Obelus Similars, but none came.

By the time she made it back to where Ampersand had shooed her away, he was gone. All of them were gone. But the screaming voice was still loud and clear, and now that she was closer, she could hear that it was accompanied by what sounded like some sort of scuffle—like a dead cow being tossed into the side of the building and dragged around on the dirt driveway on the other side of the barn—but besides the one frantic voice, the rest were silent. She pulled out the tablet again, straining to quiet her breathing, hoping that she was close enough for it to give her some kind of translation.

She was, and it did, but only one word, over and over:

[ACT. ACT. ACT.]

She darted to the side of the barn, now just around the corner from what was going on. She peered around it and spotted one amygdaline, then another, then two dozen. All flat on the ground, eyes open and glassy. There were Woodward and Bernstein, but she didn't see Kruro, or Esperas, or Ampersand. But she could feel a thickness in the air, the kind of magnetic pull that only accompanied some kind of heavy telekinetic activity. And then there was the only one speaking. It took a moment for her to recognize which one of them it was. Not Ampersand's tinny voice.

[Why don't you ACT?]

Esperas.

Her gaze askance at the tablet, her back glued to the wall, she peered around the corner of the building. Esperas was flat on his back, presumably held down by some telekinetic force. And there was Ampersand, the only one out of all of them who seemed unaffected, looking at Esperas with mild indifference. Like Esperas's pleas were beneath his notice.

She rationalized that perhaps Ampersand had sent her away because there was some showdown between Ampersand and Esperas that he didn't want her to see. That perhaps *he* was the one doing this. She moved another inch, now peering all the way around the corner, and there was Kruro in what appeared to be a telekinetic struggle with a much bigger Similar.

Obelus was a good three times the size of the comparatively

slender Ampersand, and at least three feet taller, and even still, he moved with that same eerie silence. She recognized him immediately, the wide body, the sleeker, more fluid design, the feel that his body was somehow newer. Even initially trying to comprehend what she was seeing, deep down she'd known this was the only possibility she could turn the corner to. It still felt like the ground had fallen out from underneath her.

She must have led Obelus right to them.

But how? How could Obelus have possibly known where she was?

She had led Obelus right to them. And Ampersand had known.

How?

Obelus must already have the Genome, and she followed that train of thought to its logical conclusion. And if Obelus had found the Genome, then it had found Luciana. And Luciana was dead.

No, she thought. *Don't entertain that. Can't entertain that.* She hadn't seen the Genome. She had only seen one Similar; his other Similars were nowhere in sight. But if the big one was here, where were the rest of them? Why was Obelus alone?

She remembered what Ampersand had told her only minutes ago: *Because he is like me.*

Cora could feel the energy as Obelus fixed his attention on Kruro, all the while trapping the other Fremda in an invisible bubble on the dirt. Kruro was clearly at the disadvantage. Obelus stood still as a statue where Kruro was contorting painfully, trying to gain the upper hand but unable to resist the overwhelming energy.

Ampersand just stood there, watching.

The air was thick, heavy, hard to breathe, as if she were in a tiny room full of steam. She felt like her rib cage was going to snap under the pressure. Then the energy in the air relaxed, as though Obelus let go. Or Kruro had given up.

And then Kruro became unmade. His central person tore apart, unzipped, and then he came apart at a molecular level, falling into a pile of ash. She clapped a hand over her mouth. She thought she heard Esperas make an agonized noise. Whatever it was, it didn't translate on the tablet.

She looked at Ampersand, waiting for him to move, say something, *do* something, but all he did was stand there and watch. The clearing was dead silent; even the birds and crickets stayed out of it. Obelus stilled, and the air returned to normal. But there was a calm to him, a satisfaction even, as he collected himself and looked at Ampersand. Ampersand looked at Obelus, and spoke:

[Greetings, BELOVED.]

Beloved?

Cora knew precious little about the complexities of amygdaline social structure, but she could only think of one reason why one of them might refer to the other with a term like "beloved."

Esperas was spitting rage again. The tablet was having difficulty making out what Esperas was saying; either it was outside of the tablet's known vocabulary, or, by the standards of his own language, untranslatable. The few words the tablet did translate were words like "liar," "betrayer," "filth."

Cora felt a film creeping up her throat; on some level, she was thinking more or less the same thing as Esperas.

"*You need to leave.*"

"*It is for your own safety.*"

"*Do not come back, no matter your inclination.*"

And as much as it sickened her, she had come to the same realization that Esperas had. It wasn't even that Ampersand had known Obelus was coming for them and had kept it entirely to himself. That much was blindingly obvious. No, it went way deeper than that.

Ampersand and Obelus were symphyles.

And what had he told her about the main feature of dynamic fusion bonding, a week ago, a lifetime ago? *Fusion bonding incorporates the other's energy, their brain waves. Bonding allows one to sense the energies of another.*

If fusion bonding meant one partner could sense the energy of another, had Obelus known where Ampersand was? Had he always known? Maybe it hadn't been Cora who had led Obelus to them. Maybe it had been *him.* The two even seemed to be regarding each other as old friends, or at the very least, they weren't regarding each other as enemies.

She stayed frozen in place, trying to keep her breath quiet, as she would be completely visible to Obelus if he so much as turned his head a few degrees. Ampersand could see her, though, and shot her a brief but intense glare, a look that she couldn't help but read as, *You idiot, I'd kill you if I didn't know that Obelus was about to do it for me.*

She ducked behind the corner of the building as quietly as she could. Her rational mind told her to run; her instincts told her to freeze. Had Ampersand and Obelus been in league the whole time?

No, that didn't make any *sense*!

She looked sidelong toward the body of Kruro, which was now papery scaffolding rising from a pile of ash, and realized that Obelus was going to do the same to all of them. One by one, he was going to kill them, rip them into pieces. Woodward, Bernstein, Esperas . . . and her if she didn't get away.

But not Ampersand.

She then heard Ampersand speak. She looked at the tablet.

[Have you killed the Similar to provide a dramatic show for HIM/ESPERAS, [DIRECT ADDRESS]? I am not impressed. I thought we had consigned such displays of histrionics to naturals and your hated transients.]

Silence. Every time she told her limbs to move, they refused.

[You could not expect me to allow SIMILAR to live.]
[I had use for that Similar.]
[The Similar attacked me. I had no choice but to kill them.]

Silence for a few eternal seconds, then:

[SELF has been dutifully aiding you in YOUR objective of retrieving their Genome.]

This was Ampersand's voice. By now, she recognized the sound of it, even in Pequod-phonemic.

[Without consulting me? Poor planning.]
[I do not desire your consultation. I endeavor to plead that you leave US/FREMDA be.]
[And what good are these FREMDA to you?]
[Your ASSETS should have the GENOME.]
[The natives took GENOME from us. We are searching for it.]

[NATIVES.]

Cora felt a tug at her torso, and before she could scream, her body was being dragged through the dirt around the side of the building, out into the open, the force jerking her so hard she almost dropped the tablet. She held it tightly until the dragging stopped and she was lying in the open. Obelus stood directly over her.

When Obelus was calm, he had a delicateness to him, like a ballet dancer. It was as though a jumping spider had been blown up to the size of a Cadillac, his graceful bulk not weighing him down at all. She could feel a terrified bleat trying to escape, but she stopped it, nearly swallowing her tongue. But before Obelus could touch her, Ampersand stepped between them and spoke, and the two again conversed. She caught only this:

[This is a child. Irrelevant.]
[I have seen it before, at the underground military facility.]

Obelus's bright eyes caught hers, twice the size of Ampersand's, shining in the sunset. His gaze was just as overwhelming, but his eyes weren't only betraying attention; they were showing intent.

Ampersand responded, statuesque and calm:

[I would prefer it remain intact.]

Obelus brushed him out of the way, and this time, Ampersand didn't fight him, calmly stepping aside. The terrified noise that she'd fought to hold down came out in full force, and she tried to crab-walk away from the monster, but he swiftly, gracefully reached out with his hand like a black widow readying its prey for consumption and held her down. She made a few noises of babbling incoherence, unable to look away from his gaze.

Obelus examined her neck and then pulled away from her, leaving her supine on the ground. He spoke to Ampersand again, and after a few seconds, when her muscles finally unlocked and allowed her to look down at the tablet, she glimpsed a portion of what he said:

[Its DNA was present at the vehicle caravan. It must have been wounded to leave so much blood.]

His long, meat hook fingers, so much like Ampersand's but thicker, took her arm to examine it. Obelus spoke again. Cora didn't dare look down at the tablet until Obelus looked away from her.

[But its wounds have been healed, and I know of only one in this group with the ability to heal natural wounds with such efficacy. You took great care to heal this one. Why?]
[I have use for it still.]
[It could easily be replaced.]

Ampersand stepped between them again, his air bordering on aggressive.

[I see no need to argue my motivations for something so irrelevant.]

Cora gagged, wiping the dirt, sweat, and fluids from her face. *Please don't call me irrelevant, Ampersand. He'll kill me just to prove how irrelevant I am.*

She peeked across the dirt road, a few meters away to Esperas, held down by invisible chains and positively radioactive with anger. No fear, no hope, just anger. Even across species, without speech or facial expressions, Cora could feel it. But she was far too afraid to share it.

Obelus seemed to have lost interest in her altogether, attention now on Ampersand.

[We have dealt with samples of this species so extensively when we were technocrats. I had supervised you euthanizing and dissecting dozens of these specimens.]

Cora couldn't help but look at Ampersand, and their eyes met as though he were checking to see if she'd caught that. Then he responded:

[This is their planet; performative respect of their persons is integral to gaining their trust.]

[I want to know the significance of this Terran.]

[Biological relative to one of the Fremdan caretakers.]

[Explain, then, the device in its ear through which you speak to it.]

[I used it as a vessel to communicate with NATIVES.]

[Ask it if it knows the location of the Genome.]

Cora forgot to breathe, her eyes darting to the tablet, then to Ampersand. If Obelus had noticed the tablet, he didn't think anything of it. He must have thought it was an iPod or something.

He doesn't know I can understand their language.

"*He believes you know the location of the Genome,*" said the voice in her ear. "*He asks you to reveal its location.*"

Cora's mind hit a wall, words failing her, unable to speak the truth and terrified of lying. She caught the intimation here—Ampersand knew the location, and if he hadn't given it up, he didn't want her to, either. After all, fusion bonding meant there was some sort of sensory perception with these two, but as he had explained to her before, they could not read each other's minds.

Obelus has a low opinion of humans, she reasoned. *Might as well play to his expectations.*

She blubbered incoherently, crawling next to Ampersand and grabbing one of his feet, working up a good, believable, frothy panic. "I don't know what that means, Ampersand, don't let him hurt me! Please, don't let him hurt me! *Don't let him hurt me!*"

Making it believable wasn't difficult.

She curled up into a fetal position next to Ampersand's feet, continuing to whimper little "don't hurt me's" as she wrapped herself around the tablet at an angle where she could just see the text, trying to walk a fine line between believably panicked and not quite annoying enough to kill.

Obelus moved away from them and observed:

[Histrionic communication vessel.]

Ampersand responded:

[You have observed them long enough to know they are all like this.]

[Their trust benefits you little if they are hiding your GENOME and you do not know its location.]

[After all you have put me through since the purge—SMALLEST of reparations.]

Obelus looked over at his flock of bewildered prisoners as though he'd only just remembered they were there. Most were cooperating, motionless and frightened, but Esperas was alert, livid, and confrontational, even. He never took his eyes off Ampersand.

Obelus continued:

[I do believe that you would accomplish this endeavor quicker without my presence. I do believe that the NATIVES trust you. I do not believe that you ever intended to deliver GENOME to me. But what benefit is there for me freeing you after our MUTUAL objective is concluded?]

[You don't want me dead, but you don't want to risk the possibility that I might reveal your true identity to your SUBORDINATES.]

[And if you don't, here are twenty-five more who would.]

She saw Esperas go still, and she half expected to see him disintegrate as well, unzip like Kruro had. Obelus placed a delicate hand behind Esperas's head as if he were picking up an infant, and he spoke. The tablet translated only:

[ESPERAS.]

Esperas was positively electric with hatred, and every joule of it was directed at Ampersand. Ampersand didn't even look at him.

Obelus kept on going:

[Why did you not share the truth of my identity / our bond to caste-peer, ESPERAS?]

Ampersand responded:

[It was for your protection, my BELOVED. I did not want INFORMATION revealed to your inferiors that you may not want them to know.]

Obelus spoke again:

[I require insurance you won't betray me.]
[I require incentive not to betray you.]
[What do you value, BELOVED? There is little in this universe left that you value. But I require more than insurance that you won't betray me—I require insurance you will not end your own life.]

Obelus stood up to his full height. Again, the energy in the air changed, felt less oppressive, and she saw some of the Fremda stir. He must have released his telekinetic grip on them. He continued:

[I may spare some of them as you wish, if you cooperate, deliver the Genome to me. But I must take insurance. I would take them all, but I do not have the physical means. So a fraction must suffice.]

He plucked a few Fremda from the huddle—Woodward, Bernstein, two more she didn't know. And Esperas. Cora's breath quickened, her vision became spotty, and she saw Ampersand looking back at her, his amber eyes reflecting brightly in the thin, orange light of the sun.

She knew she was going to be included with the insurance.

[I require the human for communication with the natives.]

[Your need to communicate with them is questionable at best. You can accomplish the task without communication. I will take those that are not essential to your present infiltration endeavor. If you are successful, I may return my insurance. If you end your own life, as did ČEFO, I will kill all of them. I may design a pandemic for the humans as well. Their advancement must slow. It would be cruel to allow them to continue at this pace.]

Cora didn't catch any more. She was so panicked, so focused on the tablet, she didn't notice Obelus until he was on her. She barely had the presence of mind to grab the tablet, stuffing it into her jacket as he turned her around and looked at her. He didn't waste telekinetic energy on her, instead picking her up with his hand by her torso. Her limbs fell limp, her eyes still on Ampersand while Obelus examined her like a potentially rotten piece of fruit.

The two were still speaking to each other, but now the tablet was out of sight, tucked away in her jacket. Her muscles were rubber bands on the verge of snapping, waiting for Obelus to demonstrate to Ampersand his point about human fragility. "Please," she said, though she wasn't sure who she was speaking to. It didn't matter. Both of them ignored her.

Still mid-conversation, Obelus turned from Ampersand and tossed Cora with the group he'd decided on as insurance. Esperas, as always, didn't even look at her, not even as they were each wrapped in individual darkness.

36

The air in the container was stuffy, recycled, and never enough. She had no idea where she was or how long she had been there. Hours, days, it became a blur. She could sometimes sense movement, as though she were existing outside of gravity and light, but the rules of physics insisted on intruding on occasion. She couldn't tell whether she was being ported somewhere or if she had been abandoned in the deepest ocean. It was as though all sound, all matter, all movement on the other side of the film that surrounded her had been swallowed.

After what was probably less than half a day, she began to beat on the shell of the body bag. She had no choice but to soil herself a few times, and the stuffy bag reeked of urine. She beat on the side of it until she started to feel the moisture of broken skin on her knuckles, and she screamed until she was hoarse. She knew it was futile, but just doing *something* was preferable to wasting away in her own filth.

Before Obelus had put her inside this thing, he'd taken

them to some clearing in the middle of nowhere, within a few miles of the barn. Cora wasn't sure how he moved them; it had felt like accounts of abductions she'd heard, disoriented and outside of time and space until she was facedown on the ground somewhere else entirely, and Obelus was on top of her. She felt the translation tablet being removed from her jacket. Obelus barely looked at it for a second before he tossed it away like an empty soda can. She felt a piercing pain in her neck, and then a *pop* as he sucked out Ampersand's tracking device. She felt a tiny trickle of blood coming down the side of her neck, and she bit her tongue, willing herself not to scream. When for a few seconds Obelus concentrated his attention on Esperas, she turned over and made a grab for the tablet. She stuffed it back into her jacket just before he put all of them inside the body bags and left them there.

Now, days or hours or minutes later, she again kicked and scratched at the shell that held her in the bag. This time, to her surprise, the shell of the body bag gave, and she was exposed to a shock of cold. She cried out, surprised but relieved to be free from the suffocating closeness. She could hear movement and what sounded like a violent, voiceless struggle very close by.

Not wanting to draw attention to herself, she turned over and allowed herself a glimpse. The light was dim, the sun was setting, and they were in a vast pine forest. She thought she heard the ocean, but it might have been the wind. She thought that perhaps this might be somewhere in the Pacific Northwest.

This could be a fluke, she thought. *Maybe I could run.*

A thought, another voice, as clear as her own inner monologue spoke up: *Do not move.*

Then she saw the Similars. Obelus and another Similar were standing over Esperas, and they had some sort of filament going into the back of his head. It looked like fiber-optic filament, deceptively simple. Every few seconds, his body jerked in spasms, which likely would have been more violent had the second Similar not been holding Esperas down with its foot.

Then she spotted the other hostages nearby. They seemed pinned to the ground, pulled down by the invisible magnet, and a ring of lighted filament surrounded them. Esperas's body spasmed again, and this time a terrible sound accompanied it. It sounded almost *natural,* a sound the Genome would make, nothing like the tinny, mechanical-sounding Pequod-phonemic she'd become accustomed to. When it ended, Esperas fell limp. The other Similar moved him to the little invisible dome next to the vessel where the Fremda were being held. Then Obelus turned his attention to Cora.

She scrambled to stand up, her legs wobbly from lack of use. She had often been amazed at how Ampersand, himself almost as tall as a small bus, hardly ever made noise when he moved, and Obelus was no different. It was hard to gauge intent, whether or not Obelus was contemplating the least messy means of disposing of her or if he was simply curious, but regardless, Cora wanted to blather some sort of plea.

The voice in her head spoke up again: *It would be ill advised to attempt to negotiate with him.*

She wanted to look away but couldn't, and wondered if he had put her under some kind of mind control, something that was keeping her gaze firmly fixed on his awful eyes, making her feel stripped naked. Obelus grabbed her around the waist and picked her up, taking her toward the force field with the others. He wasn't gentle like Ampersand, and his grip hurt her ribs, but she managed not to make a sound. A spot in the filament went dim as he tossed her in like a rag doll. He stared at her for a long while, then he was gone.

The gravity in the little invisible dome was so intense she wasn't even able to sit up, and it forced her onto her side. She wrapped her arms around herself and shivered, looking at her five miserable companions. It was so much colder out here than it had been in the South, which was enjoying an unusually balmy autumn. As she hugged herself, she felt something hard in the pocket of her flimsy jacket.

She still had the translation tablet.

Alive for now, she reasoned, meant that Obelus had at least been somewhat sincere on the topic of keeping her and the rest of this group alive as "insurance." She rolled onto her back, looked at the dim, overcast sky wreathed in tall pines, and tried to push past how painfully dehydrated she was. How long had Obelus given Ampersand to pay up? Had they even come to some sort of understanding? If they had come to some agreement that Obelus would return his insurance in exchange for the Genome, Cora had not caught it.

The air left her body at the thought of the Genome. The already fantastically slim chance of Cora surviving this was contingent on the Genome effectively being put up as ransom. All that effort saving her life, for nothing.

She turned to Woodward and Bernstein and started making her way toward them, but the pressure was so heavy that it was a struggle even to army-crawl. She figured that they weren't unable to move, but that they must be in some self-preservation mode, lying on their sides like insectoid fetuses. Out of the corner of her eye, she saw two Similars, stonelike in their stillness. Obelus was gone, and with him, one of the other three. Then her father's voice popped into her head, and she could so clearly imagine the cocky, smug tone he would have used: "What did the president know, and when did he know it?"

And again, she wondered if Obelus would approach Ampersand's underlings, knowing they could spill the truth about Obelus's genetic lineage. It may have been a massive stretch. But Esperas hadn't known anything about Ampersand and Obelus being symphyles, and Obelus's Similars, according to Ampersand, did not know that Obelus was Fremdan, either. That he, like the rest of their race, should be long dead.

"Hey," she whispered, keeping an eye on the Similars. "Esperas." Esperas wasn't looking at her.

She turned over and crawled on her belly toward Esperas. "Hey."

Nothing.

Cora huffed and looked again at the Similars. They appeared invested in each other and not at all in their captives.

"You will listen to me," she continued. She pulled out the tablet, placing it in front of Esperas so he couldn't avoid seeing it. His eyes didn't move or change focus. "I understand your attitude on the dangers of communication. Now more than ever, I understand it. At the end of the day, we will never be people to you. But you and I are on equal ground right now."

She stopped, cowed, when Esperas looked at her. He had never looked her, or any human, in the eye before. Woodward and Bernstein dared to sit up now as well, intrigued, but neither of them spoke.

"But that doesn't matter right now," she said. "We have to get out of here. There has to be a way we can get a message out, let Ampersand know where we are."

Esperas pulled himself up into a roosting position, never taking his eyes off her. His eyes didn't catch light the way

Ampersand's did, relatively small with flecks of blue, but shone more onyx than amber. And those eyes imparted to her an unmistakable message: *You have no idea what I've just been through.*

And she didn't. Moreover, she didn't care. She wanted a plan of attack, but she didn't even have the tiniest seedling of one.

"Say something," she said quietly. Esperas continued to stare at her.

"Stelo? Krias?" She turned the tablet to them. "Say something?" They, too, looked her in the eyes but remained silent. And she realized they couldn't speak. None of them could.

She rolled on her back, air escaping her like an old tire. Of course Obelus wouldn't want his captives to be able to speak to his Similars; the captives knew his terrible secret. So correspondingly, they were left without a way to communicate. Obelus was not going to let any person, human or otherwise, who knew what he really was survive this. Ampersand must have known that. And the desperate hopelessness she had been holding back finally overwhelmed her, and she wept.

She put the tablet away and pulled herself away from them. The realization that Obelus did not truly intend to let them survive meant she would never see Olive again. That her family would never know what had happened to her. That Luciana let her speed off into certain danger, and then she was never heard from again.

She wished she had done more for them when she'd had the opportunity. As soon as she had started communicating with Ampersand, she had contrived every means to stay attached to him, just because she wanted to know more. She wanted to be attached to his importance, and all the while, she had completely forgotten why she had agreed to help him in the first place.

"Olive, Felix," she whispered aloud, tears spilling down her cheeks, "I'm sorry I didn't do more to help you. I'm sorry I forgot about you. I love you. I'm sorry."

You are aware that humans are incapable of any kind of telepathy.

Ampersand, even as a figment of my imagination, could you please just humor me?

It is an improvident use of time.

Cora felt her face flush, and she sniffled loudly, realizing that she was having an argument with an imagined version of the reason she was in this mess. *You told me to leave when I had the chance, and I didn't listen to you. Can you really blame me for trying to make cosmic amends before they kill me?*

There could be a more fecund way to utilize your time. You aren't altogether at a disadvantage.

She looked over at the Similars and then back down to the pitiful little translation tablet.

Disadvantage?

You have tools your comrades do not.

Cora stopped breathing. She looked at the tablet, then at the Similars. Obelus was nowhere to be seen.

You are aware of my own weaknesses, weaknesses you do not share. You know the danger both to your kind and to mine, and you have stated your belief as to what needs to be done. Therefore, it falls upon you to do what I cannot.

"Do what I cannot," she whispered.

It had always been in the back of her head that if any human killed Obelus or any of his Similars, that would be tantamount to a declaration of war, with humanity as the aggressor. They could save their own lives in the short term only to doom humanity in the long run. But humanity couldn't be held accountable for the death of a high-ranking militarist if it was revealed that said militarist had been "genetically defective" the whole time. A fraud and, therefore, a traitor. Humanity could claim no accountability in that case.

It might work, if it was his own Similars that killed him.

She struggled to her feet, pushing against the oppressive gravity in the little dome, forcing her body to stand itself upright. She grabbed hold of the tablet firmly, looked up at the Similars, and yelled, "I wish to communicate!"

They turned to look at her. They seemed perplexed, as though they were dealing with a creature that simply didn't know the protocol.

Then they saw the tablet.

"I have the means," she said, "and I wish to communicate with you."

For a second, the gravity seemed determined to crush her from all sides, then she was being lifted out of the dome by the invisible hand, the telekinesis of one of the Similars.

Their eyes, like Esperas's, were dark, and she couldn't get a read on either of them. Their eyes weren't overwhelming like the technocrats', but they were calculating eyes. These weren't mindless, murdering drones.

They examined her as she tried to calm her hyperventilating. They said only one thing out loud that her tablet picked up:

[Fragile, very fragile.]

She forced herself to speak. "I want to know," she cried, with no clue as to whether it would translate correctly, "why was Obelus sent here to kill his symphyle?"

The Similars didn't move or speak, but just watched her, as

if waiting for her to finish a thought. She thought she might not have been clear enough. "Why would Obelus want to kill the amygdaline we call Ampersand, his own symphyle?"

This caused a shift in both of them. She felt her body being grabbed by one of their minds, contorted, lifted, and the tablet being taken away from her. The one on the left in particular no longer looked perplexed, but livid. He spoke:

[Misinformed.]

"I'm not misinformed," she squeaked. She couldn't breathe. "I know the amygdaline Ampersand. I was his interpreter, I spoke for him . . ." Every word was harder and harder to get out. She felt like her neck, her lungs were being squeezed from the inside. She cried out. "Ampersand is bonded to the Fremdan Obelus."

The two seemed more interested now in each other than in her—as if perhaps this had been a suspicion all along, perhaps there had been some sort of controversy. But that telekinetic grip on Cora was tight, too tight, crushing her from the outside and in. Were they having a telekinetic tug-of-war over her? "Stop," she begged. "You're crushing me. Stop!"

It didn't stop; in fact, whatever argument these two were having among themselves was being taken out on her. The agony was short but blinding. Then one of them won out so fiercely that the force from it threw her against a nearby tree, bashing her head, ripping the air out of her lungs.

Her coherency came in bursts; she tried to stop making noise, slow the sound of the ragged breaths she was pulling in. Distantly, she was curious—she'd never had a concussion before and wondered if she had one now. In her fugue, it took her a moment to see that Obelus had returned, was standing over her. He was regarding her again with the same expression he had a short time earlier. She looked to see if his subordinates were reacting, might attack him, but no. The hierarchy was still firmly in place.

It hadn't worked.

He was doing something to her neck, injecting something into it, and the pain numbed, and she, too, was silent.

Hello, Friends and Strangers,

I've been trying to think of a way to articulate this. I've spent hours trying to find words, but there are none, and time is of the essence, so I'll be direct.

We just posted a document stating that my ex-wife and three children, Felix, Olivia, and Cora, have been taken into federal custody.

Even more bewildering, the document states outright that they aren't being held under any charge except as "accessories." Accessories to what, it doesn't say. But I will state now and in front of any court: they are not now, nor have they ever been, an accessory to me.

This is unconscionable.

What can I say? I know what you've done. Now the world does. You've gone beyond trampling civil liberties; you've obliterated them.

For God's sake, they're *children*.

Release them.

Ortega, Nils. "'Open Letter.'" *The Broken Seal*. October 9, 2007. http://www.thebrokenseal.org.

By the time she opened her eyes, the intense brightness made her think that perhaps she were dead. But no, this brightness wasn't death; it was just the sky. An overcast sky. Then she heard a voice in her ear telling her: "*Remain conscious.*"

She tried to look around for Ampersand, move to call for him, but her body did not respond to her commands.

"*When you regain control of your body, and you will shortly, you need to run.*"

She forced her head to fall to her right side and saw Esperas lying on his back right next to her. Amygdalines looked so unnatural on their backs—like dead insects made of dry slate. She couldn't tell if he was alive, his glassy eyes fixed in a skyward stare, his head lolled at an uncomfortable angle.

They were no longer in the mountains, either; this place was flat, muggy, empty, with woods shrouded with stubby trees and crabgrass in the distance, the ground sprinkled with recently fallen leaves.

"*We have a much greater chance of success if you take the initiative to remove yourself and the unconscious hostages onto the semiautonomous plates after I detonate the pulse.*"

She was at the end of the line of hostages—Woodward and Bernstein on the end opposite from her, then the one she didn't know, and Esperas right next to her. One of the Similars was holding two more she didn't recognize. It took Cora a moment to realize that it wasn't two of them but one of them in several pieces.

Then she saw Ampersand—he was opposite Obelus, and Obelus was talking at him. Not to him, *at* him, Obelus's chatter seeming to bounce off his shell while Ampersand just stood there. He seemed helpless and, frankly, indifferent. He was also Genome-less. It would seem that he'd made his decision, and whatever decision that was, Obelus was not happy about it.

One of Obelus's grunts moved toward Bernstein, moving to do the same thing to him as he had to the other one—not evaporate the creature like they had Kruro earlier but just rip him apart. It made sense, she thought. Ampersand had mentioned that their ability to manipulate electromagnetic fields required an incredible amount of energy. A simple dismemberment must have been much more energy efficient.

The Similar hesitated before Bernstein; it looked almost as though Obelus and his underling were having some sort of telepathic disagreement. The grunt left Bernstein and moved to Esperas instead. He grabbed Esperas's head and locked his fingers around it like he meant to tear it off. Ampersand still didn't move or respond.

More outrage from Obelus. More silence from Ampersand. The Similar moved again, and the voice in her ear spoke:

"*I have several fail-safes if you are unable to cooperate, but our already slim chance of success is increased if you are indeed as intuitive as I hope you are.*"

She moved to respond to this but found she had no more control over her body than she had as soon as she'd regained consciousness. The Similar had left Esperas in one piece—it had now moved on to her. It was now *her* head in its claw, *her* head it was about to rip off for show. She closed her eyes. She was still so numb, her mind too bleary to be terrified.

Distantly she was aware that she was anesthetized, her senses dulled. She opened her eyes, looked at Ampersand. She was starting to believe she'd imagined even hearing his voice in her ear at all.

"*Be ready,*" said the voice in her ear. "*Run to the truck.*"

Then a bright light flashed, burning her sensitive eyes, forcing them shut. She hadn't been anticipating it, and then she remembered why it felt familiar—it looked and felt like Obelus's energy pulse. When she opened her eyes, she saw that Obelus, Ampersand, and all the Similars had collapsed into broken heaps. The one that had been standing over her had nearly crushed her.

Cora sat up, gasping loudly. A dam inside her had burst, and every ounce of blood inside her flooded to her head. Obelus was down. They *all* were. Obelus must have been using some energy field to keep her still, but whatever it was had switched off as soon as he had. She was surrounded, her mind jumbled, confused as to what was real and what she had imagined. Then she recalled the last instruction she'd gotten: *Run to the truck.*

She stood up, surprised her legs even supported her, and spun around. *The truck, the truck.* This wasn't the complete middle of nowhere—it looked like fallow farmland. There were fences in the distance, garbage everywhere. A few feet away, she spied empty beer bottles, a rusty hoe, an even rustier shovel. And there was a truck sitting on a road about a hundred yards from where she stood. It couldn't have been the truck they'd stolen back in Nevada, the red-and-gray Ford F-150, but it sure looked like it.

Ampersand must have turned the same pulse technology Obelus had used at Google, at NORAD, and again against her caravan, around on them. Obelus's first pulse had been powerful enough to knock out the power to the entire Google campus, and Ampersand had taken hours to come to, but she didn't know how powerful *this* pulse was or how powerful the Similars were in relation to Ampersand. It could take hours for them to recharge. It could also take a matter of minutes.

She ran for the truck.

She stumbled, the blood-rush to her head bringing her dangerously close to fainting, her head throbbing. She hopped up on the ledge of the truck's bed, gulping for air, and saw that there were indeed several autonomous plates resting inside. Now there was the question of how to get them where they needed to be.

She hopped down from the bed, and as she tore the driver's-side door open, she saw that she was not alone in it. There was the Genome, holding some small alien device the size of a phone receiver, chirruping a few careful alien words. The skin under that translucent, icing-like suit was no longer splotchy, her eyes clear and bright. She looked perfectly fine.

Cora all but lunged toward the Genome without thinking, causing the Genome to shrink back in fright. Cora pulled away, momentarily forgetting that she was the giant alien monster in this scenario. She put her hands behind her back. "You!"

The Genome stood back up. She held up the device in her

hand and chattered frantically in her language, more like a squirrel barking than the percussive, metallic Pequod-phonemic. The device looked like a high-tech pill bug, legs and all.

"You're the fail-safe."

Cora hopped in the truck, found the key in the ignition, and began the process of trying to start it. As it had with the murdervan after the Google pulse, the engine turned after one try. *Targeted energy pulse for amygdaline bodies,* she thought, *not for trucks from the 1980s.*

By this point, at least two minutes had passed.

Genome in tow, Cora drove the short distance back to the killing fields. So far, there was no movement in any of them, and she didn't want to think about what she might do if there were. But she felt weak, the concussion making her nauseated, and getting the plates out and where they needed to be was much harder than it looked. She grabbed one and tried to muscle it out of the truck but was shocked at how heavy it was. Having only seen these things float at Ampersand's command, she'd assumed they were light as air.

Woodward and Bernstein, being roughly the size of ten-year-olds, were the easiest to move. She started with Woodward, struggling to pick him up as he was heavier than he looked, then carrying him to the plate, collapsing his limbs as per Ampersand's instructions back in the Cheyenne Mountain Complex. Her folding job was clumsy and sloppy, nothing like the way she knew these guys were capable of moving when they were conscious. But she collapsed him as best she could in the center of the plate and stood back. The plate moved, spread itself up and around Woodward's body like shrink-wrap, and then disappeared.

She dashed to get another plate to do the same for Bernstein.

Again, she collapsed him and got him onto the plate, much quicker this time now that she knew getting them as perfectly compact as they were able wasn't a prerequisite. She noticed that the Genome was concerned not with the plates but with Ampersand and had placed the pill bug device on his back just below his neck, pressing on it as if it were a defibrillator, causing his body to jerk ever so slightly. Clearly, the Genome's instructions were to resuscitate him, not get him onto a plate.

In the few seconds it took for Cora to take this in, she saw one of the Similars' eyes shoot open. It didn't move otherwise, but there was enough of a focus to let her know that it was conscious. She charged back to the truck for more plates, moving up the line, using the size of the individual as triage—the smallest ones first. After Bernstein came the one who was still in one piece.

And then there was Esperas.

Cora slid the plate next to Esperas's inert body as she had with the others, then paused, looking back toward the Genome, who was frantically moving that pill bug device onto different spots on Ampersand's back. The Genome looked at Cora urgently but made no gesture, only changed the spot on Ampersand where she was releasing the charge. He jerked again but remained otherwise motionless.

Triage would mean saving Ampersand first. Ten minutes must have passed since the pulse—was saving Esperas worth jeopardizing Ampersand?

She moved another plate next to Ampersand and tried to shove him onto it. She managed only to turn him onto his side. The effort of pushing him nearly caused her to faint again and brought her nausea to a breaking point, and she heaved yellow bile on the pale brown grass. She grunted in loud frustration, causing the Genome to back away before going back to her mission with the pill bug defibrillator.

Cora was wasting time, and deep down, knew she was just digging for a rationalization to abandon Esperas. Angrily, she shoved his limbs up against his body and struggled to roll him onto the plate. Esperas easily exceeded two hundred pounds and was impossible to move without his limbs dragging out behind him.

Cora managed to get him onto the plate and again shoved his limbs up under him. Eventually, the plate deemed her job adequate, and it enveloped Esperas and disappeared.

There were three plates left—one for her, one for Ampersand, and one for the Genome.

She moved back to the two of them, pushing a plate next to the Genome, then stood over Ampersand's inert form. The Genome looked up at her, blathering something in her own language. Transparent panic—the same thing Cora would do if their positions were reversed. She knelt, pushing the plate right up to the Genome's feet. She slapped her palm in the middle of the plate, pointed to it, gestured to it in enough ways to be universally unmistakable. "You need to get out of here."

The Genome responded in kind—spoken language—but she didn't budge. Just pressed down on the pill bug defibrillator once more.

Cora stood up again, using her size to intimidate. "Get on the plate."

The Genome may not have understood her words, but she certainly understood the shift in tone. Her eyes grew wider, her body language more contrite and submissive, but she kept her hands on the defibrillator device on Ampersand's back.

Then Cora noticed Ampersand's eyes flicker. "Ampersand!"

He was still in the process of booting up, not quite in control of his body, his eyes opening and closing like a repeated software restart. The Genome let the pill bug device fall to the ground, speaking urgently to Ampersand. It took him nearly a minute before he was able to respond to the Genome in her own language, but he didn't move.

Then the Genome looked at Cora, a strange, implacable expression. She stepped onto the plate Cora had left for her, was enveloped by it, and disappeared.

One more to go.

"Ampersand? Can you move? Can you speak?"

He did speak, but in Pequod-phonemic. His algorithm to decode English must not have been online yet. Then she felt another movement from the Similars, this time from Obelus. More than eyes shooting open—his arms were beginning to move.

He was trying to stand up.

Cora looked at the plate she'd pulled out for herself and then at Ampersand. It had taken every fiber of her strength to get Esperas onto his plate, and Ampersand was nearly twice the size of Esperas. And he was nowhere near to being able to hoist himself onto that plate.

Cora looked around for something, anything, that might buy them some time. There was the truck, there were the scattered bits of trash. There was that rusty farm equipment—the rusty hoe and rustier shovel. Her body moved to the shovel almost of its own volition, and she grabbed it, recalling something Ampersand had said to her weeks ago, alone in the dark of that motel room in Nevada: "*When I was recovering from the pulse, I was vulnerable. You could have killed me easily.*"

Her grip around the old shovel tightened, and she turned toward Obelus. She thought of all the times Ampersand had told her humans were dangerous. The fear he had exhibited when he'd learned he had been unconscious in that van with her for several hours. The fear he *still* exhibited.

Obelus had managed to lift himself up onto his wrists, but his heft was too great, his energy near nonexistent, and he wasn't yet able to stand up. Cora's approach became more of a charge, and like a wave coming out of the ocean, she felt a primal power push her forward, lift the shovel up above her head, and using the momentum of her entire body, brought it down on Obelus's back.

The giant fell onto his stomach and did not move.

Cora's adrenaline spiked, her skin grew hot, the next wave of force in her a tsunami. She saw the monster try to move an arm to defend himself, but she beat it back. Again, he attempted to lift himself up, but another hard knock on the back sent him flat onto his stomach. Again, and again, and again, she came down with the shovel, the outer hull of his shell crumpling in on himself like aluminum foil.

"*Stop!*" It was Ampersand. She ignored him.

Obelus tried to grab the shovel, but she ripped it out of his hand easily, backed up a few feet, and rushed him, forcing him to fall onto his back. She hit him twice more to keep him down, put one foot down on his midsection to hold him. She could feel his strength returning, as she actually had to struggle to hold him down. She lifted up the shovel and thrust it down into his midsection like a spear. Obelus howled, a polyphonic shriek.

"*You'll rupture his power core!*" said the voice in her ear, much louder than it had ever been. "*You'll kill us all!*"

No, she thought. *How do I kill this thing?*

She asked the question in her mind like she expected it to be answered. Then, it was as if the answer were obvious, like she just knew. She traced a path in her mind, a strange path that felt alien to her, as if she were looking into someone else's thoughts at something she was not supposed to see. It felt almost like a schematic—a schematic of Obelus.

He is alive, she thought. *He is organic. He is vulnerable. Show me how to kill him.* And the imagined schematic told her how simple it was; she had seen it in the autopsy. Like humans, amygdalines had a large arterial nerve that ran down the middle of their necks. And something almost outside of her told her: *Sever that nerve, and he will die.*

She pulled the shovel out of Obelus's thorax, lifted it up again, and drove it down toward Obelus's neck. This time Obelus swerved, just missing the shovel plunging into the earth. Swerved, or had she missed? An intense feeling of relief bubbled up, like it was *good* that she had missed.

"*Stop!*"

She ripped the shovel out of the ground as Obelus tried to shove himself away, tried to lift his massive heft, but he was still too weak to stand. She swung the shovel up again and whipped him on the back, forcing Obelus back down onto his stomach.

The back of his head, normally protected by a force she could not see, was open, unshielded. Once again, she could intuit where she needed to strike, practically feel it in her mind's eye. It was like a soft spot in a baby's head, open and vulnerable directly to the brain. His power grew exponentially by the second—this would be her only chance. She raised the shovel back, preparing to drive it into his brain.

She felt the wind knocked out of her before she realized she was flying, and for an instant, she was coursing over the brown crabgrass, and then her back hit the dirt, and the shovel flew out of her hands. It took two solid attempts to inhale before her lungs allowed air back in. Before she even got a breath, she sat up to get her bearings. She knew the source of that telekinetic shove, and it had not been Obelus. She pushed herself up on her elbows, saw Ampersand struggling to stand up some hundred feet away, lumbering like an injured bird, still reeling from using up what little energy he had after that telekinetic push.

Cora grimaced, her resolve encasing itself in iron, and she might have gone for the shovel again had she not seen Obelus's state. He was still trying to get to his feet, pushing against the gravity of Earth, painfully, like a *T. rex* full of buckshot, but with each passing second, he stabilized, all the while keeping his eyes on her.

She considered making a run for her plate, which was presently on the other side of Obelus. Obelus shook his head as though he were shaking off the laws of gravity, steadily regaining that delicate bearing of a monstrous ballet dancer. Right next to him, she saw that his other Similars were beginning to stir.

Then he moved toward her.

Cora lunged for the shovel, figuring if she could beat him back down to the ground just once, that might give her enough time to get to the plate. She got to the shovel in time to touch it, but not in time to pick it up, Obelus now charging like a bull. She only just managed to roll out of the way.

Obelus stopped, turning on a dime as she reached for the shovel, backhanding her with his meat hooks. She fell on her back again and gave up on the shovel, scrambling to her feet and heading back toward the plate. She felt the same meat hooks grab her ankle, pulling her to the ground.

Her instincts whiplashed from flight to fight in an instant, and she made a feral noise she'd never thought herself capable of, shocking even Obelus as she turned on her back and delivered a kick into the arm that had grabbed her, a blow just powerful enough to make him let go of her ankle.

Whiplash again to flight—she was barely thinking, no strategy, all instinct. She turned to get away from the monster, did not quite make it to her feet before the meat hooks came down on her leg, this time using the force of the earth to its full advantage, skewering the flesh of her left calf, holding it in place.

Cora cried out as she came down on her side, and she thrashed, a lizard ready to lose the limb if it meant saving her life. The other of the monster's hands came down on her, this time right into her torso, skewering her innards. She was blinded, feeling the threads of her body tear apart like old paper.

Somewhere she was aware that she wasn't the only person screaming, albeit she was the only human. She looked about as though there might be some deliverance to save her from this. She only found the source of the screaming when she followed Obelus's gaze—the Genome, alone in the middle of the grass about fifty feet away, was goading Obelus. She was pulling the translucent film that covered her away from her body.

Cora felt the meat hooks hesitate before digging in farther. More ripping deep inside her. She could feel blood creeping up her esophagus, and she cried out again as though that might keep it down.

Obelus removed his digits from inside her, and Cora grabbed her torso to keep her intestines from spilling out. She turned on her side to see that Obelus was heading toward the Genome— why? The Genome was doing something to herself, but Cora couldn't quite make it out. She was so wrapped up in her own agony, so concerned with not dying, it took her a moment to realize that the Genome had torn the protective film.

Obelus had nearly made it to the Genome before another

telekinetic shove sent him off his feet. It was weak and didn't send him far, barely a stumble, but it was enough for Ampersand to grab the Genome before Obelus did.

"*Please!*" she begged. Warm liquid was pooling into her hands now.

Ampersand was heading toward her, Genome in tow, pressed up against his shoulder as if she were an infant. Even from this distance, she could hear the Genome struggling to breathe.

The semiautonomous plate was by Cora's side before Ampersand was, and she didn't wait for instruction, rolling right onto it, her blood-soaked shirt slapping onto the plate like a wet sponge as she curled into a fetal position. In seconds, Ampersand was on top of her, as was the Genome, and they were all enveloped in darkness.

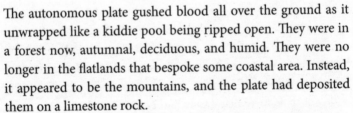

The autonomous plate gushed blood all over the ground as it unwrapped like a kiddie pool being ripped open. They were in a forest now, autumnal, deciduous, and humid. They were no longer in the flatlands that bespoke some coastal area. Instead, it appeared to be the mountains, and the plate had deposited them on a limestone rock.

Cora tried to breathe, only to feel the strands of her being ripped apart at the seams, each breath tearing at the fibers of her person, more blood spurting out from the holes in her torso. How many were there? Two? Three? There was so much blood. Ampersand was covered in it. The Genome was covered in it. It was only here that she became aware that something was deathly wrong with the Genome. The film that had covered her was hanging off her like dead skin. Her breath was heavy, labored, cruel, beginning to sound like a coffeepot gurgling at the end of its run.

Through that, the Genome was managing to speak to

Ampersand, who seemed stunned. Cora considered begging for her life but knew also even if he could give it to her, it would come at the cost of the Genome. With the return of her right mind came a stab of guilt to complement the physical pain— the Genome was dying because of her. The Genome had gotten away but had come back to goad Obelus, because Cora had gone against all common sense and tried to kill him.

Would have killed him, she thought, *if you hadn't stopped me.*

As if responding to that thought, Ampersand practically lunged at her, holding her down, and her animal instinct told her to fight him off. He shoved her forearm into her mouth, then placed her other arm over it.

"*Hold your arm in place to muffle your screams,*" said Ampersand. "*I must cauterize the hemothorax. I do not have time to anesthetize you.*"

Even the act of physically holding her body down was agony, and again, it bucked against him, resisted. And that was before the real pain bloomed in her. Heat, searing white heat. Her legs kicked and thrashed, and it was only when she felt his fingers slide out that she realized they had been inside her.

"*Be still.*"

She bit down harder on her arm and tried to do as he said. *Cauterize* was indeed the word—she could feel the heat, hear her tissue sizzling. Her screams muffled the sound, but nothing could drown out the smell. It was rank, dirty, like burned pork chop. She could hear the Genome's labored breathing next to her as she tried to speak in her own language. Cora tasted blood.

She felt the pressure in her midsection relent before the pain did, and when she took her arm out of her mouth she realized the blood she'd tasted had come from her biting into her own flesh. She wiped the blood from her mouth, looked at

Ampersand, and doubled over again in agony. She expected the pain to ebb when Ampersand pulled away, but it persisted and throbbed, the same persistent sting that accompanies any burn, but multiplied hundreds of times over. She kept her hands glued to her stomach like removing them would result in her entrails spilling all over the forest floor.

Ampersand had moved to the Genome now and was trying to repair the film. His fingers moved like a machine too complex for anyone on Earth to engineer. She had seen them work like that before when he stitched up her arm, but this carried a new energy, a sense of speed she would never have imagined could come from a living thing, even one that was machine augmented.

The Genome labored out sound, barely language compared to the complex sounds she'd been making earlier. Ampersand's machinelike stitching of the film slowed, and then he stopped.

Cora managed, "What is she saying?"

"*She is dying,*" said Ampersand. "*The concentration of nitrogen in the atmosphere is toxic to us, and she has destroyed her protective filter.*"

"Why?"

"*To goad Obelus,*" he said. "*It was a bluff. An accident. She says she didn't intend for the filter to rip. She didn't understand how fragile it was.*"

Cora felt blood rising in her esophagus and swallowed it, the copper taste lining her mouth. The Genome's gaze found Cora, and she was not strong enough to meet it, closing her eyes so she wouldn't have to. The Genome's breathing continued to slow down, sick and watery. Cora opened her eyes, yearning for the sound of the painful, liquid breathing to stop.

And then it did.

Ampersand had his hands up as though he were waiting for the Genome's corpse, limp and sallow and covered in human blood, to reanimate and pounce. The surge of adrenaline that had been coursing through her was beginning to run out. She tried to sit up, but the lightning strike of pain that accompanied her abdominal muscles contracting stopped her. And the adrenaline, the will to survive, translated in her mind as anger. "You should have let me kill him."

Ampersand's focus seemed to dissipate, the nucleus of his eyes spreading out like mist, until the glow of his eyes had faded into a gentle, homogenous amber.

"If Obelus is dead, no one's hunting you, you can—"

"*I will not let you kill him,*" he stated.

Perhaps on some level, she knew this would always be the case—there was no way for Ampersand to escape while Obelus lived. He'd hunt Ampersand down no matter where he fled. But it was a statement of fact; Ampersand would not allow Obelus to die. It just wasn't going to happen.

"If he won't let you go, then he has to die."

"*I will not allow him to die.*"

"Whose life is more valuable? Yours or his? You could do good on Earth; you could help us. You could help us prepare for the *real* First Contact. You could *save us!*"

"*It does not matter.*"

"I told his Similars the truth. I told them Obelus is like you." At this, he looked at her. "And they understood me."

The millions of reflecting surfaces inside his eyes brightened, began to concentrate in a brilliant mass.

"I don't know who Obelus was in his old life," said Cora, gritting her teeth through the sheer pain of simply sitting up. "What his position was in your old life. But I know if his identity really was a secret, they didn't know he was Fremdan or that you two were symphyles . . ."

Ampersand continued to stare at her, but the laser focus of his eyes was softening, dissipating. Then he looked to the sky.

"Maybe we can't kill him," she said. "But *they* can. And if they know he's like you, then they will."

Ampersand's gaze was still to the sky. "*You do not understand what it is to lose a symphyle.*"

"I understand enough to know that you can survive this," she said. "You've survived worse. You can survive this."

Ampersand's body shifted as though he were feeling for barometric pressure changes, and he moved over her. Carefully, he shifted the fingers of one hand under her back and the fingers of the other under her legs and backside, sending white-hot blades of pain shooting through her entire abdomen, and lifted her off the ground.

In the flash of agony at being moved, the anger melted into fear. Fear of dying, fear of him dying. Fear of simply him leaving. As fluidly as he picked her up, she put her bloodied arms on his shoulders and then around his back, her fingers smearing even more blood all over him. She placed her cheek on one of the plates where his neck met his midsection. *Please, don't leave,* she said in her mind like a prayer. *Please, don't leave.*

She hadn't had her eyes closed for more than ten seconds. When she opened them, Obelus was there, standing over the corpse of the Genome, staring down both of them.

3 9

Cora could only imagine how odd the sight of his ex-Oligarch symphyle holding a natural alien as if she were a sacred relic must look to Obelus. She wrapped her arms tighter around Ampersand's neck as though that would in any way protect either of them. The adrenaline ebbing, she was also becoming aware of how cold she was. Not the surface-level cold from being outside but something deep, like her viscera had frozen solid and the cold was working its way out.

The sky was clear, the sun's rays slanting and stinging her eyes as it illuminated Obelus from behind. He barely moved, and Cora noted that the dents she'd made in his shell with the shovel had popped back out.

Obelus moved closer in that deerlike way unique to the Similars, moving into the shadow of a tree. The light of the late afternoon sun made Obelus's eyes catch fire. They weren't identical to the coal ember of Ampersand's eyes, but desaturated somehow, like sunlight reflected off an oil well. She couldn't help but read confusion in his gaze. Here had been this whimpering animal that pissed herself at the mere sight of him, and then that animal turned around and eviscerated him when he was vulnerable. Nearly killed him.

Would have killed him had it not been for Ampersand.

The two began to converse in their own language, and the sound of it, the percussive staccato like rain on a tin roof, made her feel faint. Her body had run dry of the adrenaline keeping her falsely active, to say nothing of being out of blood. She clasped her hands behind Ampersand's neck. She could barely feel her fingers.

"*I cannot leave you on this planet with these naturals,*" said a voice in her earpiece, different from the one she had become accustomed to, deeper and more androgynous.

It had come not from Ampersand.

"*It's irresponsible of you to even suggest such a thing,*" the voice continued. "*I cannot allow that. You are too dangerous, both to them and to the Superorganism should you overtake their civilization, which we both know you would.*"

Cora drew closer to him, confused, wondering if Obelus was just trying to frustrate Ampersand or stall until his energy returned. Ampersand responded to him in Pequod-phonemic.

"*Come now, Beloved,*" said Obelus. His voice in her ear sounded less mechanical than Ampersand's did, deliberate and calm. "*If you respect the natives as much as you purport to, then you know that they consider it rude to converse in a language that they do not understand. We should speak in their vernacular.*"

Ampersand clapped back at Obelus in their language, tightening his grip on Cora ever so slightly.

"*But it is in your nature,*" said Obelus. "*You were bred to dominate, and you cannot possibly hope for any measure of assimilation without wanting to dominate them. You will inevitably become the Autocrat of this planet. It may take time, decades or even centuries, but you are their superior and far too powerful for them to resist. You may be left with no choice. How does that strike you, little one?"* Obelus angled his head and looked directly at Cora. She felt like she might slip out of consciousness any second. *"To have your life in the hands of your future Autocrat, were I so shortsighted as to allow him to stay?"*

Obelus looked at Ampersand. *"You will save this little civilization from pain, misery, and possibly extinction; you may even eventually save them from the Superorganism. You alone in the galaxy, the first to guide another species into Advancement. But the humans will loathe you for it. Every value you hold dear is in direct opposition to their perceptions of what constitutes freedom. You will overtake this planet, you will better them in every way imaginable, and you will be hated for it."*

Cora had no idea what either of them was playing at but couldn't discount what Obelus was saying. Obelus drifted his body directly in front of them.

"So you see, Beloved," said Obelus, *"it is in your best interest that I remove you from this planet. In your state of domination, you are accustomed to respect and love, not fear and hate. On this planet, you are surrounded by creatures that are only coming to learn of your existence, of the existence of any intelligence outside their own."* Obelus lifted his hand, placing one, two, three of his claws onto Cora's scalp, dragging them over her skull with a pressure just shy of painful. She looked at Ampersand.

He didn't move.

"The more they learn about you, the more incomprehensible and terrifying you will become to them. But you will grow attached to them, as I see you already have, and inevitably overtake them,

mold them, conform them to what you wish them to be. Think of all the uprisings you would need to quell, the little lives you would need to extinguish to maintain control. You would become the greatest mass murderer this planet has ever known." He held one of his fingers in place on Cora's temple, pressed in slightly, then removed it.

Ampersand was still, silent.

"*Perhaps killing does not come as easily to you as it does to me, nor does slavery, but if you stay here, you will kill, and you will enslave.*" He looked pointedly at Cora. "*It would be irresponsible of me to allow you to stay on this planet, for you, for the Superorganism, and for human civilization.*"

Ampersand responded in his own language, still unwilling to play the game of using Cora as a proxy.

"*You must, Beloved,*" said Obelus. "*I cannot let you stay here, and I cannot let you die.*"

She closed her eyes, dipped dangerously close to unconsciousness, pulling herself back on some deep sense that if she did, she wouldn't wake back up. When she opened them, she saw that the other three Similars were already descending on them, floating down from the sky like avenging biosynthetic angels. She looked up at Ampersand, wondering what the hell his plan was, even *if* he had a plan. The three Similars seemed disoriented, in the same state Obelus had been a few minutes prior, their movements clumsier than when they were at full power. They rallied around Obelus, all four Similars now towering over the two of them.

"There's four of them, there's four of them," said Cora, trying to temper her pained breathing.

"*Wait, dear one,*" he said. "*Wait.*"

Then one of Obelus's subordinates blurted something in

Pequod-phonemic. Obelus responded and turned to face his subordinates. Ampersand backed away a few paces but made no indication he was going to make a run for it. "*They are using a combination of the network language and Pequod-phonemic,*" he said quietly.

"What's going on?" she asked, her voice now almost a whisper.

"*They are insisting that Obelus kill both of us. They want him to do it. They want to watch him do it. He is explaining to them why he cannot.*"

"Why?" she breathed. "Isn't that insubordination?"

"*Because you have made them suspicious that he is not who he says he is. And right now, his behavior is very much corroborating that suspicion.*"

Cora tried to muster the courage to look at the scene in front of them. It was becoming heated, at least by amygdaline standards. Seconds of tense stillness stretched into years, into centuries, followed by a burst of the spoken language in a cluster, like metal ball bearings being dropped on a tile floor by the handful. The sound made her feel like she would shatter. But their body language was tense, and then all four of them dropped silent, dead still, like stags pausing mid-fight.

Then the three Similars lunged, and in the maelstrom that ensued, Cora wasn't sure what they had lunged at. It all seemed to happen in slow motion, claws flying, rubbery skin shredding, and so *close* she couldn't even tell who was attacking whom, just that she was fairly certain none of their spear-like fingers had gone into *her*. They weren't using their energy like she'd always seen them do before. No pulse, no invisible heat, just fighting with their strength and claws, like naturals, clawing through Obelus's carapace like he'd clawed through hers. Obelus had gained enough energy that he could attempt to fend them off, but not enough to handle all three of them. They almost instantly pinned him to the ground, ripping into his skin as if it were butter.

Ampersand stayed put for one eternal second, maybe even two before he decided to make a run for it. Cora closed her eyes, trying to muscle through the delirium, the dizziness, the pain that accompanied the impact of him running.

"*Stay conscious.*"

Cora forced her eyes open, trying to obey. "I think I'm dying."

Ampersand laid her on the ground, all the while keeping his eyes on the Similars. They were close, uncomfortably close, a city block at the most. She could feel those crude, cauterized seams ripping inside her. She felt a new drip of blood come out of an opening, but nothing compared to the torrent earlier. She was bled dry.

"Why'd we stop?" she whispered.

"*We're cloaked. They can't see us.*"

"For how long?"

"*Until they leave. They'll want to get off this planet immediately to report the 'truth' about Obelus, even though it was a truth of which the Autocrat was always well aware.*"

Obelus was subdued, and the three subordinates were now still, surrounding the body. It seemed that the Similars had only now realized that Ampersand had escaped, and they seemed to be deliberating as to what to do.

"Is he dead?"

"*They're still low on energy,*" said Ampersand. Cora was so disoriented she did not connect with the fact that he did not answer her.

"You think they'll decide this isn't worth their while and leave?" she asked, not looking away.

"*That is my hope.*"

"And if they don't?"

Ampersand didn't answer, and again, she felt the pull toward darkness, this time stronger than she'd yet experienced. The voice in her ear said to her again, "*Stay conscious!*"

With Herculean effort, she opened her eyes. Through the trees, she thought she could see Obelus's eviscerated corpse. The three Similars stood over it, one of them holding the corpse of the Genome. They seemed to be deliberating among themselves. She again felt the pull to darkness and opened her eyes again. They had disappeared.

"Are they gone?" she whispered.

"*Possibly.*"

She sensed something like deep sadness, but a strange distant sadness, a feeling that had not originated from inside her. Ampersand stood up, hesitated, and then moved toward the corpse, leaving her alone.

"Where are you going?"

She dipped back into the darkness, coming to only long enough to see Ampersand standing over Obelus's corpse. She tried to call out for him to come back but couldn't summon the energy. With no voice telling her to stay conscious, she finally gave in.

Hey, Kaveh,

Let me begin with: fuck the Pulitzers. You were robbed.

Second, I'd ask where you got the cables detailing the detainment of my ex-wife and children, but of course, there is no such thing as a secure line these days where email is concerned (hi, Sol, been a while—how's your mom?). I'll just take it at your word that an anonymous source sent them to you and give you my bottomless gratitude for forwarding them to me rather than publishing them yourself. I was going to send a bottle of wine as a thank-you but then remembered that would be in poor taste, so maybe a bottle of Martinelli's would suffice. I recognize that this could have been huge for you, and it was incredibly decent of you to send them to me. "I owe you one" doesn't even begin to cover it.

As for your question about how I plan to engage with the kids, I think in the short term, we should drop it. I reached out to Cora, and she was not receptive (she returned the letter I sent, opened but without comment, which was more or less what I expected). If she hasn't responded by now, she isn't going to.

Felix is a much better bet, especially now that he's old enough to take an interest in what I do. My plan is to initiate contact with him in the next few weeks and see how that plays—my gut tells me he's of an age and temperament that he'll be more receptive than Cora was. We don't even need him to become a flag-flying transparency militant—we just need guarantee that he and his sisters won't publicly come out against me. If he *does* decide he wants to revisit the custody issue and explore the idea of moving to Germany, all the better.

Honestly, I can't believe the detainment even happened, but I'd be lying if I said it wasn't deliriously, miraculously good timing. The detainment gave us momentum, and it would be stupid of me not to ride it. So thanks again, dude. Please don't hesitate to reach out to me if there is anything in the world I can do for you. Best of luck with the piece you're working on. Fuck the Pulitzers, but I do hope you get one.

Your bud,
Nils

Ortega, Nils. "Re: Following up on the detainment." Email to Kaveh Mazandarani, featured contributor for *The New Yorker*. October 11, 2007.

40

Cora's ease into consciousness became a plunge. She gasped and sat up, bracing for the ripping fire from her ripped-up and seared insides. There was an ache, but no ripping.

"Mom?"

Her voice came out a harsh whisper, and just saying that one word made her cough. Demi couldn't contain herself, all but falling on Cora, scooping her into an embrace. Cora braced for pain but felt hardly any. Luciana was there too, standing behind Demi, looking at Cora like she was a reanimated corpse. This was a hospital. They were in a hospital.

"Monster Truck . . . Thor . . ."

Demi coughed out a laugh. "They're fine! Neighbor took them to the vet, and then they were held at the shelter. They're fine. They're okay. Felix and Olive are with them. They're staying with Abuelita."

Demi stood up and glanced at Luciana, and Cora thought she saw accusation in that glance. She pressed into her stomach where Obelus's stab wounds had been. There was pressure, a modest pain, but even feeling through the hospital gown, she could feel that her wounds were gone. "Where is he?"

"Where is who?" asked Demi.

Cora looked at Luciana, who shook her head ever so slightly. Cora caught her meaning, and her heart sank. "How did I get here?"

"We don't know," said Demi, her tone becoming more serious. "Someone . . . just left you here. When we got the call, they said it was like you'd been torn apart and put back together."

"How are you free?" asked Cora.

Demi shook her head, looking almost contrite. "You won't believe this. But Nils."

"Nils?"

"Yeah, someone leaked a document to him proving we were in custody. Then things started moving really fast." She shrugged. "Here we are."

The revelation that Nils had been instrumental in their release should have invoked some reaction in her, but all she could think of was Demi saying, "Where is who?"

Demi hugged her again, kissed Cora's hand, then her forehead, and rested her head down on the edge of the bed; it seemed like she was struggling to look at her. Luciana stayed still, distant, an unwelcome guest that couldn't think up a graceful exit.

"I need to, um . . . I need to make a phone call," said Demi. "I need to tell everyone you're awake. I'll be right back."

Demi shot that glance again to Luciana, who didn't return it as she turned to leave the room. Cora looked up at her aunt, who didn't seem glad at all to be here.

"I'm sorry," said Cora. "For the things I said."

"*That's* what you're sorry for?"

"What should I be sorry for?"

Luciana looked at her as if she were speaking in tongues. "Cora, you've been gone for two weeks."

This, too, probably should have sparked some sort of reaction—alarm, concern, agita. Cora did certainly feel some confusion, as she did not remember any of the last two weeks, but the length of time she'd been gone felt obvious. Of course it had been two weeks. What did you expect? The damage was extensive. Her colon had been ruptured. First, she'd nearly died from exsanguination, then from sepsis. He had needed two weeks to bring her back from that.

"We thought you were dead," said Luciana, her voice breaking. "And anyway, yes, I was really hurt and I was horrified that that was the last time we ever saw each other, and thank God it wasn't. But I told you the truth. I don't know how Nils got ahold of the Fremda Memo; I don't know how he knew to look for it. That's the truth."

The two women looked at each other, and Cora realized there was a divide between them that had never been there before. She knew this wasn't all there was to it, and Luciana did, too. But they would never speak of it.

"I know," Cora lied. "I believe you."

The doctors wanted to keep her there one night, and then two, just to keep an eye on her. It was clear what had been done—she had been sewn up, her body repaired, but with a technology heretofore never seen on Earth. Sol even admitted to her on day two that there were debates being had as to whether it was responsible to let her go, not knowing exactly what had been done to her. On the surface, it seemed to be a highly sophisticated form of microsuturing, but was that all he had done? And would it hold?

And all the while, a deluge of government types from all walks of agency flowed in and out of her room like blood through veins, asking her the same questions over and over again. Where had they gone? What had happened to her? Did she have any idea where the Fremda group might have gone? Cora told a watered-down version of the truth, minus Ampersand's relationship to Obelus.

Sol was in and out all day as a part of that deluge but went surprisingly easy on her. Given that the Fremda group appeared to have departed just like they'd said they would, they were now left with all the detriments and none of the benefits from alien visitation, but at least there was no more time pressure. It took a while for her to actually be alone with Sol, let alone feel like she could bring it up, that she felt she could finally ask anyone about what had happened to Vincent Park and the other people in that caravan.

She had expected a straightforward answer, something along the lines of what burdened generals do in movies when they have to tell the families of loved ones that their son didn't make it. Instead, Sol's expression turned neutral, almost commercial. "Vincent no longer works for the agency."

Cora blinked, and waited for him to expand on that. When he didn't, she asked, "What do you mean, 'He no longer works for the agency'?"

"I mean, he no longer works for the agency."

She searched for a needle of hope in this haystack of bullshit, the possibility that her assumption that Vincent died like the rest of them had been false, but one look at Sol's expression told her there was no hope. That he was quite dead, and that no one was allowed to know about it. "Is this some . . . cover-up bullshit?"

"That is exactly what it is," said Sol, his low voice bordering on a warning. "And I can't tell you any more than that."

She caught his meaning—sometimes people die doing things no one is supposed to know about, and no one would ever know.

"Nils was the only winner, if we're being honest," said Sol. "He was already the Robin Hood of transparency, but then when someone sent him documents about the detainment . . . well, then he *really* got to play hero in the court of public opinion, and it worked. So he's having a great month, at least."

"Who sent him those documents?" asked Cora.

"This burnout shitbag that calls himself a journalist, guy named Kaveh Mazandarani. We have no idea how he got them, though, or why he didn't publish them himself instead of delivering them to Nils. Nils must have some dirt on the guy. Which"—Sol chuckled to himself—"well, if you know anything about Mazandarani, that wouldn't be difficult."

She sat up, the old familiar anxiety itching inside her, the same sense she'd experienced all those weeks ago before any of this had happened, that dread that Nils would use his public platform to try to manipulate her again. "I guess Nils will be expecting us to publicly perform some gratitude."

"Actually," said Sol, and she caught a fleck of guilt in his voice, "I think he got what he wanted from playing the family card. I don't think he'll bother you again. At least for the time being."

"How do you know that?"

He shrugged in a way that told her she wasn't going to find out. "Just a hunch."

She reached for the words to describe what she was feeling, as she'd been instructed to do after so many hours of therapy after Nils left. It wasn't anger or outrage but disappointment.

The word was "disappointment." The word was "loss." There was a part of her that had hoped that this wouldn't be the end of things with Nils. That he'd keep trying, even if it wasn't a material benefit to his career. That he wanted to rebuild this bridge as more than just a tool to elevate his public brand.

After all this time, she didn't know why she'd expected anything different from him.

. . . . .

On the second night, even after the doctor insisted that Cora needed rest, sleep eluded her. The hospital room never truly went dark, and sleep was so shallow and inconsistent she couldn't be sure if it happened. But sometime during those wee small hours, it might have been 1:30 or 3:30, something jerked Cora out of her pseudo-sleep. A presence.

She shot up in her hospital bed and looked around, ignoring the dull ache that accompanied fast movement. Though dimmed, there was hardly any corner of the room that wasn't at least a little bit illuminated. She neither saw nor heard anything, but she felt it. She couldn't even tell how she felt it.

"I know you're here."

A heartbeat passed. Then another. Then the wall opposite the foot of her bed shuddered and gave way, and the cloak fell off Ampersand. A wave of emotion crested in her. "I thought you'd left," she said. "I was so afraid you were gone."

"*Tell me how you knew,*" said the voice in her ear.

"How I knew?"

Ampersand approached the bedside, standing directly over her. "*Tell me how you sensed my presence.*"

"I don't know," she said. She moved away from him,

making herself small against the opposite rail of her bed. "I can't explain it."

"*What are you doing?*"

"Making room," she stated. "So you can lie down next to me." It was only as she said it that the absurdity of suggesting such a thing struck her. *Yes, alien being, lie down next to me as a human person, which you are not, might do.*

He hesitated, then lifted one foot off the ground and onto the hospital bed, and then the other, and he began to settle into his roost, the bed heaving under their combined weights. The whole time, he kept his gaze half-focused, soft amber light reflecting like the coals of a dying campfire. There was no awkwardness or false starts in his movements, but they were careful and slow as he settled, one arm next to her under his body, the other hand over her face until it fell onto her hairline and began a stroking rhythm. Two of his fingers, from the top of her scalp to her ear, a stroke length of ten inches. Five seconds on, five seconds off.

Cora released a breath and closed her eyes, leaning into him. He was so big, him sharing the bed with her meant he was practically on top of her. She opened her eyes, inches away from the joints and fissures where his neck met what could only be described as a thorax. The makeup of his body was still strange. There were so many more apt descriptors for this being than "human." Machine. Insectoid. Reptilian. Dragonlike. Alien. She should be horrified to be in the position she was in, but in that moment, the only thing causing her distress was the thought that this contact was temporary.

Again, she found herself contriving a reason to convince him to stay—but what was there to keep him here? An advancing civilization he'd already considered a lost cause and the corpses of his two symphyles. The person who had summoned him here, and he had died before Ampersand had even located him.

Čefo.

It was only then that it hit her—Čefo, who had ended his life the day of the Obelus event. Obelus, who had followed the same summons Ampersand had. "Čefo was bonded to Obelus, too, wasn't he?"

The rhythmic stroking stopped. "*Yes.*"

"So the three of you were a phyle," she said, unsure how to feel, remembering the time she'd asked a similar question back at Cheyenne Mountain and he had sent her away. "Obelus was the reason he killed himself."

"*Most probably.*"

"If they were symphyles . . . did he do it to keep Obelus from using their bond to find the rest of the group?"

Ampersand hesitated, then at length said, "*I cannot say for sure. It is possible. But Čefo's short-term memory was too damaged for me to have retrieved any meaningful intent for certain.*"

Cora's brow furrowed. "Why weren't you able to use your bond to find Čefo? You . . . you were here for a month before he died."

She sensed something heavy in him, something melancholy. "*Obelus had ways of tracking him that I did not.*"

A part of her wanted to pry but intuited that this was something that he wanted to stay buried. Either way, this was not the most pressing issue in her mind. "Now that Obelus is gone," she said, "would you reconsider staying?"

"*That decision is not completely up to me,*" he said. "*The revelation about my relationship to Obelus, and who Obelus truly was, has damaged my place in the hierarchy.*"

"But if you do leave, then what?"

"*I do not believe there is a 'then what.'*"

Cora's eyes burned, and she felt her face grow hot. "After all this, you'd consider just giving up?"

"*Esperas is of the opinion that with no hope of reprieve and the Genome repossessed by the Superorganism, we have reached the end of our purpose.*"

Quietly, Cora regretted having bothered to shove Esperas onto that plate. "It shouldn't be up to him. I know at least your propagandists want to stay here. I doubt they're the only ones. After all this, you *can't* just give up."

"*Why are you frightened?*"

"I don't know," she said, forcing a laugh, only now realizing how afraid she really was. "I'm trying to keep control of it, but the truth is just the idea of you leaving, or giving up on life, it's terrifying to me. I don't know why. Maybe it's the trauma talking. It's been a traumatic week, hasn't it?"

Ampersand looked down at her and hesitated for an uncharacteristically long time. "*Have you observed any other symptoms?*"

"What kind of symptoms?"

"*Emotional or mental abnormalities, starting when Obelus kidnapped you.*"

She nodded. "When I was with them, the Similars, I heard your voice in my head. I thought I was just . . . delusional with terror, but you told me, 'You have to do what I cannot.' And I took it to mean . . . the only thing I *could* do was . . . what I did do. Using the tablet to tell the Similars that Obelus was Fremdan."

"*What did this voice in your mind sound like?*"

There was an urgency in his tone, one that transcended mere curiosity. She forced a nervous smile. "Ampersand . . . tell the truth. Can you . . . get into my brain?"

"No. *What you are describing is not possible. Even the process of learning human language was an arduous one that took years. The brain waves and physiology of our respective species are even more disparate than our spoken languages. Even among our own species, what you are describing is only possible through direct neural contact. I was not sending you telepathic messages.*"

Cora felt something like disappointment. Confusion, even. Like she knew what he was saying wasn't entirely accurate or she was missing a vital piece. She'd heard that voice in her mind so clearly. Then later, when she had tried to kill Obelus, the feeling that she had known exactly where and how to do it, that she could see his vulnerabilities like hot spots.

"You did something to me," she whispered.

Ampersand's rhythmic stroking slowed and then stopped. He shaded his eyes in one long, languid blink. And suddenly, she was aware of a presence, *his* presence, the same she'd felt in the woods with the Similars, like being haunted by a ghost. "What aren't you telling me?"

"*I do not think it wise.*"

Cora pushed his hand away and wormed her way out from under him. "What won't you tell me?"

"*If I have kept things from you, or from anyone, it was for your protection. And for mine.*"

She shook her head slowly but struggled to find the words. Maybe it had been a strategy, and he had his reasons, but that didn't mean it was the right strategy. Ampersand had been correct to distrust the various government agencies— they couldn't be trusted not because of malice but because of shortsightedness, ignorance of what they were dealing with, and sloppiness. Their messiness had landed them and the country in the chaos they found themselves in presently. But between the two of them? Between "Entity Ampersand" and his interpreter? Had any good come from his keeping secrets from her?

No.

His secrecy regarding the Genome had led to the humans nearly killing her in their ignorance. His secrecy regarding his relationship to Obelus had put hundreds of people in peril and killed others. It was only when Cora—or indeed anyone—had any idea as to what they were dealing with that they could hope to come up with a useful solution. Ignorance rendered people useless. Did he want to be stuck on a planet populated by billions of ignorant, useless children?

Then she remembered the things Obelus had said to her in the forest—that this was a being accustomed to having power. That if he found something repugnant in human culture, he would only tolerate it for so long. That he wouldn't want to assimilate into humanity; he would want to control it. Her sense was that there was some validity to Obelus's words. Maybe a planet of ignorant, useless children was exactly what Ampersand wanted.

"But it didn't protect me," she said quietly. "It only put me in more danger. I mean, if you valued me—"

"*I do value you,*" he cut her off, an almost defensive edge to the voice. "*You have shown me kindness that my own kind never would. Do not think I haven't valued you.*"

She hugged herself, pressing on her healed injuries, confronting the ache like invoking it meant she could control it. "Then I wish you'd just be honest with me."

"*I do not want to overwhelm you.*"

"I think the most overwhelming barrier—just learning about your existence—is behind us. Please, just tell me the truth."

"*I want an agreement, then,*" he said, straightening his head up. "*That the information I am about to impart remain between* the two of us. You share it neither with your family, nor any human researchers, nor any amygdaline or any other exoterran you may in your life encounter. Do we have an understanding, dear one?"

She stilled, surprised that he would call her that, but feeling a swell of warmth at the endearment all the same. "I swear."

"Then know first my perspective; my mind is damaged from years of trauma. This planet frightens me. I now have a terrible mistrust of all things that I did not have when I was younger. When I met you, I was frightened. Desperate."

"I understand."

"Had you and I met under different circumstances, healthier by the reckoning of the Superorganism, I am not sure what I might have done with you. Would I have entertained the idea of communication, engagement, even empathy had I not been so desperate and lacking in resources? I cannot say. But I have come to value you, far more than even I anticipated. That is what pressured me to make the decision I made."

"The decision to even bother saving me?"

"The means by which I divined your whereabouts to save you."

She fell silent.

"As soon as I made my deal with Obelus, I knew that he intended to collect collateral to ensure I kept my end of the deal. I knew that he would take you as well, and there was nothing I could do to stop him. I went through a great deal of deliberation, and with the resources and time I had, my options were few. The pragmatic choice would have been to simply cut my losses, mourn you, and move on. But I realized in a moment, I admit, devoid of objectivity, the reason why I had been so challenged by you. Why I decided to communicate with you in the first place.

"In my decades of captivity, having all but lost my sense of *self, only a primitive natural had shown me kindness. And even after I was reunited with my own kind, this natural remained the only creature that continued to show me kindness. And I realized that, subjectively, the thing I valued above all else I had known since the purge was a kindness I had neither anticipated nor earned.*

"But I had no resources, no plan, no weapons, and no way to protect myself, let alone you. I knew that Obelus would find and remove the tracker I implanted in you. Without it, how would I be able to tell where you were or if you were even alive? I had no way to devise a means of doing so with the resources I had. None, save one."

He didn't need to finish. She'd already figured out what he had done to her. To both of them. The mere thought of it was just so heavy, she couldn't bring herself to say it: *fusion bonding.*

A sickly "Oh" was all she could manage. The two sat in thick silence for at least a minute. Finally, she managed, "You can . . . do that? You can do that with a human?"

"*I did not know whether it was possible until I tried.*"

Cora just looked at him, agog and speechless. The only thing she could think was that it wasn't like him to do something so reckless.

"*I made a decision that was more desperate and shortsighted than I might have under circumstances from my earlier life. A decision that is, for me, lifelong. But through it, I succeeded in my objective, and therefore, I do not regret it. And now I have been honest with you, as you wished.*"

Cora was shaking. "What do I need to do?"

"*You needn't do anything.*"

"I do need!" she said, then coughed at the exertion. "It did something to me."

"*That shouldn't be possible.*"

"Well, clearly, it is possible. I can *feel* you, I heard your voice . . ."

"*This I cannot explain,*" he said. "*There is no record of an amygdaline fusion bonding with a natural alien. There is no precedent for this. But what I have done should have no effect on your mind at all.*"

"Well, 'should' and 'does' are not lining up," she said, running her hands through her hair. "Whatever you did, it did something to me. It *hurts* me, the thought of you leaving. I don't know if that and the bond are related. I think they must be. I've never felt like this before. It's like, I don't know, I feel like an addict. Like if you leave, I'll go into withdrawal." She chuckled nervously, and thought of just how powerful he was. That she still had no idea what he was capable of. How consequential he could be to humanity's future. She could very well be sharing a hospital bed with the most important being who ever set foot on this Earth, if that was what he wanted.

She buried her face in her hands, rubbing the skin of her cheeks, reaching for the right thing to say. At length, she was aware of long, spindly fingers cupping her head. She let her hands fall to her lap. "Please don't leave me," she whispered.

"*I do not wish to leave you.*"

She looked up at him, at those magnificent eyes, and marveled at the sheer absurdity of this situation. Again, she thought of Obelus's words. Wondered if she was being selfish, if begging Ampersand to stay now, in the Year of Our Lord 2007, would lead to something horrible as a direct result in 2207. There were riots in the streets. The government was crumbling. And here she was begging the source of that chaos to stay.

"*But our bond will always be difficult for me.*"

On reflex, without even asking for permission, she

found herself reaching up for his "face," that delicate curve of structure that rimmed his big eyes. He allowed it, even seemed to lean into it. "Why?" she asked.

"*Given our disparate physiology, we can never communicate through high language. I will never truly know you. We will always be isolated within our own minds.*"

Cora understood what he meant. He couldn't communicate with her any deeper than human language would allow. He could never *know* her in the same way he *knew* his other symphyles. "Well," she said. "We humans somehow manage with only the limits of human language."

"*Yes, you do,*" he said. "*But I am not human.*"

I've had some version of Ampersand in my head for ten years, but the final form of this thing is miles away from where it started. I did not foresee how many people would eventually help me find the final shape of this word cloud, but there have been many over that decade-long haul. Here are some of them.

Thank you:

To my literary agent, Christopher Hermelin, who reached out to me on a hunch that I already had a story ready to go, and like Merry and Pippin, his coming was like the falling of small stones that starts an avalanche in the mountains, and who has also become a good friend. To Antonella Inserra and Elisa Hansen, who have been with this project since its earliest incarnations, and the number of drafts they have read is *checks notes* many. To my husband, Nick, who was not only an invaluable font of knowledge but also has been a loving and supportive partner through The Process. To Angelina Meehan, my creative soulmate, who immediately understood what I was going for and helped me find the book's final form, its aesthetic, its theme, and so very much else. To Pete Wolverton, who was so excited to take a chance on this book, and to Hannah O'Grady, who likewise spent so much time on this project. To Hank Green, my friend and mentor who has guided me and helped me in more ways than I can list on an acknowledgments page. To the rest of the team at St. Martin's Press, who gave an unbelievable amount of trust and faith for a debut, and the team at Titan Books. And to other folks who've either worked with me on this, helped it find its form over the years, or just been there with support or advice: Ken Munson, Aline Baumgartner, Emily VanDerWerff, Katherine Lo, Sean McCarthy, Sue Ellis, Oliver Thorn, Lindsay Ribar, Princess Weekes, John Green, John Scalzi, Philipp Dettmer, and Caitlin Doughty.

Most of all, deepest thanks to President Ronald Reagan, who deregulated the hell out of children's television programming in the early 1980s (among many other things), and without whom *Transformers* would not exist.

Lindsay Ellis is an author and video essayist on media, narrative, and film theory, and also co-writes and co-hosts the fiction-focused web series *It's Lit!* for PBS Digital Studios. After studying Cinema Studies from NYU's Tisch School of the Arts, she earned her MFA in Film and Television Production from USC's School of Cinematic Arts with a focus in documentary and screenwriting.

She lives in Long Beach, CA and tweets @thelindsayellis.

For more fantastic fiction, author events,
exclusive excerpts, competitions, limited editions and more

VISIT OUR WEBSITE
titanbooks.com

LIKE US ON FACEBOOK
facebook.com/titanbooks

FOLLOW US ON TWITTER AND INSTAGRAM
@TitanBooks

EMAIL US
readerfeedback@titanemail.com